Christopher Fowler's
Bryant & May mysteries

'Quirky and original . . . the relationship between
Bryant and May is done brilliantly'
Mark Billingham

'Imagine the *X-Files* with Holmes and Watson in the place of
Mulder and Scully, and the books written by P. G. Wodehouse,
and you have some idea of the idiosyncratic and distinctly
British flavour of the Bryant & May novels'
Black Static

'What Christopher Fowler does so well is to
merge the old values with the new . . . he's giving
us two for the price of one'
Lee Child

'Fowler, like his crime-solvers, is deadpan, sly,
and always unexpectedly inventive'
Entertainment Weekly

'I love the wit and playfulness of the Bryant & May books'
Ann Cleeves

'Invests the traditions of the Golden Age of detective fiction
with a tongue-in-cheek post-modernism'
Evening Standard

'One of the quirkiest and most ingenious pleasures
to be found in the genre: atmospheric, sardonically
funny and craftily suspenseful'
Barry Forshaw

'Witty, sinuous and darkly comedic storytelling

BRYANT & MAY
Wild Chamber

CHRISTOPHER FOWLER

BANTAM BOOKS

LONDON • TORONTO • SYDNEY • AUCKLAND • JOHANNESBURG

TRANSWORLD PUBLISHERS
61–63 Uxbridge Road, London W5 5SA
www.penguin.co.uk

Transworld is part of the Penguin Random House group of companies
whose addresses can be found at global.penguinrandomhouse.com

Penguin
Random House
UK

First published in Great Britain in 2017 by Doubleday
an imprint of Transworld Publishers
Bantam edition published 2018

A CIP catalogue record for this book
is available from the British Library.

ISBN
9780857503107

Typeset in Sabon by Falcon Oast Graphic Art Ltd.
Printed and bound by Clays Ltd, Bungay, Suffolk.

Penguin Random House is committed to a sustainable
future for our business, our readers and our planet. This book
is made from Forest Stewardship Council® certified paper.

MIX
Paper from
responsible sources
FSC® C018179

1 3 5 7 9 10 8 6 4 2

For Roger and Izabella – into the beyond!

Those intensely quiet places immured in
the very centre of London seem as still and
desolate as cloisters.

HENRY MAYHEW

At the best, city life is an unnatural life for the human;
but the city life of London is so utterly unnatural that
the average workman or workwoman cannot stand it.

JACK LONDON, *THE PEOPLE OF THE ABYSS*

Take a wretched thief
Through a city sneaking,
Pocket handkerchief
Ever, ever seeking.
What is he but I
Robbed of all my chances,
Picking pockets by
Force of circumstances?

W. S. GILBERT

1

'LIKE A KITE STUCK IN TELEGRAPH WIRES'

On a desolate, rain-battered London midnight, the members of the Peculiar Crimes Unit went looking for a killer.

DC Colin Bimsley charged up a narrow flight of service stairs leading to the raised railway line, and was near the top when sweat broke out across his back and forehead. He looked down at his boots as the station staircase truncated and rotated, churning his stomach. Stretching out his hands to the walls, he tried to steady himself.

His quarry was getting away. Even with a section of rusted iron drainpipe manacled to his right wrist, the killer was running nimbly over rails and sleepers, sure-footed in the falling rain. It shouldn't have happened like this, but nothing in the case should have happened the way it did, and now the staff of the Peculiar Crimes Unit were dealing with the farcical consequences.

Colin fell back against the wall, watching in horror as the stairs dropped. He could not move. From the corner of his eye he saw his colleagues Detective Sergeant Jack Renfield and DC Fraternity DuCaine ascending towards him.

'Hey, Colin, you OK?' Fraternity called.

'No – it's my head thing, it's back.' Bimsley suffered from

Irlen Syndrome, a perceptual problem that made him unable to judge widths and spaces, and it had kicked in just as he was coming within range of their suspect. All he could do was point upward. 'He's getting away,' he called. 'I can't go any further—'

'Stay here, mate.' Renfield slapped him on the shoulder as he and DuCaine powered past, up on to the rainswept bridge-work that ran beside the train lines. Ahead of them, the southern routes of London Bridge Station fanned out in a great brick swathe.

The yellow windows of a commuter carriage flickered past. The train was heading for Kent and the coast. It had just turned midnight. Below them the stalled traffic steamed and rocked, jouncing forward, only to halt and hoot, the drivers cursing as the traffic lights flicked red again.

The suspect was running hard along the narrow edge of the bridgework, but DuCaine's long muscular legs quickly closed the gap. Renfield had spotted the only possible escape route and was frantically calculating their chances of an arrest; at the end of the brick path was an open section of railing leading to one of the railway arch's buttresses. Even if their suspect was able to climb through, it was a long drop to the street below.

DuCaine had almost caught up with the running man. He made a sweeping grab at his jacket but the rain was in his eyes and he missed. He slipped over on to his knees. The suspect vanished into the gap between the railings and headed out on to the brick promontory beyond it.

'Leave him, Frat,' Renfield called. 'He can't go anywhere.'

Fraternity answered by jabbing his finger down: *Look*.

Renfield peered over the side of the arch and saw a single freestanding iron pillar, the top of which was about ten feet below them. If their target took the wildest of risks and managed to land on its broad capital, he could leap once more to the pavement and run back into the tunnels beneath the lines. There was a good chance that they would lose him forever.

'If he jumps don't attempt to follow him,' Renfield said into his headset. 'I don't want to be the one peeling you off the pavement.'

'Why is there even a bloody pillar there anyway?' DuCaine asked.

'Left over from the old line,' Renfield replied. 'Damn, he's going for it.'

It was too late to stop him. Their suspect had spotted the rain-slick top of the pillar and made his move. He was light and easily managed the leap, landing perfectly in the centre of the capital. Now he just had to jump downward once more and he would be home free.

DuCaine had also calculated the probable outcome. He touched his microphone. 'Is there a cordon around London Bridge Street?'

His headset crackled. *'Yeah, we've shut off all traffic, and on St Thomas Street as well.'*

Renfield hesitated, thinking that he should head back down the stairs, but he knew it would take him too long to reach the base of the pillar. DuCaine was already bracing himself for the jump.

'OK, I'm going for it.'

'Frat, don't try it, mate.'

Fraternity was there one second, gone the next. The suspect had made his second leap, and behind him DuCaine was about to land hard on the pillar he had just vacated.

Renfield looked over the edge of the railway parapet and saw their target falling from the pillar towards the ground. Right at that moment, something entirely unexpected happened. The suspect stopped in mid-air, hovering above the street with his arms over his head. It seemed insane, impossible, but there he was, suspended above the road.

'Bloody hell,' said Renfield.

His headset burst into life. *'What's happening?'* asked John May.

'Fraternity's doing a bit of parkour,' he replied. 'Suspect

made a jump for the pavement. Only he didn't make it.'

'*What do you mean, he didn't make it?*'

'Not exactly sure, guv,' Renfield admitted. 'A bit of a Peter Pan job. He's sort of floating above the road.'

Their suspect had jumped between a pair of virtually invisible steel guy ropes running between the railway arches, which had been used to suspend signs for the London Dungeon's last exhibition. He had dropped between them but the length of drainpipe manacled to his wrist had caught itself over the knotted cables. Trapped, he tried to grip the ropes with his free hand to ease the weight on his right arm, and now swung helplessly back and forth with his legs kicking, unable to move in any direction.

A few moments later he was surrounded by various surprised members of the Peculiar Crimes Unit.

'You're too late!' their suspect shouted down at them. 'It's over. I did what I set out to do. You know I did. Whatever happens now, remember this: I won.'

'He can say what he likes,' Jack Renfield told his boss, John May. 'He's hanging over the road like a kite stuck in telegraph wires. It looks to me like we've caught the Mr Punch Killer.'

2

'WHY ARE THEY ALLOWED TO BE THERE?'

Over on St Thomas Street at exactly the same time, a Metropolitan Police traffic unit was redirecting cars around a makeshift cordon of railings, red plastic barriers and ribbons, but it was proving trickier than anyone expected. Articulated trucks were being forced to tackle the small side streets running under the railway arches, and were mounting the pavements as they turned.

Sergeant Samuel Kemp-Bird was nearing retirement. What he saw around him was utter chaos. He hadn't expected to end up on point duty tonight, but there was a lot of flu about and the traffic unit was short-staffed. He had only just recovered from a bad cold himself and the damp night air was filled with diesel fumes, tightening his chest. His spectacles were covered in water droplets, and he had nothing to clean them with. The traffic was backed up in every direction and seething, the drivers on the lookout for someone to blame. The sergeant wished he was in America, where failure to comply brought the threat of arrest. Here, drivers just laughed at you and swore.

'Oi, mate, this is a joke, innit? What's going on?' a driver shouted down from the cab of his truck.

'Police are arresting someone. The arterial roads around the station are closed. Keep it moving,' Kemp-Bird called back, waving him on.

The driver kept his air brakes on. 'How am I supposed to get into the West End?'

'You'll have to go round and back up to Tooley Street, then down Borough High Street,' Kemp-Bird replied. 'Barnham Street's shut but I think Shand Street's still open.' He called to his gormless young colleague, 'Oi, Blakey, is Shand Street still open?'

'Yeah, it must be,' Blakey shouted back. 'No one's mentioned it.'

'Are you having a laugh?' The driver slapped the side of his truck with impatience. 'This is an artic, not a concertina. And that's not a road, it's a bloody tunnel. It's got a tight bend at either end and a low-clearance ceiling. I can't get through that.'

Sergeant Kemp-Bird stepped back and eyed the truck's roof. He removed his glasses and wiped them. The trucker was holding up traffic. 'You've got a good foot and a half all round, mate. You're clear to go.' He waved the vehicle on.

The driver didn't think so, not for a minute, but he was already two hours late getting his glassware into the old Covent Garden market because of delays to the ferry services, so he decided to take the traffic cop at his word. Releasing his brakes, he hit his turn signal and accelerated.

The vehicle behind him, a gleaming red Chevrolet Cruze, pulled up near the traffic cop and its window rolled halfway down. 'What's going on?' called the pretty blonde girl inside. Sergeant Kemp-Bird coughed. He thought he could smell dope over the blue exhaust fumes in the tunnel.

'Detour,' he said. 'Where are you heading?'

'Trying to get to Vauxhall. Why is it so difficult to get anywhere in this city?' She sounded as if she might also have been drinking, but there was no room and no time to pull her over – he needed to get the traffic flowing again.

'Look, just follow the truck in front to Borough High Street.' Stepping back, he waved her on.

Further along the tunnel, Sharyn Buckland pushed a strand of auburn hair out of her eyes and checked her watch again. The show had finished late, the service in the restaurant had been abysmal and the night tube wasn't in operation tonight, not that she ever caught it this late – it was too full of drunk people eating the most disgusting burger things out of paper bags. 'Stay close to me, darling,' she told the boy, adjusting the heavy box under her arm. 'We'll find a taxi in a minute.'

But there weren't any taxis. Worse still, London Bridge Road appeared to be closed off and backed up in every direction. Sharyn could see the rotating blue lights of two squad cars parked across the road in the distance. It meant that everyone would be trying to hail a cab on the other side of the roadblock, at the approach to the bridge. She wished she'd chosen something light-coloured to wear instead of a black raincoat. At least then she would stand out more.

Charlie Forester kicked at the kerb in annoyance. 'Is my father bringing me something from Hong Kong?'

'I'm sure he will,' Sharyn replied. Mr Forester never forgot to bring his son a gift, just as he never bothered to bring any-thing for his wife. What was the point? Helen Forester spent half her life stressing out on business trips and the other half putting herself back together in health spas. Sharyn had been employed as the boy's nanny since he was three, and he was now almost eight. She had severe doubts about Mrs Forester's commitment to her son. Whenever Charlie wanted to tell his mother about his day at school she looked trapped and anxious to escape. Any attempt she made to show interest seemed awkward and false. Luckily Mr Forester made up for the imbalance in parenting skills. He was just about the best father a child could ever have. Sharyn wished Mr Forester would divorce his wife and marry someone with a warmer heart. He just didn't realize there was already a devoted candidate living in his household.

Charlie stepped into the empty street and saw the barriers. 'Why aren't there any taxis?'

'They've closed the street. Come out of the road at once, please.' *There's no point in just standing around here,* she thought. *Maybe we can get an Uber. If not I'll have to find a cut-through to the station.* But her phone wasn't connecting to the internet and she wasn't sure which road would take them through to the taxi rank. Looking up, she saw the sign on the wall: 'Shand Street'. 'Come along,' she said, taking Charlie's hand. 'Your father will be home shortly. Let's see if we can beat him back.'

As she turned into Shand Street she realized her mistake. It wasn't a street at all but a low brick tunnel leading underneath the railway lines. The walls were wet and green with calcifying rainwater. The air was sickly with truck fumes.

'Sharyn, look – there's a tramp.' Charlie pointed at a bundle of clothes wedged inside a roll of corrugated cardboard.

'They're not tramps, they're homeless people,' Sharyn explained, lowering her voice.

'You mean they stay here all night?' Charlie asked in amazement. 'He's sleeping in his clothes.'

'He doesn't have anywhere to go. It's not his fault. Imagine if your mother and father lost their jobs and couldn't pay their bills – they'd have to sell your lovely house and you'd all have to sleep on the street.'

'We'd stay with Granddad.'

I bet you wouldn't, thought Sharyn. *Granddad wouldn't like having his nice Monte Carlo lifestyle compromised.* 'Just come away, please. Let's cross over.'

She pulled him closer to her and they fled to the other side of the road.

It wasn't far to the end of the tunnel, and she recalled there was a cab rank in a bay around the corner. The box beneath her arm contained a heavy toy truck. It was an encumbrance

8

but Charlie had been given it at the show, an elaborate inter-active event with pirates and prizes, and it was too big for him to carry. He'd won it by using his brains and solving a puzzle when all of the other children had merely made guesses. He was an astonishingly smart boy. His father was already making plans to have him accelerated in school. She imagined the pair of them raising Charlie themselves, Jeremy coming home after board meetings to play with the boy, the three of them living in the country, sharing a hug in a sunlit garden. She saw herself on the boards of charities, coming home to Charlie and Jeremy – and perhaps their own little girl, a new sister for the lonely child . . .

She had to release his hand to avoid dropping the package, and of course just then her mobile rang. Digging it from her bag, she saw that Mr Forester was calling, probably from the arrivals lounge at Heathrow. 'Hang on – Charlie, stay here . . .' she called, wedging the phone under her ear as the toy truck started to slide out of the end of the box.

The truck driver swung his wheel and turned into Shand Street, checking the clearance meter on his cabin ceiling. It told him that the tunnel's sloping roof was less than six inches above, because he was coming in at an angle. Straightening up, he watched as the meter dropped back to a foot, and knew he would be able to keep it there. He just had to watch out for protrusions; some of these tunnels had cable bars hanging down from their roofs. There was a lot of traffic in the tunnel, and visibility was poor.

The vehicles suddenly shunted forward. He reached out a hand and cleared the condensation forming on his wind-screen. He didn't enjoy truck-driving; the work was monotonous and his foreman at Medusa Holdings was constantly pressuring him to improve on his delivery times. He had a degree but couldn't find a way to make it pay, so for now he was stuck with long-haul deliveries—

Damn. The car in front had slammed on its brakes and he nearly rear-ended it. The trucker turned up his radio. There had just been a warning about road closures to the south of London Bridge but he had missed it. Perhaps it would come on again.

As he tried to find another news station he saw a movement from the corner of his eye. One of the homeless men in the tunnel had lurched to his feet on the left-hand pavement and was about to step out. He swung the wheel to avoid him. The clearance meter started beeping urgently.

Swinging back, the truck's front nearside tyre mounted the low kerb with a thump. Wary of shifting his load, he checked his mirror and smoothly slowed down as the homeless man wandered clear. A moment later he saw a smartly dressed woman in a black raincoat standing in front of him, squinting in his headlights, and through the fumes he sensed something else – that there was a child just below the level of his windscreen.

He was an instinctive driver. Swinging the wheel sharply, he managed to avoid the boy without shifting his load, but the vehicle behind was caught out by his brake lights. It was getting too close, and meandering in its lane as if its driver was drunk.

Looking in his rear-view mirror, the trucker could see that the car was about to hit the grey metal electrical cabinet that jutted from the tunnel wall. Those damned things were barely visible; he'd often come close to clipping them. He heard a low scrape and a thump and, sure enough, caught a glimpse of the car rocking to a sudden stop, right up against the brickwork. *Been there, done that,* he thought, but suddenly the smartly dressed woman on the pavement was yelling and he thought she was reacting to the shock of nearly being run over, but as the driver behind got out he realized that something bad might have happened. The girl was pretty but very thin, dressed in tight blue jeans and a green Superdry sweatshirt. She looked alarmed, confused. As she came around the car's driver-side headlight she reached out a steadying hand.

The trucker kept his eyes focused on the rear-view mirror. The toy lorry that lay in the gutter looked like a miniature version of his own vehicle. He watched as the girl knelt down before it, drawn by the same ominous sight, then saw the shocked little blond-haired boy standing just ahead of her car. He was holding a hand to his cheek, but he couldn't possibly have been hit. *Man, that could have been nasty,* the driver thought. *These bloody short-notice detours are going to kill someone one day.* Satisfied that the boy was OK, he was about to drive on, hoping to meet his deadline at Covent Garden's tourist market, but when he looked in his rear-view mirror again he saw there was something wrong.

It wasn't in his nature to walk away from a problem. With a sigh he looked for a spot to pull over, and prepared to miss his allocated time slot.

'Are you hurt, Charlie?' Sharyn asked, holding the boy's thin shoulders. 'Show me your face.'

'I'm fine,' said Charlie, pulling free. 'My eye's sore.'

'Don't rub it. Let me see.' She gently removed his hand from his left eye and peered into his face. There didn't seem to be anything wrong. 'It's probably a bit of grit from the road.'

'Is he OK?' asked the thin girl in the Superdry sweatshirt. She glanced back nervously at the car. 'Are we all right here?'

'I don't know.' Sharyn turned the boy to the light. She could see a tiny red mark in the corner of Charlie's left eye. 'It looks like a little speck of blood.'

'I'm OK,' Charlie repeated.

Sharyn looked down at the pavement, which she now saw was covered in tiny pieces of broken glass. 'Is that from your wing mirror?'

The girl turned and looked. She seemed dazed and unable to take in what had happened. 'No,' she said, 'I think there was like an empty bottle on top of the cabinet or something. It must have smashed.' They looked back at the gutter, where a wine label lay with shards of green glass still stuck to its back.

Suddenly Charlie Forester wavered as if he was about to faint. He fell forward, but slowly, so that Sharyn was able to catch him and keep him upright.

The girl dropped back in a state of panic. 'Oh God, what's wrong with him? I didn't do anything.' She turned and staggered towards the car.

'Wait,' called Sharyn, 'where are you going?'

'It's just shock, he looks fine, I have to go,' said the girl over her shoulder.

'You can't leave; it was still an accident. Don't you have to stay here until we've reported it?' Sharyn wanted to run after her but couldn't abandon Charlie.

'I can't, I'm sorry,' said the girl. She climbed back into the car and then it was reversing, lurching back and forward again, freeing itself and bouncing out into the traffic gap before it had a chance to close up, leaving Sharyn and Charlie on the pavement.

Sharyn turned her attention back to Charlie. Her only concern was for the boy. He was heavy in her arms. His eye was definitely weeping. Then someone in uniform was running towards them. Sergeant Kemp-Bird was out of breath by the time he reached her side. 'What happened?'

'I'm not sure – I think he's fainted.'

'Get back to the wall, away from the traffic,' Kemp-Bird instructed. 'I'll call someone.' The truck driver was walking towards them now, a look of concern on his face.

She went with Charlie in the ambulance but wasn't allowed to sit with him in the back. The EMTs did what they could, but the boy grew deathly white and lay motionless on the trolley. The supervising technician shone the beam of his penlight into his left pupil. Sliding back the window, he asked Sharyn whether she saw anything enter the boy's eye.

'I think it was probably dust from the tunnel,' Sharyn answered. 'The lady in the car that hit the wall said she saw a bottle break. There was glass all over the pavement. There was a wine bottle, probably from one of the homeless men. Why are they allowed to be there?' She looked back at the boy and grew even more alarmed. 'Why isn't he responding?'

'I don't know yet,' the technician admitted as the ambulance edged through the traffic, but he had seen something like this happen before and had a strong suspicion about what was occurring. He could see something reflecting in the left caruncle, the corner of the eye. If it was a sliver of glass from the road it could be coated in all kinds of chemicals and bacteria. It could work its way around to do serious damage, perhaps even sever the optic nerve. He'd known a sliver of glass to enter an eye, blind it and leave a patient's body one week later from under a fingernail. People who worked with glass all said the same thing: that it was a pernicious and potentially lethal material.

His worst fears were confirmed when it became obvious that the foreign particle had gone much deeper and was causing a clot. 'We need to get there faster,' he warned the driver.

Charlie Forester died on the operating table twenty-seven minutes later, and through her tears Sharyn saw another tragedy approaching. She realized she would have to confront his father about the events that had occurred on that rain-beaten night in the tunnel underneath London Bridge Station.

It was the moment when she saw all her plans, her ambitions, every expectation and dream she had for her future wiped out in a single stroke.

3

'THE COMPANY WILL OUTLAST
ITS EMPLOYEES'

Six months after his son died in the emergency unit at St
Thomas', Jeremy Forester arrived at his office just before
8 a.m., parking his black Mercedes-AMG S 65, a vehicle
worth more than his first house had cost, in his space beneath
the sign saying 'Washbourne Hollis Employees Only'. As he
killed the engine, he gathered his presentation materials and
tried to get his wife off the phone.

'Helen, I agreed to the meeting in principle but we're going
to be really busy here. We've a heap of contract renewals to
handle. Someone has to oversee the renovations on the house,
and I've got to deal with the Hong Kong flat. I let you choose
the counsellor but I've never even met this woman. How do I
know she's not just going to automatically take your side?'

'Oh, we have sides now?'

'You know what I mean.' He closed his case, bipped the car
door and headed for the lifts.

'I have no other time. I'm choosing fabrics for the gallery.
Surely you haven't forgotten? At this point we have to be seen
to be spending money.'

'Do we? I'm more concerned about closing Hong Kong. I've just arrived at work. We'll talk later.'

Jeremy knew he had lost the battle. Helen's appalling friends would encourage her to spend while he stayed in London trying to close his contracts and project-manage the house renovation at the same time, and the relationship counsellor would charge them a fortune for a series of broken appointments. If Helen's gallery failed to open on time, the house wasn't finished or the Hong Kong flat was delayed, she would blame him, and even if everything *did* work out she would still not be happy, because she never was these days. Nothing had been the same since they'd lost their son in a bizarre accident no one could adequately explain. Charlie's death had opened fissures in their marriage that were impossible to close.

Washbourne Hollis was housed in Number One, Poultry, a prestigious building at the epicentre of London that had arisen during the city's birth, and had remained in one form or another for two thousand years. The lift took Jeremy to his office. A message from his assistant Melissa warned him that Larry Vance, the head of finance, had called an urgent meeting. As he diverted there, Jeremy wondered if the month's figures had finally set him on track to become a partner. Vance needed him. It would mean that the deal's accompanying shares would pay for the house, the gallery and Hong Kong, which was good timing as he had just finished signing the paperwork.

Vance was too short and inconsequential-looking to be sitting behind an acre of Indonesian teak; it made him look like a fearful schoolboy waiting to see the headmaster. Even so, Jeremy knew at once that something was wrong. Instead of the usual tentative smile from the financial chief there was a downcast fidget, a failure of acknowledgement from the man who had mentored him for six long years.

Placing his manicured fingers on the blotter and spreading them wide, Vance finally looked up into his employee's eyes.

'Don't get too comfortable, Jeremy. I think it's better for both of us if I keep this short. I'm afraid I'm the bearer of bad news. You know I made a lot of allowances for you after Charlie died. But I simply can't any longer.'

Jeremy tried to swallow but his mouth was dry. 'What are you talking about?'

'There's no other way to say this. I'm afraid you're relieved of your duties here. In compliance with company policy, I have to insist that you immediately clear your desk.' Vance turned away, actually turned away, unable to hold his gaze. 'Don't take any files with you. You can leave your security keys with the concierge.'

Jeremy glanced about the room. Was this some kind of grotesque joke? Were his colleagues about to jump out? 'You're not serious, are you? I thought this was about making me a partner.'

'Until a week ago, so did I,' said Vance. 'I really need you off the premises as quickly as possible, Jeremy.'

Pain prickled behind his eyes. 'After all the money I made for you in the last two years? Are you insane?'

'This is not about your skills as a negotiator,' said Vance, 'it's about your choices. We've been over the books.'

Jeremy's face froze. What was he talking about? There were no actual illegalities, just a few carefully bent rules. A decision pivoted before him: Deny their existence or come clean. 'I never did anything for personal gain. Everything I did was for the company.'

'I believe you, Jeremy, but it doesn't alter the fact that what you've been doing completely contravenes fiscal policy,' replied Vance. 'If any of this gets reported we'll have the Fraud Squad on our backs in a heartbeat. You saw what happened with the Panama Papers. There has to be total accountability.'

'It's not exactly in the same league, Larry. We're talking about methods in common usage in the international business community.' He was starting to speak too quickly; he knew that. 'I needed to make our investments more profitable. What, you think that just happens by itself?'

'Let me ask you – what do *you* think will happen if the City Companies Commission gets wind of this?' He stopped his employee from framing a reply. 'Are there any other records I don't know about? Is there anything kept off-site, on your home laptop, in cloud storage?'

'No, it's only here in the office in secure e-vault files. I would never take it outside, you know that.'

'I'm prepared to accept your word for now, until there's a full internal investigation. This kind of – blindness – is something we keep a constant watch for. It's lucky for you that I noticed before anyone else did. We'll clean house as fast as we can, but I'm afraid part of that process is getting you off the premises before 9 a.m.'

Jeremy felt sweat dripping between his shoulder blades. There was a terrible sense of things falling away. 'What's my severance package? The terms are complex, it'll take a while to go through everything with the lawyers—'

Vance looked amazed. 'What are you talking about? There is no severance package, Jeremy. What you get is me keeping you out of jail, in the short term at least. That's the only deal we're looking at here, the one you should be thanking me for. Look, I know it was a rough year for you, losing your son, and I know you and Helen are going through a difficult patch, but this is an extremely serious matter.'

'It isn't what you think,' he replied, starting to feel sick. 'Did you stop to wonder whether the profitability levels on those contracts were sustainable? Where did you suppose the money came from, for God's sake?'

Vance picked up a thick envelope and plucked it open. 'Yours is the only name on any of the transactions, for which I suppose I must thank you. I just need you to sign this.' He unfolded the pages and smoothed them out before his employee.

Jeremy looked down at the sheets containing details of his

transactions and subsequent resignation. 'Please, Larry, I have debts,' he said. 'I owe money, I've a million pounds' worth of house renovations going on here and I just purchased the Hong Kong flat so that I could be there to handle clients more easily. There are substantial outstanding loans – everything was based on the assumption of me being made a partner.' He rattled the page, his fingers leaving sweat-marks. 'What if I don't sign this?'

'Then I'll have to call security and they will call the police. This was your project, nobody else's.'

'Don't do this to me,' he begged as quietly and reasonably as he could. 'I have nothing saved. I took personal risks. My own investments didn't work out. I had to borrow from all sorts of – hell, I haven't even finished paying for the gallery, so you can imagine what my wife—'

'I wouldn't wish your wife on a dog,' interrupted Vance, relishing the opportunity to be brutally honest. 'You bought her to make yourself look good. Get rid of her. Women have always been your weakness, Jeremy. Don't say you did this for us – admit that you did it for her. You know I'm sorry you lost your son, but I can't afford to be sentimental about this. I need you to sign the document and then vacate the building.'

'Let me keep the car,' he pleaded. His pen hand was shaking violently. 'Just the car.'

Vance considered the point. The car was nothing. Forester's replacement would want a new one anyway. He could concede that. And as far as his accountants could tell, Jeremy had operated alone without authority, indicting only himself. Perhaps it was the gentlemanly thing to do. 'All right,' he conceded. 'Out of respect for your work here, you can keep the car.'

The page wavered before Jeremy's eyes as he signed his career away. For one horrible moment he thought he felt tears swelling. 'I've served Washbourne Hollis well. I put its profits before everything else.'

Vance thought about this and grunted assent. 'The company will outlast its employees. But you, Jeremy – let me give you a word of advice. You need to develop a survival strategy. You're too loyal. To the company, to your wife. We'll both be fine without you. Look after yourself. Settle your debts, find a way to reconnect, but do it alone, on your own terms. Your job here will be filled within days. People will be climbing over corpses for it.'

And then the security guard was walking him down the corridor to his office and everyone was looking at him through the glass partitions because he saw to his horror that they knew, they all knew he was being fired although they probably had no idea why, and being humiliated like this was more than he could stand, because he had always prided himself on looking the best and being the best. Was there time to talk to Melissa, to admit that their night together should never have happened, and that he might never see her again?

The bubbling nausea within him really started to rise when Jeremy Forester realized that this would be only the first of the humiliations, that they would start now and keep on coming until everything was gone and there was nothing left at all, because he had always lived beyond his means, making reckless decisions when it came to loan terms. Now he owed more than he could ever pay back, so it wasn't simply a matter of seized assets and frozen bank accounts, it was smashed faces and broken legs and, God, what if they found out about the gallery? What if they discovered where Helen worked? They couldn't take what he didn't have, but they could harm his wife. Suddenly this distant woman to whom he had barely spoken lately except to co-ordinate diaries was desperately precious to him.

That was when he decided there was nothing for him to take from his office, that he would leave empty-handed and gain a head start while he worked out some kind of a game plan that would keep Helen safe and him in one piece. He would sell the car and get some ready cash; that would keep him going for a while. It no longer mattered what the staff of Washbourne Hollis thought; it was only important to stay ahead of his creditors. The loan he had taken out in Hong Kong and could not pay back was large enough to get him killed.

He began to run towards the lifts.

THE FIRST DAY

4

'BETTER VALUE FOR MONEY'

From today I will learn to take charge of my organization by blaming other people, Raymond Land repeated to himself, using one of the thirty or so mantras he had memorized from a self-help business manual called *Lower Your Expectations & Raise Your Profits* by a bearded American professor called Osbert Desanex. Having been told that he needed to run his wayward police unit like a private company, Land had taken the message somewhat too heavily to heart.

Leaning forward, he squinted at his computer screen, checked that he had the date right and the correct staff list pulled up, then touched the microphone symbol with his mouse arrow. For some reason it opened his email, so he closed down Mail because he didn't like to have two windows open at once, and tried again. This time the mouse accessed his recent history and revealed a page about Beautiful Russian Women Just Waiting to Meet You. Embarrassed, he panicked and stabbed randomly at the keyboard until a window popped up reading *Are you sure you want to shut down now? If so all current data will be lost YES NO.* He meant to click *NO* but for some unearthly reason found himself clicking *YES*, and then it was too late.

While the computer restarted he rose and went to the window. Over time Land had acquired the features of an ineffectual man, soft-boned, thin-haired and seething with small irritations. He was a visual representation of constipation, marked with the look of a fellow who knows he will never be listened to with anything other than disrespect. But for all of that, he meant well. Outside, the bedraggled one-legged pigeon that had made its nest on his windowsill stared back at him. It looked like an avian version of a very sick Camden Town punk from the late 1970s.

'I'll get you this time, Stumpy,' muttered Land. Pressing himself against the wall, he picked up a copy of *Time Out*, rolled it up tightly and reached across to the window catch. In one swift movement he slid up the sash and thwacked the magazine down on the sill. The pigeon strutted around the weapon, flicked one staring orange eye at it, warbled, then dropped a white splodge on to a photograph of the mayor.

'Why not,' Land sighed. 'Everybody else treats King's Cross like a toilet.' He returned to his desk to begin dictation.

Peculiar Crimes Unit
The Old Warehouse
231 Caledonian Road
London N1 9RB

STAFF ROSTER MONDAY 11 DECEMBER

Raymond Land, Unit Chief
Arthur Bryant, Senior Investigator
John May, Senior Investigator
Janice Longbright, Operations Director
Jack Renfield, Operations Director
Dan Banbury, Crime Scene/Forensics
Giles Kershaw, Pathology (off-site)
Meera Mangeshkar, Coordination
Colin Bimsley, Coordination

Steffi Vesta, Scientific Services
Crippen, staff cat

PRIVATE & CONFIDENTIAL MEMO
FROM: RAYMOND LAND
TO: ALL PCU STAFF

As I'm sure you know, the police service in England and Wales is currently reducing its budget by 20 per cent, while another wonderful new quango, the Police and Crime Commissioners Office, has been created by the Home Secretary for purposes only she understands, so you'll see from the attached list that there are some changes. Your former Metropolitan Police titles have been removed, so you're no longer locked into their pay structure. This doesn't mean you can make up your own job titles. I've already told Mr Bryant he can't be Sultan, Emperor or Supreme Being. I'm willing to humour him a bit because he hasn't been well, but if anyone else starts winding me up they'll soon discover the less forgiving side of my nature. I can be a right Dr Jekyll when I have to.

'He does know that Mr Hyde was the bad one?' asked Arthur Bryant as he read the memo back later.

Stay with me, it gets worse. The new pay structure is performance related, so if I can't regularly put a few biscuits in the tin you don't get any wages. As we're starting out with a deficit from the building renovations, we have to win our next case or PCU goes down. I know you've all heard that before but this time it's about hard cash, not meeting quotas. Conducting an investigation is expensive, and we have to pay for every outsourced service we use. This isn't some Swedish crime show where they only have to snap their fingers to get a bucketful of tested DNA dropped into their laps. We'll be lucky if we can run to chocolate digestives.

Now, some of you may remember that Jack Renfield used to work with the PCU. You should do, as it was just six weeks ago, before he threw a moody and walked out, leaving us all in the shit. He rejoins us after completing an exhausting month-long stint back at the Metropolitan Police Force, during which time his so-called mates filled his locker with dead fish and superglued his trousers to an armed response vehicle. As his homecoming proved somewhat less than welcoming, and the exciting opportunities afforded by a unit offering low pay and even lower esteem proved irresistible, he's come back just in time to qualify for Christmas overtime. I imagine it was this or working in an Oxfam shop, so unless he's good at pricing teapots and Harry Potter wands we're stuck with him.

Also joining us on a temporary secondment is Steffi Vesta from Cologne. She has a background in scientific services and a degree in criminal law, and wanted to spend a couple of weeks in a respected, world-class specialist unit. Instead she got us. She says she's looking forward to meeting you all and is therefore clearly out of her mind. When I say make her feel at home, that doesn't mean telling her what your granddad did during the war. I'd like to remind you that our own royal family is German, so if you want to have a go at someone, do the proper British thing and pick on the French.

The closure of the King's Cross Police Station means that we're now the only unit operating between Holloway Prison and Bloomsbury, so the City of London Police have asked us to handle public consultation sessions one morning a week. Yes, that's 'public' as in 'general public'. Janice will produce a duty roster, so be prepared for a lot of witless questions about fly-tipping and whether it's illegal to have a fire in your back garden, no doubt mixed in with some disturbing theories about immigrants from our neighbourhood's highly volatile mix of tracksuited wombles, nutcases and cat ladies, a technical term for a certain type of unmarried female that I am assured by Equality & Diversity is not yet listed as derogatory.

'He's become quite angry since Leanne left him, don't you think?' said John May. 'It's an improvement.'

You may be aware that I recently attended a business seminar called 'Policing & Profit', as the powers that be have decided we should offer better value for money to our 'customers', quote unquote. I shall be sending each of you exercises designed to increase your awareness of customer care and value. Our politicians think they can rebrand their way out of budget cuts and I'm only amazed that they haven't changed 'crime prevention' to 'product satisfaction'. Perhaps they're planning to turn the ground floor of the PCU into a Patisserie Valerie. I thought of taking sponsored advertising but I don't suppose your chances of gaining respect will be improved by having 'Barclays' emblazoned across your jackets, especially as it's rhyming slang.

You'll notice that we now have a smart new operations room on the first floor, created by the two Daves, who've miraculously managed to take out the right walls without this doss-house falling down. You'll see from my floor plan that all staff except myself and our two senior detectives will share this space in order to improve communications. Obviously Mr Bryant and Mr May will remain in their own office, preferably with the door shut. I don't want you catching any of their habits, ideas or germs. We don't want a repeat of what happened when that polio-infected rabbit got loose.

Right, a little housekeeping. The third-floor stairs are finally in place; there's just not enough of them, so be careful at the top. Speaking of stairs not going all the way to the attic, Mr Bryant insists he is almost back to his old self, which might explain why the fire brigade called me at two o'clock this morning. According to them somebody catapulted a burning chicken from our building into the Caledonian Road. I know we're a 'hands-on' unit but I draw the line at aerodynamic experiments with flaming poultry.

'Was that you?' asked John May. 'What were you trying to do?'

'I wasn't *trying* to do anything,' Arthur Bryant replied cheerfully. 'I succeeded. I'd like to see you fire a petrol-soaked capon two hundred yards into a litter bin. Two out of three wasn't bad. OK, one bounced through the door of the Hen Hut Takeaway, but I proved the point.'

'Which was?' May asked, but his partner had gone.

As of today we have a clean case slate, but I want you all ready for the week ahead. As for Mr Bryant, I believe he expects to make a full recovery, although at the moment he is still experiencing some side effects from his treatment. If you catch him in heated arguments with lamp-posts, try to show some patience.

The two Daves have now cleared all harmful materials from the basement with the exception of the eight-foot stone casket they found in the floor, which appears to have a cadaver in it. You saw what happened when archaeologists found the remains of Richard III buried in a Leicester car park, so if you don't want Health & Safety creeping around here for the next six months I suggest you keep any word of this from getting out. I'm sure we can handle one ancient body; God knows we employ enough of them. We're going to smuggle it over to the St Pancras Mortuary and let Giles work out whether it's worth flogging on eBay.

Right: the Police Benevolent Society Christmas dinner is fast approaching and we've been instructed to buy tickets. They've promised not to seat us next to the toilets this time, which will save the embarrassment of you lot sliding under the table and shuffling it to the front again. You ruined the seating plan last year, and we won't talk about the other incident, for which the words 'jelly fight' barely suffice.

I've been advised there's a change to this week's Film Club screening of *Interstellar* after staff requests for something we can all follow, so we will now be showing *Camelot*.

Finally, it has come to my attention that members of staff are planning to hold a Christmas party in the evidence room. There will be no festivities on my watch, thank you, especially not with stolen vodka and confiscated marijuana. Besides, you can't have a party without bringing other halves, and as most of us haven't got one I don't think we want to sit around in paper hats trying to be vivacious with people we see every day at murder sites. My Christmas Day is going to consist of a microwaved chicken tikka lasagne in front of Morecambe and Wise and I don't see why yours shouldn't be just as miserable.

My management manual suggests ending any pep talk with a summary, so – go and find something useful to do, try not to fall through anything and don't get us closed down this week. My nerves won't stand it.

5

'SO MUCH VIOLENCE IN LONDON'

Ritchie Jackson surveyed his kingdom.

Strong and well formed, he took pleasure in simple things: the dew on the early morning grass that shimmered like the surface of a lake when the breeze touched it; the sharp clear scent of a freshly minted morning; the wet green bushes and trees that turned the scene before him into an Impressionist painting. Ritchie's Samsung Galaxy had a high pixel rate and his photographs usually looked great as screensavers. Crouching low, he steadied his phone on the back of the wooden bench and took a series of HD shots.

Lately he had seen emerald-green monk parakeets in the tops of the plane trees. One of the gardeners told him they'd escaped from a cage at Pinewood Studios, where the birds were being used in a film, but there didn't seem to be any around today. A shame; they would have added a nice touch of colour.

Jackson's father had worked in Kew Gardens, and had told him that American greys had killed off England's native red squirrels by infecting them with a virus back in the 1920s. Survival of the fittest. A pity, because a red squirrel would have looked good against that wall of bright red *Pyracantha coccinea* berries.

He was just thinking about finding something else to put into the shot when she appeared.

It wasn't just that she was beautiful – she was, of course, in a sad way – but it was how she walked in her pristine white tracksuit with a scarlet coat carelessly thrown over her shoulders, so confident and sure of herself, with a swing of her arm and a spring in her step, as if this was her own private space where no one else would ever see her.

And he supposed it was. Like many other well-heeled streets in London, Clement Crescent had its own garden set aside for exclusive use by residents. The woman had a small white West Highland terrier on a tartan-handled leash. Ritchie had seen her here before, but her blonde hair partially hid her face and he realized that he had never seen her eyes. Her clothes could have been donned directly from a shopping bag. Even the dog was immaculate.

As he looked through his viewfinder and took the shot, he saw something else in her body language, a kind of wariness, and he suddenly felt uncomfortable about spying on her, so he lowered the phone and slipped it into his pocket. He was about to make his way back to the bushes he had been pruning. Women like her were not for men like him.

But he stopped and looked over once more. He was shielded from her by the green blades of the overgrown philadelphus bushes. Their dew brushed his shoulders, dripping water down his neck. The dog stopped suddenly and pricked up his ears.

'Beauchamp?' she said, also stopping. 'What's the matter?'

Ritchie wondered if the dog had sensed his presence. The logical thing would have been to make himself known, but instead he stepped further back into the bushes and held his breath in the still morning air.

The dog looked straight at him.

'What is it, Beauchamp?' she asked. Looking around, she reached down and unclipped the leash from his collar. Dogs were only allowed in the gardens on a leash. Beauchamp pranced towards Ritchie, then suddenly veered away, as if he'd seen a squirrel.

'Beauchamp, come back.' She took a tentative step forward but seemed unnerved. Now he saw her eyes, wide and violet. She was captivating, but somehow haunted. He looked around, thinking that if he brought the dog back the gesture might please her, but the animal was nowhere in sight. He tried to listen for its movements in the bushes but the park faced a main road, and a peristaltic line of double-decker buses was grinding past.

Beauchamp couldn't have travelled far; the gardens weren't very large. Ritchie looked for paw prints in the dewy grass. A milky sun had appeared from behind heavy grey cloud. He was annoyed to see a McDonald's bag lying in a flowerbed near the railings. No junk food was allowed in the park, so someone must have thrown it over from outside. He had a horrible thought, that Beauchamp was voiding his bowels in the newly planted herbaceous border. Following the line of bushes, he spotted his shovel and fertilizer bag, but there was no sign of the terrier.

Ritchie decided to announce his presence. When he returned to the bench and looked across the grass he expected to see her still standing against the banked berries of the *Pyracantha coccinea*. Instead she had gone. Had the dog come back?

He stayed on the path, following it around the perimeter until he reached the evergreen *Aucuba japonica* that he had not yet trimmed. He stopped, his mouth slack.

The woman was lying on her back in the middle of the gravel path, part of her scarlet coat laid over her neck. She seemed tidily arranged, as graceful as a fallen angel.

As Ritchie approached, he instinctively reached out and pulled back her lapel, revealing a raw black-red mark across her throat. He thought of giving her mouth-to-mouth but sensed there was nothing he could do; and besides, it would mean marking himself, and what if the police thought he'd done something to her?

Dropping to his knees, he tried to see if she was alive. He pressed an ear to her heart and put his hand to her neck, but there was no beat, no pulse. He needed to call an ambulance, but now his fingers were slippery with blood that had leaked from her nose and – *my God* – from the corners of her eyes, and every second he dithered she came closer to death. He felt his heart beating faster and looked around, suddenly fearful; her attacker had to be standing nearby. He had an awful, overpowering sensation of someone right behind him, but when he turned there was no one there. Nobody could get out; the garden gates were always kept locked.

She was dead long before help arrived, and all Jackson could do was sit on the wet grass, tormented, and cry a silent prayer for her.

Margo Farrier was small and sudden of movement in the way that some old ladies turn into sparrows. Genteel but lively, she had an attentive face that was quick to judge. She watched it all from her window, of course. First an ambulance and two squad cars turned up, then one car went away and some more police officers arrived, and some kind of white and yellow tent was erected on the footpath (Margo could only see its top corner from her bedroom window). Then a grey BMW stopped with three men in it, one tall and elegantly attired, flicking a handkerchief over his shoes; one stocky and shaven-headed, eating a sandwich; the last one elderly, wearing a squashed homburg and a ridiculously long striped scarf, and carrying a walking stick. When these three arrived the others avoided them and beat a hasty retreat.

The one in the homburg paused to knock his pipe out on the park gate. On *her* gate, indeed! Then he checked the sole of his shoe, scraped something off on the kerb and spat for good measure. Where did he think he was? This was Holland Park, not Hackney!

Margo rang Mr Dasgupta at number 17. 'I'm sorry to call so early,' she said. 'What's going on in the crescent? Are they plainclothes police? One of them looks like a tramp.'

'Oh, Mrs Farrier, I think it's another mugging,' said Mr Dasgupta very loudly, knowing that his neighbour was hard of hearing. 'I just went to get a newspaper and the policeman told me there was a body in the park.'

'It can't be a mugging,' said Margo, shaking her head vehemently. 'Nobody can get into the park except us and the gardener, not without a key. I hope it's not serious. There's so much violence in London, it's just awful.'

'Maybe one of those troubled boys from the estate managed to get over the wall,' said Mr Dasgupta. 'Nobody is safe these days.'

'The railings are covered in anti-climb paint,' said Margo. 'They were redone only two weeks ago. Whose body is it? Not one of the residents, surely?'

Mr Dasgupta was apologetic. 'I'm afraid I don't know. The officer said he couldn't tell me anything, but a special unit was on its way and they would come to talk to all of us.'

Mrs Farrier suddenly felt cold. 'I don't want anything to do with the police. People will think I've been up to something. I live alone, I don't feel safe.'

And yet you're always inviting strangers in for tea, thought Mr Dasgupta wearily. 'It's our duty to help them with their inquiries,' he told her, adding, 'My son has not come home yet.'

'You don't think it was him, do you? Those lads he hangs around with – well, some of them could be refugees and you never know what *they* get up to.'

'I meant *he* might be the one who got mugged,' Mr Dasgupta explained with an inward sigh. 'His friends are Indian, Mrs Farrier, not Syrian. And anyway . . .' He decided it was not worth having another argument with her about refugees. 'My son is a good boy,' he finished lamely.

'Of course,' agreed Mrs Farrier, 'but can't you go over there and ask them what's happened? We live here; we have a right to be told. If you don't, I will.'

When Mr Dasgupta demurred, Margo Farrier went for her coat. A new gardener had started a few weeks ago, a black lad, Ritchie something – perhaps he would know what was going on.

'I'm just popping out, Wilberforce,' she told the budgie. 'I'll only be a few minutes. Somebody needs to find out what's going on.'

6

'A MURDER IN THE PRELAPSARIAN PARADISE'

It was a measure of the area's affluence that while other neighbourhood parks had bandstands, Holland Park had an opera company. The neighbourhood's elegant centrepiece had landscaped gardens with statues and peacocks, an orangery and an icehouse. Nearby, the communal gardens of Clement Crescent were arranged in an arc of grand terraced houses, yet this verdant and immensely wealthy West London neighbourhood was bordered by the more vivacious ethnicity of Shepherd's Bush. The famous and the infamous rubbed shoulders, passing through each other's districts, rarely having cause to speak to one another.

The sky had a look of pained contraction, as if at any moment it might find release in a flood upon the heads of passersby. The walled garden of the crescent was always off-limits to the general public, but today it was closed to everyone except the police. An ominous patch of scuffed gravel showed at the edge of Dan Banbury's geodesic examination tent. John May looked around, waiting impatiently while the crime scene manager scraped some of the gravel into a plastic box. 'God, it's as cold as Keats's owl in here,' he complained.

'That'll be the trees, you urbanite,' said Banbury, lidding his sample. The crime scene manager was an oddity at the PCU, a happily married husband and father who enjoyed living in the suburbs and having a kickabout in the garden with his son. As a result, none of his colleagues ever enquired about his home life.

'If he strangled her, why is there blood?' asked May.

'Cartilage rupture. It's a ligature strangulation. Mechanical asphyxia. He pulled a cord around her throat and held fast. I don't think she felt much.'

May couldn't bring himself to look. 'So it's a professional job?'

'Don't just hover about outside, come and see for yourself. This isn't an act you commit after carefully studying an anatomy chart. It's the sort of wound inflicted by someone subject to violent outbursts. It's interesting that he didn't use his hands; we might be looking at premeditation.'

'You said "he".'

'Well, yes, because, you know – strength.' Banbury pointed back at the figure in the flowerbeds. 'Can you do something about him?'

'Oh – of course, sorry.' May turned to the figure that was hunched over in the herbaceous border pulling up a purple-flowered buddleia by its stem. From this distance, with his brown hat and overcoat faded by the early morning mist, it did indeed look like a rummaging tramp. Arthur Bryant's blue button eyes missed very little even when they lost their focus. The detective sidled and beguiled his way through life with an easy gentlemanly air, and although he now had fewer hairs on his head than a coconut, and those white, he possessed a sense of animation and liveliness seldom seen in men half his age. None of which went an inch towards explaining just how incredibly annoying he could be.

'Arthur, what on earth are you doing?'

'This is a weed.' Bryant rose with the uprooted plant in one pudgy hand. 'They grow out of brickwork and can pull down walls if you let them take root.'

'Would it be asking you too much to pay attention?' May pointed at the tent. 'A woman just lost her life over here.'

'She's dead but the garden's still alive.' Bryant looked around for somewhere to drop the buddleia and finally decided to sling it behind a hedge.

'You're getting dirt everywhere,' shouted Banbury. 'John, either bring him over or keep him away from the area.'

'You don't have to talk about me as if I'm not here,' Bryant complained. '"One is not idle because one is absorbed. To contemplate is to toil, to think is to do." Victor Hugo.'

May indicated the disturbed gravel. 'I thought you'd be interested in this. She put up a fight.'

'I'm more interested in the suspect. What kind of gardener doesn't know that buddleia is an invasive weed? Has anyone talked to him yet?'

'When did we have time?' asked May, exasperated. 'He's only just been taken into custody. Let him get over the shock before you hit him with questions. You'll get clearer answers.'

'Between seven and seven fifteen,' Bryant called out.

'What?'

'The time she died.'

May was brought up short. 'How do you know that?'

'The gardener phoned it in at seven twenty a.m., but he got here at seven. She's lying on the main walkway so he'd have seen her on the way in, which means she was attacked after he arrived.' He tipped his homburg and pointed to the wooden noticeboard on the railings at the back of the shrubbery. 'It's got the gardener's hours on it. Monday, Wednesday, Friday – seven a.m. to one p.m. I had to pull the buddleia out to read it, didn't I?'

'He's got a point,' Banbury admitted. 'I think you need to see this, John. The markings are unusual.' He opened the flap of the tent, which had now been properly illuminated, and ushered May inside.

Arthur Bryant could not remember the last time he had been in a London park. He looked about, marvelling at the height of the trees, the scale and age of the planting, the aleatoric shadows. In this small green city pocket he smelled damp wood, something smoky, petrichor and the lingering scent of night flowers. During the war doctors had placed soldiers with respiratory problems in large parks because the air was cleaner. What the city destroyed, the trees put back.

May stood outside the tent with his gaze averted. Banbury frowned. 'Is something the matter?'

May turned away. 'Her eyes are still wide open, Dan. Can't you close them?' The unfamiliar tone in his voice alerted Bryant, who stumped over and threw Banbury a questioning look.

'Strangulation is a bit more unpleasant than you'd expect,' Banbury explained. 'It's – well, it's an indoor crime.'

Bryant moved in for a closer look. 'What do you mean?'

'There's usually other damage inflicted first – punching, kicking, rape. It's primarily associated with partner abuse. Strangulation is intimate. It suggests anger, power and control.'

'What about the technical side of it?'

Banbury laid out a tray of little white boxes as if he was about to start offering canapés. 'Technical? OK. It would have taken around eleven pounds of pressure applied for ten seconds to make her black out, and over thirty pounds of pressure to close off the trachea. Brain death usually occurs about five minutes later. The gardener found no pulse and thought she was dead but she might not have been, quite. Not his fault. We should try to find the ligature that was used. It's not rope or wire cord, it's got small ridges that have left tiny indentations. He may have thrown it somewhere.'

'John?' Bryant sidled up to his partner. 'What's the problem, old sock?'

May looked forlorn. 'You always say we don't handle this kind of case.'

Bryant removed his homburg, not as a sign of respect but because his ears were hot. 'What are you talking about? We don't know what we're dealing with yet.'

'I do,' said May, so softly that they barely heard him. 'A woman-hater. We can't do anything in situations like this. Violence without rationality – that's for the Met to untangle.'

'It will fall to us whether you like it or not,' Bryant pointed out, smoothing down his white tonsure. 'If people start feeling unsafe in public spaces—'

'But your speciality lies in finding motives, Arthur. If there isn't one, your abilities are useless.'

'Thank you.' Bryant extracted an immense handkerchief from his sleeve and blew his nose. The noise startled starlings. 'It seems to me like you're making an excuse.'

'He's right, John,' said Banbury. 'It's not like you to be squeamish.'

Women, Bryant mouthed theatrically at the crime scene manager. 'What if it turns out there's a motive?' he said aloud. 'You'll be failing her, and possibly others like her.'

May looked down at the path, determined not to see inside the operations tent a second time. 'I don't know, Arthur. After all I've been through lately, I'm not ready for something like this.'

'Ah, so *that's* what this is about,' said Bryant.* 'We don't know the circumstances yet. If it turns out she was attacked by a drunk boyfriend I'll happily hand it straight over to the Met. They seem to enjoy sorting out dreary old domestics, and I don't.'

'Maybe you should learn more about them,' May pointed out. 'Sometimes people do the most extraordinary things. They keep disastrous relationships going just for the pleasure of hurting a partner. Cruelty becomes the only thing that satisfies them.'

---

* John May was falsely accused of murder in *Strange Tide*.

'It all sounds ghastly,' said Bryant dismissively, 'husbands clubbing their wives to death because they've walked in front of the television once too often. Let's treat this as one of our cases for now. We should be able to see what we're up against in a couple of hours, shouldn't we, Dan?'

Unhappily placed between the pair, Banbury could only shrug. 'I hope so, Mr B. There's one other thing. I think he's moved the arms and legs. Not the gardener, the attacker.'

'What makes you say that?'

Banbury tilted his head to one side, considering the corpse. 'If you drop in your tracks, that isn't how you hit the ground. This arm, here, and her leg, not folded under her but set neatly beside the other. And the gravel marks, see? She's too tidy. Almost as if she's been prepared in some small way.' He turned to May, but the detective had walked away.

Bryant considered his partner's uncharacteristic reaction. The attachments John May formed with women were on an entirely different level to his own. They were his lifeline and the source of his strength. Bryant had once thought that the roots of this bond lay in May's need to be found attractive and find attraction in turn, but in the last few years he had come to the recognition of a deeper truth: his partner's respect for women far surpassed that of most men. He was in awe of them, and grew profoundly upset when they proved to be victims of violence, a reaction unsuited to his profession.

Bryant had more layers of protection; he did not understand people and didn't expect to be understood in return, a state of affairs which suited him perfectly. Circumstances interested him, not emotions. As far as he was concerned the male animal was an atavistic, truculent creature who could not be trusted to get the lid off a sardine tin, let alone involve himself in a loving relationship. At the end of every party there was always a girl left crying, never a man.

He looked up at the curving mouse-brown bricks of the terrace. 'She died here in the shadows. There must be a lot of eyes staring down from those windows. There don't seem to be many lights on, but maybe somebody saw something. I'll wander over and have a chat with them.'

'You're not going to wander off anywhere,' called May. 'To keep everyone happy, let's do this by the book, just while you're getting back on your feet.'

'I *am* back on my feet,' said Bryant indignantly. He held up his malacca walking stick. 'This is just to give me an air of sophistication. Behold, Arthur the *flâneur* detective.' He used the tip of the cane to push back his hat and nearly took his eye out.

'Fine, but crime scene first, suspect interview, then witness statements.'

'And murder weapon,' said Bryant, turning about on his heel. 'There isn't one. I mean not dropped nearby. Unless you count this.' Bending down, he lifted an opened Swiss army knife by the tip of its blade.

'Are you touching that?' Banbury all but bellowed. 'Can you just leave it alone until after I've bagged it?'

'Well, it's obviously not the murder weapon, is it?' said Bryant reasonably. 'She's been strangled. Park sweeps always produce fistfuls of knives.'

'Yes, but not in this kind of park. The residents are too exclusive. So what's it doing here?'

'Maybe it's the gardener's. Or someone lobbed it over the wall.' Bryant looked around his feet. 'The grass is wet, the gate is locked, the railings are painted with a special oil that never dries. What can you check for prints?'

'I'll do the gate but I don't know if we're going to pick up much,' said Banbury. 'Sometimes it's worth doing car bonnets.'

'Why?'

'When people squeeze between two parked cars they often put their fingertips down on the car closest to their dominant hand.'

Bryant squinted back at the entrance. 'The gardener had to let the EMT in with his own key, didn't he? So he was locked in here with the victim and her killer. What happened to the weapon after the attack?'

'It's a garden, Mr Bryant, he could have thrown it any-where,' said Banbury, checking his camera. 'It's a cord or cable of some kind, so he probably took it with him. If he didn't, we'll find it when we get a bit more natural light in here.'

'You'd better do so in the next few minutes if you want dabs,' said May. 'According to my phone it's going to rain at nine.'

'I need you to get low shots of the grass in every direction around the path, so we can see if there are any trails through the dew,' said Banbury. 'He must have disturbed something in order to reach her, although I can't see any flattening, which means he came up the path. It's hard-packed gravel.'

'What about a shoe shape? Come on, let's have a shufti.' Bryant headed over to the tent.

'Covers on, please.' Banbury handed him blue paper shoe slips. 'Gloves too.'

The victim was in her late twenties, lying on her back in the centre of the garden's path, dressed in an ice-white designer tracksuit with an expensive-looking red woollen coat beside her. Banbury had closed her eyes but the left one had partially opened again, so that the dead woman appeared to be lewdly winking.

'She's well heeled,' remarked Banbury. 'Gold necklace, solitaire diamond wristband and rings, Prada trainers. Nothing's obviously missing, so it's not a mugging.'

'No bag,' said May. 'A woman dressed like this is bound to want a hairbrush and make-up. Manicured nails, nothing underneath them. What's in her wallet?'

Kneeling awkwardly, Bryant removed a black patent-leather purse from her coat pocket and examined its contents. 'Lots of lovely credit cards. Helen Forester, number thirty-eight, Clement Crescent, Holland Park. That's just over the road. No cigarettes, no smell. Assuming she wouldn't smoke in her flat, it would have been the most logical reason for her coming here.'

'He's right-handed. The bruising is deeper on one side of the throat,' said Banbury. 'There are a couple of tiny upright marks on the neck, possibly caused by her nails as she tried to get her fingers under the ligature.'

'She didn't come out here for a cigarette and she didn't bring a bag with her,' said Bryant. 'She didn't need one. Would anyone like a banana?' He removed a mottled bunch from the voluminous pocket of his overcoat.

May was disgusted. 'How can you think of your stomach at a time like this?'

'I didn't have any breakfast. I could murder a kipper. So, where's the dog?'

'What dog?'

'She's got a plastic poo bag hanging out of her pocket.'

'Of course. It must still be around here.' May eased himself out of the tent.

Grunting with the effort, Bryant bent closer to the body and felt in her tracksuit pockets, producing a set of keys. 'So she comes over from her flat, unlocks the gate and enters the garden with the dog. The gardener is already inside. She gets what – halfway around the crescent? The dog's ears go up – he sees someone. Maybe he hears the gate open and shut. She stops, apprehensive. It's still too dark to spot anything but she feels safe. She's in a small London park a few yards from the main road, but in a way she might as well be in the heart of the countryside. Then what?'

'Her attacker suddenly appears and runs at her,' said Banbury. 'He pulls out some kind of ligature and manages to wrap it around her throat, which he'd have to get very close to do.'

'And he's able to do this before she has time to fend him off? If the dog stopped and alerted her she would have had advance warning. Wouldn't she be wary and protect herself as he came at her?'

'Not if she knew her killer,' Banbury said. 'There are no defence marks.'

'What kind of defence marks would you find in a case of strangulation? He didn't attack her with the knife; there are no palm slashes.' Bryant chewed his banana ruminatively. 'She let him get close enough to choke her, so it was a friendly face. I'll need to get in and out of this park – can you get me a skeleton key?'

'I've told you before, Mr Bryant, I'd get you one if I could be sure you wouldn't go around opening every locked door you come across.'

'I'm naturally curious, that's all,' said Bryant.

'No, Mr B., you're just nosy.'

Outside, Bryant found his partner checking behind mossy stacks of wood. 'Any luck with the dog?'

'He must have got out.' May leaned on his arm to stand up.

'Walk with me, John. Let's think this through for a moment.' He tossed his banana skin at a bin and missed. 'There are unusual elements here. The locked park, the knife, the marks, the missing dog. I'm inclined to assume that it wasn't a drunken lovers' fight, which means this is a case for us. "To prevent crimes capable of causing social panic, violent disorder and general malaise in the public areas of the city, without alarming the populace or alerting it to ongoing operations" – our remit, engraved upon the flinty stone that replaced my heart. If people can't feel safe in residential gardens, they won't feel safe anywhere.' He sniffed the air noisily. 'It doesn't even smell like London in here. There's no CCTV and even in midwinter the cover's dense. No wonder Winston and Julia conducted their affair in rural surroundings in Orwell's 1984. A murder in the prelapsarian paradise of an exclusive locked garden square – I've never come across such a crime before, have you?'

'Only in dreadful old murder mysteries,' said May.

7

'WILD CHAMBERS IN THE URBAN MACHINE'

John May smoothed his silver mane in place and looked around. He was as handsome as he had been a quarter-century ago, with dark, sharp eyes and features that seemed better for their silver setting, as if he had finally grown into his ideal age. 'I remember investigating an attack in Victoria Park once,' he said. 'A violent altercation with a drunken boyfriend, marks everywhere, torn branches, gouges in the grass where he had dragged her by her hair. By comparison, this looks like a kind of dismissive execution. She came here to what should have been a place of calm reflection. Instead, she was choked to death.'

They walked slowly along one of the side paths behind Banbury's tent, in the dripping gloom of the great plane trees. The branches should have been bare at this time of the year, but still had their leaves. They formed a dense canopy overhead that trapped the sickly sunlight and snuffed it out.

'I don't get it,' continued May. 'Why would he wait until she was inside the park? There's a section of road where he wouldn't have been seen.'

'You mean over there, between the parked cars and the

railings?' Bryant hopped about to see between the bushes to the curving pavement beyond.

'Exactly. If he kept low behind those vans and jumped out at her, nobody would have spotted him. I mean, assuming it wasn't the gardener.'

'There certainly would have been more light.' Bryant unpacked his tobacco and began filling his Lorenzo Spitfire. 'At seven on a winter's morning there are no lamps on in here. The only street illumination is behind those trees.'

'Perhaps she disturbed someone who was already in here. Maybe he was a vagrant, which might explain why he was carrying a knife.'

'If he had a knife, why not stab her? Why kill her at all? Why not just scare her away?'

'Someone on the main road must have heard something.'

Bryant squinted up at the sky. 'I'm not so sure. We're surrounded by sound-deadening greenery. We're also under the Heathrow flight path and on a major bus route.' He stopped and slowly turned on one foot, listening. Like many low, stocky men he sometimes possessed the grace of a dancer. 'Hear that? The London engine. There's no such thing as silence or darkness in the city any more.' He allowed his fingers to brush a laurel bush, its wet leaves as shiny as plastic. 'We've made these green spaces a unique feature of England. We copied Italian designs, you know, replacing bare windswept piazzas with plants and lawns, cluttering up the vistas and creating these arbours of tranquillity, islands of pastoral freedom.'

'I suppose I never really think about them,' said May.

'You'd notice them if they weren't here. People need parks. That's why they must be kept safe. They're a national legacy. I'm surprised the government hasn't found a way to monetize them.' They made their way back to the geodesic tent. 'Dan, can I look for the weapon?'

'I wish you wouldn't, Mr Bryant,' Banbury called. 'The eliminations are going to be hard enough as it is. We've already had three EMTs and four officers in here, plus whoever else has been using the place since it rained the day before yesterday. I need to find out how this bloke got in.'

'I rather think you need to find out the reverse.' Bryant headed for a wooden bench and eased himself on to it for a puff and a ponder. 'It was either the gardener, who, let's not forget, called the emergency services as soon as he could, or someone who had a key to the main gate and let himself in behind her, or someone who was *already* in the park, possibly overnight, in which case how did he get *out*? She has flat shoes, yes?'

Banbury looked puzzled. 'Trainers.'

'And she's what, five six?'

'Give or take an inch.'

'Then we need to get her neck examined.'

'Why so?'

'The depth and angle of the ligature might give us an idea of his height.' Bryant took a laborious drag on his pipe, releasing a curl of blue smoke. 'The park's reserved for property owners granted keys by the residents' association. The railings are specifically designed to keep out lowlifes. So, how did he leave?'

'Up a tree and down the other side from an overhanging branch?' May suggested.

'Do you see any overhanging branches?' Bryant rose from the bench. 'The council always remove them. Health and safety. And where's the dog? Did he take it with him?'

As he headed back to the tent a pair of grey squirrels tumbled past. When they saw Bryant they froze, as if realizing that it might not be a good idea to get in the way of his walking stick. 'Have you got anything more for us, Dan?'

Banbury ducked out of the tent, removing his gloves. 'Nothing so far. It was very fast, which doesn't make sense. Strangulation is not a quick option, and yet she just dropped where she stood. I'm wondering if she had a heart attack.'

'Is it normal to have blood forced from the eyes like that?' Bryant sucked noisily at his pipe.

'With this level of sudden force it's not unusual,' Banbury replied. 'Something's bothering me about the ligature marks, though – they don't look right. I need to examine them more carefully with Giles Kershaw.'

'He could have got blood on himself, couldn't he? You didn't find any on the gravel?' May looked down at the ground. 'It would be good to find a witness or get a CCTV grab on him before he has a chance to change his clothes. Have you got a decent team to help you?'

'Yes, but it's going to be a long day,' said Banbury. 'We'll map out and search every square inch of the garden. It's only a small space but there are a lot of bushes.' He stretched his back and looked about. 'It's all so immaculately laid out. It doesn't look like anything violent could ever happen here.'

'You're not going to tear it up,' said a determined female voice. 'You have no right. This is private property.' Margo Farrier stepped forward and stood firm. Although tiny, she cut a formidable figure. She had wrapped herself in an ancient grey fur coat that suggested kinship with the squirrels. 'I am a resident here. Clement Crescent's garden is under our guardianship.'

'I appreciate your concern, madam—' May began, meeting her halfway. He wanted to try to keep her away from his partner, who took particular pleasure in upsetting pensioners, but Bryant was already on his way over.

The old lady held out her hand. 'I'm Margo Farrier. You've probably heard of me.'

'Why?' asked Bryant. 'Are you wanted by the police?'

'I'm on the board of the Clement Crescent co-operative committee.'

Bryant exhaled a cloud of aromatic smoke. Mrs Farrier coughed theatrically. 'You mean you decide who moves into the street?'

'We can't prevent a purchase, of course, but we can make the process awkward for the wrong sort of tenant. For the past thirty-seven years I have lived at number nineteen. You're not allowed to smoke in here.'

'I'm in the great outdoors, Gran, it's hardly a *casus belli*.' Bryant was tempted to blow smoke right in her face.

'It's not an act of war, I agree, but if we allow a pipe it'll be the thin end of the wedge.'

'Actually, we can't allow *you* in at the moment. There's been a violent assault in this park.'

'It's not a park, it's a garden.'

'Very well, this *garden*, and as the circumstances of the attack have not yet been established it's our duty to protect the residents and users of the – *garden*. So hop it.'

Mrs Farrier tried to peer around him. 'It's not the lady who walks her dog, is it? Because she's not supposed to let her dog off the leash in here. She's been told before. She only moved here in September and she's been nothing but trouble.'

'What makes you say that? Did you see her enter this morning?'

'I heard her front door go – she does have an annoying habit of slamming it.'

'What time was this?'

'About seven, I think. She's had warnings from the committee—'

'So you know her name?'

For the first time Mrs Farrier's resolve flickered. 'She's dead, isn't she? That's what the tent is for, to cover her body.'

'Would you be prepared to identify her for us?' Stepping aside, Bryant allowed her to fully see the geodesic tent.

'Arthur, this is unorthodox—' May began.

'We need to verify her identity, John. It'll be quicker this way. Go and have a word with Dan.'

Banbury covered the victim's body, leaving only her face clear. 'Hang on a second. OK, you can bring her over.'

Margo Farrier moved in, more intrigued than upset. 'Yes,' she confirmed, gripping the lapels of her fur coat tightly as if suddenly feeling a chill. 'That's Helen Forester. She was one of the new people. We've never had trouble here before.'

'Sorry to put you through that,' said Bryant insincerely. 'Would you like a banana?'

Mrs Farrier ignored the offer of bruised fruit. 'We didn't get on well. She told me to mind my own business. Even so – poor soul.'

'What do you mean, she was one of the new people?'

'She moved in only a few months ago, and with that yappy little dog. Where is the dog?'

'Do you remember his name?'

'Beauchamp, I think. Spelled like the Earl of Warwick, not the cold remedy. Such a pretentious name for a West Highland terrier. She's a tenant, not an owner. She said she was going to buy her flat, but – I don't know – she must have changed her mind.'

'I think we need to get you out of here, Mrs Farrier.' May took the old lady's arm and led her away. 'For all we know, the person who attacked her could be in here.'

Mrs Farrier's eyes widened in fright. 'You think he's still inside the garden?'

'For your own safety I'd prefer it if you went back to your home. I'll be happy to escort you. We'll need to talk to you a bit later.'

'Yes, I suppose so,' she said, quavering just a little. 'I hope you find him.'

May walked her back, mainly to make sure that she didn't touch anything. 'Do you have a key?' he asked gently as she was standing before the gate without making an attempt to unlock it.

'Of course. I'm sorry. I didn't mean to be rude when I said we didn't get along. It was just the dog. The committee has rules. How did you get in?'

'We have the gardener's key.'

'You don't think it was him? He's new. He's, well – coloured.'

'We won't know anything for a while,' May said.

'She was getting a divorce,' Mrs Farrier volunteered. 'The

husband came around a couple of times. You've never heard such language.'

'They argued?'

'He was outside very late one night and shouted at her, right from the street.' Mrs Farrier bridled at the thought. 'One doesn't expect that sort of behaviour here. It's always been a decent neighbourhood.'

'What did they argue about?'

'I think he must have needed money. He said he'd come back for it and she couldn't stop him.'

'What did she say?'

'I couldn't hear very clearly.' Mrs Farrier's eyes watered. 'And now she's gone to meet her maker.'

'Best not to dwell on it,' said May. 'Perhaps you should make yourself a nice cup of tea.' He waited on the pavement, watching until she was inside.

Arthur Bryant tossed his banana bag at a bin and missed. 'You don't think he's still hiding in here somewhere, do you? I mean, it's not that big. What could he do, dig a pit and cover himself with leaves?'

Banbury rose and looked over Bryant's shoulder. It seemed to be getting darker, not lighter. 'It wouldn't be logical to stick around. Would you?'

'If I didn't have a way of getting out, I wouldn't have much choice, would I?' Bryant replied. 'Look at it, flowers and lawns, it all seems so safe. Parks weren't always, of course. Racist and homophobic attacks were part of everyday life in parks, as well as assaults on lone women. I honestly thought we were getting past all that, then along comes something like this. You know what they used to call parks? Wild chambers. Wild chambers in the urban machine.'

Together they stared off into the dankness of the rain-ticking bushes.

8

'GARDENS AREN'T SUPPOSED TO BE LETHAL'

Janice Longbright walked into the freshly painted operations room and threw her bag on to a chair, only to find Jack Renfield standing before her, as awkward as a coal miner in a cake shop, looking around for somewhere to sit and something to do with his great meaty fists that wouldn't break or spill anything.

'Move my bag, will you?' she told him. 'Stick it on the floor.'

He did as he was told. 'Blimey, what have you got in there, bricks?'

'Just the one. What are you doing here, Jack?' There was no animosity in her voice, only curiosity. She set down her coffee and removed her coat.

Renfield blew through his mouth, raised his dimple and let his eyebrows creep upward in a catalogue of awkward male responses. 'I got a call to come in. You've got a new case and Raymond is short-staffed.'

'Are you back for good? Or is this a temporary thing?'

'I think his idea is to see how it goes.'

Longbright pointed to the opposite desk. 'Fraternity was

going to take that space but he's moved on. He's going to specialize. You may as well have it.'

Renfield didn't budge. He couldn't have looked more awkward if he'd been caught donning drag on the *Titanic*.

'Look, I don't want there to be any bad feeling between us, Jack. What happened before—'

'Water under the bridge, Janice, I assure you.' It was an unfortunate turn of phrase, seeing as they'd been standing beside the canal when Renfield had announced he was leaving her and the unit. 'I'm not here because of you. Don't think that. This is work. You've got a job to do and so have I.' He cut the edge of one palm against the flat of the other, showing he meant business.

'But that's just what I mean, pretending that nothing happened—'

'No, I know what I did and it was harsh, I admit that, fair play, and you've every right not to talk to me again,' Renfield blustered. 'I got uncomfortable and scarpered. I thought it wasn't for me, all of this . . .'

Longbright folded her arms and stared at him. 'All of what, exactly?'

Renfield blew again, waving a hand. 'Oh, you know, everybody arguing and Mr Bryant setting fire to things, and those workmen tearing up the floors and cats everywhere. But going back to the Met . . . When I heard you were short-staffed it seemed right to come back.'

'So my feelings weren't a factor, then?'

'You? God no, I'd almost forgotten you were here, to be honest.'

He had certainly not forgotten that Janice was here; how could he when she haunted his sleep? He admired her – that was the word for it. She was an admirable woman, full of hip and lip, good-humoured, smarter and braver than anyone he knew, but he feared that she would never need him, and now that his weakness had been exposed he was in her thrall. The sensation made Renfield uncomfortable. He was a good man, but not always a modern one.

'Hm.' Longbright gave him what her mother would have called an old-fashioned look. 'I get why you went. I'm not sure I understand why you've returned, so let's just see how it goes, eh?'

'Yeah, great, yes, I mean of course, whatever. But we can be friends, yeah?'

'Friends – I think so.'

'Friends, cool, sure.' He jumped up and clasped her hand like a teacher congratulating a pupil on prize-giving day, held it fractionally too long, then released it as if he'd been electrocuted. 'So, we're all together in this space now?' As conversational segues went it wasn't the smoothest.

'Raymond's keeping his old office, and John and Arthur have their own room because nobody wanted them in here with us. Are they back yet?'

Renfield smiled. Janice was the only one who dared to call Mr Bryant by his first name. 'I think so,' he said.

'Then let's get everyone together and find out what's going on.'

Happy to have something to do, Renfield nodded a little too vigorously and went to work.

The furniture in the old briefing room was pushed to the back because several of the floorboards were still raised. Since one of the workmen could be heard gonging a pipe somewhere under the carpet, the group gathered as if stepping through a minefield. They were joined by a six-foot-tall woman in her late twenties. The sides of her head were shaved in a Camden cut, leaving a thatch of thick blond hair on top that made her look like a river bird. She had an extraordinarily long neck and wore a nose ring, which would have been considered a health and safety issue in any other police department.

'This is Steffi Vesta,' Raymond announced with pride.

'She's from . . .' He racked his brain. It was a town in Germany that had something to do with grooming products . . .

'Cologne,' said Steffi, with only the faintest trace of an accent.

'Yes, well – she's going to be with us as Christmas cover, seeing how a British specialist unit operates, so try not to make her uncomfortable.'

Steffi turned and gave the group a confident smile. Colin grinned back, but stopped when he saw that Meera was watching him. Steffi's skin was as smooth as a dinner plate. She looked far too young and healthy to be working in a run-down police unit in King's Cross. It made Meera feel sick to look at her. She felt her lip curling.

As everyone took their usual places they surreptitiously watched the door like a congregation waiting for the bride to arrive. As soon as the detectives entered, Raymond Land leaped up and ushered them to a pair of seats before taking a proprietorial place in front of the room's whiteboard.

'What's happening here?' Meera asked from the side of her mouth.

'Raymond's doing a business management course,' said Colin. 'Janice reckons he's trying to assert himself. He's bought a pair of glasses because he wants to be taken seriously.' They stifled their laughter together.

'Right, you lot,' said Land, tapping the whiteboard. 'We've got a female Caucasian, Helen Forester, twenty-nine-year-old head of a public relations company, found strangled in the gardens of Clement Crescent, Holland Park, at approximately seven fifteen this morning while she was out walking her dog. Dan's still at the scene and hasn't put in a report yet, but he reckons somebody came up the footpath and surprised her because the dew on the grass had only been disturbed by the dog, which incidentally is missing. So far Dan's found nothing in the bushes or the surrounding area.'

'Not true,' called Bryant. 'We have a Swiss army knife. It may not be related but there are prints on it.'

Land pursed his lips and allowed for a stage pause, unhappy about being interrupted. 'Mrs Forester rents a house in the crescent,' he continued. 'These are properties subdivided into very expensive flats. White-collar, professional, more than half sold to overseas buyers. Mrs Forester was in the middle of a messy divorce. We haven't spoken to the husband yet, mainly because he no longer works at his old office and his mobile number is dead. He's not officially a suspect but he was overheard fighting with her a couple of weeks ago, so can somebody try to find out where he is?'

He looked down at his notes and withdrew a pair of tortoiseshell glasses so preposterous in design that everyone stopped listening and stared at them.

'Helen Forester walked the dog at the same time most days. There was an ongoing dispute about that with the neighbours, who don't allow unleashed animals in the communal gardens. The lady who identified her, a Mrs Farrier, heard her front door slam at around seven a.m. The problem is, the garden gates can only be opened with a key. To obtain one of these keys you have to be a resident in the crescent, and only one key is allowed per property. The residents' association is extremely strict about that.'

'How many keys in total?' asked May.

'How do I know?' said Land. 'I'm just telling you what it says here.'

'How did her attacker reach her?' asked Renfield. 'Did he climb over the wall?'

'I haven't started questions yet, have I?' Nettled, Land stabbed his glasses further up his nose. 'The railings are high and impossible to climb, so the killer must have a key. Mrs Forester was found by the gardener, who is . . . Why isn't his name up here on my board?'

'Ritchie Jackson,' said Longbright, reading her notes. 'He saw her just before the assault and very soon after—'

'So where was he when the attack occurred?' asked Renfield.

'He says he was on the other side of the lawn taking photographs when she walked past with her dog,' Longbright replied. 'When he heard her call for the dog he came back and found her lying on the ground. He knew she was dead but was scared of disturbing her, and stayed by her side while he rang the emergency services. He didn't see anyone else, and can verify that the gate was locked when he arrived. The sun was coming up but it was misty and the light was very low. Dan's found two sets of tiny blood spots, one beside Mrs Forester and the other from Jackson, who says he tore his hand pulling out some brambles.'

'Don't gardeners wear gloves?'

'He hadn't put them on yet.'

'What was he doing spying on her anyway?' asked Land. 'Bit of a perv, is he?'

'He was taking shots of the gardens,' Bryant piped up. 'It's his hobby.'

Land looked mystified. 'Why would he be lurking around snapping pictures of shrubbery first thing in the morning?'

'He's interested in plants, you mounter,' snapped Bryant. 'Oh, I meant to think that, not say it out loud.' He turned to May. '*Mounter*, a provider of false information, 1780, obsolete.' Lately Bryant had decided there were too few appropriate insults in the current English dictionary and had been studying archaic slang to improve the strength of his invective. 'Ritchie Jackson graduated from horticultural college with a degree in environmental science, then trained as a photographer at Goldsmith's, but he didn't finish the course. He took on short-term work, contract stuff, but still likes to take photographs and recently submitted several to an exhibition—'

'Can we stay on topic?' begged Land, exasperated. 'We don't need to hear about this bloke's pastimes, we just need to know whether he got off spying on girls.'

'Don't be such a roof-scraper, Raymond,' said Bryant. He glanced back at May. '*Roof-scraper*, someone who misses all the important details, spectator standing at the back of a gallery, 1909, colloquial.'

'What are you saying about me?' Land demanded to know. 'No, don't look at your friend, I'm talking to you.'

'Arthur's still not feeling a hundred per cent, I'm afraid,' said May hastily. 'When Ritchie Jackson arrived for work this morning, he says, the gates were definitely locked. He drank a coffee, took some shots of the lawn and his new planting, and he also took this.'

He rose and tacked a blown-up photograph on the whiteboard. It showed Mrs Forester in her white tracksuit and scarlet coat, side profile, the white terrier running ahead of her on its lead. The brightest light source came from the top deck of a bus which could be glimpsed through the dark green branches of the trees behind her.

'Why did he take the picture at all?' asked Bryant. 'If he's often there and she walks the dog most mornings, they must know each other. So why sneak off this shot?'

'He obviously fancies her,' said Land. 'Why else would he creep about taking photos on the quiet?'

'Are you sure you want to make him a suspect?' asked May. 'As soon as he found her body he called it in. And it's a good thing he took the photo, because there's this.' He walked to the board again, drawing a circle on the photo with a red crayon. 'Look in the bushes.'

Everyone came forward to see. Land tried to remember if there was any advice in his management manual that would help him take back control of the meeting, but his mind had gone blank.

'There's a man's face right here.' May pointed out a shadowy oval between the laurel leaves. 'Steffi's digitally enhancing the shot for me. The contours are clearly delineated but his features are indistinct. He's crouching, looking up in Mrs Forester's direction.'

'I may be able to get more detail from it,' said Steffi. 'He's on his – what are these parts?' She tapped her thigh.

'Haunches,' said Colin.

'Yes, he is on his haunches in the bushes right behind her, watching.'

'Oh, man, that's really creepy,' said Meera.

'Jack in the Green,' said Bryant.

'What, you know who this is?' demanded Land.

'I was merely citing the garland-covered May Day participant, the trickster embodiment of natural fertility in English folklore,' said Bryant.

'Well, can you not? We don't need you dragging in mythological figures. Steffi, can you get any more out of this?'

'I think perhaps I will manage a facial contour and an approximate height,' said Steffi, nodding.

'How do we go about finding him?' Renfield asked.

'John's going to talk to Mr Jackson while Meera and Colin interview the keyholders,' Bryant said. 'Janice, I need you to run a background check on Mrs Forester and pull together a list of names. Steffi and Jack, you help Dan. See if you can come up with anything more from this picture and from the gardens. Your main priority is to find the husband, but let's dig out anyone else she might have seen recently – family, friends, the lot.'

'What about me?' asked Land, once more feeling like the last pupil to be picked for the team. 'I'm the boss here, I should be of some use.'

'Why don't you stay here and keep the press and the Home Office off our backs?' suggested Bryant. 'I think they're going to be interested in this one. It would be an enormous help.'

Land waited for his most senior detective to add an eighteenth-century insult, but nothing came. *Maybe his health scare has had a beneficial effect after all,* he thought, happy to do as he was told for once.

'Trillibub,' muttered Bryant as he left the room. 'A portly fool, 1800, derogatory.'

*

Ritchie Jackson had no faith in the police. He swung back and forth on his stool, his hands between his knees. He was a solidly built, tall young man, but awkwardly set and uncomfortable with strangers. Now he was anxious to get back to his garden.

'Well, there's not too much damage on your CV,' said May, reading the page Longbright had given him. 'A drunk and disorderly and a caution for possession, nothing to get excited about.'

'Yeah, surprising considering,' Ritchie murmured, swinging back and forth.

'Considering what?'

'I don't need to remind you about the odds of a black guy getting stopped in a wealthy area.'

'That may happen in Holland Park, Mr Jackson, but we're in King's Cross,' said May. 'You're in the big wide world here, not Little England.'

'That's comforting to know.'

May studied his witness. He was scruffily dressed in a bagged-out grey jumper and mud-streaked jeans, and had dirt under his fingernails, but looked powerful enough to take a life.

'Show me the cut on your hand?'

Ritchie held up his right palm. 'I was on my way in and saw some branches that had come loose overnight. I tried to pull them loose and they sprang back. Hazard of the job.'

'What did you use?'

'I've got a Swiss army knife that I use for pruning.'

'Where is it now?'

Ritchie looked blank. 'I had it earlier. I must have put it down somewhere.'

'How many times had you noticed Mrs Forester in the garden before?'

'I don't know – a few.'

'Five, ten, what?'

'Maybe half a dozen times.'

'Over how long a period?'

'A couple of months, I guess. She usually came in before I got there.'

'How do you know?'

'I'd see her leaving. I think she went early knowing that most people wouldn't be up. She liked to let her dog off the leash.'

'Did she ever say hello?'

He shook his head. 'To me? No. I'm the invisible bloke with a rake in one hand.'

'But she knew who you were?'

'I don't know. I guess so.'

'What's the foot traffic like in the garden? You get many people coming in during the day?'

'Not many. It always seems a bit of a waste to me. I guess there was a time when all the houses in the crescent were occupied by families, but you don't see many lights on now. Everyone's at work or in another country.'

'The usual.' May nodded, tapping a pen against his list. 'Overseas investors and single professionals. I guess they're not the kind of people who take walks in parks. Even so, you must see some of the same faces.'

'Not that many. I don't know anyone's names apart from Margo Farrier, because she heads up the committee and I have to follow her planting schedule. And Professor Clarke at number forty-two, who hired me from the agency. And there's an elderly Indian gentleman, I can't remember his name. I keep all the beds and borders trimmed according to Mrs Farrier's plans, and I have to know the names of everything I plant because she tests me. So yeah, we sometimes talk.'

'Why did you take Mrs Forester's picture?'

Ritchie shrugged. 'I'd already lined the shot up to frame the winter planting in the flowerbed. I was looking for some colour to go in it. She walked into the frame wearing that red coat.'

'My colleague thinks it's odd that you let the buddleia remain.'

Ritchie laughed. 'There are over a hundred different species of the butterfly bush. It's also known as the bombsite plant because it sprouts in rubble. It's usually invasive but ours is a sterile seed variety. Mrs Farrier likes them because she says they remind her of London after the war.'

'Ever photograph Helen Forester before?'

'No, man.' The gardener pointed to his phone. 'You've got all my shots going back nearly a year. It's mostly reference for the planting. I have the rest marked with dates and locations on my hard drive. You can go through them if you want.'

'What do you do on the days you're not at Clement Crescent?'

'I help out in other parks and gardens. Wanstead, Syon, London Fields, Bishop's Park, Kensal Green, all over. I don't just do gardening. I do some seasonal delivering and I design websites for mates.'

'When you took the shot, did you realize there was someone else in it?'

'No, I couldn't see much in the background. The light source was limited.'

May walked to the window and looked out. It had started to rain hard, which would make Banbury's job more difficult. 'So you didn't see anyone else this morning?'

'No.'

'Does anyone ever manage to climb into the gardens? Do you get any break-ins?'

Jackson pulled at a thread on his sweater, thinking. 'The railings were repaired and repainted recently because some women had tried to get in and dig up the plants. They had baby buggies with them, loaded with flowers they'd cut from people's front gardens. I'd heard about some Albanians doing this over in Hackney but never in Holland Park before. We chased them off.'

'How did the workmen get in and out?'

'I let them in; they never had keys.'

May stood thoughtfully for a moment. Banbury had

checked the gardener's shed and had found only secateurs, fertilizer and shovels.

'There's one thing,' said Ritchie. 'It may be nothing. I'd seen Mrs Forester coming in through the gate a couple of times. Before she unlocked it she always looked around, left and right, like she was doing something wrong. I don't want to say anything bad about a dead lady, I just remember noticing. It was like she was checking for someone.' He shook his head in wonder. 'Man, who'd have thought you could lose your life just walking a dog? Gardens aren't supposed to be lethal.'

'Was she always alone apart from the dog?'

'She just had Beauchamp. That was its name. You know, one of those upper-class names like Cholmondeley, spelled different to the way it's pronounced. A white West Highland terrier.'

'How do you know it was spelled differently?' said May.

'What?' Ritchie looked confused.

'You must have seen the name written down.'

'Oh, right. Yeah, maybe I saw the collar, or Mrs Farrier told me.'

'Do you ever get homeless people in the garden?'

'No, I told you, they can't get in. There's a whole privacy thing about places like Clement Crescent. They have a history – Mrs Farrier would be able to tell you.'

'OK,' May said finally, turning off his tablet. 'Off you go. We've got your details in case we think of anything else.'

Ritchie slowly rose, as if he couldn't believe that was all there was to it, and shook May's hand with awkward formality.

'Don't get too excited. You're not off the hook yet,' May warned. 'We'll have to recall you at some point.'

'But I haven't done anything wrong,' insisted Ritchie. 'OK, I took a photograph when she wasn't looking. That's not a crime, is it?'

'No,' May agreed, 'but moments later she was dead, which puts you in the picture whether you like it or not.'

9

'ALL IT TOOK WAS A MURDERER ON THE LOOSE'

'Are you sure you're up to driving?' May asked as he clambered into Victor, Bryant's scabrous yellow Mini. 'If you think you're likely to have any more hallucinations, you would say so, wouldn't you?'

'You worry too much,' said Bryant cheerfully. 'My driving's as good as it's ever been.'

'That's what I'm afraid of.' As May shut the door a large piece of rust dropped off its base.

The car had a manual choke and always had to clear its throat before starting. 'The dreams feel very real when they happen, and only occur when I'm in a sort of reflective alpha state,' Bryant explained, smearing the windscreen with his coat sleeve. 'My mind starts drifting and things appear to me – sights, sounds, smells, even touch. It feels so real that I have trouble discerning reality from fantasy.'

'So no change there, really,' said May.

Bryant lurched away from the kerb and out into the traffic without bothering to look or signal. He'd come to anticipate the chorus of horns greeting his entry into the traffic stream, rather as bugles announced the arrival of Caesar.

'I don't suppose we know yet if Helen Forester had a lover or anything of that sort?' May glanced around nervously at the looming proximity of buses.

'She has an older sister,' answered Bryant. 'No close friends, though. Her employees reckon she was following a career plan that didn't make much of an allowance for relationships. I got the feeling they meant that included her husband.'

'That makes it trickier. You're going the wrong way.'

'No, this is the fastest way to the St Pancras Coroner's Office,' said Bryant confidently.

'I mean you're actually going the wrong way.' May pointed out of the window at the steady stream of hooting vehicles coming towards them.

'They're always changing the road layout here,' said Bryant, unconcerned. 'It becomes two-way again after the next block.' He stamped on the accelerator.

'What are you doing?' May yelled, sliding down in his seat.

'If we get there faster we'll have less chance of hitting anything.' Bryant crunched the gears. He suffered from a level of anatopism usually only found in very bad eighteenth-century explorers. 'I was thinking about what you said, to wit: Why would he attack her *inside* the park? I can only come up with two reasons. One, because they had an argument and he lost his rag, which would make it unpremeditated; and B, because if he attacked her outside there was a risk of someone coming along the pavement and identifying him, which makes it planned. After all, the street is public, the garden is not. What's this fellow's problem?'

A lorry driver leaned out of his window, swore at the Mini and waved two fingers at it. 'Get back on yer own side of the road, mate.'

'*Lack-linen dumbsquint!*' Bryant shouted. 'Mid-eighteenth-century, sexual.' He swung a hard right and they jolted into the Euston Road. 'Actually, you're right, there is a faster way than this. I tried to find it once and ended up in Birmingham.

Or was it Barking? I don't know – somewhere ghastly. But if you pick the park, you see, you rather nail your colours to the mast.'

'What do you mean?' May asked.

'I mean you have to use a key to get in, and that limits the suspect gene pool. Dan tried climbing over the railings and couldn't even get halfway up. Ruined a new pair of strides apparently.' He pulled up on a double red line. 'Open the glove box, there's a chap. Any of them will do.'

May did as he was told and extracted several parking passes including 'Disabled', 'Emergency Electrical Repair' and 'Bulawayo Consulate Diplomatic Vehicle'.

'So what are we looking for,' asked Bryant, 'a spurned lover, a business rival or some total stranger who committed murder on the spur of the moment and could easily do it again?'

'That doesn't narrow it down much,' May replied.

The detectives made their way up the meandering path through the graveyard of St Pancras Old Church. 'It never ceases to amaze me that a place like this can still exist in central London,' said Bryant. 'There was a Roman encampment on this spot, you know.'

'I know, you told me,' said May. 'Several times.'

Bryant would not be dissuaded. 'Their temple converted to Christian worship in the year 313. The sons of Bach and Benjamin Franklin, John Polidori, Mary Wollstonecraft, Dickens, Hardy, Byron, Shelley and Gilbert Scott, the chap who designed the red telephone boxes – all of them ended up here in this unassuming little side park. Don't these green spaces fill you with the enrichment of manifold destinies?'

'They give me chilblains.' May looked at him in amazement. 'You really are back to your old self, aren't you? All perked up and raring to go, and all it took was a murderer on the loose.'

Bryant laughed. 'My drug of choice. Mind you, this particular vista is starting to lose its Victorian aspect now,' he said, pointing at the curved blocks of new steel-and-glass apartments that had been built on the other side of the canal. The 'luxury loft lifestyle studios', or FutureSlums™ as Bryant disparagingly referred to them, provided the investment opportunities for speculators that had sent London's property prices to celestial heights.

Bryant stepped up to the ivy-clamped Gothic arch of the coroner's door and leaned on the bell for a while.

Rosa Lysandrou suddenly appeared. 'One short ring is sufficient,' she snapped.

'God, it's you,' said Bryant, clutching at his raincoat. 'For a moment I thought Mrs Danvers was back. You almost gave me a heart attack.'

'Almost doesn't count,' replied Rosa, not budging from the threshold. The Greek housekeeper had been lavender-polishing the chapel crucifix when the doorbell rang and she hated being interrupted when she was shining Jesus.

Bryant's blue eyes narrowed. 'You're looking very pale, Rosa. Doesn't she look pale, John? Working in a mortuary doesn't agree with everyone. You need a bit of life, get a job in a pub or something. Don't tell me you haven't pulled a pint before with those arms. Take up a hobby. You could play poker with that face, or darts. Get some fresh air; go for a walk around the graveyard. On second thoughts, better not, there are old people around. Can Giles come out to play?'

'Mr Kershaw is a very busy man,' said Rosa, folding her arms. 'Are you here for a purpose?'

Bryant rolled his eyes heavenward. 'What are any of us here for? I often wonder, don't you? No, of course not, but perhaps it's not for us to decide. We toil away all our lives, accumulating the wisdom of the ancients, only to have someone shovel dirt in our faces and leave garage flowers on our headstones.

> 'Farewell my pleasures past,
> Welcome my present pain,

> I feel my torments so increase
> That life cannot remain . . .

'Anne Boleyn,' he finished.

'Death is not the end, Mr Bryant,' said Rosa, opening the door with slow menace.

'I don't know – it slows you down a bit.'

'For some of us this earthly life is merely a waiting room.'

Bryant stepped inside. 'Not your waiting room, I hope. You've still got back issues of *Punch* and *Titbits*.' He sniffed the air. 'Are you wearing a new perfume or is it just damp in here? Kindly announce us and put the kettle on.'

'You shouldn't keep teasing her like that,' said May as Rosa trudged off to warn Giles Kershaw that he had visitors. 'You know Jack Renfield once went on a date with her.'

'No wonder he used to look so miserable. She probably took him to a horror film.'

'I don't know why you're always so mean to her.'

'Sorry, it's my inbuilt response to the pessimistic mindset.' Bryant pulled out a log of chocolate nougat and tore open the purple wrapper. 'Being alive is reason enough to be joyful. Do you want half of my Aztec bar?'

'They haven't made those for years,' said May.

'Well, I haven't worn this coat for a while.' He looked about. 'God, it's depressing in here.'

'What do you want, a pinball table?'

'It would be a start. I wonder if we'll get tea before it's time for Rosa to climb back on the church roof and start spouting water again. Ah, Giles.'

'Gentlemen!' Kershaw strode towards them in his lab coat, blond of hair and pink of cheek, a picture of health and vitality, like some 1950s brochure extolling the benefits of naturism.

'You always look so fresh,' said Bryant. 'Do you sleep in cellophane?'

'No, Mr Bryant, I lead a pure and blameless life.'

'I hate you. Have you seen me lately? I look like I won the wrinkle lottery. Have you had a chance to look at Mrs Forester?'

'Yes. Come through. Dan sent me your photographic evidence of the killer. Is there any way of making the shot clearer?'

'Steffi is having a go but she doesn't think we'll get much beyond ethnicity, sex and height,' said May.

'Steffi?'

'Yes, a very attractive young German lady. Kindly stay away from her.'

'Maybe I can get you a cranial type and rough age group.' Giles opened the door to the mortuary. 'I need you to see the victim again.'

'What have you got so far?' asked May, heading towards the covered body.

'You can see the ligature damage quite clearly.' Giles folded back the material and tapped Helen Forester's blackened throat with the old telescopic stick he always carried with him. 'A thin ridged cord of some kind, angled upward to the back of the neck, which suggests he was a different height to her.'

'But not of abnormal height,' said Bryant, 'meaning that he didn't pull himself over the railings to gain entry to the gardens.'

'No, but I think he must be very strong. The cord cut deeply, actually slicing the flesh. Of course people find the strength to do terrible things when they're het up. It was a vicious act. Strangulation's usually a spontaneous outburst of temper, but I don't think this was.'

'Why?'

'Well, it's the only strike point. He choked her first try. No facial bruising. There's something else.' He reached down and carefully turned her head to one side. Around the back of her neck a series of dark spots ran in a perfectly neat line, right on the ligature mark. 'It looks to me like she was wearing a necklace and he grabbed her very hard, pulling her to him and leaving these tiny bruises. Maybe it allowed him to hold her in place until she died. What bothers me is that they aren't normal.'

'Why not?' asked Bryant, intrigued.

'They just don't look right. Threaded pearls or beads would break, wouldn't they? You'd have found them scattered around.'

'Not a very scientific hypothesis, Giles.'

'Sometimes it's hard to say exactly what's different – the uniformity of the markings perhaps. You didn't find anything at all unusual at the site?'

'It was unusual insofar as we didn't find anything usual.' Bryant picked up a large china eyeball and peered into it. 'No signs of a struggle, no ground disturbance, no weapon.'

'What do you know about her?'

'Not much yet,' admitted May. 'She was the head of a PR company based in Hammersmith, mostly working on American soft-drink accounts, very well paid. Not really the kind of job where you make enemies. She was a very dedicated worker. Her colleagues never saw her outside of the office. Her divorce was just going through. She'd been setting up an art gallery, but it was being financed by her husband, so the separation put paid to that.'

'Where is the ex-husband? Has anybody spoken to him?'

'We're trying to get hold of him now but it's proving trickier than expected. He may not be avoiding us, but it's starting to look that way. No lovers have surfaced yet. It's early days. Janice has turned up a couple of acquaintances and a sister, but they haven't seen her for a while.'

'Could this have been a case of mistaken identity?' Giles wondered. 'What do you think, Mr Bryant?'

'Railings,' said Bryant, setting down the eyeball.

'I'm sorry?'

Bryant rarely felt the need to explain his thought processes and usually ignored blank looks from his colleagues, but decided he should make an effort today. 'Gardens like the one in Clement Crescent once had wooden stakes around them designed to segregate the population. Later they were replaced by permanent railings. Our fair city was segregated. Ladies of gentility weren't allowed to parade unescorted, so communal gardens provided safe havens, somewhere they could sit and read without being approached by ruffians. People could see there were, quote, "thieves without and nothing to steal within". Right up until the 1960s there was a sign in Montpelier Square banning all street cries. God forbid we disturbed the gentlefolk inside. The squares all came with locks and keys, and remain under the guardianship of house-owners to this day.'

'Lovely though it is to see you back on form,' said Giles, 'I really can't see how this is relevant.'

'Well, it's not just about privacy.' Bryant dug out a tube of Love Hearts and offered them around.

'What do you mean?' May asked.

'Churchill suggested getting rid of all the railings during the First World War. Campaigns began to have the railings removed.'

'Is this like the wartime initiative to melt down saucepans and make Spitfires?'

'Yes, but there was a bit more behind the idea. It fitted with the socialist ethic of taking away the privilege of privacy and opening London's land to all, so the subject of removing railings became a political hot potato. The parks' users argued that without railings the new automobiles could smash into parks and kill children, but the railings were removed to supposedly make armaments in almost every London park and square – except for the ones around Bedford Square, because the Duke of Bedford was a pacifist.'

'Forgive me, Mr Bryant, I still don't quite see where you're going with this.'

'I'm trying to show you the bigger picture.' Bryant checked his Love Heart. It read, 'CRAZY GUY!' 'As soon as the war was over the railings were put back, much to George Orwell's disgust. He saw their removal as a democratic gesture and longed to get rid of all the keys, so that the poor could enjoy what the rich had kept to themselves. London's history is filled with squabbles about the removal and replacement of dividing lines, right from the time of the Enclosures. They were the physical separations of class, created by the idea that every man's home is his castle and every scrap of garden attached to it an Eden.'

'Nope,' said Giles, 'still not getting it, Mr B.'

'All right, let me make this simpler,' said Bryant, as if having to explain himself to an inattentive classroom. 'Those outside represent chaos. Those inside, order. Therefore we have a motive. Helen Forester, wealthy, successful, moves from a six-million-pound house in Primrose Hill to live alone in an expensive rented flat in Holland Park that she plans to buy, and is seen every day in her private garden by someone outside who envies her lifestyle. We may not find our suspect among those who already have keys. Last month local residents persuaded the police to move a cardboard city from the end of Clement Crescent. We need to find out who was evicted. As for the railings, they're no longer welded in. They're designed to be removed and returned. You can still gain access to some private spaces by lifting them out.'

Realization dawned. 'Has anyone checked to see whether the railing poles can be removed from the outside?' asked Giles.

'Dan and Jack are on it right now, old sausage,' Bryant replied, popping the sweet into his mouth.

10

'SOMETIMES HIS IMAGINATION GETS THE BETTER OF HIM'

Jack Renfield clambered out of a holly bush with a black plastic bag in his fist. 'They didn't take any names,' he reported.

'What, from the cardboard encampment? Nor should they. Being homeless isn't against the law.' Dan Banbury took the bag from him and added it to the small pile of items he'd found in the shrubbery. If they couldn't identify any of the vagrants who had erected makeshift homes against the railings of Clement Crescent, they could at least sift through the debris that had made its way into the back of the park's bushes.

'If this had gone to the CID, they'd have a hefty team going through every blade of grass looking for evidence,' said Renfield. 'Just because we fall under the City of London we have to use our own staff for searches. You'd think they'd want to hang on to a case like this.'

'You're joking,' said Banbury. 'Only half of the officers in the CID are fully trained. Expertise shortage. As soon as they get qualified they bugger off for better jobs abroad. With our success record they're more than happy to let us take over. I was talking to one of the beat cops about the homeless. He says they were pretty harmless. Most of 'em just wanted to get some sleep. Messy buggers, though. Upset the neighbours. They attached their cardboard boxes to the railings with cable ties. The ligature marks on Helen Forester's neck had ridges, so it's worth checking out.'

So far about 60 per cent of the garden had been marked off into squares, each of which was tagged once it was examined. Outside, the dull roar of buses made the pair aware of passing time; it was now 11.45 a.m. and raining lightly.

They had checked the railing spears and found all but two solidly welded into place. Even with the loose ones removed there wasn't enough of a gap for anyone to squeeze through. Renfield squelched about, looking for anything else that might have made its way into the garden. So far they had only found junk-food boxes, plastic bottles and old newspapers.

'I guess when the council repaired the exterior they decided to fix the railings,' said Banbury, climbing off his knees and giving them a stretch. 'Anyway, there have to be easier ways to get into the garden than by dismantling them. Don't get me wrong, I'm loyal to old Bryant and I'm glad he's back on form, but you have to take his theories with a massive pinch of salt. Sometimes his imagination gets the better of him.'

'I never have any idea what he's on about,' Renfield admitted.

'You came back, though.' Banbury folded away his equipment box.

'Yeah, well, the Met was pretty boring after this. Funnily enough, they don't like being lumbered with serious investigations. They prefer quick in-and-out stuff.'

The crime scene manager tried to sound casual. 'How's Janice?'

'What, you mean how is she after I walked out on her? I didn't break her heart and she didn't push me down the stairs, so I think we'll be OK. Was she upset about me going?'

'She stapled your socks to a tree and gave everything else to a homeless bloke.'

'Why didn't she give him the socks as well?'

The CSM packed his bag and zipped it shut. 'She said she wouldn't wish those on anyone.'

Renfield toed the flowerbed and kicked something unsavoury into the bushes. 'I couldn't help it, Dan. The two of us were getting under each other's feet, and the shambolic way the investigation was being run got to me. The Met wasn't a picnic, either. I settled straight back into my old ways, drinking after shifts and heading home with a kebab, and I realized I'd changed. The unit changed me. Believe it or not, life was less interesting without you lot.'

'You're lucky Raymond took you back,' said Banbury. 'He's normally not so forgiving.' He knelt by a cleared space in the bushes and set down his laptop. 'This is the spot where our suspect was crouching. The soil's still soaked.'

'So, prints.' Renfield leaned forward with his fists on his thighs. 'Can you get a good cast from his shoes?'

'We don't do that any more, mate. We construct three-dimensional CAD shots from the photography. It's more accurate and better for wet surfaces. You can see definite trainer prints here.' A chart began to unscroll on his screen. 'There you go, Adidas ZX Flux Originals, one of the most popular shoes in the country, size forty-two.'

'Hang on, you've got something else there,' said Renfield.

Banbury studied his screen but could not spot anything unusual. 'Where?'

'Not on the screen. Try your eyes.' Renfield indicated that he should look beyond his laptop at the actual soil behind it. Reaching in through the branches, he carefully lifted a scrap of wet brown cardboard with the blade of a spatula. 'It's underneath where he was crouching. Might have already been there, or maybe he dropped it while he was waiting for her. Can you unfold it?'

'I'll have to conduct an examination under lab conditions, otherwise it won't be admissible.'

Renfield wiped mud off his trousers. 'I thought the PCU didn't obey the rules.'

'Mr Bryant always tells us to follow the broad intention of the law, not its letter, but I think we'd better wait for this one,' said Banbury. 'I checked the drains for discards and got nothing beyond a few cigarette ends. I take the point about the attacker coming into the area from outside, but to gain access he still needed a key, and that limits us to the keyholders.'

Renfield peered along the neat repetition of pillared entrances. 'There are twenty-four houses subdivided into flats. That's about 144 keys.'

'Probably not that many. The garden keys have to be assigned after approval. The agent says a lot of tenants don't bother to collect them. She reckons she can work out exactly how many keys are in current use.'

'So when do we start checking?'

Banbury nodded in the direction of the houses. 'Colin and Meera are on it right now.'

Colin Bimsley sat down on the step and pulled the lid off his coffee. 'Have you got any Category Twos so far?'

He and Meera had created a list containing the details of every householder in the crescent, and had divided it into those who occasionally visited the garden and those who never used it at all. They then subdivided the former category into people who had entered it in the last two weeks. Nobody had lent their key to a third party; with the formidable Mrs Farrier around they probably didn't dare.

'Not a single bloody one.' Meera climbed down beside him to check the pages. 'Maybe someone's lying. How likely would you be to admit you lent your key to someone else? The old busybody, Farrier, hardly ever goes out and reckons she knows everyone who uses the place. She told me she goes in there and counts the flowers after anyone's been in, just to make sure none have been stolen. According to her there are only four or five regular users.'

'What about Helen Forester's own key? There's no way of knowing if anyone else got hold of it and made a copy.'

'It's on the same ring as her house keys. Why would she lend it out?'

'Maybe she had another one cut for a boyfriend or something.'

'What, so that when he's up for a booty call he could go for a stroll round the tulips instead?'

Colin took a sip of his coffee and balanced one boot on top of the other. 'This is a waste of time. I reckon he just followed her in and slipped into the bushes. If she was watching the dog she might not have noticed.'

'Then how did he get out? She still had the key on her.'

'Maybe he climbed one of those bloody great trees and shinned along a branch until he was on the other side of the railings, then dropped on to the roof of a parked van.'

'Except that the trees only run along the flat side of the crescent facing the main arterial road, and that bit's covered by CCTV. And there's a row of shops on the other side. Not exactly discreet.'

They sat back and looked over at the crescent, the black railings with dense verdant perennials behind them, the towering plane trees and the immaculate emerald lawn beyond. 'Creepy, isn't it?' said Meera. 'I don't trust trees. We never had a garden. My mum can't even keep the window box alive. You don't think it's a class thing, do you?'

'What do you mean?'

'Someone with a chip on their shoulder bashing the rich bitch in the private park.'

'A bit extreme, isn't it? She wasn't doing anybody any harm.'

'Maybe she was,' Meera wondered. 'What about a dognapper?'

'Nah, *101 Dalmatians* was set in Primrose Hill, not Holland Park.' Colin pulled Meera to her feet. 'Come on, let's do the last four houses. I like having a good nose around people's hallways. I just saw one lined with antique Chinese vases. No crack houses here, eh?'

'Not so many offers of tea, either. I suppose it's all lapsang souchong. I couldn't live here. It's all too up itself for me. I like my scruffy flat.'

'At least you're sharing a nice new operations room with me.'

'I'm glad old Bryant didn't move in with us,' said Meera. 'He leaves cups of tea everywhere. How can anyone smoke and eat at the same time? He's always covered in mud or ink or food. And what's with the insects in boxes? I can tell whenever he's been past because there's usually something broken or faulty left behind, and sweets everywhere. He's like . . .' She tried to come up with a comparison. '. . . a tornado hitting a toyshop.'

'You can come and visit my flat sometime if you want to see tidy,' said Colin. 'I'm a very neat person.'

'Yeah, you're not bad,' Meera conceded, cradling her coffee.

'So would you? Come and visit?' His eyes were honest and hopeful. Colin worked on the assumption that if he asked Meera 110 times, she'd say no 109 times and then slip up on the 110th.

'Yeah, I might,' she replied, tossing her cardboard cup into a recycling bin.

In order to prevent the pause that followed from becoming pregnant with meaning, they set off to finish the interviews.

Meanwhile, high above Piccadilly Circus, directly behind the blinding LED Coca-Cola sign that turned the road below blood red, Arthur Bryant seated himself in a gloomy waiting room filled with African masks, brocaded pelmets, tassels and net curtains. He didn't like being kept waiting. He turned over a pot to see who had made it and the lid fell off.

'I know you're out there, Mr Bryant,' called Dr Gillespie. 'For heaven's sake, come in. It's like being haunted.'

The doctor's office only had one window, and that was blocked by the Dilly's garish signage. 'So, no after-effects?' he asked, peering over the top of his glasses at his patient's notes. 'Anything you want to tell me?'

'Physician, I healed myself,' said Bryant, seating himself and looking about for an ashtray.

'There isn't one,' Gillespie told him. 'Put your pipe back in your pocket. Better still, throw it in the bin. I looked into your treatment. I still don't quite see how you did it.'

'That's because it wasn't entirely legal.' Bryant reluctantly pocketed the pipe. 'Some of the drugs I had to take still aren't approved. I've had no side effects apart from a dicky bladder, and I can deal with that by avoiding opera and rollercoasters. I'm fully recovered. Better than ever in fact.'

'I'll be the judge of that.' Gillespie tried to add a note to Bryant's file but he was wearing a finger splint and couldn't hold the pen upright.

'What have you done now?' Bryant asked.

'This?' Gillespie raised his prophylactic digit as if noticing it for the first time. 'Shut it in the freezer door.'

'That was clumsy of you.'

'Not me, my wife. I was trying to get my tortoise out. She's got a mean streak.'

'Your tortoise?'

'My wife. Have you not met her? She can be very—'

'Opinionated?'

'Homicidal. Do you think you've been suffering from hallucinations?'

'Only when I open your bill,' said Bryant.

'Because Mr Land told me you had' – he groped for the appropriate word – 'lapses.'

Why can't Raymond ever keep his big mouth shut? Bryant thought irritably. 'No, nothing. I feel healthier than you. I imagine everyone does.'

'I'm supposed to put you through your OPRM. You know that, don't you?'

'Remind me?'

'Your objective performance-related medical, Mr Bryant. I take it you want me to sign you off and get this document back to the CoL and the Home Office?'

'. . . Yes.'

'You didn't hesitate there?'

'This isn't a quiz show,' snapped Bryant. 'If you sign it I'll go back to work and I won't have to bother you again.'

'Unless you make a mistake in the course of your duty, and I'm investigated for giving you the all-clear. You see my point?'

Bryant exhaled theatrically. 'You're a bit of a tappen, you know that? What do I have to do to get the all-clear?'

Gillespie slid over his notes and turned them around. 'Just sign at the side here. It's an extra condition to say that you take full responsibility for any problems that might arise from your self-treatment.'

'Take responsibility,' Bryant repeated. 'That's not something anyone seems prepared to do any more in this brave new world, is it? Very well, if that's what you require.' He snatched up the doctor's pen and scrawled across the page. 'There, now you have nothing to worry about.'

'And again on the last page,' said Gillespie doggedly.

Bryant obeyed.

'And at the bottom.'

Bryant fairly stabbed at the paper.

'And initial it.'

Bryant banged at the page and rose. 'In return I expect total patient confidentiality from you. Do you think you'll be able to manage that for once?'

Gillespie didn't look too sure. 'I'll act in your best interests,' he said finally.

Bryant shook the doctor's hand. Gillespie flinched sharply. 'You just gave me an electric shock,' he complained.

'Ah, yes,' said Bryant, happy to have inflicted damage. 'I'm emitting static. A side effect of my treatment. I seem to be disrupting phone signals as well. The mysteries of human science, eh? You could take a look at my feet while I'm here. It's all the walking. I'm starting to move like an old elephant.'

'That's not part of the deal,' said Dr Gillespie, closing the detective's file and savouring this one small victory. 'Go and see a chiropodist.'

Bryant headed out into Piccadilly, where the lunchtime office crowds had appeared and were weaving around each other in their manic hunt for sustenance. *I wasn't going to tell him about a few ridiculous lucid dreams,* he thought. *If I can work out what brings them on and learn to control them, he'll never need to know. The one benefit of maturity is discovering just how crafty you can be.*

He located his phone and called the unit, shouting over the noise of a road drill, several police sirens, a howling electric guitar and a man selling Jesus through a megaphone. 'Janice, have you had any luck with the background check on Mrs Forester?'

'Bits and pieces, nothing useful yet,' she replied. 'Dan's back, though, and he's got something he wants you and John to see. Where are you?'

Bryant was a man who was rarely willing to answer a direct question. 'I'll be there in twenty minutes,' he promised. 'Put the kettle on, I'm desiccated.'

At that moment, Dr Gillespie was already breaking patient confidence by putting a call through to the PCU's chief.

'I'm not sure he's ready for duty at all,' he complained to Raymond Land. 'Perhaps you should put him on gardening leave.'

'Are you saying that my most senior detective is not fit for his job?' Land asked, leaning back in his chair to keep an eye on his pigeon.

'No, it's just that he's become extremely insulting.'

'Become?' Land had never thought of Bryant as anything else.

'He called me a *"tappen"*. I don't know what it is but I'm sure it's rude.'

'Yes, he's taken to employing arcane words lately. Hang on, I'm looking it up.' Gillespie heard the tap of a keyboard, then a suppressed cough of laughter. 'It's a rectal plug. "An obstruction or indigestible mass found in the intestines of bears during hibernation. A tappen prevents bears from defecating while asleep. Also used to refer to someone who wilfully holds up business and stops a system from working efficiently." I think he's got your number, old man.'

Land found himself talking to a dead line.

II

'A SERIES OF UNFORTUNATE CIRCUMSTANCES'

Dan Banbury had dried and flattened the two-inch slip of cardboard from Clement Crescent, and pinned it to the light box in the operations room. 'There's no reason to assume it's his. Except that it was underneath his foot. But you have to admit it's intriguing.'

The detectives took turns to examine the page.

'It's not very clear,' said May.

'I'm used to looking at this sort of thing,' said Banbury. 'He used a biro so I went from the pressure rather than the ink. I typed it out for you.'

The page read: 'RSC: FHG26 FP28 CCG29 CSNP2 APC4 GTNR8 EHP10 GP11.'

'RSC? What's that, the Royal Shakespeare Company?' asked May.

'Can't be,' Banbury replied. 'Unless those are Shakespeare text references.'

'Trust me, they're not,' said Bryant. 'For example, Henry the Fifth's St Crispin's Day speech would be Act Four, Scene Three, lines eighteen to sixty-seven, so there are too many numerals.'

'Could they be map references?' asked May.

'What, two letters, three letters, four letters?' Bryant shook his head. 'The numbers progress largely in pairs.'

'To make it even more intriguing, there was something on the other side of the card – a set of twelve numbers so randomly arranged that I didn't even bother copying them out,' said Banbury.

'Hm. I may have a book for this.' Bryant headed off to his room with May following. He aimed for a low shelf containing a number of dust-caked volumes, quickly sorting through the titles.

'These are in my rarely read section,' Bryant said. 'Let's see what we've got. *Rum, Sodomy & the Lash: My Nights at Tory Party Conferences, The Little Book of Swiss War Heroes, Britain's Most Embarrassing Diplomatic Incidents (Vol. 7: E–F)* and *Is That Mine Floating or Is That a Floating Mine? Wartime Coastal Humour*. Ah, here we are. *Tompkin's Standard Guide to London Postal & Telephone Codes 1860–1951*. I knew it would come in handy one day.'

May waited impatiently while his partner sorted through half a dozen pairs of spectacles, settled on the right ones and roamed through the pages of the bright yellow volume. 'Nope,' he said finally, slamming it shut, 'nothing that remotely corresponds. I'll have to examine these in more detail. I suppose it could be a standard substitution code.'

'So now what do we do?' May asked.

Bryant tapped the side of his pug nose. 'The book doesn't have the answer, but I know a man who does.'

On Monday afternoon Dan Banbury printed out his photographs from the garden and laid them around the briefing room. He preferred to keep all work on his laptop but produced separate pages for the detectives, who still believed in getting a feel for a crime scene by writing on big pieces of paper with fountain pens.

'You didn't find any other footprints apart from the trainer mark in the bushes?' May walked from one shot to the next.

'I didn't think I would,' said Dan. 'How we use parks in this country is very different to almost anywhere else.'

'What do you mean?'

'We're always slightly embarrassed about walking on the grass even when we're allowed to, and tend to stick to the paths. That probably even applies to killers. It's simple conditioning. The dew was unbroken except for paw marks, so I think she stopped and took the dog off the leash. Her attacker came in through the gate and only left the path to step into the bushes and wait for her.'

'There's always a big list of things you can't do in parks,' said Bryant, studying the shots. 'No cycling, no ball games, no skateboards. They're green and neat but not much fun, especially with our weather.'

'Then why do we have so many of them?' asked Dan, laying down another photograph of a herbaceous border.

Bryant unwrapped a sherbet lemon, thinking. 'Our communal spaces were modelled on formal English gardens, which were exclusive and expensive to maintain. They weren't places for recreation but for reflection. Crowds are associated with chaos and loss of control.' He peered at a photograph of an immaculately pruned rose bed. 'Look at this, picture-perfect. English gardens took inspiration from Poussin and Claude Lorrain, presenting an idealized view of nature. We created places where you could promenade in your finery past lakes with swans, striped lawns and rose beds. We plonked fake temples and Gothic ruins into idyllic pastoral landscapes. In the Middle East and the Mediterranean, parks are there to provide relief from the sun, which is why they're used after dark. And the activities that go on – rollerblading, tightrope-walking, yoga, acrobatics, smoking dope, cycling, dancing and playing musical instruments – your average English park-keeper would be having a conniption.' His fingers traced the violet petals of a ceanothus shrub. 'You know, when the British first took up residence in India they tried to re-create their parks from home, laying lawns that went brown and importing flowerbeds that instantly withered. Their wives paraded in crinolines and dropped like flies. If it was an English garden, English rules applied. The policy of "Look, don't touch" remained in place.'

For once John May did not interrupt his partner. It was good to have Bryant back on form again, showing an interest in everything around him, even when he drifted off topic. 'Dan, this Mrs Farrier, the head of the garden committee,' Bryant said. 'She issues Ritchie Jackson with a typed-up planting schedule?'

'That's right. There was one in his toolshed. I brought it back with me because it has a scale map of the gardens.'

'Good man.' They pegged it beside the photographs. Bryant studied the roster in silence, then went to the pictures of the flowerbeds. The others had no idea what he was looking for.

'You said Jackson is passionate about his plants, didn't you? So he's not likely to make a mistake?'

'I imagine not,' said May.

'Then why does this rose bush' – Bryant tapped the photograph – 'have a nameplate saying that it's a Shropshire Lad, which I happen to know is a thornless peach rose, when it's quite clearly been marked down on Mrs Farrier's plan as an Apothecary, which is thorny and deep red, the original rose of the House of Lancaster?'

'Blimey, people do make mistakes, Mr Bryant,' Banbury protested, but the old man was right; someone had removed one of the green plastic nameplate stakes and stuck it in front of the wrong rose bush.

May picked up his phone. 'Colin, are you and Meera still in Clement Crescent? I know this is going to sound daft but just do it, will you?' He gave them instructions to find the rose bush and search underneath.

Five minutes later Colin called back to say they had found another knife, and that this one was more unusual, almost a foot long, with the blade sharpened on both sides.

'He needed to be able to find it at a later date so he pushed it into the earth and marked it with the rose stake,' said Bryant. 'This doesn't look good for Ritchie Jackson. Dan, see if you can get prints from it.' He pulled his homburg and scarf from his pocket and prepared for the outdoor onslaught. 'I'm off to see a gentleman called Dante August. Back in an hour.'

'I'll say this for him,' said May, watching him go. 'He certainly bounces back. Does he seem all right to you?'

'I ask him why we have gardens and he gives me a bloomin' history lesson,' said Banbury. 'So yes, I'd say he's back to normal.'

Longbright put her head around the door. 'I've got Jeremy Forester on the line.'

'How did you find him?' May grabbed his notes and headed for the operations room.

'We didn't, he found us,' said Janice. 'We've pinpointed his phone. It's an unregistered handset. He's on the move, not far away. We can grab him.'

'No, don't do that.' May put the call on speaker. 'Mr Forester, I assume you know what's happened,' he said, seating himself before Longbright's monitor so that he could keep Forester's details in front of him.

'Melissa called me. She, ah – she was my assistant. Do you have any more information? Where was Helen found? Can I see her?'

May was not inclined to share too much information. 'Where are you?' he asked.

His voice was uncertain and hesitant. 'Look, I'm in a bad situation. I didn't hurt my wife. You have to believe me.'

'When did you last see her?' May looked across at Longbright, gesturing. *Do we know exactly where he is?*

'Square Mile,' said Longbright quietly. 'Near the Bank of England, heading away from the river.'

'I saw her a couple of weeks ago. We met one evening at her flat,' said Forester.

'How were things between you on that night?'

'Relatively civilized.'

'You didn't shout at her from the street?'

'We had a few cross words but it was nothing serious.'

'We need you to come in,' May warned.

'I can't right now. I need to stay on the move.'

'Why? Give us details of your movements this morning and we'll be able to clear you.'

'I can't do that. You're going to try to trace this call.'

'We already did,' said May. 'We're not coming after you. At this stage I just want to talk, OK? Do you have time to do that?'

Silence. Then: 'Yes, fine.'

'You were fired from your job – what happened?'

It wasn't the question Forester had been expecting. 'I'd worked there for seven years,' he said. 'They didn't like the way I handled their business.'

'Tell me what happened, Jeremy. Talk about anything. I need to understand what's happened here.'

Another silence. Then a deep breath. 'OK. Let me see. I drove home from Washbourne Hollis and lied to my wife. The thought of telling her the truth was too exhausting. I still loved her, desperately so, but she changed – we changed. Money changed us. Helen could smell financial problems like a deer senses earthquakes. As a kid she watched her father's businesses go bankrupt. She learned a lot from that, became very hard-headed. She thought I had too much respect for my bosses. I disappointed her – I know that. But it's not what wrecked our marriage.'

May was about to jump in, but decided to wait and listen. Bryant had taught him to have patience.

'I couldn't bring myself to tell her I'd lost my job. It didn't even occur to me that my behaviour was strange. Each morning at seven thirty I'd climb into my car and drive to work, parking in the basement of the NCP across from my office. Then I went upstairs to a corner café for coffee and a croissant, followed by a walk around the City. I'd return at lunchtime to eat a sandwich in the car. I kept my phone in meeting mode. Finally I'd drive home and go to my study. I'd sit up all night with my door closed, trying to find a way out of my debts. I sold the Mercedes, sounded out a few connections on LinkedIn and drained my current account. I lost weight. I polished my shoes every night but my clothes never seemed clean enough any more. Then I got beaten up.'

'What happened?'

'One of my creditors had been tipped off as to my whereabouts by someone – I don't know who. Two guys followed me from the tube station at Chalk Farm. They shoved me into an alleyway for a good kicking, loosened a couple of teeth and tried to make me sign some property papers. They ran off when a police constable walked past. I went home knowing they would soon be back, and next time they might come to the house. Two days later they found me in the café near my old car park and handed me a schedule with a series of account numbers. They told me that if I missed any payments I would have one of my eyes removed. They weren't the worst of my creditors.'

'You didn't report any of this?'

'I guess my body was less badly bruised than my ego, which took another blow that night when Helen confronted me with a statement of missed payments, along with an order from the bank to vacate our house.'

'What did she do?'

'Well, she didn't scream or cry. She just looked as if she'd always known that something like this would happen, that I'd finally lived down to her expectations. That look – it devastated me. The very next morning she packed a bag and left. After that, all communications came through her lawyer. I left behind the Primrose Hill house and everything in it. I hung around the city at night, sleeping in cheap hotels, then hostels, and finally in the alleyways behind hotels. That was when the real nightmare began.'

'What happened to your wife? You don't think your creditors went after her?'

'The idea had crossed my mind, but it seemed a bit far-fetched.'

'Do you know if she had enemies? Anyone who might wish her harm?'

'Not to my knowledge.'

'Did relations between the two of you become any more amicable?'

'It was a divorce. Everything went wrong. See, there's something else. We'd lost our son, our little boy, Charlie. In a way, you were involved.'

May was bewildered. 'What do you mean?'

There was a sigh, a pause. 'It was back in February. Raining hard, very late. Your unit was looking for someone at London Bridge Station. Your officers had closed off the surrounding roads. My son and his nanny had to walk through a tunnel. Charlie was nearly hit by a diverted truck, and the car behind crashed into a wall rather than run into the back of him. Something hit Charlie in the eye. He was taken to St Thomas' Hospital, but this tiny speck that nobody could see somehow found its way to his brain and caused a blood clot. He died a few minutes later.'

The memory of the event came flooding back to May. They had been tracking the Mr Punch Killer. After they'd caught him, word had come through of an accident in one of the tunnels that ran beneath the railway arches. An inquiry had quickly settled on a verdict of accidental death, but the traffic supervisor had subsequently been placed on gardening leave.

'I can't imagine how upset you must have been.'

'A series of unfortunate circumstances. That was what the police told us.' The line went quiet. For a moment May thought Forester had hung up, but the man was trying to control his emotions. 'The tunnel was badly lit and filled with fumes. It should never have been used as a traffic detour. There were no signs explaining where pedestrians should go. As a result, my child's life was lost.'

'What happened to the nanny?'

'Sharyn blamed herself for what happened. I didn't stay in touch with her. At that point Charlie was holding our marriage together.'

'When was the last time you spoke to your wife?'

'I called Helen a week ago and left a message. I'm sure you have that. I wish we could have talked one more time. And I wish it was anyone but you investigating her death. I must go.'

'You need to come in,' said May. 'There has to be a formal interview.'

'That's not possible at the moment.'

'You don't have a choice, Mr Forester. Either you do it willingly or we fetch you.'

'This isn't how it looks. My life is in danger.'

The line went dead.

'Janice, get him here,' said May.

'His signal just vanished,' said Longbright. 'We've no one in the area but I'll try.'

'Do you have Mrs Forester's voicemails?'

'Yes. Jeremy Forester asked to see her urgently.'

'Anything else on him?'

Longbright checked her notes. 'Some background stuff. He was the CEO of a company called StarMall SEA. They built shopping centres all over South East Asia. Then he went to Washbourne Hollis, where he stayed until he was let go back in August. Smart chap like him, you'd think he'd have some collateral squirrelled away.'

'How much was his wife due to get in the divorce?'

'I don't have any figures yet,' said Longbright, 'but she told a colleague that after the settlement she was planning to set up a new company and buy the flat in Holland Park outright. And there was a gallery being purchased in Hoxton. As far as I can see, none of it went through.'

'Any luck finding a lover?'

Longbright held up a crimson-varnished fingernail. 'Funny you should ask. She was seen with an orchestra conductor named Charles Haywood Frost. He's your best bet. At the moment he's based just around the corner from here, at the Kings Place concert hall.'

'Then that's my next port of call,' decided May. 'You'd better forewarn him.'

'I already did,' she said, swinging back in her chair.

May grinned. 'What would I do without you?'

'Starve, for a start.' She handed him a cling-film-wrapped sandwich. 'Shippam's crab paste on rocket.'

May paused in the doorway. 'You know, it has to be Forester.'

'You can't be sure of that,' said Longbright. 'Not from one phone call.'

'I need to know why he left his job and what he's so afraid of. His son died right around the corner from us, and now his wife turns up dead. You and I would call that a tragedy. Arthur would call it a conspiracy. Get digging.'

He returned to his office and wrote out some fresh interview questions, but could not stop thinking about the night they had trapped a murderer at London Bridge, and the separate drama that had been unfolding a few hundred yards away. He tried to imagine how the past and present tragedies might be linked, but came up with nothing.

Sometimes the trickster city spawned extraordinary events and dared you to connect them when there was really no link at all.

12

'LIKE GOLDFISH INTO A BOWL'

The Jerusalem Tavern in Clerkenwell was an itinerant pub. Since the fourteenth century it had wandered off a number of times, finally settling down in its present location in 1720, but it had only recently been returned to what Arthur Bryant called 'a proper boozer', with the usual perquisites of a falsely imagined past: freshly aged counters, newly roughened wood floors, olde worlde cabinets and stools. As such it created a typical London paradox: a place that was rooted yet rootless, ancient but new, false and real. And like all pubs, on a wet day its interior appeared to shrink. Denied the appeal of standing outside with a pint in hand, its drinkers apologized profusely as they squeezed past each other like wet cats, trying to reach the bar.

Bryant had played the senior citizen card and bagged the only pair of seats by the open fire. He had arranged to meet Dante August, the curator of the Museum of London's recent 'Street Life' exhibition. The tiny pub suited August, as he was an extremely small wild-haired man with delinquent eyebrows and a loud high voice, developed by his determination to be heard if not seen. Like many small men he had an ageless quality that pegged him somewhere between forty and sixty.

'So, you've a fellow hiding in a park waiting for an opportunity to attack young ladies, and this was under his foot?' August flattened out the photocopy of the note, donned his reading glasses and examined it with his nose almost touching the paper.

'I thought it might be some kind of thieves' code,' said Bryant, attempting to separate himself from his scarf, 'a way of working out who he can rob.'

'Did he steal anything from his victim?'

'No, although he may have threatened her with a weapon first; we found a rather peculiar ornamental dagger planted in a rose bed.'

'Well, this isn't a thieves' code, I can tell you that,' announced August, sitting back up and blinking his distended eyes back into their sockets. 'The belief in a housebreaker's code of ethics comes from the idea that Russian criminal families have brought their habits to this country. The real codes are mostly made up of circles, squares and triangles, not letters and numbers.'

'Don't they just indicate homes with valuables or fierce dogs?'

'Supposedly, but it's hard to tell how much of that is urban mythology. The use of thieves' codes has been exaggerated by overexcited tabloid journalists. Our lives are peppered with false beliefs, Arthur. Fear of foreignness was once our defining characteristic. This is something else.'

Bryant raised a pint of bitter so cloudy that it appeared to be deliberately hiding something. 'I tried a substitution code,' he explained, 'but I didn't get anywhere.'

August took a chewed yellow pencil stub from behind his ear. 'There are other ways to break cyphers. Assuming the paper was his, why did he throw it away?'

'He could have dropped it, or simply finished with it.'

'Which means that these pairs of numbers – 26, 28, 29, 2, 4, 8, 10, 11 – are probably dates, because it's the eleventh today. And where you get dates you get locations. So if they're places we have several recurring consonants, P, G and C.' He made some calculations on the back of a receipt.

'The death occurred in Clement Crescent,' said Bryant. 'An old lady scolded my partner for calling the site a park. She said it's a garden, which is different. P and G – park and garden?'

'What do you know about the man who left this?'

'Very little,' Bryant admitted. 'He wears bright trainers that look like sponge bags with laces.'

'If he was sleeping rough in parks, it could be a list of the other places where he's been hiding out. Can you get the internet on your phone?' August made it sound like a fabulous but barely feasible idea.

Bryant cracked his knuckles in preparation. 'It's a bit touch and go, Dante. I tend to have an electromagnetic effect on gadgetry. Last week my bottom phoned someone in Taiwan.'

'Oh, that happens to everyone, Arthur. I keep ordering pizzas every time I bend over. Try finding London Gardens Online for me and type in FHG.'

It took Bryant several goes, but he got there. 'Fenton House Garden. It's in Hampstead.'

'And FP?'

'Finsbury Park.'

After putting their heads together and trawling through the rest of the initials, a picture emerged. Their target had plotted a course around London, visiting Culpeper Community Garden, Camley Street Natural Park, Abney Park Cemetery, Gunnersbury Triangle Nature Reserve and something called Emslie Horniman's Pleasance, a *pleasance* being a French term for a secluded garden.

'So he keeps on the move to avoid detection,' said Bryant, tasting his pint. 'The first thing to do is find out if there have been any attacks in those parks. The progression's wrong, though. If he deliberately set out to visit Clement Crescent, the last one should read CC. He's gone off-piste. Why?'

August smashed a bag of salt and vinegar crisps flat with his fist, tore it open, rolled a pickled egg in the crumbs and handed it to Bryant. As an accompaniment to a decent pint it was hardly delicate but shockingly delicious. 'I'm afraid that's rather more your area than mine. I can help you with his environment, though.'

'Be my guest,' said Bryant, nibbling his crunchy pickled egg.

'London's greenery is complicated. Parks are not gardens and gardens are not squares. They cover forty per cent of the city and form the so-called lungs of London. There are over 250 officially designated parks alone.' August ticked off his fingers. 'Then you've got burial grounds, woodlands, ancient forests, secret gardens, informal community parks, tended meadows, play areas, crescents, allotments, polygons, circuses, heaths and commons, each with a different character, and many are still separated by our old friend the English class system.'

'Of course they are,' said Bryant, whose childhood in the backstreets of Bethnal Green had been marked by a moment when the local children had all stopped playing to watch in awed silence as a gentleman passed by in a grey silk waistcoat and watch chain. The detective had been an outsider then, and still was now.

'Gardens were for communal use,' August explained, clenching his eyes and releasing them in what proved to be a disturbing physical tic, 'but squares kept out the rabble and provided bosky dells where like could meet like, so that the social classes wouldn't have to mix. There are still hundreds of them all across the city and most go unnoticed. Some parks, like Hyde Park, are as old as London itself – both Hyde and Green Park have ancient tree circles. They remain for the general use of all, while others, like Victoria Park in the East End, were constructed to keep out "diseased miasmas". It was believed that pestilence travelled through ill humours, and the parks could provide a germ barrier between the sick poor and the healthy rich.'

'But some of the places on this list aren't used by the rich,' said Bryant. 'I've been to Abney Park Cemetery many times and I know it can be a pretty rough, wild corner of London.'

'Well, yes,' August agreed. 'There are all kinds of liminal spaces. At the bottom of the list you had the pleasure gardens, which were more like disreputable funfairs, with concert halls, skating rinks, cafés and beer halls that turned rowdy after dark. In such areas base human nature was quick to surface, and the lands were used for liaisons.'

'That wasn't just limited to the working-class parks, surely.' Bryant licked his forefinger and dusted it around his crisp crumbs.

'No, of course not.' August's great eyes rolled. 'Russell Square was rife with sexual goings-on after dark, and in Samuel Pepys's time Green Park was littered with copulating couples. As for Cremorne Gardens near Battersea, James Whistler might have painted his *Nocturne in Black and Gold* there but it was little more than a meat market. Look at photos of Soho Square between the wars – they show a wild, uncultivated spot. Green Park still had grazing rights for sheep. Nobody rented out chunks for corporate events and film shows, as they do now. The royal parks were charged to "improve" their users, which is why there are still concerts of popular classics at lunchtimes. The squares were seen as extensions of the typical London house; they were overly pruned and domesticated, like the Ladbroke Estate in Kensington, which was designed so that children could be dropped into them like goldfish into a bowl. We're so used to seeing these places and assuming they're safe that we barely notice they're there.'

'So if our killer moves from one secluded green space to the next, why does he need the piece of paper to guide him?' Bryant asked. 'Why not just head to the quietest spot and wait for a victim?'

'Parks are not fungible,' replied August. 'Each has its own

character. Perhaps he has done this before and plans to do it again, and matches each park to the nature of his victim.'

'Do me a favour, Dante, don't try to be a detective.' Bryant looked into the fire's dancing flames. 'Maybe he just sleeps in the parks. They're sheltered and separated from the street by hedges, and if he gets in and out at the right time he wouldn't be disturbed. But why keep a shorthand list? Dante, is there such a thing as a homeless person's code? Could this be a recommendation list of which places are safe, and on what dates?'

'I suppose so,' replied the academic, 'although I've never heard of such a thing. Tribal groups appear and vanish with such speed in this city that it's impossible to catalogue them all. I do try, though. While I was assembling the exhibition for the museum, many of the street groups I was planning to feature broke up or re-formed under new identities. Online social networks have made street life much more fluid. The classes have become more permeable.'

'I have to get back,' said Bryant, draining his pint. 'I'd like to say you've been a great help. If you think of anything useful, let me know. He's going to do it again.'

'Why do you say that?' August asked.

'Because he thinks he got away with it,' said Bryant, gathering his hat and scarf.

Kings Place on York Way was one of the few new buildings of which John May wholeheartedly approved. It housed a national newspaper, two concert halls, an art gallery and a restaurant, and its airy atrium led to the sky-reflecting canal basin, where the winter air was filled with sweet woodsmoke from houseboats and barges. As he walked across the pale marble tiles May could hear the raw brass of a modernist piece by Michael Nyman being rehearsed on the floor below.

Charles Haywood Frost met May in the atrium's coffee bar. He so resembled a music lover's ideal representation of an orchestra conductor, tall and elegantly slender, with an alarming mass of curled black hair designed to flop forward during bows, that it was hard to tell which came first, the image or the man. Either way, he seemed very young to be commanding an orchestra.

'This is the first break I've had today,' he complained, settling with a cardboard coffee cup on the other side of the table. Beyond them, excited schoolchildren disembarked from a barge on the basin. 'We're rehearsing Tavener's *The Protecting Veil*. Critics always underestimate just how punishing minimalist works are on members of the orchestra.'

'They're pretty hard on my ears, too,' May replied.

'Oh, you'd be surprised,' said Frost. 'We get a lot of unlikely converts. It's an exacting musical form, but it's fascinating to watch in live performance. A piece can really come alive in this space.'

May studied the smiling young man sitting opposite him, restlessly jiggling his left leg. 'You do appreciate that this is a murder investigation?' he asked.

Frost's face froze. 'Yes, of course, how stupid of me. You must think me utterly inconsiderate. I didn't know Helen for very long.'

'But you were lovers.'

'We weren't partners in the conventional sense. My work is more important to me than anything right now, and Helen didn't want a formal relationship. I understand she was changed by the loss of her son. She blamed herself for not being there when he needed her. She told me Charlie's death altered the course of her life.'

'How did you meet?' asked May, moving his coat to allow a pair of violinists to seat themselves and their instruments.

'She came to a Vaughan Williams concert and I remember noticing her after, sitting in the front row in tears. *The Lark Ascending* is a pastoral piece; it doesn't usually make people break down, so I talked to her. Her husband had bought the tickets for their wedding anniversary but they were divorcing, and she had come alone. I consoled her and I suppose that's what I became, a source of consolation.'

'Do you know if she had any enemies at work? If she was getting trouble from her husband?'

'She told me nothing about her working life.' Frost rested long fingers along the arms of his chair. 'Obviously I never met the husband, although I know he had very strong feelings about her.'

'In what way?'

'They fought a lot after their son died. I think he had an affair with his assistant. Nothing serious, a one-night stand. He confessed to Helen but I imagine his timing couldn't have been much worse.'

'What else do you know about him?'

'He made his money from a company that developed shopping malls in South East Asia, but ran it into the ground, then worked for some property firm in the City. From what I understand the nanny also had a soft spot for Mr Forester. She blamed Helen for being a bad mother and so on. Look, I was on the outside of it all and that suited me fine.'

'You two seem to have had little in common. What was the attraction?'

Frost seemed genuinely at a loss. 'Helen liked music. She was lonely. She was easy to be with. We weren't involved in each other's lives, which made being together simpler – if that makes any sense.'

May understood perfectly. London was full of uncommitted men and women who kept their personal and public lives separate. 'Mr Frost, I need to build up a mental picture of Helen Forester. In these cases we tend to come in after it's too late to fully understand someone, so we have to work backward through the people who knew them. Anything you can tell me would be helpful.'

Frost chose his words with care. 'She kept people at arm's length. I imagine she was very different before she lost her son.'

'The boy's nanny,' said May, checking his notepad. 'Did Mrs Forester tell you anything else about her?'

'We went to dinner with her and her boyfriend. It was an uncomfortable evening. I couldn't understand why we were even there.'

'What do you mean?'

'Helen talked about work. The nanny talked about children. They didn't have anything in common.'

'They were linked by Mrs Forester's son, Mr Frost.'

The conductor looked as if the thought had never crossed his mind. 'I suppose they were. Something odd happened to the husband.' He looked away to the barges drifting past beyond the glass. 'He was kicked out of his company and they hushed it up.'

'His boss is unwilling to talk to us,' said May, although he had written 'Forester Asst' on his pad.

'Apparently he had trouble telling his wife what had happened, and carried on going to work as if nothing was wrong. When she found out, it caused the final split between them.' He looked at May uncomfortably. 'Why would anyone do something like this? It wasn't a sexual assault, was it?'

'No, but she may have known her attacker,' May admitted.

From the bottom of the stairs a bell rang, making Frost start. 'I'm afraid that's my rehearsal cue.'

May watched Frost leave. The conductor had a commanding presence. It was not difficult to imagine him walking into a hotel with Mrs Forester, greeting the staff with natural self-assurance. May had run a check on Frost's background before the meeting: Harrow and Cambridge, then the Conservatoire de Paris and a smooth step into conducting his own company, the Orchestra of New Minimalism. He was thirty-one years old and heading for international fame. His liaison with Helen Forester had already been forgotten.

As he walked back to the unit, May thought about the Foresters: a high-flying couple committed to their careers, their only child being cared for by a nanny, and the sudden terrible loss that had made them re-evaluate their lives. Bryant was an academic, not a psychologist. May sensed that his partner was struggling with the case. Perhaps it was up to him to find out what exactly had happened to Helen Forester in a small London park, and why.

He made one more stop before meeting up with his partner, to see Melissa Byrne, Forester's assistant. He met her in a fake-artisanal chain coffee shop across the street from her office. Byrne was in her mid-twenties, slender, dark and attractive enough to worry any wife. She had come out without a coat, and sat hugging her arms on the chair opposite, anxious to leave.

'Jeremy was released for violating financial regulations,' she explained. 'That's all I know. He was marched out of the building, so it had to be serious.'

'How did you get on with him?'

'Let's just say I wasn't being paid enough to share his passion for making the company money. He had kept me working late a lot. He refused to believe I was actually working at home on Fridays and never once asked me how I was, even when I'd been in hospital.'

'But you were shocked when he was dismissed.'

'Of course – anyone would be. I called him to see if he was OK but he never answered his mobile. Eventually I got up the courage to call the house phone, and his wife picked up. She didn't know where he'd gone. After he was fired nobody could get hold of him.'

'Why were you trying?' May asked.

'Well, we worked together, I was worried . . .' She knew her reply sounded lame.

'Was it during a business trip that the two of you slept together?' Byrne's eyes hardened. She was still deciding how to answer when May continued. 'Melissa, you said it took courage to call the house phone. I know he told his wife about it. Do you think if he hadn't, it would have turned into something more between you two?'

'God no, that was a mistake! Our flight was cancelled because of a French air traffic control strike. We were stranded overnight in the Hotel Adlon in Berlin. We were both kind of angry and got drunk.'

'What were you angry about?'

'I'd just been dumped by the guy I was seeing and he'd had a fight with his wife over the funding of an art gallery. Why would he have told Helen? I mean, what was the point?'

'I guess he loved her,' said May.

'Well, she's dead now, and he's lost everything,' said Byrne bitterly, 'so who cares what happened once in a hotel room?'

13

'IF A FISH MURDERED A LADY FISH'

The mature trees and unruly grasslands of Green Park separated it from other open spaces in central London.

The meadows behind Piccadilly had once contained wilder prey than the surrounding raucous streets; highwaymen, hunters and duellists took the lives of animals and citizens alike. The fields had contained lodges and libraries, an icehouse and the two vast temples of Peace and Concord, both of which were accidentally exploded in fireworks festivals. This licence for wildness had been tamed by the arrival of two grand houses on the park's borders: Buckingham Palace and the Ritz Hotel. Yet there remained something undomesticated about the place. Unlike most other parks, Green Park had never been closed to the public at night.

Tonight two figures could be glimpsed between the trees, climbing towards Constitution Hill. Passing joggers might have imagined that these gentlemen of mature status were spirits strolling through the grand golden gates on the way to their club for an evening snifter, followed perhaps by a partridge pie, but if they had stopped they would have overheard a conversation about death and darkness that was all too real.

'The blade that was buried under the rose bush has an ornate red and blue enamelled handle,' said John May. 'Dan says it's handcrafted and unusually well balanced, probably an illegal import.'

Bryant batted his stick at a pile of leaves. 'Is it valuable?'

'We can't find a match on any database, so it's not a stolen antique. It looks modern but seems to have been specially prepared for its owner. It's been sharpened by a professional. We have a list of specialists but it only covers London.'

'You checked that it wasn't Ritchie Jackson's, I assume? He wasn't using it to trim plant stalks or something?'

'Apparently not.'

'Not a nice thought, is it?' mused Bryant. 'Some chap creeping about the bushes in London parks with a hand-tailored foot-long blade, waiting for lone women to pass through the shadows.'

'And yet he strangled her. It doesn't make sense. Either he targeted Mrs Forester and it'll prove to be an isolated incident—'

'No, no, no,' Bryant protested. 'You don't carry a specialist knife and hide in parks to attack just once. He'll do it again. Giles feels there's a sexual element to the attack, which I find mystifying. Forester showed no signs of sexual assault.'

'There are other components in the psychology of sadism that may not include sexual assault,' said May. 'It could be someone who has abnormal sexual responses.'

'Please don't tell me this case is going to be all about *relationships*.' Bryant led the way into the park's great tunnel of lime, chestnut and plane trees. 'I don't do relationships. Domestic crimes are for the Met to sort out, not us.'

'Why do you always say that?'

'My dear fellow, because they're *simple*; the victim and killer are known to each other, and they're normally to be found at the location where the crime occurred. Murder is an assault that goes one step further than it meant to, that's all, and all the plods have to do is bang it through to the Crown

Prosecution Service as quickly as possible without traumatizing everyone involved.' Bryant turned to look his partner in the eye. 'We were appointed for a higher purpose, John – to deal with the kind of criminal activity that has public consequences, not to lock up thugs who've accidentally buried their wives for incorrectly folding the tea towels once too often.'

'No wonder you've turned down every dinner offer from my sister,' said May. 'She'd have nothing to say that wouldn't bore you, and you'd have nothing to say that wouldn't upset her.'

'I never learned how to be good at relationships,' Bryant admitted. 'I used to watch my father knock my mother around and thought it was what all married couples did, until the day I had to fetch a policeman. It got even more confusing when I arrived back home with him in tow. My mother accused me of bringing shame to the house. "What will people think of us?" she said, hiding her black eye. How could I begin to comprehend that? I can teach myself everything I need from books except how to understand other people.'

'No, Arthur, you understand them perfectly well, you just don't like what you find,' corrected May. 'Which makes it all the more amazing that you chose to become a detective.'

'Well I didn't, not really.' Bryant kicked at a dead branch. 'The unit wasn't set up to solve crimes so much as to locate them and report on their circumstances in order to create predictive patterns. It was a scientific and academic unit. The job changed around me and I ended up where I never expected to be. It was a lucky thing you stayed on.'

'I've learned a lot from you,' said May.

'Oh, in what way?' asked Bryant, shamelessly fishing for compliments.

'About seeing the bigger picture, for a start. Damn, it's starting to rain. Tell me why we're in Green Park?'

'Because the code said GP, not CC, which means he diverted from Green Park to Clement Crescent. I admit it's a long shot.

I suppose GP could also stand for Gladstone, Gillespie, Grovelands, Gunnersbury and Greenwich Parks. But this is the only central London one, and therefore the most likely.'

'I don't know how we can be expected to find a man we can't identify from the gardener's sole photograph. It's too big an area for us to cover even with Jack, Colin and Meera helping.'

'Forty-seven acres,' Bryant interjected, 'actually the smallest of the royal parks. It was a swamp once, a burial ground for lepers. Charles the Second formalized it so that he could walk from Hyde Park to St James's without leaving royal soil. They say it doesn't have any flowerbeds because his missus, Catherine of Braganza, caught Charlie-boy picking the flowers to give to another woman. Cath had every single bed dug up and banned all flowers from the park in perpetuity. It's a nice story, but probably not true.'

'Arthur, I work in a police unit, not a florist's.' May looked about. 'Where are the others, anyway?'

'They started off by the RAF Bomber Command Memorial and are supposed to be making their way over towards us. I'm not expecting anyone to spot our suspect, I'm just hoping we might find some evidence of his presence.'

May gave a snort of disapproval. 'That's a bit vague, isn't it? He's been following this pattern of parks and dates for weeks, we don't know why or what for, and you expect something to just drop into our laps?'

Bryant wasn't answering. Instead he was pointing further down the tree-lined avenue into the grey murk.

'What?' said May. 'I can't see anything.'

'Presbyopia,' Bryant informed him. 'Thank God for age-related longsightedness. Here they come.'

Emerging from the evening rain mist towards them were Officers Renfield, Bimsley and Mangeshkar. In Meera's right fist was a tartan leash, on the other end of which was a white West Highland terrier.

'It's Beauchamp,' she told them. 'He's got his name on his

collar. We found him tied to a tree branch over there, all tangled up in the bushes.' She pointed into a fenced-off patch of woodland. 'It's where the gardeners incinerate the leaves.'

'We've roped the area off,' said Jack Renfield. 'He doesn't seem to have been there very long – he wasn't in any distress. He didn't even bark, did you, boy?' He ruffled the dog's fur. The Westie ignored him.

'So our suspect brought him here, tied him up and left?' said May. 'That doesn't make sense. Any marks on the ground?'

'We had a good look in the grass and the surrounding area but couldn't see anything,' said Colin. 'It's all loose bracken and foliage. Dan's on his way here now. We asked the park-keepers if they'd seen anyone. One said he saw a lanky black bloke with tied-back dreads, late twenties, hanging around earlier.'

'Did you show him Ritchie Jackson's photograph?'

'After he gave us the description, yes. He thinks it might have been him but can't be sure.'

'That's it, then,' said May. 'We have to bring Jackson back in.'

'What, the gardener did it?' said Bryant, feigning incredulity. 'Just like that?'

'He fits the description, Arthur, he admits seeing the victim alive in Clement Crescent, he knew the dog and he could get in and out of the garden.'

'So you're dismissing the hiding figure in Jackson's photograph?'

'Jackson took the picture himself,' Renfield reminded them. 'He could have set the whole thing up. He knew what time the Forester woman was due in the garden. He planted something in the bushes—'

'Like what, pray tell?'

'I don't know, a photographic blow-up of a man's face. And then he made the boot print himself. You know, to put us off the scent.'

'Oh, well, that's genius!' Bryant leaned his fists on his walking stick and looked heavenward. 'He set up an alternative suspect, then left a written clue that would lead us here, where he'd tethered the victim's dog in order to incriminate himself.'

'Jack's got a point,' said Colin. 'You don't know what his reasons might be. Maybe he wants to get caught. Like, to stop himself before he strikes again.'

'Am I surrounded by blithering imbeciles?' Bryant asked a rowan bush. 'That's like saying if a fish wanted to be caught in a net it would leave a series of clues along the riverbank for the fisherman.'

'I don't think that analogy holds up, Mr Bryant,' said Colin, raising a tentative digit. 'If a fish murdered a lady fish and then swam off, erm, taking the lady fish's dog—'

'Colin, stop trying to use unopened parts of your brain. If Jackson wanted to be caught he could turn himself in or just not deny that he did it.'

'Jackson's a big man, maybe he doesn't know his own strength,' said Renfield. 'Suppose he thought he was in with a chance and tried to pick her up, she turned him down and he lost it?'

'So he had a knife on him but decided to strangle her instead?' Bryant shook his head. 'The knife wasn't his – it just doesn't fit. We haven't found the actual murder weapon yet. And why leave the dog here?'

'A killer can hurt a woman and be kind to a dog.' Renfield crouched beside the West Highland terrier, scuffing his ears. 'He could still be in the park. If he decided to take his own life he might tie the dog up somewhere first, mightn't he?'

They began a search of the meadowlands. It was now crepuscular, silent and nebulous, as if the park had started to fade from the memory of a dying man. Visibility had fallen with the night, so that the trees loomed before them as if emerging from rainclouds. A flurry of emerald-headed ducks made Meera jump.

'Do you know exactly where this chap was seen?' asked May as he reluctantly followed the others, risking his hand-made shoes by stepping from the path into the former sheep pasture.

'The park-keepers couldn't agree about that,' said Meera. 'What if he changes his mind and goes back for the dog? Maybe someone should stay by the tree.' Beauchamp sensed he was being talked about and raised his ears, looking eagerly from one face to the next. Finally they fanned out, into the deep cover of the trees, with the senior detectives following behind.

'I have to say that this feels like a very disorganized way to conduct a murder hunt,' said May, 'a handful of officers wandering about in long grass on the off-chance of bumping into him.'

'You don't complain when we send our staff off to climb about inside bonfires and graveyards, so I don't see why a park should bother you.' Bryant sniffed. 'This is the way we work. It's the Churchillian spirit of lateral thinking. Originality is a great British strength. We come up with the brilliantly imaginative ideas that drive the world, then give them away for virtually nothing in order to retain our position as a second-rate nation run with the economic vision of an Armenian pastry shop.'

'So you're feeling better then,' said May drily. 'Stay here.' He headed off to catch up with Renfield.

Redwing, starling and fieldfare batted about in the branches overhead, sending down showers of raindrops. Rising breezes brought the leaves to susurrant life. The park was almost deserted now. Overhead, the green canopy flexed and eddied like seaweed in a rock pool.

It felt as if time had folded back on itself; Bryant wearily lowered himself on to a damp wooden bench and waited for the others to report back. He saw the soft yellow glow of the grand mansions that lined the eastern edge of the park, heard only the rustle of legs striding through grass, a call and response, then silence. The damp chill bit into his bones.

This is what it must have been like during the Civil War, he thought, *the Parliamentarians and the King's Men stumbling across each other in straggling groups, chasing through the sward. A musket shot, a whinnying horse, voices carried on the wind. I must not drift,* he told himself. *I can't afford to be whisked away to 1650 right now. No more hallucinations – I need to concentrate on the investigation at hand.*

The voices he heard became clearer. One, he realized, belonged to Colin Bimsley. 'I've got him, Mr Bryant!'

Heaving himself to his feet, Bryant set off in the direction of the yell as the others converged on the same spot. They found their youngest officer sitting astride a tall middle-aged black man in a dark overcoat, his face obscured by a thick woollen scarf. Bimsley turned over his protesting suspect and pulled out his wallet, tossing it to Renfield.

'Let him up, Colin,' said Renfield. 'He's not our gardener. He's a Nigerian bishop.'

Profuse apologies followed as the nonplussed clergyman was uprighted and dusted down. The bishop pulled himself free from their embarrassed attentions, swore spectacularly and went on his way.

The rain increased, soaking and weighing down the landscape. As it appeared to be setting in for the evening, May called off the search until first light. By that time he felt sure that any clue – if any there had been – would have dissolved into the dark soil of the surrounding grassland. It was as if their murderer had found the perfect place to hide in plain sight, within London's wintry wild chambers.

THE SECOND DAY

14

'WE'RE THE PROFESSIONALS'

Leslie Faraday, the epicene Home Office liaison officer and budget overseer of London's specialist police units, plucked the glossy invitation from his desk and examined it carefully. The Tate Modern was hosting a charity auction tonight, selling powerful images taken by war photographers in order to raise awareness of the plight of orphaned children in the Sudan. *Just what I need,* Faraday thought. *This is perfect.* He folded the invitation in half, then in quarters, and slid it under the leg of his wobbly desk.

Everybody underestimated Faraday. When they looked at him they saw a fat idiot. It was an opinion that was confirmed if they bothered to study his track record: conducting a fact-finding tour by visiting the poorest towns in Wales in his Bentley, failing to recall the capital of Germany during a European debate, charging his pet falcon's knee operation to expenses. But he had the feral instincts of a survivor, honed by a lifetime spent in the civil service. Charged with keeping the Peculiar Crimes Unit in line and thus decreasing the likelihood of them embarrassing the government yet again, he could be trusted to find a way of doing so while simultaneously promoting government agendas, and as he received word of the PCU's latest investigation, an idea struck him.

London's public spaces had never been systematically mapped, but it was taken for granted that the freedom to share and enjoy open greenery was a basic right. However, it was a right that was currently under threat.

In his previous positions Faraday had vociferously advocated the expansion of POPS – privately owned public spaces. These were areas that looked public but were not, wherein the rights of users were decided by corporations. He had endorsed and encouraged the creation of PSPOs, public space protection orders, which bestowed broad powers to criminalize behaviour which was not usually considered criminal. Hackney Council had already attempted to make sleeping rough an offence within designated areas, but dropped its plans after local groups served the council with a petition signed by eighty thousand residents.

If orders could be introduced into the parks, Faraday knew he could tender private security firms to police such spaces. If he could temporarily close a number of gardens and squares, he would be able to gauge public reaction and start the ball rolling. What he needed was a way of alarming the general public enough to make them welcome state interference. And here was news of a brutal murder in a London park . . .

This could be just the beginning; after employing private security firms his colleagues would be able to sell adventure courses, tree walks, minigolf, cafés, skate areas, climbing walls, parkour training, yoga classes, open-air gyms and advertising space, all priced accordingly. For an average family, the cost of visiting a London attraction was currently around a hundred pounds. There were already plans to place levies on small businesses that had the benefit of being near parks, giving them the right to hold corporate events in return. The next logical step would be to place offices *inside* parks, as they'd tried in Hackney.

This time the business model would be better. Parks were in the middle of a funding crisis that would allow the commercial world to step in and take over. The days of going for a stroll in pastoral splendour without paying through the nose for it were finally coming to an end. The more snouts he could get into the trough, the better his chances of promotion became.

He wondered how long it would take to get a blanket closure order in place. The royal parks might prove a problem but the rest could be dealt with through allies in councils. By the end of the week he could have a lock on every gate, and the blame would ultimately be laid on the doorstep of the Peculiar Crimes Unit. With a frisson of excitement he saw that the PCU could be got rid of in under a week, so long as they failed to make an arrest.

He began to sketch out his plan on a notepad. The closing of the parks would cause outrage across the capital, and such relief when they reopened that no one would stop to analyse the proposed new measures. Picking up the phone, he speed-dialled the one person who could be relied upon to unwittingly feed him information: Raymond Land.

The investigation was now one day old. Much had been achieved, but the first mistakes had already been made. Early on Tuesday morning, Land went to the Ladykillers Café for his usual bacon roll and found Steffi Vesta seated alone, pensively hovering a fork above a plate of fried eggs. Removing the woollen cap he had lately taken to wearing in an attempt to hide his bald patch, he pointed to the opposite chair. 'Mind if I join you?'

'Please,' said Steffi. 'They have no rösti. I like rösti with my eggs.'

'Never mind, have some brown sauce,' Land suggested. 'How are you getting on?'

'Well, I—'

'Because I must say it's good to see a fresh face at the unit, someone who isn't touched by all the' – he windmilled his hand vaguely – 'well, it's been a bit of a year, as I'm sure they've told you, what with my detectives arresting respected public figures in Claridge's of all places and getting locked in a vault under the Ministry of Defence, then ruining a Thames pageant and being charged with murder and, well, the whole lot of us getting caught up in the banking riots and my top female officer almost burned alive. The last thing I needed was poor old Bryant going insane – he got better, but that's not the point; it takes a toll on us as a unit, and every time we upset people by blowing something up or burning something down it reflects badly on me. And naturally I have no one to talk to about it, because of course the buck stops at my door, or where my door would be if it wasn't still missing. It didn't help that my retirement application got turned down or that my wife went off with a Welsh flamenco instructor, not that I could ever really talk to her, and now I have this internal investigations officer sexually harassing me – I mean, nothing's actually happened but the implication is that she'll drop the charges against us if I, that is if we, well, you know' – Land rolled his eyes knowingly – 'so I had to move to a bedsit in Shepherd's Bush and it was difficult to concentrate at work with kittens everywhere – I mean *everywhere*, because Crippen turned out to be a girl – and now there's this corpse in the basement. So no, things haven't been easy, and I can't help wondering whether it's nobler in the mind to suffer the slings and arrows of outrageous fortune or to take another kick in the nuts.'

'I have only been with your unit for one day,' said Steffi, eyeing her congealing eggs, 'so it is not really possible to form an opinion—'

'No, fair play to you, appreciated, but as they say, uneasy sleeps the head that wears the, um, hat.' He waved his fingers in the vicinity of his ears. 'I'd never quoted Shakespeare in my life until I met Mr Bryant. He has us all at it. Whenever he's around everything sort of gets *infected*. I thought by now I'd be coasting towards a nice little nest egg in a dead-end department nobody cared about until he and his partner, who in many ways is just as bad if not worse because he's an enabler – is that the right word? – invite everyone to chuck in their two bob's worth, and suddenly we've got spiritualists and pyromaniacs offering us their advice on murder cases, which plays havoc with my budget because you can't put a tarot reader down on expenses, can you? I thought it would help if I took a business management course, and in one of the exercises you have to sum up the core strengths of your team in three words, and all I could come up with were "erratic", "irresponsible" and "potentially dangerous", which is four words, but you get my drift.'

Steffi looked down again at her cold plate. 'My breakfast is' – she sought the right word – 'hardening.'

'Yes, of course, I'm sorry.' Land rose to leave. 'I'm glad we could have this little chat. Please feel free to talk to me whenever you need to. My office door is always – well, if I can find it.' He paused, seemed about to speak again, then changed his mind and headed out of the café, leaving behind an utterly mystified employee.

'The Foresters lived in Primrose Hill,' said Longbright as May set down tea mugs on her desk. 'I spoke to the neighbour. She didn't see much of either of them – they were often out of the country at different times, so the son was left at home with the nanny. I tracked down the car Jeremy drove – a high-end Mercedes that disappeared back in September, sold to a cash buyer in St John's Wood, so I guess if he had any hidden assets he couldn't access them.'

'He should have traded the car in.' May emptied sweetener into his coffee.

'I think he panicked. The pair split up and the house was sold at auction. It went for a lower figure than expected.'

'So they needed the money fast.'

'It matches my dates for Mrs Forester, who moved into Clement Crescent in late September.'

'Selling the house, starting divorce proceedings, moving –

it all happened very quickly.' May saw that Longbright had already created a detailed timeline for all those involved in the case so far. Without her organizational skills the place would fall apart. 'Did you have any better luck with his company?'

'I spoke to his boss, Larry Vance. He was very keen to stress that they'd reached a mutual decision to part in August. He refused to go into the details, said it was a corporate matter. I tried to talk to a couple of other colleagues but they weren't happy about giving out information, either. They've clearly been warned not to speak to outsiders. I got the impression that Forester left under a cloud, so I did some checking with his bank, phone records and a couple of debt-collection agencies.' She pulled out a sheaf of papers. 'Have a look at these, then think about how much you still owe on your mortgage. You wouldn't have wanted his money troubles, trust me.'

May examined the figures and gave a low whistle. 'That's quite a string of zeroes,' he said. 'He told me he was in danger.'

'He took out loans from several companies, at least one of which doesn't officially exist, at least not in the EU,' said Janice. 'Do you think he might have been in fear of his life? He agreed to buy his wife's flat in lieu of alimony, but didn't even get to the starting line on that.'

'Do we have no other contacts for him?'

'The numbers and email addresses I got from Helen Forester's computer don't work.'

'What about his parents? Somebody must have something.'

'If he realized he couldn't repay his loans and went on the run after losing his job, he probably cut all ties with his former life.' Longbright turned back to her laptop. 'Let me see what I can do.'

As May headed back towards his office, Beauchamp chased Crippen down the corridor. The startled cat darted into Raymond Land's room followed by the West Highland terrier. There was a yowl, a bark, a crash and a loudly yelled epithet that managed to combine vulgarity and blasphemy, so May judiciously closed his office door.

His partner was draping an immense green scarf around his coat rack and divesting himself of several wet layers, starting with a shapeless trench coat and ending with a fisherman's jumper that looked as though it had been partially devoured by a goat.

'I've been thinking about our man in the park,' Bryant said. 'He's on the run. The piece of paper he threw away listed safe havens. Where did he get it from? What if someone's been giving him advice on places where he could hide? Is there even such an organization?'

'It looks like we've reached the same conclusion,' said May. 'Jeremy Forester is our man in the park. That's why he won't come in; he knows we can place him at the crime scene. He sold his car but the house had a hefty mortgage, and he was supposed to pay for his wife's flat as part of the deal, which by my reckoning would leave him owing . . .'

'Over two point seven million, not counting the money he owed on his Hong Kong property and the accruing interest on his loans, which I can't work out without knowing the terms,' said Bryant, patting his pockets. 'Have you seen a sausage roll anywhere?'

May picked up a suppurating paper bag and handed it to him. 'We need to show Ritchie Jackson a headshot. Maybe it'll jog his memory.'

'There's something else,' said Bryant. 'I had another look at the dagger found in Clement Crescent. The handle has panels that at first I thought were purely decorative.' Clearing a space on his cluttered desk, he unfolded a pair of photographs and laid them flat, then opened a leather-bound volume entitled *Dynastic Seals & Motifs*. 'Here's the top side and the reverse. You'll see that the patterns are different. They're known as chops, Chinese seals called *xìngmíng yìn* that bear the owner's name and can have legal significance. It's a Chinese throwing dagger, originally manufactured around 1880, very popular in its time but not the sort of thing you'd keep at your fingertips. This is a decent reproduction.'

'How do you know it's a throwing knife?'

'The clue is in the enamelling,' said Bryant. 'The blade is high quality but the handle weighs less than you'd expect, and the finish is cheap. The thing about throwing weapons is that you don't get them back. There are three kinds: blade-heavy, handle-heavy and balanced. Blade-heavy knives are the easiest to use. They're show knives, mostly used in circuses. You hold the light end and throw the weight. The throw line – that's the distance between you and the target – is short because you need a lot of power. There's an art to it but it's not that difficult once you've mastered the basics. Forester was regularly in Hong Kong and could easily have purchased one. So could one of his creditors.'

'So he was going to throw a knife at her, but changed his mind at the last minute and strangled her with something else that he realized was less likely to identify him.' May was frowning.

'And then he buried the knife, switching the names of the roses,' said Bryant blithely. 'I know, I don't believe it either. Colin and Meera have interviewed all the keyholders in Clement Crescent. None of the keys have been lost, even briefly. They also showed photographs of the knife. Colin says that a Mr Dasgupta might know where it came from. He made a statement. I wrote it down somewhere. Hang on.' Pulling tobacco, sweets and what appeared to be a Victorian cistern handle from his pocket, he uncrumpled a piece of grimy-looking paper and flattened it out. 'Oh, this appears to be a note from Brad Pitt.'

'What, *the* Brad Pitt?'

'Yes, my next-door neighbour.* He says to stop playing

* A long-standing matter of confusion between Arthur Bryant and his neighbour, who had sarcastically identified himself to the detective, only to end up regretting it.

Pirates of the Caribbean at three o'clock in the morning or he'll fetch me a punch up the bracket. I think he means *The Pirates of Penzance*. I always put on Gilbert and Sullivan when I'm thinking. Mr Pitt's not a music lover. Do you want to hear what Mr Dasgupta had to say or not?'

'Yes, of course I do,' said May, vaguely irritated.

Bryant turned over the note. 'He said he'd never seen it before.'

'Then what did you mention it for?'

'Because he ran it past *his* neighbour, Mrs Farrier, and *she* says the knife is hers, and that it's been in the family ever since they were in China – her parents were in the Foreign Office – only here's the thing: she thinks it went missing from her flat sometime last month.'

'Does she have many callers? Could someone have taken it? Can she narrow down the time frame?'

'Not really. Mr Dasgupta thinks the old lady is a few ducks short of a funfair – she's getting on a bit and is always losing things. He says she's wary of callers and never lets them in to check her gas pipes, but randomly invites strangers in for a cup of tea. Perhaps she admitted a familiar face, one of the neighbours, say, and the knife was swiped while her back was turned.'

'That doesn't make sense,' said May. 'Why would anyone worm their way into her home just to steal a knife they then didn't use?'

'There you have me, old bean. Kleptomania or part of some bigger plan?' Bryant unwrapped his sausage roll and bit into it, dripping oil on his desk.

'Why must you always overcomplicate things?' May asked. 'You hate the idea that there might be a simple, logical answer. A kid abandons a knife in the garden, and you assume it has to be part of the case.'

'It's not a bread knife, it's a professional weapon.' Bryant dug pastry from his dental plate. 'Jeremy Forester didn't murder his wife. Domestic crimes take place in the home, not in a communal garden.'

'You can't be sure of that,' said May. 'She let him get close; she didn't raise her hands to fight him off. She has no bruises other than the ligature mark around her neck. You have to ask yourself about the husband: what was his state of mind? He got fired from his job due to some kind of financial irregularity, then he faked going to work so he wouldn't lose face. When he was finally caught out by his wife she told him she was leaving him. He'd already lost his son. What else did he have holding him together? He sounded desperate on the phone. Arthur, we're looking for a panicked fugitive. I'm sure he's the man in the bushes, and he went to the park specifically to kill her.'

'Then why would he hide from his own wife?' Bryant asked. 'He'd seen her two weeks earlier, he was shouting at her from the street – so now he suddenly disappears into the bushes?'

'Because just as he's about to strike he sees Ritchie Jackson watching,' said May. 'He could even have hired Jackson to do it because he didn't have the guts to kill her himself.' He threw Bryant a pack of tissues but it was too late; there were pastry flakes and oil patches all over his desk. 'Why else do you think Forester refuses to come in and talk to us? How are we going to track him down, Arthur? He's off the grid. His credit rating is dead, his cards have all been withdrawn, he doesn't even have a registered Oyster card or a mobile number any more. He's out there somewhere and up to something. And he's trying to dictate terms to us? Who the hell does he think he is?'

Bryant waved the thought away. 'He's a frightened man, John. That's what scared people do. Before this he had a future filled with privilege and now he has nothing left. He's not equipped for a life on the streets, going from park to park. He'll have to come in eventually.'

'Then let's hope he does before anyone else gets hurt,' said

May. 'I don't appreciate being given the runaround. For God's sake, we're the professionals.'

From Raymond Land's office came more barking and what sounded like a lamp falling off a desk.

15

'THE PLAYGROUNDS OF THE RICH'

'I don't know why I have to come along,' said John May, donning his coat. 'This is your area, not mine.'

'I thought it would be good for you.' Bryant looked about for his homburg and found he'd been sitting on it. 'You haven't been joining me on my jaunts much lately. You should occasionally remind yourself how I work.'

'I know how you work,' said May. 'You flip through your address book of academics with no social skills and poor personal hygiene, select one at random, overshare the case details with them, then sit back and listen while they rant about psychic resonance imaging or Blakean land geometry or some such deranged tosh.'

'Then you might be pleasantly surprised today.' Bryant beamed and reached out a hand. 'Come along. We're going to Tavistock Square. It's only a short walk from here, and I can get a pipe in.'

The slender parkland in Bloomsbury was young as such London spaces went, only a couple of centuries old. It was nicknamed the Peace Park because it contained a statue of Mahatma Gandhi, a cherry tree planted in memory of the victims of Hiroshima and a commemorative stone laid by conscientious objectors. A bust of Virginia Woolf also stood beneath the trees; the writer had lived across the road until her home was hit with a Blitz bomb. The park's flowerbeds contained medicinal plants, which were appropriate as the square was home to laboratories and hospitals, even a former horse hospital, and the benches were daily filled with lab-coated doctors having a crafty smoke.

'My friend works in a neurolinguistic laboratory by the old Italian Hospital,' Bryant explained, thrashing his stick at some litter, 'but he has several specialist side subjects. Ah, dear fellow!' He held out his hand to one whey-faced smoker rising from a bench to greet them. Although young, their contact's gaunt face was already permanently creased from the effort of avoiding smoke. 'This is Walsingham Pew,' said Bryant. 'My partner, John May.'

'Pleased to meet you,' said Pew, carelessly flicking his fag end into a rhododendron bush.

'I hope I haven't pulled you out of anything urgent,' said Bryant.

'No, not at all, I'm between lectures and was going to pop out for a cough and a drag anyway. I read through your note. I think I can help you.' He hacked and spat into the rhododendron. 'God, I have to give these things up.'

'Why do so many people in the medical profession smoke?' May asked.

'It's obvious, isn't it?' said Pew, shucking another cigarette into his palm. 'We all think we're gods.' He pulled out a scan of Bryant's paper scrap. 'Your man here – and it is a man because I showed a colleague and he says the handwriting is chock-full of male signifiers – is not a member of the Royal Shakespeare Company but the Rough Sleepers Community. It's an organization founded by the homeless to warn others of the pitfalls of rough sleeping. It finds them safe overnight havens, many in parks. Right now rough sleeping is on the rise, and nearly half of the homeless have no contact with aid teams. We see them coming in all the time. It's such a traumatizing experience that many hide themselves at night. Guides like this help them to find places where they won't be harassed. A lot of people feel safer outside than in, particularly if they're in danger from someone else.'

'Is there any pattern to the choice of these "safe" parks?' Bryant wondered.

Pew took what appeared to be a painful drag on his snout. 'They pick the ones with sympathetic keepers and plenty of shelter on wet nights. Your fellow was simply working his way through the weekly list, which I hope will rule him out as a suspect.'

'Don't try to do our job, matey,' said Bryant jovially. 'It could still have been an unpremeditated attack.'

'Do you mind if I have a word with my colleague for a moment?' said May, grabbing Bryant by his collar. 'How much have you told him?'

'I always leave out names,' Bryant replied. 'I think. He needed something to go on.'

Pew overheard. 'Mr May? I'm sorry, but we live in a world where people sleeping on the street only get attention if they're queuing for new phones. At least they're interviewed by film crews. Meanwhile, a quarter of all Londoners have key poverty indicators, and a great many are in inadequate housing. There's a fifty per cent shortfall in new housing targets. That's why people vanish. They don't do it because they suddenly fancy a bit of fresh air. If your suspect proves to be a rough sleeper and the press gets wind of it, homeless kids will be kicked unconscious at night.'

'Tell me more about the Rough Sleepers Community,' said Bryant, calming Pew with a friendly hand on the shoulder.

'It covers many parks and quite a few London squares.' The technician dug into his lab coat and pulled out the flap of a cigarette carton. 'I have someone who may be able to help you find your man. Her name is – well, we just know her by her code name: GPS.'

*

Their next stop took them to Seething Lane Garden, below Fenchurch Street Station in the city's Square Mile, but when they arrived the detectives found the site closed. They followed its painted wooden wall but failed to discover the means of ingress. From all around them came the noise of jackhammers and drills, the grind and screech of cut steel. The area bristled with yellow cranes. It looked as if the city was being attacked by mechanical monsters.

'Over here,' called a girl's voice. 'Push against the picture of the cheese.'

The detectives found themselves looking at a print of a large round Parmesan. Shoving against it, they watched as the wood parted and a roughly cut door swung inward.

The girl was short and slender, with unnaturally black hair sticking out from her red knitted cap and the kind of flushed urchin face that could be discerned in the backgrounds of old Cruikshank sketches. She might have been one of Fagin's crew. She wore black dungarees and work boots – a smart move, as the inside of the site was thick with mud. 'Follow me,' she called over her shoulder. 'It's drier over the other side.'

The detectives made their way to a low corrugated metal shelter and stepped in. Unexpectedly, they found themselves in what looked like an old naval headquarters, with boxes of supplies covering the floor, timetables and charts pinned on the walls. They made their introductions, although GPS offered nothing more than her nickname.

'I'm sorry, it's a bit cramped in here.' She pushed back some cartons to make room. 'We keep on the move and this became available at short notice. The workmen were taken off the site last night so we're making the most of it.'

'Where are we?' asked May, looking about.

'The old Navy Office stood here back in 1656,' GPS explained. 'The story is that Samuel Pepys buried his wine and Parmesan cheese for safekeeping on this spot during the Great Fire. That's why there's a bust of Pepys at one end of the garden and a picture of a cheese on the wall outside. We cut our way in with a specially adapted hacksaw, so yes, we bend a few laws. I hope that isn't going to be a problem.'

'I don't think that falls under our remit,' said May.

'Why is the garden closed?' asked Bryant.

'They're building an extension to a hotel underneath it at the moment. There's room for some of our female sleepers while the site's unoccupied, but only for a few nights; they're installing security spotlights at the end of the week. It's important that they put back the old rose gardens.'

'Why?' May asked.

GPS pointed. 'On either side of the gate were beds of red roses commemorating the date in 1381 when Sir Robert Knollys was allowed to construct a bridge across Seething Lane. The City charged him a rent of one red rose annually. There's still a ceremony of roses organized by the Thames lightermen. Another of those peculiarly pointless London habits.' She wiped a smear of mud from her wrist. 'Well, they'll soon have their nice gardens back and we'll have one less place to recommend. Perhaps they'll even remember to plant the roses. So many nice historical gestures vanish between the brochure and the building.'

'Why are you putting people in squares and gardens, though?' asked Bryant. 'Why not in empty houses?'

'The councils are working with private companies to keep properties locked,' she explained. 'Every last square inch has been monetized, and empty buildings are patrolled. The number of squatters in London has dropped dramatically. I suppose it's probably a good thing. In this day and age you can't be expected to live without heat and water.'

'Parks were always sanctuaries for dissidents and rebels.' Bryant had to raise his voice above the beep of a reversing digger.

'I think in some sense they still are,' GPS agreed. 'There's another London you lot never see. Go down the Hyde Park underpass at night and watch the traffickers dropping off

Africans, Romanians, Bolivians, all sorts. Seventy per cent of the illegals stay out of sight, and they don't hang around in the centre. They're in Edmonton, Walthamstow, Peckham, Beckton, Plaistow, not around here. They work because they have to, and right now we need them. They often have support networks created from their own ethnicity, but the truly vulnerable kids fall through the cracks. The homeless are treated like germs in the city's body. In the late 1980s the young around here had money leaking out of every orifice. Now they're poor and powerless. Bad timing, tough luck.' She looked from one to the other. 'So, how can I help you?'

'We're looking for a man called Jeremy Forester, although he may be hiding his identity,' said Bryant, handing over a photograph. 'He was using one of your lists. How would he have got hold of it?'

GPS examined the photograph. 'We're not exactly under-cover. We have a website and a Facebook page, and there are other organizations that connect the homeless with us. Their lawyers offer us covert advice, and we even get help from within the Metropolitan Police. With all the building plans being pushed through, we never know what's going to become available next. The playgrounds of the rich get built on plague pits.' She tapped the picture. 'I've seen this guy a couple of times. Hang on.' She called to a young man with a shaved head who was packing a crate of sandwiches just outside the door. They conferred for a moment.

'He was in one of the churchyards near St Paul's, maybe at St Mary Aldermanbury,' GPS confirmed. 'We saw him wandering around and I asked him about his situation.'

'How did you know he was a rough sleeper?' May asked.

'Trust me, anyone who sleeps outside more than three nights in a row gets an unmistakeable look, even in an expensive suit.'

'He was wearing a suit?'

GPS pushed back her cap, trying to recall the meeting. 'There was something about him that didn't add up. He said he'd lost a high-powered job in the City and he couldn't tell his wife, only she found out and left him. After he sold his house he tried to find somewhere to crash, but no one would help.'

'So what didn't add up?'

'A man like that – he obviously knew people. Living in parks is something you only do when you're out of options.'

'When was this?' asked May.

'I'm not sure, maybe a month ago, a bit more? Someone told him about us and he started using our open-air guides to find shelter. But he'd clearly had money – I mean, he had a phone for a start. That's quite unusual. The people we deal with don't have basics like sanitary towels and toilet paper. We deliver the absolute essentials for survival and still have to put up with a lot of abuse.'

'Why do you think no one would help Mr Forester?' asked Bryant.

'I asked him if he had friends he could stay with. He said something about not being able to take the risk. I told him we might be able to place him on a more permanent basis in return for putting in a few hours here each week. We're involved in the foraging movement: we collect the food super-markets throw out and distribute it to parks. We clean up after ourselves wherever we go. It's not just civic-mindedness – we can't leave a trail. The police would stop turning a blind eye if we made any trouble. But your guy turned us down. He seemed to think he'd be OK soon.'

May folded away the photograph. 'Did he say why, or where he was going next?'

She shook her head. 'I got the feeling he was waiting for someone or something. He said he was angry with his wife, that she'd let him down. It's not unusual to hear that. People look for reasons why their circumstances have changed. Often it happens very quickly.'

'If you do hear from him again—' May began.

'I know the drill. If you'll excuse me, we've a lot to get

finished here.' She went to help her workmates unload crates.

'So there you have it,' said May as the two detectives walked back along Pepys Street. 'When Helen Forester found out her husband had been lying to her she moved to Clement Crescent. He followed, told her he wouldn't be able to pay for the flat and asked her to bail him out. She already knew he'd been unfaithful with his assistant, so I imagine she said no. And he killed her.'

'I must admit it looks that way,' replied Bryant, digging out his rolling tobacco.

'But what?' said May.

Bryant's blue eyes widened. 'I didn't say there was a *but*.'

'But there is, isn't there? I can always tell with you.'

'Very well. Why wouldn't he have killed her in the flat?'

'Maybe he thought he'd disturb the neighbours and get caught. Maybe he called there and she wouldn't talk to him, so he waited until she was out in public.' May raised his shoulders. 'Hey, it happens. Many years ago I fell in love with a stripper who worked at the Doll's House in Carlisle Street. I followed her home, rang her doorbell and asked if I could take her out. I called several times but after a while she wouldn't open the door to me.'

'I don't blame her,' said Bryant, shuddering at the thought.

'So I waited for her in the street. I knew which bus stop she used.'

'I can't vouch for the young lady in question, but wasn't that an incredibly creepy thing to do?'

'First I was lovestruck,' said May. 'Then I was actually struck. Her boyfriend emptied a crate of rancid crabs over me. He worked as a porter at Billingsgate Fish Market.'

'What an incredibly poignant story of love's young bloom,' said Bryant.

'I was thirty-four,' May replied.

Bryant shot his partner a look of wrinkled disgust. 'Let us

leave behind these sordid tales of your amorous stalkings and concentrate on our suspect,' he suggested. 'You do understand now why I asked you to come along, don't you?'

May thought for a moment and came up blank. 'No.'

'You witnessed my incisive interview technique.'

'Only insofar as I saw that you don't have one.'

'That's where you're wrong,' said Bryant vehemently. 'I extracted all the information I needed. Now all we have to do is find out one simple thing that will help you to decide about Jeremy Forester.'

'I'll bite,' said May. 'What do we need to find out?'

Bryant looked at him as if the answer was obvious. 'How many steps lead up to Helen Forester's flat,' he replied.

They headed for Tower Hill Station.

16

'WHY ARE THE SIMPLEST CASES THE HARDEST TO CRACK?'

Steffi Vesta quickly discovered that her fortnight at the PCU was to be very different from her two years spent in Cologne's Bundeskriminalamt specialist forensic unit.

For a start, the unit was piled with all kinds of esoteric rubbish, from a stuffed Abyssinian cat to a wax fortune teller in a glass cabinet. Apparently most of it belonged to Arthur Bryant, who provided a vague but unsatisfactory explanation about cataloguing memorabilia. In the meantime Steffi set up her laptop and tried to understand what she had taken on.

In attempting this feat, she quickly realized that all rational efforts to define the unit's operating procedure were doomed to failure. She had always found the English to be entirely paradoxical. They refused to be guided by hard data and relied instead on a combination of common sense, goodwill, humour and wishful thinking. This made them flexible and forgiving, but indiscriminate and fatally shortsighted. Nothing operated on a common standard. Weights and measures, health and safety, law and order, everything was negotiable; there was no consistent norm and even less at the

PCU, which exhibited all of these national symptoms *in extremis*.

So when Janice Longbright asked her to head down to Clement Crescent to interview Mrs Farrier, as everyone else was busy, Steffi agreed to do it even though she had never interviewed anyone in her life. It was only later, after the case had been closed in the most bizarre and surprising manner, that she looked back on her first week and realized just how much she had learned by being propelled from her orderly desk job into the rampant pandemonium of the outside world.

Her first lesson in understanding how the unit muddled its way through investigations came upon her return, when she found Longbright on her knees in the building's attic, shifting damp-stained boxes.

'I'm looking for interview forms,' she explained. 'Did you get any answers to Mr Bryant's questions?'

'I believe so,' Steffi replied. 'Wouldn't it be easier to print new ones?'

Janice blew a lock of bleached blonde hair from her eyes. 'It would be if I hadn't spilled nail varnish inside the copier. Don't worry, I'm used to this. How was Mrs Farrier?'

'She recognized Mr Forester when I showed her his photograph.'

'Does she remember him calling on his wife?'

'He visited but did not enter the building. She saw him in the street outside on two separate occasions – of that she is quite certain. She never spoke to him herself.'

'So he had no way of taking the knife.'

'I think not,' said Steffi. 'She showed me where it had been, on her mantelpiece. She said it had belonged to her father, who split firewood with it, but she used it to open letters.'

'And she doesn't know when it disappeared?'

'No, she only remembers it being there two weeks ago.'

Janice dragged the last of the boxes back in place and sat on her heels. 'If Forester didn't get into his wife's flat or

Mrs Farrier's, how did he get hold of a key to the gardens?'

'You did not ask me to find this out,' said Steffi reasonably.

'No, but presumably you had a nose around.'

'No, I did not have a *nose around*, I did as I was asked.'

'Steffi, that's not really how we operate. We tend not to wait for warrants. So there was nothing worth borrowing?'

'What do you mean, "borrowing"?'

'Virtually all evidence is admissible here, outside of opinion and hearsay.'

'I did not know this.' Steffi looked at the mess that surrounded them. 'You seem to do everything. Does no one else help?'

Janice pulled an old paint-tin lid from the knee of her jeans. 'I ended up looking after the incident and operations rooms because no one else knew how to run them. I take care of the action book, but I'm also part of the inquiry team. I'd prefer it if we only ran online searches, but Raymond and Mr Bryant won't read them. They like using pens and bits of paper.'

'But this is all most inefficient.'

'Not if it keeps everyone up to speed.' Janice caught sight of herself in the old mirror that leaned against the wall. Who was she to talk about efficiency when she looked such a mess? The fresh-faced young German made her feel sloppy and slow-witted. She rose and tried to swipe off some of the dust.

'I find your investigation system very . . .' Steffi groped for the appropriate terminology.

'Unstructured?'

'. . . ridiculous. Is this the right word? Also illegal. I noticed Mr Banbury did not have a cordon log at the murder site. How is it possible to ensure that there is no loss of evidence?'

'He'll remember, Steffi.' Longbright tapped the side of her head.

'In Cologne we would have thirty people on the murder team. You can manage with a staff of ten?'

'There are twelve if you count the two Daves.'

'But they are workmen. Are they not repairing the basement floor?'

'Yeah, but sometimes we let them man the phones.' She was aware of how awful that sounded.

Steffi's unblemished brow produced a furrow. 'I think I will need to study this further. It is unlike any system I have experienced before.'

'Everyone says that.' Janice tried not to catch sight of herself in the mirror again. The wall behind her had been painted white but was already stained with damp. 'You'll either get used to it or walk out in tears.'

Steffi nodded. 'Very well. I may leave.'

Longbright watched her go, and all but collapsed. She had spent her entire career justifying the unit's actions to non-believers, and the sensation of possibly being wrong overwhelmed her.

Returning to the operations room, she tried to fix her hair and searched for her bottle of Leopard Girl Jungle Gloss. Her nails were chipped.

'You OK?' Jack Renfield set down a white plastic bag filled with foil containers.

'Just tired,' she said. 'What's this?'

'Chicken jalfrezi. I know it's early for lunch but I didn't see you eat breakfast.'

'I forgot.' Janice lifted a corner of the top lid and smelled chillis, cardamom, turmeric and limes. 'Did you cook it yourself?'

'Curry in a Hurry on the Cally Road, £4.99, free poppadom and a sauce that can stain teak.' He planted a heavy thigh on the corner of her desk. 'How's it going?'

'I have a feeling that if Steffi lasts the week, I won't.'

He broke off a piece of poppadom and munched it. 'What do you mean?'

'Forget it.' She shook the thought away. 'Two suspects, one missing, no forward strategy.'

'Hey, less than forty-eight hours, we're still in the hot zone.'

'Only just. The boys tell me they're on it.'

'You're the only one who calls them boys.' Jack handed her a container. 'The oldest cops in London.' He shook his great square head in wonder. 'Somebody must be looking out for them.'

'Who's eating Indian?' Arthur Bryant stuck his head around the door looking like an old glove puppet. 'I hope you brought enough for all of us. John just walked me past a dozen cafés and wouldn't let me stop anywhere.'

'Arthur – where have you been?' Janice dug a spork from her desk and handed Bryant the container. He helped himself to a spoonful of glutinous meat and wiped orange sauce from his lapel. Jack felt vaguely jealous.

'Eliminating suspects from our inquiries,' he answered, 'if I could find them. Jeremy Forester's still in hiding, and the only thing that's stopping me from issuing a warrant for his arrest is the suspicion that we won't get anything from him if I do. He must have tried to borrow money from his wife. She'd stopped taking his calls so he went to her flat, not daring to be seen at the front door. Why? Because there are eight steps up to the porch. He would have had to wait under a bright light in full view of the main road and the houses on either side while he pleaded with her on the intercom. He couldn't risk such exposure, which was why he planned to hijack her in the park.'

'So he could have killed her,' said Janice.

'Except that he never met eagle-eyed Mrs Farrier and didn't steal her letter opener, because she only ever saw him in the street.' He returned the tray. 'Thank you, that was awful. So somehow he got into the gardens and waited for her, knowing that she'd walk the dog. Then Ritchie Jackson turned up and started taking pictures, forcing him to hide in the bushes.'

'Don't you think that's a bit of a wild coincidence?' Renfield asked.

Bryant looked surprised. 'Not at all. Helen Forester always walked the dog at the same hour, and both her husband and the gardener had solid reasons for being there. Helen was attacked and fell to the ground – and what do you think happened when her husband emerged from the bushes? The dog ran to him. It was his dog! It probably wouldn't leave him alone. So when he went to his next safe haven in Green Park he had to take the dog with him, which was why he had to tie it up there. We'll probably pick up plenty of CCTV footage of Forester and the terrier, but it won't prove anything.'

'How are we supposed to find him?' asked Renfield.

'Maybe he left some kind of clue in the Mercedes,' said Bryant. 'We know where the car is. And we could have another crack at Forester's former work colleagues.'

'You're sure he went to his wife for money?' Longbright asked. 'A man like him must have cash squirrelled away all over the place.'

Bryant broke off a piece of poppadom and crunched it noisily. 'I think you're right. He needed to see her about something else.'

'Jackson's sticking with his story,' said Renfield, 'and I think he's telling the truth. He didn't see anyone else. Why are the simplest cases the hardest to crack? What do we do now?'

'We take the dog for a walk,' replied Bryant.

17

'LOSS OF RESPECT CAN MAKE A MAN DO TERRIBLE THINGS'

'What do you mean, they've taken the dog for a walk?' said Raymond Land, still eyeing the malevolent pigeon on his windowsill. 'Bryant's not gone potty again, has he?'

'He's trying to find Forester,' Longbright explained, dumping the Clement Crescent interviews on Land's desk. 'He's got Colin and Meera talking to park-keepers, and we're distributing E-FIT images at every green space on the shelter list.'

'What good's that going to do?' Land ignored the interviews, choosing instead to heft an ancient volume of the *Yellow Pages*. 'By the time anyone spots him he'll have moved on.'

'Do you have a better idea?'

'I do, as it happens. Nobody survives on the streets for long without help. Somebody let this bloke sofa-surf before he started hitting the parks.' He carefully opened the window. The pigeon watched impassively, then took a tentative step backward.

Longbright was doubtful. 'Forester doesn't have any close friends. We tried talking to his colleagues and they all said they hadn't seen him. They shut up at the mention of his name. Even the assistant John spoke to says she has nothing else to add.'

'Then they either hate him or they're scared,' said Land, not unreasonably. 'You say he carried on driving into work after he was fired.'

'Yes, until he got duffed up in his car park.'

'So there's a gap between the date of his contract termination and the time when he started following this rough-sleeper group's advice.' He slammed the directory down on the sill. The pigeon sidestepped it and eyed him with disdain. A gust of wind blew the interview papers everywhere.

Longbright decided that although her boss had lousy aim, he might have a point. She paused in the doorway. 'By the way, Leslie Faraday was just on the phone for you. He wouldn't speak to anyone else. Did you catch the call?'

'Er, no.'

'It's just that he only ever rings to make trouble.'

Land attempted to look busy. 'Get on with those interviews, will you?'

Longbright shrugged and left. She and Vesta caught the tube to Brook Green, a sliver of verdant parkland that existed beneath the polluted haze of Hammersmith, now in a state of wintry bareness. Like many of London's more haphazard open spaces its grass had been cropped, its bushes pruned until it resembled a lonely pensioner's front garden. The pair followed an Edwardian grey-brick terrace around the park's edge. 'How well do you know London?' Longbright asked Vesta.

'Not well at street level.' Vesta checked the house numbers. 'Of course I have made myself familiar using online walk-throughs. I did not think we would come here on the Underground.'

'It's usually quicker and we don't have to pay. You don't mind being taken away from a desk?'

'Not at all. I like being outside.' Vesta looked up at the houses with uncertainty.

'After a few months of trudging about in the rain you might change your mind.' Longbright sniffed. 'I think I'm coming down with a cold. When I was in Cologne it was always raining.'

'You have been to Cologne? With the unit?'

'No, I was a hostess in a nightclub on Zülpicher Straße. I wore a strapless satin gown and persuaded drunk businessmen to buy Chinese cognac. It was all very immoral and paid for my police training.'

Vesta looked rather shocked. 'Oh. This is not an English thing to do, I think.'

'You'd be surprised at what English people do.' Longbright counted the door numbers.

'We have more resources in Cologne but perhaps not your freedom.' Vesta studied her companion. Longbright struck her as heroic and unappreciated. Why did she stay?

'The PCU won't be much of a career stepping-stone for you,' Longbright warned.

'But there are perhaps lessons to be learned, even if they are illegal and ridiculous. You are not married?'

'Just to my job. I'm not sure anyone's special enough to deserve me.'

'I too am single. For now it's the right thing. There are always sex partners to be found if you need pleasure, yes? Also I play in a band.'

'Oh, what kind of thing do you play?'

'The trumpet.'

'No, I meant—'

'Ah, I see. I play German jazz-funk. It's a police band.'

'What's it called?'

'The German Jazz-Funk Police Band. You should come and hear us. We are very good, every note perfect and all in the right order. This is the house, yes?' Steffi held open the gate. 'Shall I conduct the interview?'

'I'll do this one,' Longbright suggested. 'You'll soon get plenty of practice, don't worry.' She decided she rather liked

Steffi Vesta. Having an outsider around made her take a step back and look at herself. *Like that's a good idea,* she thought.

Helen Forester's sister Catherine was small, grey and as wide as a gate. She was five years older than her sister and less well cared for, exhausted and disordered, with eyes predisposed to disappointment. She looked as if she'd been crying. Her kitchen was filled with the smell of stewing beef and so many saucepans and cooking pots that there was barely any room for the three women to stand.

'I'm sorry about the mess,' she said, gesturing helplessly. 'My partner prepares meals for the community centre. I have some folding chairs somewhere. I've been trying to clear up but, well, now with Helen – is there any news at all?'

'Mrs Forester's husband has been placed at the crime scene,' said Longbright, 'so we have some questions about him.'

'That's awful. He can't have been involved, can he? In spite of everything that happened between them he still loved her. I could make tea – perhaps we should find a place . . .' She tried to locate anything that would serve as a table. A small black cat rubbed itself against her legs.

'When did you last see your sister?' Longbright asked.

'Let me see – it's hard to remember . . .' Her anxiety was palpable. She looked about for somewhere to sit but nothing seemed suitable.

'How long roughly?'

'About three weeks, although she often called – she worried about me. I have panic attacks. Ever since I was little. We grew up in the countryside. The city isn't good for me. Helen always liked it more.'

'Do you get on with her husband?'

'No, I can't say I care for him.' She reached over and reduced the heat under one of her saucepans.

'Why not?'

'I suppose he's always frightened me a little. He's very ambitious. He likes to show off and take chances. I suppose his job taught him that. I think much of their relationship was based on status.'

'When your sister visited, did Mr Forester come along?' Longbright asked.

'Only the first few times. I didn't see much of him. My partner didn't like him. After Charlie was born they made no attempt to change the way they lived, and you have to with a baby, don't you? They travelled a lot, but not together. Their schedules didn't allow them to be at home very often.'

'Would you say Charlie was neglected?'

Catherine touched the fine gold chain at her neck, trying for the words. 'No, he had the best care, the best toys – but Helen wasn't the maternal type. She never put Charlie's needs first.'

Longbright made a note. 'Can you give me an example?'

'She held his second birthday party at that club, Soho House.' She thought for a moment. 'It was like a work event, champagne and canapés and all the right people – for a two-year-old! That boy didn't have a normal loving environment. Helen didn't like us looking after him.'

'Why not?'

Catherine looked about herself helplessly. 'I don't think she saw us as good role models for him. We don't move in important circles. But I often went to the park with Sharyn and little Charlie. I didn't tell Helen. It was our secret.'

'This was the boy's nanny, Sharyn Buckland? You were friends?'

'She was very kind to me. She doted on Charlie. She couldn't have children of her own. But it was awkward. She had a soft spot for my brother-in-law, you see. I think she always hoped that he would divorce my sister and turn to her. She saw me as an ally.'

'Was Mr Forester attracted to her?'

'I shouldn't have thought so. If he was, he certainly never acted on it while he was married.'

'How can you be sure of that?' asked Steffi.

'I told you – he still loved Helen. It was his saving grace. Besides, she would have known and told me. She told me about the assistant, Melissa. But she knew it was only one night.'

'How could she be sure about that?'

'She just knew. Jeremy spent a fortune on an apartment in Hong Kong. I saw the photographs – an incredible place. He couldn't meet the payments. But he wouldn't do anything to Helen.'

'What makes you think that?'

Catherine looked astonished by the question. 'You wouldn't hurt someone you still cared about, would you? That's why he hid the loss of his job, surely? Because he couldn't bear to reduce himself in her eyes.' It was clear that she considered the idea unimaginable. 'It was Helen who asked for the separation, and he had to agree. Things deteriorated very quickly. The bailiffs came. She only had days to get out of the house. To think that you're always going to be well-off and then to discover you have nothing – it must have been a terrible shock.'

'Did your sister have any enemies?'

'Not that I know of.'

'What about Sharyn Buckland? Do you have any way of contacting her?'

'After Jeremy lost his job she didn't bother staying in touch. I imagine she started a new job somewhere else.'

'Did you think they might have gone off together?' Steffi asked. Janice was surprised; the thought hadn't crossed her mind.

'God, no, not for a second. I mean – Sharyn was with Charlie when he died. The tragedy was a huge barrier between them all. Jeremy was heartbroken by the death of his son. I'm sure he felt guilty for not having been there. He was returning from Hong Kong that night and his flight was delayed.' The room suddenly felt underheated, as if thoughts of loss had opened windows to the chill morning air.

'I think we've covered everything for now.' Longbright handed Catherine a PCU card. 'If you hear from your brother-in-law or think of anything else that might be useful, please call this number.'

'When will my sister's body be released?' Catherine tugged her cardigan more tightly around her shoulders as they headed back to the front door.

'Within the next twenty-four hours, so you'll be able to make your arrangements then.'

'I still can't believe something like this could have happened.' She shook her head in disbelief. 'Strangled. Jeremy told me that was why they met.'

Longbright stopped. 'What do you mean?'

'He said it was the first thing he noticed about her. Helen had such an unusual neck. Like yours, so long and white.' She pointed to Steffi's throat. 'He bought her an emerald necklace; it was his first gift. He said her neck was her best feature.'

The thought stayed with Longbright after they left.

'Is that normal?' she asked Steffi as they started back towards Shepherd's Bush Road. 'I mean, do guys compliment you on your neck?'

'All the time,' said Steffi. 'I had a boyfriend, he used to call me his white river bird. Tell me, do all English people apologize so much for their houses?'

'All the time,' said Longbright. 'Apologizing is considered polite.'

'It was not how I expected you to gather evidence. You gave her privileged information about Mr Forester being at the crime scene.'

'What were you expecting?'

'Forester's sister could be in collusion with the suspect, no?'

Longbright turned her collar up against the rain. 'I needed to gain her trust so that she would surrender information quickly and willingly. She's not colluding with him.'

'How is it possible to know such a thing?'

'Steffi, trust me, you can tell. The way she looks and lives, the kind of person he is, they have nothing to share except the memory of a wife and sister.'

They set off in the direction of Hammersmith tube station. Steffi's long stride meant that Longbright had trouble keeping up with her. 'This is surmise, and would not be acceptable in my unit,' said Steffi. 'I speak your language but there are many things I don't understand here.'

Longbright cast a sidelong glance at her companion. 'Like what?'

'Your Mr Bryant.'

Longbright laughed. 'You're not alone there. I think John and I are the only ones who truly appreciate him.'

'How old is he?'

'Only John knows that.'

'He has no respect for formal procedures, I think.'

'No, it's not how he works.'

'Then how does he work?'

'He examines old books and talks to strangers and makes connections no one else has noticed.'

'But this is not a practical method of investigation.'

'You're right. You won't find it in any instruction manual. No one else is able to do it, not even John. It's like watching a magic trick. You see all the movements but you can't duplicate their effect. Perhaps you'll witness him in action. Right now, we have to concentrate on finding Forester.'

'I have heard of similar cases to Mr Forester,' Steffi said as they crossed the road. 'There was a businessman in Munich who lost his job and carried on going to work for two whole years. Imagine! He put on a suit and tie, and drove to the company car park from his house each day, and sat in his vehicle until it was time to go home. His family lived in Schwabing, which is an expensive part of the city. His three children were in private schools, his wife and friends supported all kinds of charities, and he couldn't bring himself to break the news to them. They found out eventually, of course.'

'What happened?' Longbright asked.

'He shot his whole family dead,' said Steffi with a shrug. 'Then he turned his gun on himself. These things happen. Loss of respect can make a man do terrible things.'

18

'THERE ARE DARK ROOTS TO THIS CASE'

'I don't know why we had to bring the dog with us,' said May, watching in annoyance as his partner tried to extricate his legs from Beauchamp's tangled leash. 'This isn't a Disney film. He's not going to tell us where the killer's hiding.'

The terrier kept his noisy nose to the ground, trying to follow traces from the path in Clement Crescent into the musty gloom of the dripping bushes. 'Beauchamp needs to be exercised,' said Bryant, 'and I wanted to take another look at Helen Forester's flat.'

'But why? Dan has already been over it.'

'He looked for blood spots, stains, bits of alien dust and irregular website visits. He doesn't have a devious mind.'

'What do you want to look for?'

'Clement Crescent wasn't on the rough sleepers' list. Forester chose to make this an extra stop because his wife lived here. He was desperate enough to cross the city and risk visiting a spot where his creditors knew he might show up.'

May waited. The dog crouched, its legs trembling. Bryant struggled long and painfully with a plastic bag. Finally May exploded. 'Well?' he cried.

Bryant looked up innocently. 'Well, what?'

'Why did he risk coming here?'

'I would have thought it was obvious.'

'If it was obvious I wouldn't be asking you, would I?'

'I don't know. You might be humouring me.' Bryant scooped Beauchamp's leavings into his bag and knotted it. 'People must really adore dogs to fondle their warm bowel movements every day. Forester needed something more important than money. Let's go up.'

After only a day the flat had already assumed a stale, unlived-in atmosphere, but a faint trace of perfume could be discerned in the bedroom. Dan Banbury had stacked and sealed half a dozen plastic boxes in a corner of the dark hall, ready for removal to the PCU. Bryant headed for the kitchen with the dog.

'Do you think that's wise,' called May, 'just when Dan's finished clearing the site?'

'I want to see where he goes,' said Bryant. There was a clatter of crockery. 'The caddy's empty. What kind of person runs out of teabags?' He tutted. 'Utterly lacking in moral fibre.'

'You're wearing gloves, I hope.'

'This isn't the murder site. Lincolns? Nobody likes those. You can learn a lot about a person from the biscuits they choose.' Bryant replaced the packet in disgust and unclipped Beauchamp's tartan leash. The terrier snuffled off at speed.

May folded his arms, amused. 'And now we just hand the detective work over to Lassie?'

'Attar of roses, made from damask or cabbage roses. It's a heavy, old-fashioned scent that's rather fallen from fashion,' Bryant declared. 'You must have noticed that Janice wears it, along with a lot of peculiar garments she seems to have salvaged from the wardrobes of old actresses. It was Helen Forester's perfume. It's an oil, so it has a tendency to stick to surfaces. Beauchamp is looking for his mistress.'

They followed the dog from room to room as he whined and scratched and circled about. When he sat outside Mrs

Forester's wardrobe looking up at May with beseeching brown eyes, the detective was impelled to open the door. The dog shot inside and fell silent.

May peered in. Beauchamp had curled up in a corner. Puzzled, he moved the dog and felt underneath. 'There's nothing here.'

'I have a torch.' Bryant lowered himself to the floor with a grunt and shone his beam into the corner. Scrabbling at the base of the wardrobe, he lifted a cut section of wood and pulled out a shoebox. 'Well done, Beauchamp. What have we here?'

Taking the box to the dressing table, he donned gloves and pulled off its lid. Inside were an antique perfume bottle, a jewellery holder and a thick A4 envelope. He tipped the contents on to the table. 'What is it that impels us to stash away our treasures in boxes?' he wondered. 'It's the paperwork for her divorce proceedings, ID documents and so forth. Ah. And something I imagine Jeremy Forester was desperate to get back – his passport, and this.'

Carefully tucked inside the passport wallet was a gold credit card issued by the Royal Bank of Hong Kong.

'She wouldn't give him the passport,' said Bryant, 'but he couldn't admit to needing the credit card as well, because of the declaration of wealth required by the pending divorce settlement. He had money and a means of escape, but couldn't access either.'

'Then he must have been very angry with her,' said May.

Jeremy Forester was exhausted. He had not had a decent night's sleep in weeks. His skin felt coated in a film of sweat and ground-in dirt that no public bathroom tap or sliver of hotel soap could remove. He needed a hot shower and a change of clothes. People were starting to avoid him in the street.

The situation was an escalating nightmare; he had money in the bank that he couldn't withdraw, overseas investments he couldn't touch and property that was no longer his to sell. He didn't even have any loose cash because someone had stolen his wallet while he was wandering through the crowds at Waterloo Station, trying to fill the hours of his day.

He changed his routine constantly, forcing himself to stay away from the places he knew. He couldn't afford the risk of being seen. Helen had always looked after the house bills and documents, and without his passport he was stranded in the country.

Nothing in his hitherto comfortable life had prepared him for this. In the last few weeks he had come to realize that he possessed no practical skills at all. He had been trained to negotiate contracts, make presentations, balance figures and hire others, not feed and clothe himself. He'd always told people that he was a survivor, but living well had nothing to do with survival.

Everything he had taken for granted was now a challenge. He didn't know how to get the simplest thing done, and was desperate enough to consider stealing. Out of cash, friends and escape routes, he had even missed his chance to pick up this week's park guide from the Rough Sleepers Community. Without it he did not know how he could eat, or where he could sleep. He couldn't risk visiting a legally registered charity in case they shared his details.

To a man who was used to having a twenty-four-hour concierge service the learning curve was steep and unpleasant. His former colleagues proved not to be friends. They didn't even care enough about him to be enemies, and only became engaged when discussing company politics. He saw himself reflected in them. The same tunnel vision that kept him focused on hitting financial targets had fatally undermined him as a normal human being.

The realization forced him into a desperate decision. He headed north to Melissa's flat, hoping to catch her as she came home from work.

The battered-looking Victorian houses that lined Hornsey

Lane were partially hidden behind tall hedges. Checking the address, he loped across the road and tried her doorbell but there was no answer, so he slipped into the front garden to wait.

Half an hour later a black taxi pulled up outside and Melissa Byrne stepped on to the pavement with an armful of Miss Selfridge shopping bags. For a brief, disconcerting moment Forester had a glimpse of his old life. He knew he looked different; moving from a heated car into a temperature-controlled building had allowed him to wear a black suit and white shirt all year round. Now he was wearing a charity shop sweater and jeans, and his hair needed cutting. The idea of spending fifty pounds on a trim and shave had become fantastical.

He knew he had not been good to the women in his life, but now the balance of power had changed and even Melissa, who worked at home on Fridays but was mysteriously never near a phone, and couldn't book restaurants without getting the days confused, had the upper hand. He wondered if she was bearing a grudge or would try to help him. Knowing that he smelled unsavoury and looked possibly dangerous in his muddy clothes and wild-haired state, he resolved to keep his distance so as not to alarm her.

Melissa already had her key in the door when he called out to her. She turned in surprise and took a moment to recognize him. She did not appreciate complications in her life. 'What are you doing here?' She stayed on the step, refusing to release the key from the door.

'I know you must have wondered what was happening,' he began unsurely.

'They told us you'd been released for violating company policy.' She continued to slowly turn the key.

'I can promise you I acted in the company's best interests.'

Melissa didn't care whether he did or not. She had no interest in his career.

'I've been going through hell. You have no idea what it's

like. I lost everything, Melissa. I'm sure you've heard all kinds of stories about me and you're going to hear worse in the coming days, but I'm not who they say I am. Please, I need you to trust me.'

Melissa did not see why she should. Her position at Washbourne Hollis was better without him, so why should she jeopardize it? He was toxic now, and the taint would rub off on to her.

'I'm sorry, Jeremy, I feel bad for you but I don't see what I can do.' She pushed open the front door and prepared to close it behind her.

'There are people coming after me. I need some money – not a lot, just some cash to get me by. I have plenty in my account but it's locked. I can pay you back when I get into it.'

'I'm really sorry,' she said, trying to match the sight of this pathetic pleading figure with her memory of their drunken night together. 'I really don't see what I can do—'

He lost his temper. 'Jesus, you've got enough money, look at all this crap you just bought! It wouldn't kill you to help me out.'

She had been about to offer him what she had in her purse, but now her heart froze. 'You never treated me like a real person, Jeremy, not even in Berlin. You only come to me when you need something.' She stepped inside with the Miss Selfridge bags and shut the door behind her.

He was still deciding his next move when he heard a car pull up. He turned in time to see a heavily muscled Chinese man in his late twenties exiting a red Porsche and heading towards him, walking at a steady rate that suggested he would intercept his quarry whatever happened. His face was as blank and smooth as marble. He was incapable of keeping his gloved hands at his sides; his black suit was so tight that it would surely rip if he raised an arm.

Forester knew he had been a fool not to think that someone would be waiting for him. He looked at his options. The lane was lined with mature oaks and elms that kept the wet pavements in shadow. There was no one else around. He set off, keeping the parked cars between himself and his pursuer. The man had now drawn level and was looking for a way to squeeze between the vehicles and grab him.

Ahead, spanning the six lanes of Archway Road, was Hornsey Lane Bridge, a forty-foot-high steel and stone viaduct that appeared much higher because of its vertiginous views down to St Paul's Cathedral and the Gherkin. It was soon to be fitted with anti-suicide fences because it had proven too easy to climb, but for now there were only ornamental railings.

Forester carried on walking. When he heard the sound he first thought that someone had kicked a stone against a car. Then it occurred to him that it might be a gunshot. A wave of fearful disbelief swept over him. Would someone actually fire at him in broad daylight?

The second clatter against the window of a builder's van made him turn.

He watched as the knife spun on its hilt before coming to a stop on the tarmac, pointing at him. The man behind the cars reached into his belt and pulled out another silver blade.

You've got to be kidding, Forester thought. *Not again.*

They knew he had no way of clearing his debts. Was he more useful to them with a knife in his back? He wondered if they had figured out a way of reclaiming the Hong Kong property without him. The knife-thrower was a rather theatrical touch even for someone employed by Sun Dark.

He remembered the previous time they had encountered each other. He had been crossing the western quarter of Hyde Park when the man had walked towards him and thrown the dagger. It had landed between his feet, its tip burying itself two inches into the ground. He had pulled it free while the man stopped to watch before walking away, a warning Forester understood all too well.

'Wait, wait,' he said, stopping on the pavement and

turning with his raised hands towards the Chinese man. 'This is crazy! What are you doing? Get me a meeting with your boss. I can sort this out.'

The next knife cut his left hand between the third and fourth digit, and the pain was at a level he had never before experienced. The blade was razor sharp, and stung like a deep paper cut in the soft flesh at the base of his fingers. Blood sprayed on to his sweater. So there was to be only one warning. This time he was to be injured, the next killed. As a system of persuasion it was fairly faultless.

He had no choice but to start running again.

As he hit the approach to the viaduct, drawing level with the black iron railing, an insane thought entered his head. The arterial road below was used by trucks, which were forced to reduce their speed as they reached the converging lanes that led to Shepherd's Hill. He looked down at the drop to the northbound traffic lane, and his resolve failed. Only for a moment, though, because the next knife glanced off the roof of the Nissan behind him and nicked his right arm, slicing through the material of his sweater to the skin beneath.

Climbing on to the balustrade would place him in clear view of the knife-thrower, but if he timed it right, only for a second. He was approaching the iron column of a lamp with spikes fanned on either side of it to prevent jumpers, but saw now that they might protect him.

Looking over the edge of the bridge once more he realized that the traffic had slowed to a crawl – and coming out from under the bridge was a furniture truck with a Plexiglas roof that allowed daylight to enter its storage area. One swift but shaky step took him to the top of the balustrade. He felt another sting, smaller this time, on the side of his left knee. Without looking back, he swung around the fan of spikes and pushed himself out as far as he could above the roadway, leaping into the fume-filled air above the dual carriageway.

*

'We've got Forester,' said Jack Renfield, stopping in the doorway of the detectives' office. 'He's in University College Hospital. At first they thought he'd tried to kill himself but it looks like an accident.'

'Why, what did he do?' asked Bryant, pushing back his chair. May was already grabbing his coat.

'He jumped off the Archway Road bridge. He landed on the roof of a truck, fell off the back and was run over by an ice cream van. Not very dignified but at least the driver was able to pack his broken leg in Raspberry Ripples until the EMT arrived.'

'But he's alive?'

'Yeah, just not in one piece,' said Renfield. 'He's in the ICU.'

'That's a nuisance,' said Bryant unsympathetically. 'Can he blink?'

'No, Mr Bryant,' said Renfield, 'he can't blink, he can't do anything, he's out cold. It gets weirder. He has knife cuts in his left hand, right arm and left knee. The bloke who chased him there was chucking daggers, and didn't stop to pick them back up. Dan's looking at several big razor-sharp buggers, the same as the one in Clement Crescent, so as we suspected, Mrs Farrier's memory of her so-called "missing knife" must be wrong. These are mainly found in one London store – a Chinatown supplier who makes speciality knives for high-end restaurants.'

'We've got the CCTV,' said Banbury, sticking his head in. 'It's set up.'

Everyone trooped into the operations room, where Raymond Land joined them in confused curiosity. Banbury ran the footage from his laptop on to the large screen, pausing it at the point where Forester jumped. 'It's a pity it's in long shot but there are no camera mounts on the bridge itself. You can clearly see it's him, but watch.'

He hit play again. Moments later Forester clambered up on to the balustrade, clutching his arm. He paused for just a moment, looking over the edge, then threw himself out. Four seconds after he made the leap a smartly suited figure arrived at the edge of the bridge and peered over.

'His pursuer just walked away,' said Banbury, 'so I'm assuming he came from a car. He looks to be of Chinese descent, but we only have a partial on his features. The camera was too far away and the definition is rubbish.'

'Why was Forester there?' asked May.

'His former assistant lives just up the road. Apparently he was waiting for her when she arrived home. She says he ran off before she could do anything.'

'Did anyone else at Washbourne Hollis know why he was fired?'

'No, but there was plenty of gossip going around. The subject of embezzlement came up a lot.'

'So that's it,' said Land with an air of grateful finality. 'Forester got himself into debt, tried to make up the lost money, was caught with his hand in the till and given the boot. His wife found out he'd lost his job and demanded a divorce, so he choked her to death. Then this loan shark comes after him so he tries to kill himself.'

'He might have panicked, but he was trying to escape,' said Bryant. 'You can tell from the footage that he thought he could land on the lorry.'

'But he still killed his wife, didn't he?' Land asked hopefully.

'No, he went to Clement Crescent to get his stuff back and leave the country, but she wouldn't help him.'

'All the more reason to kill her if you ask me,' said Land, but no one was asking him.

'Which brings us to the dagger.' May held up the evidence bag containing the first knife. 'This one matches the ones thrown at Forester on the bridge. Same enamelled handles, no fingerprints.'

'You're not suggesting that this Chinese bloke was also in the garden on Monday morning?' Land made a noise of disbelief. 'Just how many people were in there?'

'No,' Bryant replied. 'Forester is the link. My guess is he encountered the knife-thrower earlier and picked up the dagger, keeping it for protection.'

'So he could have taken it to Clement Crescent to attack his wife.'

'Don't be absurd, *mon petit tête à claque*. We know he still loved her. As he was sleeping rough, he probably kept the knife on his person for defence, but in the chaos of what happened on Monday morning, he lost it.'

Land snorted so derisively that he had to wipe his nose. 'By "lost it" you mean "buried it under a rose bush"?'

'No, of course not, but that part is easily explained.' Everyone waited, but of course nothing was forthcoming on the point. 'Forester confronted his wife in the gardens because he couldn't allow himself to be seen outside the flat. He asked her to return the passport wallet but she refused. It's ludicrous to think that he would kill her without going back to the flat and searching for it. Instead, he ran off. Her keys were still in her pocket. It may look like a simple domestic to you but there are dark roots to this case.'

'If he hadn't done anything wrong, why didn't he call the police?' asked Land, mystified.

'Because he witnessed the murder,' said Bryant. 'And it was someone he knew. That's why we have to talk to him.'

19

'THE SHRUBBERIES ARE FILLED
WITH ASSIGNATIONS'

The wind was high in the trees, breathing secrets through the branches. Arthur Bryant stood looking in through the great black gates that led into Mecklenburgh Square. Alone among central London's green spaces this one had always struck him as strange and slightly forbidding. Nobody ever walked around here. Beyond the hedges were great dark elms and towering plane trees that seemed to have entirely outgrown the garden.

The after-effects of his medical treatment had left him with troughs of tiredness, so he had left the unit early to walk back to the flat he shared with Alma in Bloomsbury. Looking around, he recalled investigating a bizarre murder involving a houseful of UCL students living in the square. He wondered if any of them were still in residence, or if they had all graduated and gone. It was an area where everyone moved on.

His memory was unfathomably selective. He remembered every case that had involved the unit, but was unable to retain the name of a single cabinet member below the level of prime minister. His knowledge of the city's past was as phenomenal as ever; he knew what had happened to Lord Byron's remains and which Westminster house had been occupied by Oliver Cromwell. He assumed it was common knowledge that London had once boasted a Turkish hammam in Jermyn Street and a museum of geology in Piccadilly. The city's secret history was there for all to find, but these days only a handful of specialists could be bothered to look. London's lost characters were to him close companions, from the body-snatchers of Blenheim Street to the running footman of Mayfair and the rat man of Tottenham Court Road. He saw Queen Elizabeth I dancing alone on rainy days in Whitehall Palace and female barbers shaving beards in Seven Dials, but he could barely recall his mother's face.

Bryant's nature was now so far removed from that of any normal person in the street that when he turned on a television he had absolutely no idea what he was seeing. He clung to one incontrovertible truth: that human nature never changed. Those neon TV shows filled with prancing, scream-ing ninnies were merely seventeenth-century puppet plays transposed, their presenters an updated version of the fops and mountebanks from centuries past. If you knew people, he told himself, you could solve any mystery. A city's character lay in its people.

The gardens of Mecklenburgh Square were closed to all except keyholders, but now that Dan Banbury had obtained a set of all-purpose keys for him, he intended to use them on every locked door in the city. He was going to nip inside and have a quick nose around, just out of curiosity, when the gardens suddenly transformed themselves into a park.

He had been expecting the return of the lucid hallucin-ations Dr Letheeto had warned him about, but had not suffered one in a couple of weeks and had been lulled into thinking they might not recur. As he approached the entrance the trees spread wider and wider before him, the railings toppled and vanished, and fairy-lit avenues flickered into sight, seductively snaking to the interior, drawing him forward.

Music played in an unseen bandstand, the sound made harsh by a hurdy-gurdy and fiddles. A wavering orange light shone between the trees. Bryant held out his right hand and turned it over, marvelling. The air felt suddenly warm. Pushing the iron gates apart, he stepped from the street on to the gravel path and began making his way towards the music.

He stopped in the middle of the footpath and stared. A lady of some eminence was promenading with her escort. He wore a deep blue tricorne hat and a startling pink suit with a cream brocade waistcoat. She was the epitome of grace, dressed in a sky-blue centre-parted dress with a bodice covered in tiny sewn flowers. Around the 1660s, then, Bryant decided, as wigs for women were not yet back in fashion, although the lady wore yellow ribbons in her curled locks. The couple were heading towards a circle of red and yellow lanterns where musicians played.

It was the time of tea palaces, spas and skittles, the era of the pleasure garden, but where was he meant to be? Not at Ranelagh, for that had a rotunda and an artificial boating lake, nor at the Cremorne in Chelsea, which sported ruins, cascades and triumphal arches. Flambeaux and lanterns lit the way. He could only step forward and marvel at the sight.

Why am I seeing this? he wondered, trying to make sense of this latest glimpse into London's past. At least he could now cope with the visions, which he knew had a chemical cause. They were patched together from the historical knowledge he had absorbed and sprinkled with scraps of dreams, but it didn't make them any less extraordinary.

'Is it not amusing to see how a feast unites everybody? Appetite is the great leveller.'

Bryant turned to find someone his own height, but young, in his late twenties, full-lipped, long-nosed and rather bug-eyed, his bone-pale face half buried beneath a dry-looking wig of brown ringlets. In one hand he carried a pair of beribboned grey leather gloves.

Bryant experienced a shudder of excitement. He had read that Samuel Pepys was fond of spending his evenings in the capital's pleasure gardens. He was standing shoulder to shoulder with a man familiar from countless paintings and sketches. His mouth dried at the prospect of a conversation with London's greatest witness to history.

'I came to gather some pinks from the Jardin Printemps, but rather wish I had gone to the Fox-Hall now.' Pepys sighed. His face was unexpectedly kind. 'Here the young bucks are too fondly making nuisances of themselves. Look how they scale the supper boxes to petition their wenches! There is a place for such sport, la, but we gentlemen of quality must abstain. One should never try to separate a maiden from her mutton.' He released a squeak of a laugh.

'Mr Pepys – you are Mr Pepys, I take it?' Bryant asked. 'Why do Londoners love the parks so much?'

Pepys looked as if he had never considered the question. Bryant was reminded of the often disingenuous entries in his diaries, the remarks of an ordinary man, albeit one with the king's ear, caught up in a lifetime of extraordinary events. 'I would have thought the answer obvious,' said Pepys. 'It is the pastoral in the urban which brings out the beast in man.'

'Then perhaps we should all move to the countryside,' said Bryant, enjoying himself now.

'Lud, no! London is my domain. A fish kept in a glass of water will live for ever.' Pepys unfolded a handkerchief and passed it beneath his nose. 'These counterfeit pleasures will not last. Already they are becoming spoilt by nature.'

'What do you mean?'

'Why, all of this.' Pepys's forefinger jabbed at the flickering scene before them. 'The dandies strutting like forcemeat laced into corsets, using the bushes as jeroboams, these fubsy mother-midnights pretending to be maidens.' Before them passed a pockmarked old woman got up in the mauve gown of a much younger girl. She held a silvered mask before her, and leaned on an escort half her age. 'That's it, milady,' Pepys yelled delightedly, 'keep your vizard high to hide the worst and show the better face!'

Some linkboys with torches danced past, their lights splitting the shadows. Taking Bryant's arm, Pepys led the detective on to the sheep-shorn grass. 'The refinement of the gardens is giving way to base urges,' he warned. 'They always reassert themselves. Have you not seen?' He pointed off to one side. Bryant followed the line of his finger. Each grass hillock was occupied by unbuttoned couples in the throes of delirious carphology. Many of the women were in advanced states of undress, their clothes splayed about on the bushes, their pale breasts jouncing.

'To see the line of loose-boxes outside the gardens one would think there was a sale of common goods on offer, not a concert of Jenkins's gavottes,' said Pepys. 'The shrubberies are filled with assignations. What an age this is, and what a world! The designers of these Arcadian delights encourage such sport. Did you know there are fountains that piddle upon you as you pass, making the ladies shriek with delight? La, there you have it.' He sniffed hard and replaced his handkerchief. 'I am not a prude, of course, I love my ladies and must find them, especially when my wife has her month upon her. Even so there is a time and a place, and it is not at a public entertainment. Have you had chocolate? It's rather good.'

Bryant wanted to know more of the man behind the diaries, to see the paradoxical humanity of him, a man unfaithful yet jealous, domineering yet needful, intelligent in learning yet banal in observations. It was not possible, of course, because he could not see more than he already knew. When he turned to look all he saw was a fleshy pleasant-faced young man in a suit of brown satin.

The warm summer breeze lifted the leaves, the torches blustered and ladies laughed as they pressed down their skirts. Bryant whirled about and Pepys was gone, puffed away in a gust.

Time was warping again, moving forward fast.

From the dark walkway to his right a lady emerged in a dress that appeared to have been stitched from green and purple handkerchiefs. In her powdered periwig was a miniature galleon. He heard the scroop of silk, the twitter of false laughter, the yap of a miniature spaniel. Two men wore black leather masks and were dressed as harlequins. The perfume of roses filled the air, artificial and smothering. Torches flickered out and relit themselves. *What now?* Bryant thought.

Other pairs materialized on the path. Judging by the escorted ladies who were approaching, sporting the fashion of wide skirts arranged in frilled layers, it was now the late eighteenth century, probably around 1770. The layout of lanterns and trees had changed, so that the rectangular promenade of avenues and paths ran around a great ellipse.

A masquerade was taking place within the darkened grove ahead. Bryant could smell roasting pullets and spitted lamb. Walking into the brilliantly lit clearing, he found himself before a number of garish yellow and crimson buildings constructed in different styles: Gothic, Chinese and Greek. They were flimsy and flat-looking, like theatre sets that might fall down at any moment. An elaborate curving white colonnade contained supper boxes, where diners could see and be seen. The music was faster and more raucous.

Bryant was hot now. Tearing at his striped woollen scarf, he removed it together with his overcoat and hung them on a convenient branch, then unbuttoned his cardigan.

The next enclosure was guarded by a ticket-seller. A pair of ragged children tried to duck inside, and the ticket man threw a stone at them from the grouch bag at his waist.

The detective could only watch and marvel. He recognized where he was – in the Vauxhall Pleasure Gardens, at a time long past the height of their fame. Someone was singing a much later music hall song, 'One Half of the World Don't Know How t'Other Lives', accompanied on an accordion.

And there in front of him was the most astounding sight yet, a great rococo edifice of white fretwork, set about with scalloped balconies and covered in chandeliers. There were musicians' stands in one part, and in another ices were being sold. In a cleared part of the grass lolled a scarlet hot-air balloon. On the other side a pair of pugilists waited for a crowd to gather. But as he watched, one wall crumbled and faded, to be replaced with a reeking meat stand and a dog pit.

Bryant knew that the fortunes of the gardens had fallen in time, that they had become the haunt of bawds, thugs and pickpockets, and now were in their dying stages, but what was he supposed to learn from such sights? What was it all meant to mean?

As he continued to watch, a fight broke out between two ruffians in mud-stained calico shirts while a young woman looked on. She gave a sudden scream of laughter, but the rough and tumble was now in deadly earnest and blood-spattered, the shock of scarlet blossoming on white linen. One pugilist spat a tooth, and the fight began again, this time involving the woman, who clung to her lover's opponent and was kicked aside. She clumsily rose, and moments later the boxer had his hands around her neck, throttling the life from her. It was quite clear that the ruffian had learned to enjoy the punishment of women.

I'm seeing this for a reason, thought Bryant. *It's something I know which can't yet surface – it's speaking to me through these visions.*

As the young woman fell to her knees in front of him, her hands clawing at her throat, he thought: *There will be another murder.*

20

'A HUMAN BEING IS NOT A TURKEY'

'He came home without his topcoat or his scarf, Mr May,' said Alma Sorrowbridge, 'just in his shirtsleeves and cardie. It can't be more than five or six degrees out there tonight. Where's he been? Where are his clothes? And he's been playing that awful noise all evening. Perhaps you can talk to him. I've given up.'

Bryant sat shivering in front of Alma's horrendous mock-flame-effect electric fireplace while Gilbert and Sullivan's *Ruddigore* played on the stereo.

'What happened tonight, Arthur?' May asked gently, pulling a chair alongside him. 'You left early but it took you an hour and a half to get here. Where did you go?'

Bryant heard his old friend speak, but struggled to pull his attention back into the present. 'I was in Mecklenburgh Square,' he said finally, 'although I don't remember much about how I got back here. I was warned there would be side effects from my treatment.'

'The hallucinations? I thought you said you could control them.'

Bryant pulled his dressing gown tighter. 'I can, at least to a point – but what if they get out of control?'

'Do you think they might?'

'I'm not sure. I saw another girl killed in a park tonight. I mean I imagined it. It's not second sight, I'm not seeing something that hasn't happened yet, but that's what it feels like.'

May was puzzled. 'Then how do you account for it?'

'Over the years I've read a lot about London parks, and of course I've read the Pepys diaries – the shorter version, at least – but what I see is somehow more than the sum total of my memories.'

'It's your subconscious,' May told him. 'Think of all the knowledge you've accumulated in your years. You always joke that you've forgotten more than anyone remembers. What if your medication is drawing out that knowledge?'

'I can't simply stop taking it,' said Bryant. 'I'll have to learn to live with the effects and harness them somehow. The hallucinations are iatrogenic. They're caused by the treatment itself.'

'You don't believe the investigation is over. Jeremy Forester didn't kill his wife because she denied him his passport.'

'No, that's merely the reason why he was present in Clement Crescent yesterday.'

'And you don't think the gardener had anything to do with it?'

'You've met him, John. Jackson doesn't move in their circles. You couldn't call him anything more than a general suspect.' There were five categories for persons of police interest, and Jackson was only on the second rung by dint of his presence in the gardens. 'The problem for me is his testimony. If he saw Mrs Forester both before and after the attack, why didn't he see the actual murder take place? Why didn't he spot anyone else in the garden? And then there's the viciousness of the act. Dan says it was sudden, close and overwhelming. It suggests an opportunistic assault. Am I trying to impose order on the behaviour of a madman?'

'You know it can't be,' May countered. 'It must have been

planned because the killer needed a key, and we're no closer to understanding how he gained entry.'

'Oh, I know how he did *that*.' Bryant waved the question aside.

'You do? Were you planning to tell me?'

'Yes, I just forgot. Here.' He rose from his armchair and headed over to the Victorian writing desk that he had made Alma lug into the sitting room. Shaking out one of the drawers, he removed a paper sachet and a candle, then drew down a leather-bound volume from the shelf behind him. May watched in puzzlement as he riffled the pages.

'The lock on the gate to the gardens,' Bryant said. 'It's called a Belfry and it's quite old. Belfry mostly made padlocks for British Army vehicles in the 1950s, but quite a few were fitted to gates after the war. The one on the gate at Clement Crescent takes a pipe key – that is, one with a hole in the end of the shaft into which a pin inside the lock fits. I had two hypotheses. First, that the key was removed from one of the residents, copied and replaced before they knew it had gone. I immediately thought of old missus busybody, what's her name, Farrier. But it turns out she was worried about losing it so she kept it tied to the zip of her purse, which means it was never out of her sight. I checked with the only key cutter in the neighbourhood. He said that it's a specialist item and he would have to order in a copy, but no one had requested such a key. Which brought me to the second idea. I spoke to Coatsleeve Charlie.'

'Good Lord, is he still around?' May exclaimed. 'I thought he was put away after the Belgravia blackmailings.' Charlie had sent plaster busts of Churchill and Shakespeare to various lords and civil servants in Belgravia, none of whom knew that the busts had microphones planted inside them. Even the judge had commended him on his ingenuity.

'He's still detained at Her Majesty's pleasure but I raised him on the blower. He told me there's a really simple way to crack a Belfry.' Producing a key from his pocket, Bryant lit the candle with a match and held the key over it. 'This is a standard blank. You simply carbonize the end, and then . . .' Checking that the key was stained black, he picked a padlock from the desk and inserted the key, wiggling it back and forth. 'There you are.' Withdrawing the key, he showed it to May. 'There are four leaders – the little bars that drop down and fit the cut key – you can see the marks where they've tapped against the carbon and rubbed it away. Now you just have to cut the key by hand to those depths.'

'And you think he did all that?' asked May.

'Have you got a better idea?'

Alma came in with a tray of rock cakes and looked around suspiciously. 'Are you burning things in here again?'

Bryant looked at her wide-eyed. 'No,' he lied, quickly snuffing the candle's wick with his fingers.

'You know what happens with you and fire. There's a dirty great hole in my bedsheets from your pipe.'

'Inferior cotton, madam. If you didn't go to second-rate stores for your linens they wouldn't prove so incendiary. This place is a death trap.'

'Mr May,' Alma implored, 'can't you do something? Last week he poisoned my aspidistra and got carbolic acid all over my whatnot stand.'

'I was trying to re-create a rare toxin,' Bryant explained.

Alma was unconvinced. 'The smell was something chronic. We had the gas board round looking for a leak. I was going to cook a nice bit of halibut at the weekend and found him in the kitchen bashing it flat with a poker. He says he's experimenting, but what kind of experiment involves flattening a fish?'

'It has the texture of human flesh,' said Bryant. He turned to May for support. 'At the University of Pennsylvania scientists tried to work out the minimal stimulus required to sexually excite a male turkey, and found they could remove all of the female's body parts without the male losing interest, until they were left with just a head on a stick. If you recall, they found a severed head in the canal last month. Parts of the body had been chewed by fish—'

'Can you not bring up body parts where there's food about?' cried Alma, exasperated. 'A human being is not a turkey. Or a halibut. You have no idea what I go through, Mr May. This is a council flat; we're not allowed to make any alterations. He took the floor up!'

'I wanted to see if a corpse would fit underneath it,' said Bryant reasonably.

'And you encourage him,' she accused. 'Every day there's a new problem. He should never have had that locust farm in here. There used to be topiary by our main entrance. Then the drains caught fire. And he threw next door's cat out of the window.'

'It was on a parachute,' Bryant pointed out. 'It's amazing how they always land on their feet.'

Alma would not be mollified. 'Mr Pitt downstairs thinks I've got Care in the Community people up here. What am I supposed to say to my ladies from the church when they come round for hymn practice?'

'You could invite him to attend,' said May, amused.

'And have him telling them about the seven levels of hell again? Bringing out his picture books of demons pulling the heads off toddlers.'

'That was the illustrated *Malleus Maleficarum*, madam. A rare and marvellous artefact. I was trying to teach them about Asmodeus, the spirit of vengeful lust.'

'They don't need to know about lust, they're married. You frightened the life out of them. It reflects badly on me. When I'm finally called to meet my maker he's going to say, "No, you lived with Mr Bryant, you can't come in."'

'He won't be going by your postcode, you silly woman,' said Bryant.

Alma's eyes brightened. 'So you admit he exists. That's why you came to church with me last week.'

'I like going to St Gandalf's—'

'St Andrew's.'

'Same thing,' said Bryant. 'In order to stop myself from going mad or falling asleep during your vicar's fist-bitingly dull sermon I drew on my inner mental resources and ran through the evidence in a theoretical murder investigation. It's the perfect retreat from reality. Now, we have work to do here, so hop it.'

Alma rose and adjusted her intimidating bosom. 'If you'd like some warm lavender cake, Mr May, just knock on the wall.'

'So where do we go from here?' May asked when they were alone once more.

'Right.' Bryant perched on the edge of his armchair. 'If the killer made his own key it's because he specifically planned to kill Helen Forester in the park, yes? And that means this is about gratification, not expedience. It's where he needed to be.'

'But why?'

'I think he wanted to pose her in an idyllic natural setting as she died,' said Bryant. 'In my hallucination I saw couples making love on the grass. It's a recurring symbol in British life, like Titania's bower. It reminded me of something that happened when I was twelve years old. I'd bunked off school and had come up to Hyde Park with some pals – it was wilder and more overgrown then than it is now. I ended up wandering into the long grass by myself. It was in August, at dusk. There were people coupled together, a demobbed soldier and a girl, almost hidden until I stumbled upon them. The man shouted; the girl laughed. I was shocked, but there was something else in me, some frisson of excitement.'

'You? I find that hard to believe.'

'That's not my fault. Feelings were never discussed in our family. My mother considered sex less important than making sure she had clean net curtains. My sex education had consisted of my father coming into the kitchen one day and asking, "Do you know about the birds and the bees?" When I shyly nodded he said, "Thank Gawd for that," and went outside for a fag. But here it all was on shameless display in the open air. To this day some part of me links parks with illicit passion.'

'You're not alone.' May helped himself to one of Alma's rock cakes. 'I think the associations exist for many people.'

Bryant withdrew a book from the side of his armchair. In it was a woodcut of lovers entwined in the roots of a tree. 'London has a long history of public licentiousness. The Elizabethans, the Georgians, even the Victorians.'

'You know a little too much about the past, Arthur.'

'It's true, and I know very little of the present.' Bryant shook his head ruefully. 'It's all second-hand knowledge and no first-hand experience.'

'Then perhaps it's time to turn the case over to the Met,' May suggested.

'We've already done what they would do, John. Jeremy Forester was desperate enough to beg his assistant for help. He was acting like one of those Hitchcock characters – a case of mistaken identity, on the run from both sides.'

'Are you saying you want to rule out both Forester and Jackson?'

'No, I can't. They were witnesses. But we have no clues. Dan says we aren't going to get any DNA from a wringing wet garden. Please tell me we don't have to resort to psychological profiling. Winnowing out the most crooked needle in a vast haystack of damaged people is just something I'm not very good at – you have to be a Baryshnikov.'

May brushed rock-cake crumbs from his shirt. 'A Baryshnikov – what's that?'

'Oh, they always said that Mikhail Baryshnikov and Rudolf Nureyev were equal opposites. Baryshnikov was capable of maintaining his stamina for an extraordinary length of time while Nureyev weakened faster – but Nureyev could spike his performances with the kind of energetic leaps that Baryshnikov couldn't achieve. It takes long-term stamina to find a serial killer. You look for years, maintaining a steady pace, sifting through suspects until you narrow down the search pool to a single culprit. I can't do that. I'm a Nureyev.'

It was typical of Bryant to compare detectives with ballet dancers; he thought differently to everyone else. Even so, May knew it was true. He would never have the patience or energy to locate such a murderer.

'You think we're looking for a serial killer?'

'No. Helen's husband was being hunted by loan sharks, John, let's not complicate the situation further. The only person who can help us now is lying in the University College Hospital.' Bryant closed his book and replaced it.

'But you said you thought someone else was going to die,' May reminded him. 'If Jeremy Forester is unconscious and you're ruling out Ritchie Jackson, who exactly are we looking for?'

'Whoever else was in that garden yesterday morning,' said Bryant. 'And we're running out of time. There's a rumour going around that Leslie Faraday has a plan to close us down. He knows we still have a few government allies, so he's planning to turn the public against us.'

'How could he possibly do that?' asked May.

'I'm not sure yet. Perhaps by removing something they value and blaming the unit for its loss.'

May worried at a knuckle, thinking. 'What could he possibly take away from people? All we've done is investigate a death in a . . .' Realization dawned. 'The parks.'

'Exactly.' Bryant clapped his hands. 'He was behind the attempt to privatize park security last summer. What if he tries to reintroduce the bill by playing up the risk to the public?'

'Then we have to give him no reason to act.'

'It may already be too late for that,' said Bryant, quietly pushing the door shut.

'What do you mean?'

'I think he's getting information from someone inside the unit.'

'Who would be so stupid?' May asked.

In his office, Raymond Land looked at the note on his screen: *Faraday wants you to call him back urgently.*

21

'SHE WAS WALKING DEAD'

At half past ten on a Tuesday evening there were few people in the wet streets. Sharyn Buckland kept to the brightly lit areas while trying to decide what to do for the best.

It wasn't safe to go back to the town flat. There were plenty of anonymous Travelodges on the Euston Road where she could stay overnight under a false name before heading out of the city first thing in the morning. She had friends in other parts of the country and a brother who lived in Dartmouth, although she rarely spoke to him. There were people with whom she could stay. This was what London came down to: the number of real friends you could call at short notice to help you out. There really weren't many.

Tottenham Court Road was a wasteland of demolition and reconstruction that left her feeling exposed and unprotected. The road's few remaining department stores had closed for the night, and the wet pavements were now deserted. Her suitcase was in a left-luggage locker at King's Cross. She had no idea when it would be safe to return to London. Four days earlier she had visited Helen Forester to tell her what she had discovered, but even as she had arrived in Clement Crescent she'd realized the hopelessness of her position. How could they go to the police without evidence? She and Helen had never been close, but there was no one else in whom she could confide.

Helen had almost succeeded in convincing her that she was imagining things, but now, in a stroke of awful irony, her death provided proof that her fears had been real.

It appeared that Sharyn had massively underestimated the seriousness of the situation. It was impossible to know how long she had been watched and followed, or how much danger she was in. Part of the story remained elusive. There had been an error of judgement, a mistake, a misunderstanding, a sequence of seemingly ordinary events that had somehow provided an opportunity for murder.

How easy it would have been not to notice that anything was wrong. If she had kept her mouth shut and looked the other way, Helen would still be alive now.

The emptiness of the road was making her paranoid. A chill wind blasted at her back, virtually pushing her into a side street. Skirting the puddles, Sharyn crossed over and headed towards the British Museum, past a row of small, pretty hotels on Montague Street. Her red overcoat had been a bad choice – it had made her too visible. What if she'd been seen coming out of the tube? She was as bright as a flag.

Russell Square Gardens were supposed to close at dusk, but were often open after dark because the winter light disappeared as early as four p.m., long before the surrounding offices emptied out. It was much easier to cross Bloomsbury in a diagonal line, skirting the central fountain, and the paths were usually full of students. Besides, it took forever to walk the long way around the square.

The gardens were busy and well lit. Just inside the gate a girl approached her and asked for spare change. She had the gaunt features of a washerwoman in a Victorian photograph. There was no light in her sunken eyes. Her bleached hair was tied into a ponytail with a rubber band, above the collar of a grubby blue Puffa jacket.

Sharyn was about to apologize and brush past when the idea occurred. Digging into the pocket of her jeans she produced a twenty-pound note. The girl was so disconnected that at first she could not understand what Sharyn was saying, but it only took an instant to make her appreciate the deal. Her nicotine-stained fingers twitched as she tried to take the money. Sharyn walked away wearing the girl's jacket, which was thin and reeked of stale sweat and cigarettes.

When she reached the far side of the gardens she found a damp wooden bench behind a trellised walkway and sat down. She could see the red coat plainly from here. The girl seemed in no hurry to leave the park, and it was easy to see why; this was where she operated, accosting tourists who came in through the gates heading for the opposite corner, where the great Gothic frontage of the Hotel Russell loomed like some fantastical edifice from a Bram Stoker novel.

Approach and rebuff, over and over. The junkie darted forward every minute or so, trying to catch unwary pedestrians by surprise, but her wheedling put them off. They slipped past without giving her money.

The Puffa jacket let in the cold night air. *Maybe I was being paranoid,* Sharyn decided, watching the girl's unsuccessful attempts to elicit cash for another minute before rising. She was reluctant to leave the scene and found herself almost willing something to happen.

The Hotel Russell had a bar overlooking the gardens, so Sharyn headed there. The doorman cast a glance at her shabby coat but said nothing. She sat by the window, sipped a fiery Mae Nam and enjoyed the sensation of the rum lighting her throat. The peculiarity of exchanging clothes with a stranger and covertly watching her while sipping a cocktail in leafy Bloomsbury did not escape her. By turning off the standard lamp beside the table, she was able to bring the gardens into sharper focus.

She cupped her hands against the glass, peering across the

road, trying to see if she could still spot her red coat between the trees.

The girl remained in place under a yellow lamp, repeatedly snubbed by those who passed. Sharyn almost admired her determination until she remembered what drove it. A couple walked briskly into the gardens and the girl moved forward once more, only to be ignored, the woman walking around her as if avoiding a piece of street furniture.

The next figure moved jerkily along one of the walkways. Sharyn watched as the red coat turned. The shapes of their bodies moved so close that they seemed to merge. Something white flashed. The girl's arms went up, then came sharply down.

Sharyn stepped back from the glass, almost tipping the table over. Her cocktail landed messily on the carpet. She pushed herself against the window, trying to open it, but successive layers of paint had sealed the frame.

As she watched in horror the red coat flared and spun, then dropped. The figure beside the girl moved away swiftly, shifting awkwardly, more animal than human, to be lost in the murk of the trees a moment later. That was when Sharyn knew that the little junkie who haunted Russell Square Gardens had fallen, and now lay beyond reach in the muddy flowerbed beneath the lime trees.

'I bloody hate this time of year,' Meera Mangeshkar complained as she and Colin Bimsley made their way across the muddy grass of the cemetery at St Pancras Old Church. 'The light's so bad I feel like I'm on the *Alien* planet – Sigourney Weaver's in the mother ship telling me where to go.'

They had left for the night and were bundled under scarves, heading in the direction of the cheap Indian restaurants on Drummond Street, when the call came in that a body had been taken to Giles Kershaw for examination, so Longbright had asked them to swing by and report back.

'What, a butcher's at a junkie's corpse followed by a chicken jalfrezi? Sounds like the perfect night out to me,' said Bimsley, ringing the bell of the St Pancras Coroner's Office.

Giles Kershaw opened the door wide and admitted them with a sigh. 'Let me guess, old Bryant sent you over to check on me because he thinks it's a related killing,' he said, leading the way. 'Tell me I'm right.'

'Actually it was Janice's idea,' said Colin. 'I'm just following instructions, Mr Kershaw.'

'Then you can give her the full report.' The coroner handed him an envelope. 'I've emailed it to Bryant but he doesn't usually respond so I have no idea whether he ever receives them.'

'He's not great with computers,' said Meera.

'Of course not, they've only been in popular use for a quarter of a century. I'll tell you what I've told him in this.' He tapped the envelope.

'Could we come in so you can tell us?' Colin asked. 'It's bloody freezing out here.'

'No, you can't,' said Giles. 'Rosa's just mopped the floor and she'll go bananas if I let you plant your size twelves all over it.'

'So you're scared of her, too.'

'Did I ever say I wasn't? We have a young woman, Paula Machin, a twenty-seven-year-old registered heroin user with a string of minor convictions, last known address 140, Torrington House, Building C, colloquially known as the Fritzl Suite.'

'You mean the rehab centre off the Cally Road?'

'The very same. She was found strangled in Russell Square Gardens almost' – he checked his watch – 'two hours ago.'

'And is it?' asked Meera.

'Is it what?'

'A related killing?'

Giles waggled a finger between them. 'How much do they tell you two?'

'You used to be based full-time at the unit,' Meera replied. 'We share everything.'

Kershaw shrugged. 'You know I'll check. There's a strong likelihood of the deaths being linked, and not just because of the park setting. Machin's throat has the same ridged marks I found on Helen Forester. I don't suppose it took much to kill her – she was a very sick young lady. She's covered in unhealed scars and hadn't eaten in two days. Dan's over there right now, and I imagine the old man won't be far behind – maybe you should take this straight over to him.'

'There goes my chicken jalfrezi,' said Bimsley.

Dan Banbury had cordoned off the perimeter walkway and was working beneath an arc lamp that threw stochastic shadows across the privet and hornbeam hedges. A nearby statue portrayed the Duke of Bedford in preposterous Roman attire.

Arthur Bryant stood with his hands in the pockets of his spare winter overcoat, twisting and ducking one way, then the other.

'What?' asked May, puzzled. 'You're like a dog looking for squirrels. I can almost see your ears moving. What are you doing?'

'I'm trying to see what she saw,' said Bryant. 'This is a cut-through for students. She knew they were more likely to give her money. The doorman at the hotel says she was a regular.'

'So why are you doing your worry face?' May asked.

'I can't help being wrinkly, these are my features,' Bryant replied. 'It's just . . .'

'What?'

'Alexander McQueen.'

'I'm sorry?'

'The doorman says Machin was always dressed the same summer and winter, in jeans and a cheap blue Puffa jacket. That was what he noticed most about her, apart from her ability to bounce back from the nastiest brush-offs. So why was she found in a designer overcoat worth £2,250?'

'Well, I guess she stole it.'

'She was a junkie, John. She wouldn't have been able to get into any high-end venues looking the way she did. It's too cold to take a coat off outside, and something like that doesn't get left on the back of a pub seat. So where did she get it?'

'Maybe it's a knock-off, a Chinese fake.'

'I had Giles send a shot of it to Janice. She says the coat is the real thing, and it certainly didn't belong to Machin because it's two sizes too big. I wouldn't argue with Janice when it comes to fashion.'

'There are always anomalies—' May began, his breath condensing in the chill night air.

'And they contain the truths we fail to see,' said Bryant. '"What is essential is invisible to the eye" – Antoine de Saint-Exupéry. What's the news on Jeremy Forester?'

'He's still unconscious.'

'That's tiresome. Can't we slap him awake? Did you speak to the head nurse?'

'Yes, and it's the same one you upset the last time you went to the University College Hospital,' May pointed out, 'when you went to interview Shoulders O'Keefe about the Hatton Garden job.'

'I have no recollection of that,' said Bryant.

'You sat on his drip. You must remember. He passed out.'

'He tried to bribe me.'

'He offered you money to go away. There's a difference.'

Bryant walked back to where the body had been found. 'It's the same MO, isn't it, Dan?'

'Looks like it,' said the crime scene manager, pointing to a street lamp bristling with raindrops. 'He was standing under the trees over there. I've lifted some trainer prints. Adidas ZX Flux Originals, worn on the right side, the same as in Clement Crescent.'

'Then it can't be Forester. He's out cold in a hospital bed,' said May.

'His wife was taken by surprise,' Bryant reminded them,

'and so was this street-smart, feral girl who wouldn't let anyone creep up on her.'

'She was walking dead, Arthur, skin and bone, easy to take down, a natural victim.'

'But why?' Bryant insisted. 'Why on earth would he do a thing like that?' Bryant had no idea how to respond to the notion of someone who might kill for pleasure. It was his blind spot and his greatest weakness.

'If it turns out that we're looking for a man who enjoys the sexual thrill of murder,' May said carefully, 'I think you have to stand down from the investigation.'

'Wait, you can't just—' Bryant started to protest.

'Hear me out,' said May. 'You always say you have to find the logic behind the case before you can crack it, and you admit that you have no understanding or appreciation of psychosis. If he's attacking at random, driven by impulse, you have no hope of finding him.'

'He kills without damaging them, John. He doesn't commit any kind of sexual assault.'

'Maybe it's as you said, killing them in parkland is enough.'

Bryant ground the tip of his walking stick into the gravel. 'He's acting for a solid reason.'

'You're saying that because you don't want to give up the investigation. I think you're wrong.'

'You always think I'm wrong.'

'Only when you *are* wrong.'

'But I'm normally right.'

'You go through a lot of wrongs to reach a right.'

'But the rights make up for the wrongs.'

'Can you two stop arguing about who's right or wrong for a few minutes?' called Banbury, exasperated. 'You're like a couple of bloody five-year-olds.'

'Then for heaven's sake find us something to work with,' snapped Bryant. 'We have to keep this out of the press for as long as we can.'

'I've got some scuff marks where he lifted her off her feet,' said Banbury, 'and something else. Some little metal pellets, the sort you get in air rifles.'

'Let me see.'

'No, I'm bagging them for forensic study first.'

'I don't need forensic evidence to know that he killed them both,' Bryant managed before Banbury shot him a filthy look. He turned to his partner. 'Remember I told you that the parks were once referred to as London's wild chambers? They provide the opportune locations; they're free zones where anything can happen. But the heart also has chambers. He has a personal motive.'

'You're frightened that if he doesn't, you won't ever be able to understand what drives him,' said May, looking over to where Dan was marking off patches of gravel. 'We should have been able to prevent this. You always look for logic, Arthur. This time there may not be any. There are a lot of crazy people out there.'

'Oh, come on!' Bryant slammed his walking stick into the path. 'Two deaths in two days, both in parks, both with the same MO? There's obviously a connection.'

'Then why can't either of us see it?' May asked.

'Because it's like this place.' Bryant peered into the darkness beneath the trees. 'Reason needs order. In here, the shadows move. *Or in the night, imagining some fear, How easy is a bush supposed a bear!*' '

THE THIRD DAY

THE THIRD DAY

22

'EVERYBODY HAS TO PAY SOMEONE'

Wednesday's dawn sky was striated with bands of black and yellow, a reminder, if any was needed at this time of the year, that England's location in the northern hemisphere had more in common with that of Norway and Iceland than with that of Spain or Italy, despite what the habitués of London's cafés chose to believe.

Renfield and Longbright followed the footpath into the Torrington, watched from the upper terraces by hooded teenagers. The estate had been built in 1967 and comprised four shabby grey blocks built around a quadrangle of threadbare grass. At one end stood the rehab centre. A rusty broken shovel propped against a wall was a cruel reminder that a gardener had once been employed to tend the green.

As they negotiated the maze of waterlogged tunnels and dimly lit staircases connecting the buildings, a hammering grime track leaked from a shattered upstairs window. It was hard to imagine that the place had ever felt safe. When the Torrington gained a reputation for trouble the government cut off its cash and looked away. Half a century later it was so badly run down that most of the residents had moved out, and the last few families awaited relocation. The gangs had taken over, running postcode wars at night. They were no longer visible on the street but shifted in the shadows, forming incomprehensible alliances and loyalties. The council had moved the residents block by block, providing them with new homes somewhere in London's hinterlands.

'Didn't they give this place a makeover a couple of years ago?' asked Renfield, looking about.

'A few concrete flower boxes and a lick of paint,' said Longbright. 'They're planning to get everyone out by next summer. I can't wait to see how they turn this into luxury apartments. Look out for number 140.'

They headed up on to the first-floor walkway, where half the light panels were broken, the other half flickering and buzzing. The thought of having to inform Paula Machin's family about the circumstances of their daughter's death filled Longbright with foreboding, but instead the door was opened by a young bespectacled Chinese student.

'She stayed here sometimes,' he confirmed. 'I pay the rent.'

'So she sublet from you?' asked Renfield.

'Not sublet, no. I sublet from the Cypriots.'

'Who are the Cypriots?'

'Some guys who live in the next street – I don't know. Two brothers called Stanisopolis. I pay them on time. Around here everybody has to pay someone.'

A familiar story emerged. The original families had moved out and a brokered sublet had evolved with the council's tacit consent so that coffers could continue to be filled until the wreckers arrived.

'I asked her to leave,' said the student.

'When was this?' Longbright asked.

'Two nights ago.'

'Why, what was the problem?'

'She was doing this.' He tapped the crook of his arm.

Janice showed him a photograph of the red coat. 'Ever see her wearing that?'

'No, nothing like that. I never saw her in warm clothes.'

'Anyone ever call for her? Any family?'

'No, no family, no friends, nobody ever.' He thought for a moment. 'She stole from everyone. She was not a good person. But it wasn't her. It was this thing.' He tapped his arm again.

'Why would he strangle a junkie in a busy park used as a shortcut?' asked Renfield as they left.

Janice slapped her gloves together, trying to warm her hands. 'Maybe he felt the need and had to act on it at once.'

'Which means there may have been dry runs first,' said Renfield. 'Where was Ritchie Jackson while all this was happening?'

'I already checked,' said Longbright. 'He says he was home alone in front of the TV and can't remember what he watched, and *somebody* was definitely in. His electricity records back him up.'

'Then let's start with him and move on to Forester the second he wakes up.'

'You know what's really odd about this whole thing?' said Longbright. 'It should have been the simplest case in the world. A dead wife and a missing husband involved in a nasty divorce. Why can't the most obvious answer be the right one?'

'Because life is never convenient,' said Renfield. 'Forester couldn't have killed Machin.'

'Then whatever we're missing is buried deeper.'

'Or it's right in front of us,' said Renfield. Crossing the Caledonian Road against rain and traffic, they headed back towards the unit.

Steffi Vesta had been walking around the PCU, passing from one chaotic room to the next, trying to understand what she had been drafted into.

The building struck her as a microcosm of London: not one job had been satisfactorily finished, no single rule applied anywhere, everything was off-kilter, nothing quite made sense. She made extensive notes, attempting a comprehensive study that could be submitted to her senior officers in Cologne. Instead she received answers to questions she hadn't asked and was given extraneous information that led nowhere. And old! To her young eyes the detectives seemed positively primordial. Raymond Land talked very loudly and slowly to her, as if she was a Martian. At least John May was helpful and possessed an air of modernity, but Mr Bryant smelled of peppermints and marijuana and barely registered her presence, not bothering to look up from his books when spoken to, throwing arcane words around like 'dolly-mop' and 'scobolotcher', wandering outside in the middle of a sentence and returning only to ask her if she knew anything about hedgehogs. And she never knew if he was joking; when he asked her if 'bandwidth' had something to do with fat musicians, she knew he had to be pulling her leg. Surely everybody knew what bandwidth was? Nobody else seemed to find this odd. Clearly they had all been working together for such a long time that nothing struck them as unusual.

In the morning's first meeting she raised her hand.

'Miss Vesta, now what's the matter?' asked Raymond Land, who was already growing tired of the permanently confused look on her face.

'The man who attacked Paula Machin used the same operational method, yes?' she said.

'Well, *obviously*,' said Land rather rudely. 'We've already established that.'

'But this coat looks as if it would belong to Helen Forester, do you not think? It is very similar to the one she was wearing when she died.'

'You mean he only goes after women in red coats?'

'I don't know, but is it not worth talking to Forester's sister to see if she had such a coat?' She cast a hopeful glance at Longbright, who seemed to be her ally.

'Worth a try,' said Janice. 'We'll get on it.'

But before the lead could be followed up, the week's events took a disastrous turn.

23

'THEY'RE CLOSING THE PARKS TONIGHT'

Raymond Land tipped back his chair and folded his business manual open to another chapter, entitled 'Removing Dissent in the Workplace'. The volume had been sent to him by Leslie Faraday, who suggested it might help him run the PCU more efficiently.

Land studied the manual in minute detail, making copious notes. As a result, he felt that he knew more about the efficient running of the unit than he ever had in the past, and was ready to apply his learning. He was confident that he alone had the power to turn their fortunes around.

Unfortunately, what he didn't know was this: in 1944, the forerunner of America's CIA, the Office of Strategic Services, issued a business manual aimed at sabotaging foreign industries. It was intended to be dispensed to citizens who were sympathetic to the Allies but living in Axis nations. Through an accident of fate too unbelievable to be detailed even in these memoirs, the manual's contents somehow made it into a training course entitled *Better British Business Management*, and the repackaged volume, filled with advice that actually meant the reverse, had ended up on Raymond Land's desk with a note from Faraday, who had taken it at face value. Land had perused it and cherry-picked the ideas that appealed to him, including the following:

All work should be passed through the proper channels. Never permit shortcuts to be taken in order to expedite decisions. Whenever possible refer all matters to committees of at least six people for further consideration. Always refer back to the precise wording of resolutions decided upon at the last meeting and reopen the question of the advisability of that decision. Urge your colleagues to avoid haste. Insist on perfect work and after careful consideration, reject all flawed plans. Advocate caution and responsibility at all times.

It seemed like eminently sensible advice to him, even if he couldn't quite grasp how it would make others respect him more. There was something else that Land did not know: in his eternal quest to have the PCU closed down, Faraday had spotted what he felt was its greatest weakness – Land himself.

When the phone rang on his Whitehall desk that morning, Faraday was in the middle of lowering a McVitie's chocolate biscuit into his tea with the precision of a crane driver setting down an RSJ, and the lapse in concentration caused it to break in half.

'What do you want?' he snapped irritably, trying to fish out the soggy biscuit with a pair of nail clippers.

'You asked me to keep you updated on the investigation,' said Land.

Faraday cursed as he dropped the clippers in his tea.

'The woman killed in the park. There's been another one, and we're sure the cases are linked.'

'Oh, dear. The same park?' He folded some sheets of toilet paper in half and began dredging the remains of his biscuit out on to them.

'No, this time it's a much more heavily used spot. The gardens at Russell Square, in Bloomsbury.'

'How close are you to making an arrest?'

Even Land could see the expediency in being economical with the truth. 'We have a couple of suspects under scrutiny . . .' he began.

'And in the meantime the parks are open, leaving the public at risk. I see.' Feeling a surge of elation Faraday pushed his tea aside and returned to the plan on his notepad. On it he had written:

> *City of London – Approved*
> *Westminster – Approved*
> *Kensington & Chelsea – Approved*
> *Camden – Approved*
> *Southwark – Pending*
> *Tower Hamlets – Pending*

'Yes, but of course you couldn't close the parks,' said Land, almost as if he was reading over his shoulder. 'For a start, we'd get the blame.'

'On the contrary,' objected Faraday, nettled. 'We have to get them closed as quickly as possible. People are in danger. I think we can get the gates locked by tonight.'

'But if you do that there'll be riots.' Land began to get an inkling of what he had started. 'Perhaps we should have a committee meeting. This isn't a decision to be undertaken lightly. We'd need to discuss it with at least six people.'

'No, I want all of them closed at once. Except for St James's and Hyde Park, obviously. The royals – you don't want to have to handle their PR departments, quite the most high-handed bunch I've ever had the misfortune to—'

'Not the main parks,' said Land, attempting to dam the flow of disaster heading his way. 'Perhaps just the small ones.'

'You say women are at risk, yes? There could be more than one attacker. Have you been reading the papers lately? Bombs going off all over Europe. And Turkey. Or is Turkey in

Europe? I can never remember. We could be dealing with a terrorist group.'

Land suddenly saw that he'd been played for a fool. Faraday had built his reputation by driving through dubious initiatives and buttressing them with acolytes who saw him lighting a path to promotion.

'I already have the plans drawn up,' he said, closing his ear to Land's burbling prevarications. 'I'll get on it straight away. Keep me informed of any further developments.' Replacing his phone, he set about making the calls that would seal off the city's parks by nightfall and close the PCU's doors by the weekend.

'Have you seen this?' asked Longbright, entering the detectives' office and reaching past John May to tap at his keyboard. 'Breaking news. It hit the *Hard News* website first, which probably means it came from Leslie Faraday.' It was well known that Faraday had the site's editor in his pocket. '*Police to close Central London parks from sunset tonight.* Just the very thing we wanted to avoid.'

'This isn't about public safety,' said May. 'He has an agenda. But while he's trying to drive the initiative through, he won't be watching us. What do you think, Arthur?'

Bryant had his nose almost touching the pages of a huge volume which lay sprawled across his overcrowded desk. 'I don't speculate,' he said without looking up.

Steffi Vesta saw Longbright sitting in with the detectives and cautiously entered, handing them a printout. 'Paula Machin's previous convictions include three for shoplifting, but she never took clothes,' she said. 'Her parents are both registered addicts. According to them she'd been beaten up by her boyfriend and thrown out of his flat a couple of weeks earlier. Shall I bring him in?'

'As soon as you can,' said Longbright. 'I'll cover the interview.'

Jack Renfield appeared in the doorway. 'Have you seen the

news?' he asked. 'They're closing the parks tonight. We've got a leak.'

'This is not a Marx Brothers film!' barked Bryant. 'Everybody out. You have a nice new communal room of your own. If you're confused about matters relating to standard investigative procedure, get Raymondo to arbitrate. I am trying to work here.' He raised the cover of the book as if it offered an explanation. The title read: *An Anecdotal History of London's Pleasure Gardens*. 'As for the leak, it's bound to have been him – he can never keep his mouth shut. Wait, wait. Do we have any shots of the Machin body *in situ*?'

'Dan will have them,' said May. 'He should have sent them to you.'

'Very possibly. My computer is having some kind of nervous breakdown. It keeps replaying old Norman Wisdom films. Perhaps Dan could have a look at it.' Bryant returned to his book. 'Two murders, it's not enough.'

'How many would you like there to be?' asked Renfield. 'Five, a dozen?'

Bryant removed his trifocals with an air of impatience. 'Two is a coincidence. Three is a pattern. I checked all attacks in London parks over the last five years and there are no other strangulations. At the moment the MO is the only real link we have. The attacks occurred at different times to women from very different social backgrounds. Which is why I need to explore an alternative route.'

'May we be privileged to know the route you're looking into?' May asked.

The detective set his book aside as if having to be torn from a conjoined twin. 'Look, I couldn't begin to explain my thought processes to you,' he replied, tapping the stack of volumes next to his unused computer. 'I've still got to get through *Licentiousness in London Parks 1800–1945*. There's a lot to take in. Then there are the sheep to consider.'

May had put up with Bryant's investigations into the

history of Victorian public conveniences and Egyptian street furniture, but this was pushing it. 'Sheep? Is that the best you can do?'

'Sheep do what they're told, but more importantly they all look alike. You see my point, I'm sure.' There was a lot of head shaking. Bryant sighed theatrically and held his partner's gaze with a steady blue eye. 'The gardener, Ritchie Jackson. Search his storeroom and see if you can find what he uses to stake his roses. Plastic ties have ridges on one side.'

'You think he's involved after all?'

'I didn't say that. If Jackson isn't the killer he may know who is – he might just not be aware of it. As for Forester, what if the people to whom he owes money decided to hurt him through his ex-wife? We really need to talk to him.'

'Now's your chance,' said Longbright, checking her phone. 'He's awake.'

'Do you want to come with us?' asked May.

'No,' said Longbright. 'Jack and I are going shopping.'

'We're not the only McQueen agent,' said the stick-thin sales assistant at Selfridges, 'but we're the only ones who sold this particular model. It was a couture one-off unveiled at London Fashion Week in February last year. If you care to follow me I'll find you the name of the purchaser.'

They waited while the assistant logged into the system.

'Who buys all this clobber?' asked Renfield. 'I suppose if you're a seventeen-year-old Japanese anorexic or a human skeleton with a tufty beard and a topknot you're sorted, but if you're a middle-aged extra-extra-large male you're utterly shagged. There is literally nothing in this store for me other than the toilets.' He examined a rack of what appeared to be artfully torn string vests in shocking pink. 'Look at the state of that, it wouldn't see you out.'

'It may come as a great shock to you, Jack, but women don't buy clothes to "see them out", as you put it.

Clothes don't have to last for ever. And the harder it is to wear, the more skill you need to pull it off.'

'That looks as if it would fall off. I need skill to pull off those pants you bought me. They're not big enough for a squirrel to keep his nuts in, let alone—'

'It was sold to a lady named Helen Forester,' said the assistant, pointing to her screen.

24

'AN AWFUL LOT OF TRAGEDY IN ONE FAMILY'

'Forester's medication regimen will prevent anything he says today from being used as evidence against him, you know that,' said May as they entered the hospital ward. 'We should really wait another day.'

Bryant squeezed antiseptic gel on to his hands. 'We haven't time to wait. We need to know who was in the park with him.'

'Why should we believe anything he tells us?' May searched the bed roster. 'He probably blames his wife for his son's death. After all, she abdicated responsibility for the boy, handing him over to Sharyn Buckland. We know the nanny saw more of the child than she did.'

'So Helen Forester shouldn't have had a career, but it was all right for her husband to succeed?'

'All I'm saying is that there are good reasons why he shouldn't want to tell us the truth.'

The head nurse met them in the corridor. 'The van driver on the Archway Road was very lucky,' she told them. May always found it amazing that nurses could seek out the positive elements in any tragedy. 'He didn't lose control of his vehicle even after Mr Forester landed on his roof.'

'How's Forester doing?' Bryant asked.

'He won't be taking tango lessons any time soon. But he should be home in a couple of days. He was lucky. I saw a chap go under a refrigerated truck once. You couldn't have filled a shopping bag with what came out of the other side.'

'You're new, aren't you?' May was trying to read her name tag without his glasses and failing.

'Yes, Mr May, my name is Ellen Shaw, I'm a good Protestant girl from Dublin and I know all about you, so I'm keeping far out of your reach. Didn't you date one of the *very* senior nurses here once?' She grinned and pushed open the door.

'Can we get some English Breakfast tea?' Bryant asked.

'Budget cuts,' Shaw countered with a dazzling smile. 'And I'm not English. Get your own tea.'

'I like that one's spirit,' said May admiringly.

Jeremy Forester had been placed in a public ward overlooking the streets of Bloomsbury, where there was always someone to keep an eye on him. He was still hooked up to an IV drip. His face was so swollen and blackened that the frame of his skull was lost beneath inflamed flesh. He had no cards or flowers from well-wishers.

'It's not been a great year for you, has it?' asked Bryant, sitting on the edge of the bed. 'No grapes going, I suppose? Your assistant says you told her there were people coming after you. She saw someone from her window. Who are they?'

'Owed – money,' Forester rasped, painfully turning his head. May gave him a sip of water from a plastic beaker.

'We've been going through your accounts. You lied to your creditors. You can't be surprised about them targeting you.'

'Thought – they would take longer – find me.'

'Well, *experientia docet*, as they say – you learn by the experience.' Bryant had a rummage through Forester's locker but failed to turn up anything of interest. 'It would be useful to have a name and description of the fellow who came after you. The CCTV footage shows someone of South East Asian descent.'

'Sun Dark.' Forester searched for his water straw.

'That's his name?' May asked. 'How do you spell it?'

'Opposite of moon, opposite of light,' said Bryant. 'Very Manichean. Mr Dark is a bit of a legend. So you borrowed money from a triad society. What made you think that would turn out well?'

'Thought I could – make the money back,' said Forester, starting to cough. 'Came for – my wife.'

'Wait, you told us you didn't see who attacked your wife. Are you saying now that this chap was in Clement Crescent?'

'Could – be. Not – sure.' Forester coughed again. 'Someone.' May wiped his chin.

'What did you see?'

'Short man – moving strangely – she just dropped at his feet. Over in – a second.'

'But you didn't get a good look?'

'No – too dark.'

'What do you mean, he moved strangely?'

'Hard to – explain. Hunched over her, studying her.'

'How did you get into Clement Crescent?'

'Girl has keys – all keys.'

'You mean GPS?' Bryant was annoyed with himself. Of course – it made sense that she would 'liberate' keys to the closed parks. 'Did you ever hear the name Paula Machin?'

'No – who—' Forester had another coughing fit, and had to be raised up.

'We think he attacked another woman,' said Bryant. 'Same MO.'

'Arthur, he's had enough,' said May quietly. Forester's swollen eyes were starting to close. 'Come on.'

'He killed my wife,' coughed Forester, reaching out a hand to them as they rose to leave. 'Please – find him before he comes back – for me.'

*

'Well, what do you reckon?' May asked his partner as they entered UCL's great white atrium.

'The story about Sun Dark is convenient,' Bryant replied. 'If Forester blames his wife for his downfall and chose to kill her, he could be implicating his creditor, knowing that we'd follow it up. A killer shifting the blame on to a criminal organization? That would be a first.'

'And a last, I imagine,' said May, buttoning his coat. 'Wouldn't it leave him in a worse position than being a suspect?'

'Not if it gets rid of his biggest problem,' Bryant replied. 'Maybe he's planned a way out. Of course if he was that smart he wouldn't have jumped from the bridge.'

'Perhaps he panicked.'

'True. Sun Dark is famous for the severe default terms of his property loans. He once strung a debtor over a railway line on a fishing rod, but the stories may be apocryphal.'

'I've never heard of this chap,' May admitted. 'How come you have?'

'I sometimes peruse the *South China Morning Post*,' Bryant explained. 'You soon start noticing when unusual names recur. Triads are most associated with trafficking and prostitution, but lately they've been making moves into property. They're known to use number twenty-nine, Harley Street. It's a property with over two thousand companies registered out of it, some of them bogus or fraudulent. It appears that throwing daggers are the kind of theatrical touch Sun Dark favours.'

'So where does this leave us?'

'Well, it leaves me with one last appointment tonight,' answered Bryant. 'There has to be a reason for choosing the parks. I need to talk to an expert.'

'Funnily enough I was planning on doing something similar,' said May defensively.

As they left the hospital Bryant dug around for his pipe,

thinking. 'Right about now they'll be starting to close all the gates, and a lot of angry people will be looking for someone to blame. We need to end this fast.'

'It's just spin,' said May. 'We can distance ourselves. It's not our decision.'

Bryant stopped on the steps. 'You know how Faraday works. He'll say they had no alternative because we failed to catch the killer. We're part of a bigger game, John. He's not thinking about the public, he's found a way of making political capital out of the closures.'

All over the city, crowds had begun to gather around the city's squares.

The evening briefing session took place during the detectives' absence, and without Bimsley or Mangeshkar, who were still at Russell Square Gardens.

'Nobody ever tells me where they're going,' Raymond Land complained. 'Miss Vesta, you've only just arrived here. Who told you to go off by yourself? No, on second thoughts don't—'

'Mr Bryant—'

'—answer that.'

'—said I should use my own initiative. I spoke to Miss Machin's old boyfriend. There is an English word with which I am not familiar, but I understand that it applies to him. *Scumbag*. I think this is right, yes? I showed him a photograph of the coat Miss Machin was wearing. He said he had never seen it before. But he wants it back. He is not so clever, I think.'

'We ID'd the coat to Helen Forester,' Longbright explained.

Land grudgingly accepted the good news. 'So how did the Machin girl get hold of it?'

'We had a confirmation from Forester's sister,' said Renfield. 'Helen Forester gave a McQueen outfit to her nanny as a thank-you present when she left the household. She said that as they both wore the same dress size, she wanted her to have it.'

'So she *did* get on with the nanny,' said Land.

'Sharyn Buckland was there when Helen's son died,' Longbright pointed out, 'so the gift feels a little like a guilt payment. Buckland came up in our conversation with Helen's sister, Catherine. The nanny had a thing for her employer's husband.'

'Do we know if the feeling was mutual?'

'I have no reliable information on that.'

'Well, can you get some?' Land looked around irritably. 'And would somebody locate my detectives, for God's sake? They're not answering their phones. I tried finding Bryant via the tracker Dan hid on him but it says he's in Scotland, which can't be right. Why does nothing work properly around here?'

Longbright ignored him. 'I've been trying to contact Sharyn Buckland to find out where she lost the coat, but so far no luck. What if it's the connection?' She dug out her phone and made a call. 'Mr Bryant, both of the dead women were dressed in red.'

They waited while Longbright updated the detectives. Land was appalled. 'How can she get through on her first try when I can't ever get hold of him?'

'Maybe he blocks your calls,' Renfield suggested. The room went quiet while everyone listened to Longbright listening to Bryant.

'What is he saying now?' Land demanded to know.

Longbright ended the call. 'He says of course Buckland was the target, not Machin, and does he have to do everything himself. Oh, and he said something about sheep.'

'The cases are linked,' said Bryant, pocketing his phone as they walked along the Euston Road, 'which means the killings are premeditated, which rules out your idea of someone randomly stalking London parks. What's more, the killer didn't know that Helen Forester gave the coat to her nanny.'

'How do you figure that?'

'He couldn't have thought it belonged to Forester because he'd already killed her. Oh, we're heading into darker seas now. The son, the mother, the nanny. An awful lot of tragedy in one family, don't you think?'

'The son wasn't murdered,' said May. 'It was an accident, and before you say anything, it was the kind of accident nobody could fake. The doctors who attended to him confirmed that.'

'They didn't confirm that it wasn't murder because the question was never on the cards, they just said it was reported as an accident,' Bryant pointed out, looking about for a taxi. 'I looked at the medical report, too. Do you want to check any further into Ritchie Jackson's background? Maybe we'll find out that he was connected to the nanny as well as to Helen Forester.'

'Right now our first priority is finding Sharyn Buckland,' said May. 'Either her coat was stolen or she deliberately switched it, in which case she knows something that's attracted the attention of her former employer's killer. We're still one step behind. There are more cameras in this city than virtually anywhere else on earth, so how is it that first Forester and now Buckland can evade us? How long is your meeting going to take?'

'That depends on whether my informant gets drunk,' replied Bryant. 'I'll meet you back at the PCU.' They parted on the corner of Euston Road and Gower Street, heading for their separate encounters.

Back at the unit's HQ, Dan Banbury had pinned an aerial map of Russell Square Gardens on the wall of the operations room.

'The park's litter bins were full and it had been windy, so although we found a few promising bits and pieces at the site, we don't have anything directly connected to the case. However, there was this.'

He held up a clear plastic envelope containing a used cinema ticket.

'The dirt around its edge matches the soil from one of the trainer prints, like the piece of card that was dropped in Clement Crescent, so it seems he's shed another piece of litter, which suggests to me that he's nervous and distracted. We've been checking the CCTV trying to find him, but it doesn't cover the whole of the square. I thought we'd pick the victim up somewhere outside its railings but no luck so far, and after tonight we won't even be able to get back inside the park without an official application. We're running checks on all hotels, B&Bs and hostels in the area. Steffi's got a list of Buckland's credit cards, Oyster card, shopping loyalty cards, online sites – so far nothing, which means she must be sticking to cash for now, and that means she doesn't want to be found. There's a boyfriend, but he's been out of the country and hasn't spoken to her since last Thursday. Buckland told him she wouldn't be around for a few days because she was going to visit her mother in Great Yarmouth, but the mother hasn't seen or heard from her. Her last transaction was a withdrawal of two hundred pounds from an ATM in King's Cross Station on Friday night at nineteen seventeen, then nothing.'

'The old lady, Margo Farrier.' Longbright checked back through her notes. 'Steffi, didn't she say something about Helen Forester having a visitor on Friday night, a well-dressed woman?'

'Mrs Farrier thinks it was Sharyn Buckland,' said Steffi. 'She stayed for perhaps one hour, no more.'

'So Buckland calls on Forester, Forester is murdered and her husband is hunted down,' said Banbury. 'The chain of events starts with the nanny. Do we have anything on this Asian bloke, Sun Dark?'

'Nothing,' said Renfield. 'Mr Bryant's the only one who's ever heard of him, and he's not sharing information at the moment.'

'What on earth is wrong with you people?' Land burst out suddenly. 'It's the twenty-first century and we can't get hold of anyone or find anyone, or persuade them to talk. It's ridiculous.'

'This is what happens in England, I think,' said Steffi unhelpfully.

'Good God, they used to have eight posts a day in the 1880s, and telegraph boys running all over London, efficiently delivering messages and supplying sexual favours. Has nothing advanced? I thought Bryant's tracking device was supposed to remain on him at all times.'

'It seems he attached it to a vehicle that's now in Aberdeen,' Longbright admitted.

'Well, start finding these people, can't you?' Land pleaded. 'This knife-chucking Fu Manchu bloke, or this amorous Mary Poppins woman, Sharyn Buckland – and the gardener, get him back in. And while you're there it would be quite useful to know whether my detectives have decided to abandon the case and go tossing the caber somewhere north of the border. I've got Darren Link breathing down my neck to close the investigation now that Faraday's shutting the parks.'

'When is that due to happen?' asked Banbury.

'As of this minute,' Land said disconsolately. 'He's using the restriction as an example of our failure, says we couldn't protect the public so extraordinary measures had to be drafted. We've stepped into his trap without realizing what he was up to.'

'Then do we not have to close the investigation at once?' asked Steffi, looking around. 'Surely that is not possible?'

'Ask this lot,' said Land, folding his arms. 'Two old ladies got machine-gunned in North London this morning. They died under a hail of bullets from a semi-automatic rifle while they were sitting outside the Karma Café in Wood Green having soya lattes, shot by a seventeen-year-old piece of plankton involved in a gang turf war. The Met made their arrest in under half an hour. We get a dog-walker and a junkie strangled to death and after over fifty hours we don't even have any proper suspects.'

'How did they make an arrest so quickly?' asked Longbright.

'The gunman shot himself in the foot,' Banbury explained. 'They're always doing it. They copy those gangsta rap videos where you see singers holding their hands up with the first and middle finger of each hand pointing down, not realizing you can't fire a gun like that, and blow their toes off.'

'That doesn't change the fact that there are kids running around trying to turn parts of London into Mexico City,' said Land, 'and what have we managed to achieve so far?'

'A total shutdown of all London parks, thanks to you,' said Longbright. 'This isn't a gang war, Raymond.'

'Then what is it?' Land countered.

'You're the unit head. And you're the leak, aren't you? You said, "*We've* stepped into his trap." It was you.'

'Now look here, I certainly never intended—' Land began, blustering. 'You don't seriously think I would—'

'Perhaps you could help us by not speaking to Faraday any more.' Longbright shot him a look of deep disappointment and led the way from the briefing room.

25

'LIKE MIDNIGHT FOXES, WE ADAPT'

Arthur Bryant had arranged to meet up with the editor of *Mephiticus*, a periodical of acidic prose and limited appeal that was mailed out to embittered academics and hermetic eccentrics from its premises in Bloomsbury.

Barney Calman was over fifty and still lived with his mother above his office. His grey-flecked hair revealed the tread of time, and he was not the first to own his clothes. He excelled in all enterprises that were unprofitable, and consequently was not an easy man to deal with. Permanently broke and perpetually complaining, he cadged fags, pints, meals and change, robbing Peter to pay Paul, then robbing Paul again, anything to ensure that another copy of the magazine could be mailed out to his dwindling readership. Even after the announced death of the printed word some fifteen years ago, London was awash with such esoteric tribal magazines.

'Here you go,' he said, handing a copy of the magazine to Bryant across the pub table, 'the latest issue, just for you. There's a piece on the ecstatic nocturnal peregrinations of William Blake that you may find interesting.'

'Cheers,' said Bryant, preparing to fold it in half to fit inside his overcoat, ready for binning on the way home.

'That'll be £12.50.' Calman held out his hand until Bryant dug into his pocket and found the money.

'I haven't got change of fifteen.' Bryant held out a tenner and a fiver.

'Don't worry, I'll put it towards the next issue.' Calman shoved the money into the pocket of a jacket that looked as if it would have gone on to the pre-loved rack of a Dickensian rag shop.

They were sitting in the snug bar of the Scottish Stores in King's Cross, formerly a table-dancing dump called the Flying Scotsman that Bryant used to cross the street to avoid, home to desperate women grinding topless for fifty-pence pieces collected in beer glasses. During its rehabilitation a few months ago, sheets of hardboard had been removed to reveal a perfectly preserved Edwardian boozer, a rare example of the past returning.

'God, I think I preferred King's Cross when it was full of strip joints,' Calman complained. 'Anything's better than clench-arsed hipsters in pirate beards drinking craft ales with stupid names. What did you want to see me about?'

'I've been reading up on the history of the city's parks and open spaces,' Bryant began, not quite knowing where his sentence would finish, 'and I wondered if they had any particular association with death.'

'Well, the scythe-bearer is everywhere in London,' said Calman, noisily slugging the froth from the pint of Affable Alf's Organic Ale that Bryant had bought him. 'God, I'd like to knock the brains out of the topknotted twerp who invented craft beer. This is like licking piss off a nettle. The last hanging on Tyburn's triple tree at the corner of Hyde Park was in 1783, and by then around sixty thousand people had died. The soil under Marble Arch was soaked in their blood. The city was always poorly lit but the parks were darker and full of michers.'

'You mean petty thieves,' said Bryant, proud to show off his newfound knowledge of arcane slang.

'The dark attracts dark behaviour.' Calman sniffed, and extracted quite the most disgusting tissue Bryant had ever seen. 'In old England, forests had a host of symbolic meanings. They were places of sanctuary for Robin Hood and for the banished duke in *As You Like It*. They represented the realm of magic in *A Midsummer Night's Dream*. But they're also associated with wild spirits and sometimes appalling violence. The rape and mutilation of Lavinia in *Titus Andronicus* takes place in woodland.'

Unlike his partner, Bryant was entirely at home here, listening to academic theories involving myth and history. He was able to overlay them on any investigation without embarrassment. He regarded anything that helped him to reach a conclusion as a useful and legitimate tool.

'A park may contain a wooded area or copse, and a copse can be a place of death,' Calman continued. 'The tale of the Children in the Wood is one of the most ancient of all stories, with parallels in Horace and repetitions in Shakespeare, Drayton and Webster.' He blew into the tissue, blasting it to bits, then returned to his ale.

'Are we talking about the pantomime *Babes in the Wood*?' Bryant asked, watching Calman's beer sink at an alarming rate.

'That, too,' said the publisher. 'There are several versions that tell of a murderer. In one a ship's chandler kills two children, a boy and a girl, in woodland at the behest of their uncle, and hides their bodies beneath leaves. The tale increased in popularity around the time of Richard the Third, for obvious reasons, but interestingly several wooded areas in London lay claim to the location of the tragedy. In some variations their bodies are covered by robins and turtle doves. There was a popular ballad about it still sung in the eighteenth century:

> 'No burial this pretty pair
> Of any man receives,

Till Robin Red-Breast piously
Did cover them with leaves.

'It was an appealing idea to many.'

Bryant indicated to the barman that they needed another round. 'Why would that be?'

'The image of virginal innocence being stolen away in pastoral surroundings is a particularly attractive one,' Calman explained. 'Creepy, of course, but so is everything working back from the Victorians. While the ladies sewed pictures of maidens swooning in leafy bowers and knights watching chivalrously over them, their husbands were out rogering servant girls in the nearest patch of long grass they could find.'

He set aside his empty glass, exchanging it for a full one. 'London's parks may have been filled with pretty posies but they were put there to keep the poor away, to guard against their diseased breath and add jolly promenades for land-owners. Cultural historians like to describe attractions like the Vauxhall Pleasure Gardens as havens of courtly entertainment, but they were really just amusement parks where you could get pissed and laid. So if you're wondering why this fellow attacks women in parks, and you must be because why else would you bother to get in touch with me when we hardly ever speak, you're barking up the wrong tree.'

'You think he's just doing what men have done for centuries: finding the darkest spot in the metropolis and taking advantage of it,' said Bryant, loosening his scarf.

'Of course. When you take a good look at this city you'll notice how little it changes. Did you know we still have fifteen hundred gas lamps in operation? But London is losing its dis-repute. The old Soho clubs were once the opposite of guilds and masonic lodges. They encouraged disorder, anarchy, drinking, gambling and above all promiscuity, and their inhabitants spilled out into the night and into the parks, look-ing for someone to slap or shag. What have we got now?

Japanese bubble-tea bars.' Calman stared into his empty glass as if he had just lost an old friend. 'Children worked in factories on the riverbanks, dying of mercuric poisoning so toxic that their skeletons turned bright green. Now the waterways are home to swans and herons, and you can run their length in Lycra to your fancy new apartment. In search of the real London we avoid the tourist fakery of Camden and head for Dalston, Spitalfields, Whitechapel, because we secretly like a bit of rough. And, like midnight foxes, we adapt, sliding between worlds of darkness and light. If you're ordering more beers after this I'll have one of those pork pies to go with it.'

Bryant reluctantly dug into his pocket. 'I suppose you think I'm a foolish old man looking for poetic answers when the truth is far more base.'

'You should have been an academic instead of becoming a policeman,' said Calman. 'I suppose I'm not the first person to tell you that. I can't blame you for seeking a higher purpose in our frailties. There is one thing.'

Bryant had a third pint delivered and watched in amazement as the publisher downed it. 'What's that?' he asked.

'You know why parks are still here with us in the twenty-first century? Why they haven't been ripped up by property developers and filled with blocks of flats?'

'Because there would be a national outcry?'

'Yes, but why? I'll tell you.' The publisher leaned closer. 'Because the government knows they stop city workers from going insane. Wooded areas are for reveries and fantasies, for people with crushed spirits to dream in. Dickens believed in the "democracy of dreamers" – the idea that at night in London there's no difference between rich and poor because we all need to exercise our imaginations. No difference between those at home in pressed linen sheets and nightwalkers wandering the darkened alleys like the undead. No difference between those who slumber above and the vast armies of corpses resting below.'

Bryant came away from the pub thirty pounds lighter and,

he thought, none the wiser – until the following week, when he looked back on the meeting and saw that it contained the seeds of a darker truth.

Meanwhile, taking a leaf from his partner's book, John May had headed to the low cream-coloured neoclassical building that housed the Institute of Contemporary Arts in Pall Mall, hoping to discover whether something more was motivating their killer. To that end he had arranged to meet Laura Shoemaker, one of the city's leading behavioural specialists. She was as pink and plump as a pastry chef, but her eyes were sharp and calculating. Dressed in flattering black, she drew forth curiosity in others.

'I'm not sure I'm going to be of much help to you,' she warned as they headed to a table. Behind them, workers were installing blown-up panels from comic book artists for an upcoming exhibition. Above Shoemaker's head was a gigantic red and yellow atomic explosion with an immense grawlix followed by the letters 'ROARRRR!' plastered across it. 'You're looking at two deaths. It's not a big enough research sample.'

'My partner said that, too,' May was reminded. 'He built his reputation by developing a set of intuitive techniques that should be taught in every police training college, but he's still regarded with suspicion. You know, Sir Arthur Conan Doyle invested his fictional detective with observational skills that were eventually adopted by the Metropolitan Police. Arthur came up with an equally game-changing approach to detection that's taken a lifetime to refine: he intuits solutions from a dozen or so factors that include time, place, history and personality as well as traditional elements like motive and opportunity. He thinks that if you scratch London's surface you'll find a city beneath it that hasn't changed in a couple of thousand years.'

'He could be right.' Shoemaker smiled at the thought. 'A few weeks ago a national poll found that of two thousand randomly selected adults, sixty per cent couldn't name the current prime minister. That's about the same as in the late eighteenth century.'

'Arthur has a mental attitude that allows him to see how and why crimes occur,' May explained. 'But there's one thing that bypasses his ability to understand: the madness of passion. To him everything has a logical reason. You make a study of the irrational, which is why I've come to you.'

'That's not strictly speaking what I do.' Shoemaker gave an order to the gallery's café owner. 'It's more a matter of finding patterns in irrational behaviour. Don't look so uncomfortable, Mr May. I'm not about to lead you down the path of pseudoscience.'

'I just need to understand what we're dealing with,' said May, feeling as if his mind had been read.

'If it's someone with a violent behavioural pattern, there are certain things to look for,' Shoemaker agreed. 'The first murder will be the defining one. Before they cross that line they might not have consciously thought about killing anyone. There could be test runs. The first is the hardest; the rest come easier, but depression usually follows the kill, and gradually the highs are reduced. Killers talk about "crossing over" to a point from which they can never return.'

'What triggers it in the first place?' May found that their coffees had been delivered in paint-streaked jam jars on an artist's palette, together with a bill for six pounds.

'A number of elements have to fall into place,' Shoemaker answered. 'Stressors – the pressures we face in daily life – can build up, facilitated by stimulant abuse. More than half of all male attackers have had a fight with a female just prior to the trigger moment.'

'So what's going on in our attacker's head?'

'He may have entered into a dissociative state where imagination takes over from reality. He often starts trolling for victims without realizing it. A killer may firmly believe he acted on the spur of the moment because he's blind to the fact that he's been preparing for months. Sometimes the victim's age is important, or a certain look. Were the women similar in years and appearance?'

'They were both blonde and slim, about the same build. Is there any significance in the locations chosen?'

'A third of all such killings take place in parks or on open ground. How did they die?'

'They were strangled with ligatures – we haven't found what he used.'

'That's unusual.' Shoemaker took a sip from her jam jar and appraised the matter coolly. 'If the hands aren't used, the killer usually improvises with an item of clothing taken from the victim. They weren't missing anything?'

'We don't know exactly what they were wearing but no, I don't think so.'

'Were the ligature marks the same in both cases?'

'Yes, they're unusual – the material has some kind of ribbing on it, maybe a necklace or a sink chain.'

'He may have fetishized a particular item and chosen it specifically as the method of killing. That suggests a degree of organization. I know this must all sound painfully generic to you . . .'

'Maybe I can apply it to our list of suspects,' said May doubtfully. 'Is there anything unique I should look out for?'

Shoemaker's eyes grew even darker. 'Were these quick kills?'

'Yes, very. But they were in public places, so they had to be.'

'Then you're not looking for a sexual sadist. There's no time for him to derive pleasure from seeing someone in pain. Did he take anything away with him?'

'Not that we know of.'

'Could he have considered either of the women "immoral"?'

'We think one was a case of mistaken identity. But she was a junkie, so maybe.'

'There have been cases where the killers of addicts have left bodies displayed with the track marks on their arms exposed in order to shame them. Are you OK?'

May wiped his forehead and found it covered in sweat. 'I have to tell you something,' he said. 'A short while ago I was accused of a similar crime. I was with the deceased shortly before she died. It was an unusual situation but not unique in our profession.'

'And you think something has changed in you.'

'I don't know how to explain it,' May admitted.

'It's called transference, Mr May. You're empathizing with the victim. I know your partner doesn't have a reputation for being very empathetic—'

'That's putting it mildly.'

'But *you* do. Did this accusation involve someone with whom you were intimately acquainted?'

'You could say that, yes.'

'Then I have a suggestion for you, although you won't like it.' Shoemaker set aside her coffee and rose. 'Get your team taken off the case. Give it to someone who doesn't care about it as much as you do. If there's another attack, and from what you've told me it sounds likely that there will be, the perpetrator will enjoy taking you down with him.' She smiled a little ruefully. 'Thanks for the coffee.'

'I'm sorry it came in a jam jar,' said May.

'That's OK,' said Shoemaker. 'Their chicken wings are served on typesetting boards. One person's attempt at originality is another person's stress trigger.'

The chain was threaded through the railings in a series of clanking loops, and the padlock was placed through the chain and closed with a key. The warden of Bloomsbury Square stepped smartly away and pocketed the key in his jacket. The gates of the square were now closed until further notice. A great roar of disapproval went up from the crowd. People from every walk of life had assembled around the railings and had remained silent until now, but the sealing of the lock was their cue to express anger. Arms were raised in protest, placards appeared, torches were lit and suddenly fists contained rocks.

All across the city, outside every garden and square, the same scene was occurring. Only the eight royal parks remained open, but in the face of massive government cuts, Leslie Faraday knew that these would not prove immune for long.

The taking of London's last great spaces had begun.

26

'HE DOESN'T LOOK THE TYPE'

Before it became the centre of London's Chinatown, Gerrard Street had been the home of the literary club at the Turk's Head Tavern, where Samuel Johnson met Joshua Reynolds. The former location of artists, essayists, jazz players and glamour photographers had housed French hotels and gay bars, patisseries, a trumpet shop and the actress Glenda Jackson, who took a flat there for a romantic comedy. The real Chinatown had been in Limehouse, where London's Chinese population set up shops for sailors uncrating tea and opium. Only Chinese males were allowed to settle, so a bizarre idea blossomed: that they were kidnapping Caucasian girls and selling them into slavery.

With the new diaspora came integration. Now Gerrard Street was like every other Chinatown in the western world, a pedestrianized avenue of restaurants and supermarkets, with rows of vacuum-packed jackfruit and pomelos and glistening Peking ducks on butchers' hooks, bordered by lacquered crimson gates and golden lions. The dodgy pubs and semi-legal drinking dens had vanished, but there were still passageways and basements where few westerners were invited.

In one of its back alleys, behind the dim sum parlours, Jack Renfield and Colin Bimsley waited to meet a contact who had promised to talk to them about Sun Dark.

'How do we know he's going to tell us the truth?' asked Bimsley, bouncing on and off a kitchen step slick with cooking oil, waiting for someone to answer their knock.

'Don't worry, I have a copper's sixth sense that informs me when blokes are lying,' said Renfield. 'It's only women who have the eerie power to cloud men's minds. Speaking of which, how are you getting on with Meera?'

Bimsley sucked his teeth, thinking. 'To be absolutely honest, I'm not quite sure where I stand any more. I mean, she seems to like hanging out with me but we never get any closer.'

'You mean you haven't got your leg over.'

'I wouldn't have put it as crudely as that, Jack, but no. She came over to my gaff at the weekend and we watched *Game of Thrones* together. I thought the saucy bits might get her in the mood.'

'What happened?'

'She picked all the topping off my pizza, finished my beer and fell asleep. How's Janice? Is she going to take you back?'

Renfield scratched at his chin, considering the question. 'I don't reckon so. She's still pretty annoyed with me. Anyway, we can't all be going out with women from the unit – it looks like we lack imagination. Do you ever see anyone else?'

'No.'

'Why not, loyalty?'

'Fear of being caught. She'd set fire to me, then wait ten years and come after my kids. The thing is with Meera – I love her.' Bimsley surprised himself so much that he said it again. 'I love her.'

'Then you need to tell her as soon as possible.'

'Why?'

'Tax relief. And you're in a dangerous job. She'll need the pension.'

The door opened and they found themselves confronted by a Chinese man dressed as Fu Manchu. His face was rouged and he wore grotesque blue eye make-up, a tall lacquered black wig, a slender drooping moustache and red silk robes.

'Are you the cops?' he asked in a broad cockney accent, scrutinizing the astonished detectives. 'Come in, mate, I'm Lee, the geezer you made the appointment with. Sorry about the outfit, I'm playing the Lord High Executioner in *The Mikado*. We just finished rehearsals. These sleeves are driving me bleeding mad.'

'Is it OK to talk in here?' asked Bimsley as they stepped inside a narrow black-painted corridor.

'Yeah, no worries, all our staff are Bubbles. You know, Greeks. They don't give a toss what we talk about. You wanna drink?'

'Well, we're technically off duty,' Renfield began, shrugging to Bimsley.

'Cool, I'll get some lagers in. You like Romanian beer? Get sat down in there.' He indicated the private room of a restaurant on his left, and returned a couple of minutes later with a tray of Ciuc beers. The smell of crispy fried duck was in the air. 'I'll be glad to get out of this sodding outfit,' he said. 'It's nylon. I nearly electrocuted myself on the radiator. It's for the Soho Theatre – they got a bollocking for casting Caucasians so we stepped in to help out. About this bloke you're after. You're not gonna get near him.'

'Why not?'

'The CCTV shot you sent over – that wasn't him, for a start. It's one of his lads. He's got heavies all over the place. Nobody knows what Sun Dark actually looks like. He never leaves Switzerland.'

Renfield caught Bimsley's eye. 'I thought he was based in Shanghai and Hong Kong?'

'No, he runs a consortium in Geneva and he puts out a lot of misinformation. He's part French; his name is actually Sun Darque. Q-U-E.'

'Is he in the habit of slaughtering his debtors? It seems a bit drastic.'

'Not usually. If someone rips him off they just get the innards kicked out of them.'

'How do you know about it?' asked Colin, popping his beer.

'The consortium owns four restaurants in Gerrard Street. One of our lads defaulted on a loan last year.'

'What happened to him?'

Lee winked. 'Well, he doesn't go to glove sales any more, if you get my meaning. No one can touch Sun Dark. The companies he owns here are clean but he has informants all over the place.'

'So he's not involved in human trafficking, then, which is what we heard?' asked Renfield.

Lee pulled his robe away from his neck, fanning himself. 'I know what you're thinking, sinister Orientals, all a bit Yellow Peril – it's just an image he likes playing up. He's a property developer, a businessman, hard to catch out.'

'The guy in the CCTV footage,' said Renfield. 'Who is he?'

'I don't know his name but we see him around a lot. He fancies himself as a bit of a hard-core Jack the Lad. But he ain't a killer. If he'd caught your bloke he'd probably just have broken his arm.'

'He threw a bunch of knives at his victim.'

'Oh, yeah, and that. He was probably told to put the frighteners on his target,' said Lee. 'But he's under instruction not to bring down trouble. I can't vouch for what he gets up to in South East Asia but here Dark's businesses are legit.' He glanced from Bimsley to Renfield. 'Look, you seem like nice lads, but you're wasting your time with this. Dark will want to make sure his investment is returned. Loan sharks have sharp teeth, big surprise.'

Folding his hands into the sleeves of his robe, Lee saw them back into the alley.

'Well, that was weird,' said Bimsley as the pair headed back towards Leicester Square. 'An Oriental bloke impersonating an Englishman playing an Oriental.'

Renfield gave him a funny look. 'What do you mean?'

'*The Mikado* is about the English. Gilbert and Sullivan, innit? They only came up with the idea because Japanese imports were fashionable in London households.'

'God, now you sound like old Bryant.'

'After a while he starts to rub off on you,' said Bimsley. 'You should try reading a book occasionally.'

'Nah, you can't play games on a book.'

'We wasted our time here.'

'Hard to tell. If Sun Dark's that slippery, who's to say his informants aren't playing the same game?' Renfield slapped him harder on the back than he meant to. 'For now Forester's our only real suspect.'

'How do you work that out?'

Renfield stepped aside to allow a vegetable porter through. 'He brings the chaos of gangland London into his household because he's greedy and overambitious, right? He loses his job, gets into a lethal debt spiral, panics, kills his wife and nanny in a mistaken-identity Lord Lucan-type deal, fails to get hold of his passport and tries to do a runner. End of.'

Bimsley wiped his cold nose on the back of his glove. 'We'll see.'

'What do you mean?' asked Renfield.

'Have you never noticed? Most major investigative units come on board after the crime, but we always seem to get involved while they're still unfolding. If it ends here, maybe you're right. But we still have to find a way of proving it. Besides, you're forgetting the gardener.'

'What, Jackson? Come off it.'

'He was there when Helen Forester died.'

'Nah, he doesn't look the type.'

'*Doesn't look the type?* That's not very scientific, is it?'

'You don't need science to spot a walking apology. He's the

sort of bloke who'd buy a non-lethal mousetrap. He likes *plants*, Colin.'

They threaded between shoppers drifting past the tinselly tourist shops of Newport Court, their windows filled with waving ceramic cats, and headed for Leicester Square tube station, arguing all the way.

While the staff of the PCU became increasingly disoriented and lost in the undergrowth of circumstances surrounding the case, the general public were taking action. All across the city protest groups had begun chaining themselves to park railings, and eighteen police officers had been hospitalized. News stations were warning of an escalation in violent clashes.

Leslie Faraday was unavailable for comment.

THE FOURTH DAY

27

'I HAVE A HEAD FOR THE PECULIARITIES OF HISTORY'

Thursday dawned with grudging apricity. The sky was clothed in pink and silver, as gaudy as a Christmas cake. Ice rimed the branches, starred the pavements and crystallized litter in sharded gutters. The canal water had hardened, its surface as cloudy as an antique mirror. Geese and moorhens skidded about on it, more awkward than teenagers.

Looking down on King's Cross you'd have noticed an odd phenomenon: every other roof was covered in white frost, forming a patchwork quilt, an indicator of which properties were owned by overseas investors and which had warm families inside.

Arthur Bryant was always frozen in midsummer, so now he layered himself like a shoplifter in Primark.

'I'm surprised you can move about in all that,' remarked May as he picked his partner up from the flat in Harrison Street.

'It's bad weather for the chest,' Bryant explained as he attempted to wedge himself into the passenger seat of his partner's BMW. 'I'm not taking any chances. I'm wearing my string vest, undervest, thermals, shirt, cardigan, scarf, jacket and topcoat. If I fall over you'll have to help me up. We need to hurry.'

'Why, where are we going?' asked May, starting the engine.

'Colin just got a tip-off on Sharyn Buckland,' said Bryant, trying to drag his seatbelt over his stomach. 'Someone saw a woman fitting her description a few minutes ago at Fenchurch Street Station. He and Meera have gone on ahead.'

'How do they know it's her?'

'It's complicated,' snapped Bryant impatiently. 'Do I really have to explain?'

'Yes, it would be helpful.'

'Sharyn Buckland made costumes for the Muswell Hill Community Theatre on Monday evenings, and her sewing partner . . .'

A truck overtook them, drowning Bryant out.

'. . . performing with Les Norman and his Bethnal Green Bambinos . . .'

They passed three workmen drilling a hole in the tarmac of the Euston Road.

'. . . in a charity production of *The Duchess of Malfi* . . .'

May's thoughts drifted. He'd meant to take his shoes in to get them resoled.

'. . . to return the sequined headdress before she got fined . . .'

He wished he'd had breakfast.

'. . . and paid with a credit card at the station which was immediately flagged on to the system.'

'So someone recognized her,' he said impatiently.

'Yes, but not from the payment, from *The Duchess of Malfi*. You weren't listening to a word I said.'

'Every other word. Something about sequins. Let's see if we can get to her first.' May put his foot down and they headed south-east across the city.

Helen was dead and nothing would bring her back, but the circumstances of that death made no sense. Sharyn Buckland thought of herself as a calm and rational woman, a fundamentally *English* woman, someone who wanted nothing more special than the realization of reasonable expectations: a home, a partner, a child, order and peace. Instead, her life had taken a terrible turn.

It didn't seem possible that she could be at risk, but Helen and the junkie girl were both gone; Sharyn had heard about the first murder and witnessed the second – had tangentially caused the girl's death, in fact – and now she in turn was being followed.

Sharyn chewed at a cuticle, worrying about her next step. What if she went to the police? How could they protect her? Nothing had been right since little Charlie had died, and the situation was worsening daily. She looked around. The streets were emptying as people vanished into their offices to start the working day.

She needed to sit in a calm place, a safe place, and think it over. St Olave's was one of her favourite spots in the City because it lacked the melancholy atmosphere of larger churches. Grateful to have someone to talk to, the lonely verger had told her lots of odd stories about the place, and she had taken to coming here whenever she felt conflicted.

She paused beneath the stone archway leading to the churchyard, the one with three grinning skulls at its centre, and passed inside.

The neatly manicured churchyard was empty; nobody used its benches in the winter. The sound of traffic faded away. As she walked towards the church's doors she had the distinct impression of a shadow moving to her right. She stopped and turned slowly, listening. She heard the steady drip of rainwater dropping from a downpipe, then a ruffle of dead leaves like the breathing of corpses.

The feeling of being watched returned.

She continued towards the doors, her skin prickling. There was another dry rattle, and a shift in the gloom.

Something whistled through the air close to her head.

She felt a sting at her throat and watched in horror as the dark figure divorced itself from the bushes and something dropped over her with impossible speed.

May checked his phone. 'If it's her, she's heading along Crutched Friars. There's an old church on the street – Colin's ahead of us. He'll meet us at St Olave's.'

'It's been there since twelve hundred and something,' said Bryant, tapping spatulate fingers on the dashboard. 'It escaped the Great Fire of London. Samuel Pepys had a stair-case built from his office so that he could reach it without being rained on. He's buried there, under a table. Queen Elizabeth the First gave the wardens silken bell ropes because they had rung the loudest bells in London to celebrate her release from the Bloody Tower. I'm boring you.'

'Not at all,' said May, hanging a left. 'I love your abstruse arcana. I'm all ears until we reach our destination. Pray continue.'

'Well, it seems Mother Goose is also buried there, I mean the woman who played the original pantomime character, and the grave of Mary Ramsey is there too – she's the woman who brought the Plague to London.' Bryant warmed to his subject. 'And there's a memorial to the grocers of Fenchurch Street who supplied the tea crates for the Boston Tea Party, although I'm not sure why they wanted to celebrate that. Charles Dickens called the church St Ghastly Grim. In 1941 an incendiary bomb dropped by the Luftwaffe melted the bells, and they were remade by the Whitechapel Bell Foundry, who had provided them in 1662.'

'Hm.' May pulled up at the lights. 'What's your home phone number?'

'No idea.'

'Incredible.'

'I have a head for the peculiarities of history,' Bryant admitted. 'All London churches have these oddities attached to them, it's just that most people don't bother to find out.

I don't care about my phone number. What's going on?'

Colin Bimsley was running towards them, and yanked open the driver's-side door.

'I was too late,' he said, nearly in tears. 'I was too bloody late. She's gone. Sharyn Buckland is dead.'

28

'LONDON IS FULL OF COINCIDENCES'

A rivulet of rain weighed down a single hornbeam leaf, and a perfect drop fell on to the upturned face below.

It was a kind face and rather ageless, as all kind faces tend to be. Her skin was pale where it was not pink, except for a single line of purple lividity at her neck. She had passed her life searching for something that had remained just beyond her grasp, so it would be tempting to say that she was finally at peace. But she was not; she had been denied a conclusion and robbed of dignity. She lay half in the bushes with her legs folded under her, her eyes wide to the sky. The raindrop had fallen into her left pupil and run down her cheek, so that she appeared to be crying. Perhaps she was.

The two detectives sat side by side in the church of St Olave, unmoving, waiting for Dan Banbury to finish. They could see their breath condensing before them. The still chapel air smelled of polish and candle wax.

'Colin will blame himself,' said May quietly. 'You know how he empathizes.'

'We caught the Mr Punch Killer because of a single gesture,' said Bryant. 'The tiniest of clues, discovered at the last possible moment.'

May turned to look at him. 'What do you mean?'

'All the work we put into catching a calculating murderer who then got away from us. Jack and Colin took up the chase, do you remember?'

'Why are you thinking of it now?'

'If it hadn't been for that investigation, Helen Forester's son might still be alive.'

'I don't understand.'

'It was raining hard.' Bryant gripped the back of the church pew, remembering. 'The visibility was terrible. Nobody could see where they were going. We had to close the surrounding roads at short notice and divert all the traffic. I instructed the transport police to switch vehicles through the tunnel under London Bridge Station. I didn't think about the consequences. The boy and his nanny were forced to change their route. What if this isn't about Jeremy Forester losing his job, but losing his son?'

'You're saying it's *our* fault?'

'No – not directly.' Bryant pulled his moulting striped scarf a little more tightly around his neck. 'We were misled by the death of Paula Machin. That was a stupid, avoidable mistake. I should have realized earlier and found Sharyn Buckland sooner.'

'It's not your fault,' said May. 'You couldn't have done any more.'

'There's a resonance . . .' Bryant coasted his hand through the cold air. 'Such a strange sensation. I've overlooked something. I've seen it, been close to it – a face, a conversation. After my illness I felt different. I came back, but things had changed. My attitude, my sensibilities – I always felt that I saw this city from the inside, but parts are starting to elude me. This city belongs to others now.'

'Everybody feels that at some time or another,' said May. 'The world speeds up.'

Bryant appeared not to have heard him. 'I've learned certain things – we need courage and compassion in order to age well. But I see that young woman lying in the bushes and I cannot understand how anyone can be so cruel. It's like looking back at the lives of women before they had the same rights as men – I can only pray we see this time with the same sense of heartfelt shame. Politicians can't improve our lives; it's up to us. We'll survive long after policies have crumbled to dust.'

'I can't decide whether that makes you a conservative or a socialist,' said May.

'I'm a humanist,' said Bryant, 'but I'm not doing a very good job at the moment, and it's going to get harder. The parks are locked. Faraday is causing insurrection. The police commissioner will blame the Home Office, and Faraday will step in with a plan. But what, exactly? He has a history of trying to privatize public spaces, so my guess is he'll trade the provision of private park security for a stake in the property. Meanwhile, we have to find another way of catching our killer.'

'We'll do it,' said May. 'You can't let this destroy us. Buckland knew something that caused her death. We'll avenge her, I promise.'

For once, Bryant had no response.

Ritchie Jackson had another interview at the PCU later that day, and wasn't happy about it. The young gardener twisted about as if tethered to his chair, waiting to discover why he had been brought back yet again.

'Am I a suspect or not?' he asked. 'How many times can you do this to me? I already told you everything I know.'

'Did you, though,' said Bryant, closing the door behind him. 'You failed to mention the knife you hid.'

Jackson said nothing, waiting to see where Bryant went with the claim.

'Mrs Farrier said she had lost a paper knife, and I first assumed it was the one we found in Clement Crescent. But Jeremy Forester was attacked by someone using throwing daggers. I think Forester had it with him in the gardens and you found it in the grass, where he'd dropped it. Then, when you had to call the police, you buried it in the flowerbed.'

'So what?' said Jackson. 'It wasn't the murder weapon.'

'Then why bury it at all?'

Jackson's eyes were truthful. 'I found it under one of the bushes and put it in the shed,' he said. 'I'd mislaid my regular penknife. I was going to use it to trim stalks. But when your mob stormed into the crescent I suddenly realized that you'd find it covered in my prints, so I stuck it under the roses and changed the name tags so I'd find it again. I didn't want trouble. That's why I didn't mention it.'

'Fair enough,' said Bryant. 'Now we come to the main reason why you're here. My operations director dug a little deeper into your past on the PNC database. You were fired from your old job and lodged a formal complaint against Bermondsey Police. What happened there?'

'You obviously know, or I wouldn't be here,' said Jackson, folding his arms.

'I'd like to hear it from you.'

'All right. I was a long-haul lorry driver working out of Covent Garden. Our journeys were timed, and we were fined whenever we arrived late. I already had a couple of marks against me after getting held up by traffic police one night. I was coming into London Bridge, returning from Holland. The road layout had been changed and we were diverted into a tunnel beneath London Bridge Station. It was a miserable night, visibility was bad, and in the chaos there was an accident. I missed my delivery window and my load shifted, damaging some of my cargo. I was fired, so I lodged a complaint. After the inquiry the traffic police were exonerated from any blame.'

Bryant handed him a photograph. 'Have you ever seen this woman before?'

Jackson took his time. 'I can't be sure.'

'How about this?' He passed Jackson two further shots.

'She looks like the woman at the accident, the one with the boy who died that night.'

'Do you know her name?'

'I've no idea, but I saw her arguing with the girl who had the crash. I followed the ambulance to the hospital, but there was nothing I could do.'

'Her name is Sharyn Buckland. She was Helen Forester's nanny, and now she's dead.'

'You're joking.' Jackson took another look at the photographs. 'This is about that night?'

'It's starting to look that way,' said Bryant.

Raymond Land had always liked six o'clock. It was the golden hour, going-home time. The offices started closing, the pubs filled and a general air of jollity invaded the streets, even when it was raining. Steffi had expressed surprise at the way in which Londoners could stop for a chat on the pavement without even noticing that it was tipping down.

Now, though, Land had come to dread the thought of everyone leaving. He looked out at the bedraggled pigeon on his sill, balancing on its good leg and its raw pink stump, one orange eye glaring at the raucous students hammering pints outside the pub opposite. He and the bird had more in common than he liked to think. They were both uncared-for, and neither of them had any reason to be anywhere else. The office and its accompanying windowsill were all they had left.

He was saved from any further morbid thoughts by the return of his detectives.

'Ah, Raymondo, my little *klootzak*, still here I see.' Bryant had rediscovered a little of his former spirit after the success of the interview. 'It's after six. I assumed we'd lost you to your Thursday night Zumba class. Let me run something by you.' He rarely sought the opinion of the unit chief because of his ability to compress the largest number of words into the smallest amount of thought. 'Sharyn Buckland – are you remotely interested in where we're up to?'

'Of course,' said Land. 'For God's sake, bring me some good news.'

'She was killed in the exact same manner as the other two.' Bryant raised his eyebrows meaningfully, a gesture that was lost on his boss. 'What do you see here?' He threw a magazine on to Land's desk.

'It's a copy of *Tatler*,' said Land, confused.

'Flick through it.'

The unit chief did as he was told.

'What's the first thing you notice?'

'I don't know – a bunch of over-entitled twits drinking somebody else's champagne,' said Land.

'What you see is conformity,' said Bryant, fishing through his pockets for boiled sweets. 'You'll have noticed that this precious stone set in a silvered sea has a caste system not much different from India's.'

Land thought of his rejection and humiliation at the hands of certain civil servants. 'Well, I wouldn't go so far as to say that.'

'Each class has its own tribal style, yes? But middle-class and working-class women are often hard to tell apart these days. Why? Aspiration creates uniformity. Looks and styles are copied. We're sheep. What unites a nanny, her employer and a drug addict? They're all thin and blonde, have similar builds and hairstyles and, thanks to heels, are roughly the same height. It's a type defined by its era, just like all those young men who currently sport trimmed beards and skinny jeans. Sharyn Buckland duplicated her employer's look, and Machin was in turn mistaken for her. That suggests a predator hunting an idealized female form, yes?' He popped a pear drop into his mouth and clattered it against his false teeth. 'But against that we now have a strange coincidence: the way in which two men and two women are connected. Almost a year ago, Ritchie Jackson saw Sharyn Buckland on the very night that Helen Forester's young son died. He was there at the scene and even went to the hospital with them. He didn't volunteer that information at the interview, of course, because he didn't know that Buckland was Forester's nanny. So what are the odds on Ritchie Jackson and Jeremy Forester, the man Sharyn Buckland adored, both being present for Helen Forester's death?'

'Stop trying to make it sound so mysterious,' said Land. 'Three of them were virtually family and the fourth – OK, that's a bit strange, but London is full of coincidences. I bumped into my ex-wife yesterday.'

'Oh, where?'

'She passed me on Tottenham Court Road with her new young lover. Leanne has gone blonde and lost loads of weight. I was standing in a shop doorway eating chips out of a paper bag.' He looked forlorn. 'She saw me and started laughing. They both did.'

'Anyway, back to something more interesting,' said Bryant. 'In all of this there's been no mention of Lauren Posner.'

Land checked his notes. 'I've got no one by that name. Who's she?'

'She's the girl who swerved behind Ritchie Jackson's truck and hit the electrical cabinet underneath London Bridge Station – the one who inadvertently caused Charlie Forester's death after a sliver of glass entered his eye. It was a million-to-one chance. We found a CCTV shot of her and ran a match. She was in our files because two months later she killed herself. Posner was religious and badly affected by the death. I want to look into the matter.'

'The last thing we need is you going off on another tangent,' said Land. 'Shouldn't you be concentrating on Forester's relationship with his wife? And Jackson, what exactly was he up to, creeping around the bushes with a camera snapping off photos of Helen Forester – was he obsessed with her?'

'No, Raymond, *mi pequeño pendejo*, because there's absolutely no hint of sexual impropriety.'

'He could have stopped because he realized that Jeremy Forester was watching him. And why didn't Forester do something to protect his wife? Have you carried out a re-enactment yet?'

'Certainly not,' said Bryant. 'You know I don't hold with such naffery.'

'I want one held first thing in the morning. Get Steffi to arrange it. Is that everything?'

Bryant paused in the doorway. 'Did you know that Ritchie Jackson lost his job because of us?'

Land was taken by surprise. 'No, I've heard no mention of that.'

'It was the night we caught the Mr Punch Killer. Traffic had to be diverted under London Bridge Station, and nobody checked all the height clearances on the new route. Jackson got around the back of Guildable Manor Street and slammed on his brakes. The arch was tall enough to pass under, but it had a steel cable pole sticking down from the brickwork and could have torn a hole in his roof. The sudden braking caused his load to shift. He was carrying cases of handmade glassware to Covent Garden Market, and was late getting back because out of the goodness of his heart he went via the hospital. When he went to unload the truck he found that some of the cargo had smashed and he was fired on the spot. Jackson provides a direct link between the two intended victims.'

'Thank God,' said Land. 'You can do some proper police work for a change and be a bit more realistic, instead of spending all your time rooting about in filthy old books and talking to autistic academics.'

'Reality is for those who lack imagination, *ma vieille limace*.'

When Bryant returned to his office, he found John May working at his laptop. 'Oh, there you are,' he said. 'The pulse quickens, the sap rises, I feel the bit between the teeth once more. We have a new avenue of exploration.'

'Oh?' May sat back and gave him his attention.

Bryant dug out his pipe and stuffed it with Old Holborn Captain's Shag. 'You know I am a man not in complete harmony with the normal. My thoughts tend to veer off like supermarket trolleys and my conversations with Raymondo usually prove fruitless.'

'Yes.' May wondered where this was going.

'I have to admit that this time he may have a point. I've been burying my head in my research rather too deeply. It's the part I enjoy most. Murder has such obvious motives, but sometimes our cases have something deeper behind them. I catch a glimpse of it, a vibration from the past, and I'm off.'

'I know,' said May indulgently. 'And you're often right to do so, but I think this investigation has a much more basic foundation. We're going to find that Jeremy Forester caused his wife's death. Dan says there are DNA traces of him—'

'Of course there are,' said Bryant. 'He went to her flat to try to get his passport back.'

May raised his hand. 'Let me finish, Arthur. He may have indirectly been the cause. This chap Sun Dark has connections to Forester's company. They built their malls on his land, deals were done, Forester owed them money. We're going after the company records, but Dark's lawyers have a pretty sophisticated set-up and it'll take us a while to obtain the necessary permissions. I've had some further information on Ritchie Jackson. His ex-girlfriend Sofia called Janice while you were interviewing him. She nearly got a restraining order put on him because he was stalking her. She's coming in tonight. There's a lot to be done, and I could do with your full attention.'

'Very well.' Bryant lit his pipe, sending a plume of burning embers across the room. 'I'll put aside my history books and we'll do it your way. I want to talk to anyone who knew Lauren Posner. *C'est le temps pour fumer une pipe enchantée.*'

'No, not your marijuana plant,' cried May, eyeing the

diseased-looking weed in the flowerpot under his partner's desk.

'It's for medicinal purposes,' Bryant insisted. 'I need to keep my strength up.'

'Well, that won't do it.'

'No,' Bryant agreed, 'but it'll stop me from getting depressed if we fail.'

29

'HE SAID I LOOKED LIKE AN ANGEL'

Steffi Vesta expected to pull long shifts, but the staff of the PCU never seemed to go home. They ate, slept and showered at work. Yesterday Colin Bimsley had wandered in wearing a vest and shorts, eating a bowl of cereal. Meera sat in the evidence room watching detective shows on a confiscated television. Janice came out of the bathroom with her hair in curlers. Mr Bryant wore carpet slippers. Raymond Land did jigsaws. Some old ladies came by to bless the new roof patio. Towels were dried on radiators, socks were hung on make-shift clothes lines, milk was delivered with bottles of gin. It was like some horrible student hostel.

Clearing her desk of half-eaten pizza slices, Steffi put on her coat and went to join Janice Longbright for her interview with Ritchie Jackson's former girlfriend.

As the two Daves were still painting the interview room, Longbright had taken her witness to the Ladykillers Café on the corner, hoping that the ironic Home Counties decor would put her at ease. Sofia Anzelmo fitted Bryant's description of the killer's type: blonde and slender, dressed in a skirt and black leggings. Her plucked eyebrows gave her a look of per-manent surprise. Only her accent revealed her as Italian.

'After I broke up with Ritchie he wouldn't leave me alone,' said Anzelmo. 'He was very persistent.' She shifted uncomfortably on her counter stool. The barista served them decaf soya lattes in dainty floral teacups and two pieces of hemp-seed cake on a plank.

'How long were you going out?' asked Longbright, taking notes.

'Nearly two years. He wanted us to move in together, settle down and have kids, but I wasn't ready for that.'

'How did you let him know?'

'We went for a drink and I tried to break it as gently as possible, but he didn't appear to understand what I was saying. So I had to tell him there wasn't a future for us. He was more shocked than I expected. I thought I'd finally got through to him, but the next night he turned up at my parents' flat. My mum really likes him, so she let him in and then told me I should be nice to him.'

'I'm afraid mothers have a habit of doing things like that,' said Longbright.

Sofia broke off a piece of cake, but was too agitated to eat. 'I just couldn't get him to go away. I blocked his number but it made no difference. He started following me home from work. He was never threatening, he was just always – *there*, like a clinging shadow. He kept sending me notes and always seemed to turn up in the neighbourhood when I went shopping. I mean, I felt sorry for him but I heard he'd done this before.'

'You said you *nearly* got a restraining order. You didn't get one?'

'No, partly because of my mother, who took his side, partly because he'd never threatened or tried to hurt me in any way. His persistence made me feel uncomfortable. I thought I could deal with it myself and go to the police if the problem continued.'

'But you didn't.'

'No, he finally gave up. He couldn't see what he was doing to me. I felt sorry for him.'

'Why?'

'He'd had a bad time at home – his mother had walked out when he was eight or nine; his father was a drunk. He didn't seem able to keep jobs for very long. Maybe I shouldn't be saying all this because he deserves a break, but when I heard that he'd been photographing the woman who died . . . well, his behaviour just seemed' – she searched for the right word – 'consistent.'

'So he pestered you. You're sure there was no threat of physical violence? He never tried to contact you on social network sites?'

'No, nothing like that.'

'If you didn't think he was a danger, why did you come here?'

'Because of the photographs,' said Anzelmo. 'There was a report on the news that Mrs Forester had been photographed just before her death. I know where Ritchie works. That's how I met him, you see. He took a photo of me in Holland Park. He said I looked like an angel. I said that would make me dead, and he just laughed.'

She removed a folded piece of paper from her bag and smoothed it out. Anzelmo was in the centre of the shot, seen from the side, fecund greenery forming a lush backdrop behind her. Longbright couldn't help noticing how remarkably similar it was in construction to the picture Ritchie Jackson had taken of Helen Forester.

As Leslie Faraday battled his way through the placard holders outside the House of Commons he decided he was sick of do-gooders. The something-for-nothing brigade was on his back again. Shutting the parks had been misconstrued by some to mean that his allies in the civil service were planning to start privatizing them, when nothing could be further from the truth.

All he wanted was a little piece of the action. He had all the figures in a folder: London was home to the world's largest urban forest. Some eight million trees existed in the green spaces that took up nearly half the city. In High Barnet there existed a tree that was two thousand years old! In the thirty-three boroughs there were more than thirteen thousand species in three thousand parks, thirty thousand allotments and three million gardens, and what was the one thing you never saw in all this green space? Children! The little buggers were indoors on their PlayStations while all of this beautiful, usable land went to waste.

London was desperately short of spaces capable of hosting large corporate functions. Chunks of Hyde Park and many of London's squares were now closed for private hospitality events in the summer, but how many more could play their part in enticing sponsorship? He just needed to push the door open wider, set aside a dedicated area in every park, garden and square for use by businesses and in time the rest would follow. Most green spaces were shut at night, and all that profitable time was lost. By locking the parks the government was reminding the public that usage was a privilege, not a right.

Faraday knew he would be forced to reopen them after the PCU had gone and the case had passed to the CID, but the new security force was ready to go. They would need to be quartered in the parks, which meant new buildings. He could get prefabricated ones erected in days. From there, it was simply a matter of expanding outward. Utilities, construction, contracts to be awarded . . . the next few weeks were going to be very busy indeed.

Locating his limousine, Faraday made for the door and was hit with a barrage of eggs.

He turned to see who had attacked him and was confronted by a bunch of West Indian church ladies armed with produce and placards reading 'Nature belongs to God not government!' He dropped himself into the back seat of the limo just as the rest of the crowd realized who he was and came running towards him.

'Drive over them if you have to!' he shouted at his driver. Somebody filmed him through the window, lip-read his words and posted the comment online before he made it back to the office.

It made no difference; Faraday was triumphant. In the folder on his lap lay the remaining permissions he needed to extend the closures to every park in London.

As he sat back in the purring black Jaguar, he turned back to the list of company directors who he knew would be interested in grabbing a prime piece of London real estate.

30

'WHERE DO YOU PLACE THE RESPONSIBILITY?'

As the detectives approached the entrance to the British Library, they might have been forgiven for thinking that Arthur Bryant's hallucinations had taken corporeal form and burst out into the real world; the foyer was filled with giant red and green mushrooms, and trestle tables were laid out with sandwiches and cakes for a Victorian tea party. They entered just as the Mad Hatter and the Queen of Hearts arrived with Tweedledum and Tweedledee. A jazz band was playing the theme from *Frozen*.

'Welcome,' said a young woman dressed as a giant green caterpillar, an effect spoilt only by her Nike trainers. 'Are you joining us for our Lewis Carroll celebration?'

'No, I am not, madam,' said Bryant sharply as he unlooped his scarf. 'We're here for—'

'Bryant!' boomed Ray Kirkpatrick, charging over with his arms outstretched and crushing him in such a bear hug that the detective's boots left the floor. Dropping him, the ursine academic waved a hand over the Wonderlandians. 'Look at this bloody shambles. It's exactly what's wrong with libraries. They're treating *Alice's Adventures in Wonderland* as if it's the only Victorian book anyone can recall. These twerps have modelled themselves on the Disney version, not the original Tenniel drawings. Populism in action – this is what happens when you allow your programming to be dictated by the kind of people who eat crisps at home. No wonder kids don't read any more, they're too bloody embarrassed.'

'How would you like to join us for tea?' asked the Mad Hatter.

'How would you like a knuckle sandwich?' asked Kirkpatrick, bunching a fist at him. 'It's a total pain in the arse having to walk past them every morning. You're not even allowed to touch their biscuits. I got into a punch-up with the dormouse yesterday. He doesn't like it when you stamp on his tail. Go on, get back in the sea!' he shouted at a girl dressed as a walrus.

'It does seem a bit over the top,' May agreed.

'Over the top? I expect my libraries and churches to be like my ex-wife: unlovely, unforgiving and underheated when you're inside them. I'm assuming you're here with the details of some gruesome bloody murder? Last time I saw you, you were looking for a killer and asking me about Dickens. What is it this time? Let me guess: you're after a mad bomber and want to know about Charlotte Brontë.'

'We're not here for you today, I'm afraid,' said Bryant. 'John and I have arranged to meet a chap called Duncan Aston.'

'That's a pity. I always enjoy hearing about your warped version of policing.' Kirkpatrick had a scratch around inside his immense beard, pulled something out and flicked it at the Cheshire Cat. 'Come on, I'll swipe you in.' Grabbing both of them by their arms he yanked them through a crowd of schoolchildren. 'Get out of the way, you damned homunculi! Duncan works in the maps room upstairs, room B230. Is he a suspect? Have we a lunatic in our midst?'

'Sorry to disappoint you,' said May as they climbed the stairs. 'We're conducting interviews. Are you here full time now?'

'Nah, I'm just filling in until Motörhead starts advertising for a new frontman. I'm analysing Elizabethan playscripts on Thursdays and Fridays, gigging with my band on Mondays, fixing websites on Tuesdays and Wednesdays and working as a film extra at the weekends.'

'I think I saw you in *The Revenant*,' said Bryant. 'I loved the bit where you dragged Leonardo DiCaprio around by his spine.'

'Go ahead, mate, have your laugh. I've got four jobs that just about keep my head above water. What will you have when the PCU goes?'

'Who said it's going anywhere?' asked May, puzzled.

'I guess you're still not reading the papers.' Kirkpatrick lifted a confused child aside, setting it down the wrong way around. 'The *Evening Standard* reckons you're being investigated over this business of closing the parks. They say the civil disobedience is all your fault.'

'I must admit I never thought it would get the go-ahead,' said May.

'There's going to be a massive protest rally in Westminster tonight. It's the thin end of the wedge. I imagine the mayor's office will start charging people to walk along the sodding streets before privatizing the Thames and putting ten-pound entry turnstiles on all park gates. They already charge for the New Year's Eve celebrations we've prepaid in our taxes. At least the congestion charge does what it says on the tin: you pay a tenner to sit in congestion. They'd make us pay for the air if its quality wasn't so shit. Here you go.'

He pushed open the door to the antique maps room.

The detectives found themselves in a windowless municipal office with eyeball-parching light panels. The wide desks held books of old maps that looked impossible to open or even hold flat. In a half-hearted attempt to brighten the environment, the walls were filled with poor quality Monet and Degas reproductions. Duncan Aston glanced up as they approached but didn't rise. He checked his watch.

'Sorry,' he said, holding out his hand to each of them, 'which one is which?'

'I'm Mr Bryant, he's Mr May,' said Bryant.

'I was going to come down and meet you and got caught up in this. You tend to lose all track of time in here.' Aston indicated the inked vellum map laid out on his desk. He was bespectacled, thin and sun-starved, with a complexion that suggested he would benefit from being in a room with natural light. In the habit of working in the isolation of deep concentration, he sat in a slouch and averted his eyes as if the mere idea of a conversation made him impatient for it to end.

Seeing the great map, Bryant was instantly diverted from the task at hand, as May feared he would be. 'What is this?' he asked, intrigued.

'New York's birth certificate,' Aston explained, glad to be asked. 'The so-called Duke's Plan, presented to James, Duke of York, after whom New York was named. As you can see, Manhattan was already in place. That's the town wall that gave its name to Wall Street, and there's the canal running up the middle which became Broad Street. It feels very Dutch, unsurprisingly.'

'It's in good nick.' Bryant peered at it through his trifocals. 'Smells funny, though.'

'Vellum is cured goatskin. The map was protected by a curtain before we inherited it as part of the king's topographical collection in the 1820s.' Aston daintily peeled off his white cotton gloves. 'It's getting a bit of rot now, so we're treating it. What can I do for you?'

'We're investigating the deaths of Sharyn Buckland and Helen Forester,' said May.

'This is about Charlie Forester, isn't it?' said Aston. '"The little boy with everything to live for." We may not get out much but we get all of the papers delivered up here.'

'His mother and nanny are both dead,' said May. 'Lauren Posner was the young lady who—'

'Please don't say it.' Aston raised a hand. 'Don't say my

girlfriend caused his death. Let's not bring all that up again. She had to live with the press's accusations.'

'Can you tell us what happened?' asked Bryant.

Aston's mood clouded. 'Do I have to? It's all on record.'

'We'd like to hear about it in your own words.'

The map restorer gave a shrug. 'Lauren was bright and fragile. Her parents pushed her hard. When she was young she was given extra tuition every evening and weekend. They wouldn't let her take time off even in school holidays. Piano, ballet, Spanish, French, the sciences. She studied theatre and wanted to be an actress. My mother had been a classical actress, so I could understand what drove her. But things went wrong for Lauren. At eighteen she suffered a nervous collapse. She was never the same after that.'

'How old was she when you met her?'

'She'd just had her twenty-fourth birthday. We met through a mutual friend at a book launch and hit it off at once. She wasn't easy to get along with. I was fairly well equipped to deal with her because I'd had my own share of problems in the past.'

'Mainly alcohol issues, I understand,' said Bryant.

Aston's attitude cooled at once. 'You've been checking up on me?'

'Part of the job, I'm afraid. How long were you living together?'

'About three years. Lauren was very sensitive, a practising Catholic, and the accident affected her badly.'

'But it *was* an accident.'

'So I understand.' He didn't sound entirely sure. 'Lauren had a job in a charity shop in Greenwich. She couldn't handle any kind of pressure. She'd been talking about moving out of London and living somewhere less crowded, perhaps by the sea, but I didn't want to commute.'

'Let's go to the night of the accident,' said May gently.

'I think it was the first weekend in February, Saturday night. We'd arranged to go to a party in Blackheath. Neither of us liked parties but a friend of Lauren's was leaving to work in Cape Town and she felt she should say goodbye. I had to be at work the next morning – we often work early on weekends here because you can concentrate without being interrupted – so we said we'd just stay for an hour. We lived in Kilburn, which meant crossing London. When it was time to leave she said she was enjoying herself and didn't want to go, but I'd had enough and left. She said she'd see me at home.'

'Did you argue about this?'

'No, not really – we were in different moods, that's all. I got home, watched some TV and went to bed. She got back a couple of hours later. She was in a terrible state. She explained about the accident.'

'What was your reaction?'

'I told her she shouldn't have left the scene and should have gone with the ambulance. We talked about it for a while, by which time it was late, and she wanted to sleep.'

'So she didn't know at that point that Charlie Forester had died.'

'No. Even so, I told her she should go to the police the next day, just to give details and explain why she'd left, you know, in case they came looking for her.'

'But she didn't go.'

'I don't know what happened but she ended up not going. And the police never called. I thought they would, but they didn't.' He looked from one of them to the other. 'It wasn't her fault. There was a detour under the station and the truck in front of her suddenly slammed on its brakes, so that she was forced on to the pavement. There was an elderly officer on point duty, due for retirement, a Sergeant Samuel Kemp-Bird. I remembered reading about him because it was such an unusual name. Linguistics is rather our passion up here. Anyway – where was I?'

'It wasn't her fault,' reminded May.

'That's right. Lauren said her car never went anywhere

near the boy. It hit a – what do you call those things? A box full of telephone cables. But the wing mirror cracked and a bottle was knocked off the top of the cabinet, and somehow a sliver of glass flew out and hit him.'

'From which, the wing mirror or the bottle?'

Aston shrugged. 'I d-don't know.' May now understood Aston's reluctance to talk; his stutter manifested with the effort of recounting the story. 'The c-coroner's report was inconclusive. The glass worked its way around the back of the boy's eye and s-severed the optic nerve, causing a clot, which then entered his brain – something like that. The surgeon found a tiny piece of glass but couldn't identify its origin.'

'Why not?' asked Bryant. 'If it came from the wing mirror—'

'We w-weren't kept informed about it,' Aston explained. 'We only knew what we read online. By this time Lauren had returned the car – it was her brother's – and he had replaced the mirror. She thought that the glass was more likely to have come from the empty wine bottle on the cabinet because, you know, it was m-more breakable. There were homeless people sleeping in the tunnel, and I guess one of them had been drinking. But by that time the detour had been d-dismantled and the road had been washed clean. I suppose it's irrelevant how the thing got into his eye. When Lauren found out that he'd died she began to blame herself. I couldn't understand why the police didn't look for her. Then I read that the traffic officer had got himself into trouble.'

'How?' asked Bryant. He tried to curb his habit of wandering around picking up random items, but in a space filled with rare literary artefacts it was a sore temptation.

'It turned out that he'd been having problems with his sight and had recently failed a medical. He wasn't supposed to be on duty, but I think the matter was hushed up.'

'From what we know, there was a lot going on that night,' May pointed out. 'The police weren't informed that the boy had died. Someone should have taken a statement from Ms Posner but she slipped through the system. It happens.'

'I keep thinking that maybe if they had come and cleared the matter up with her, things would have been different,' said Aston, growing weary of discussing the subject. 'Instead she became more and more upset. She went to see her p-priest several times.'

'Do you have his name?'

'Father Michael Flynn at St George's, but you'll get nothing from him. "The seal of the confessional is inviolable." That's all I got.'

'Why did you see him?'

'It was just after Lauren killed herself. I wanted to know what advice he'd given her, but of course he wouldn't tell me.' There was a bitter edge to his voice. Aston pressed a thin hand on the rising corner of the map, smoothing it back into place. 'When she died it felt like a comment on my own failure. Why couldn't I see what was happening to her and stop it?'

'So you think she killed herself as a result of feeling responsible for the accident?'

Wary of others working around him, Aston lowered his voice. 'Mainly that. I found out what had happened from her mother. Lauren had written a letter to her parents and mailed it, but of course it arrived too late. She said she couldn't live with the burden of knowing that she'd caused the boy's death. I'm sure her parents would show it to you. I have her father's work number somewhere.' Aston opened a drawer and passed over a card.

'Why do you think the boy's death affected her so badly? Did she have any reason to think it was something other than an accident?'

Aston's voice became flat and emotionless. 'I don't know. How does anyone ever know? Nothing was clear-cut. Nobody was sure where the glass came from. The press said he'd got dust in his eye from the tunnel, but that's because they were running an anti-pollution campaign. They didn't mention the glass at all. They wanted to use his death as a catalyst for change. When something odd like that happens and everyone is pushing their own agenda, where do you place the responsibility?'

'Ms Posner didn't suggest a theory to you or to anyone else?'

'No. But I wondered about the nanny. She should have felt more responsible than Lauren.' Aston touched the edges of the map with tenderness, anxious to get on.

'Was Ms Posner drinking that night, at the party?' asked Bryant. 'Was that the reason why she stayed on?'

'She used to have a problem with alcohol,' said Aston carefully. 'It's in her medical records. She was trying to stay sober but had had a bad week at work and slipped off the wagon. She told me she wouldn't drive. She seemed all right when she arrived at my place, but she was probably over the limit.'

'So that's why she didn't stay with the boy. What happened in the time that followed?'

'Things just kept getting worse. Her mother, her friends, we all tried to get her to see someone. When she couldn't handle the guilt any more she swallowed a handful of sleeping pills, washed them down with vodka and sat on a bench in Greenwich Park, looking out at her favourite view. She just went to sleep. The doctor said it was peaceful. So the tragedy didn't end on the night Charlie Forester died.'

'I'm afraid it still hasn't ended,' said Bryant, rising and retrieving his homburg.

'All I have left is this.' Aston pulled something from beneath his sleeve. 'It belonged to Lauren. I can use it here.' He tenderly placed the handkerchief under the edge of his palm. 'It stops the ink from smudging.'

31

'WE'RE THE ONES WHO HAVE TO CARE'

'I didn't think they'd do it – nobody did,' insisted Colin, pushing his way back through the shouting crowds that had once more gathered around the railings of Russell Square Gardens. 'They're bloody crazy.' The students, union groups and coachloads of elderly day-trippers had now formed an unlikely alliance and were chanting a variety of awkward slogans, including 'Two, four, six, eight, we don't need our parks with gates.'

'The papers are whipping this up,' Meera said. 'They knew there would be protests.'

After it had become known that a third woman had been found strangled, Faraday's PR machine went into overdrive. Nobody could deny that something needed to be done, but nobody felt that closing off public spaces was the right answer. This was clearly what Faraday had hoped for. Unlocking the gates and introducing private security would be welcomed as a perfect trade-off. However, his machinations had set him on a collision course with the Metropolitan Police, who had been made to look useless.

'They're trying to make a point,' said Colin, 'to remind everyone who owns the parks that it's a right that can be taken away. Let's get out of here before it all kicks off. Some of these pensioners can get really nasty.'

Colin and Meera were taking a break before heading into their evening shift and, like many others in the city, wanted to see what was happening around the locked parks. The low clouds were flavescent with reflected light. The top of the Shard glowed inside an angry swirl of vapour. It felt like a night for disobedience. Hundreds of red balloons bearing the legend *Public Not Private* had been tied on park railings everywhere. A Maginot Line of police in hi-vis canary-coloured jackets was fighting to hold back a troop of stroppy seniors from Cardiff. One constable had to be hospitalized after being hit with a pot of clematis.

'I want to go back to St Olave's churchyard,' Colin said. 'Will you drive me there?'

Meera tried to keep up but he strode ahead. 'Why?' she called above the crowd noise.

'I was the one who found her, Meera. Do you know what that's like? If I'd got there a few minutes earlier, if the traffic hadn't been so bad – it's just like that kid she was looking after. He wouldn't have died if she'd walked a different way to the station with him.' He waited for Meera to catch him up. 'My old gran used to tell us a story about a bomb falling into her street during the war, just as she was crossing it. She said she nearly turned back to the house to get her hat, but she didn't. If she had, she'd have been killed.'

'Yeah, but everyone of her age has a story like that, Colin. It's just chance. The boy died because a dozen different elements lined up. It was unlucky, that's all—'

'These women,' he said, silencing her. 'They weren't unlucky, Meera, they were stalked and killed. Darren Link always says the unit is too slow to react. It's because Mr Bryant spends his time going through mad old books instead of doing what we do, churning data and digging into rubbish bins to try to prove guilt the hard way.'

'I thought you were his biggest fan,' said Meera, unlocking her Kawasaki.

'I am, but he's too slow to catch someone like this. He reckons this guy isn't striking randomly because he went after the nanny twice. But what if he's just doing it because he's fixated on a small group of women and his demons are driving him to kill? Three deaths in four days – what will he have done by the weekend?'

'He won't be able to do it in a park any more,' she said, starting the bike. 'Get on.'

They kept away from the darkling crowds and pulled up outside the churchyard a little after six. Beyond the tall iron gates nothing was visible. 'Now what?' she asked. 'Even the doors here are locked.'

'Then we go in over the railing.'

'What's the point? What are you expecting to find?'

'I don't know, OK? I just need to see. You can wait here if you want.'

She switched off the bike. 'No, I'm coming with you. Help me over.'

Putting a boot in his locked hands she scrambled over the railing, helping to pull him up from the other side.

There were no lights showing through the stained-glass windows of the church. Here on the path beneath the caliginous bushes, it was so gloomy that Colin needed to use his torch. As they followed the walkway around it grew darker still. At the far end of the shallow garden stood another gate that led to an alley running along one side of the church.

Puzzled, Meera went over and pushed against it. 'It's open,' she said, looking back at Colin.

'This way.' Colin headed for the cover of the trees. Dan Banbury's plastic ribbons could be seen roping off the spot where the nanny's body had fallen.

Meera caught up with him. 'Why *are* we here?' she asked.

'I want to help the old man.' Colin withdrew his phone and

checked the settings. 'Mr Bryant wasn't happy with Dan's shots of the site. He made a fuss about taking them from a different angle.'

'Why?'

'He didn't say. You know what he's like; it's impossible to figure out what's going on in his head and he'll never give you a straight answer. I think he has ideas even he can't explain. I reckon he's on to something but doesn't want to tell anyone yet.'

Dropping on to one knee, Colin aimed the phone and fired off a series of shots, the flash flattening the scene with bright cold light. It showed tufts of grass, leaves, a disturbance in the gravel path.

'What's that?' Meera asked.

Before either of them could get any closer the bushes parted and a hunched shape rolled towards them, unfurling and rising. The figure of a man rose and lashed out, connecting with Colin and knocking him off balance. Meera threw herself at his back but slid off, and then they were all running, the figure ahead, she and Colin just feet away.

He beat them to the opened gate and slipped through, trying to pull it shut behind him, but Colin caught the bars and prevented them from closing. They dashed down the narrow path at the side of the church, squeezing past a brick outcrop that extended almost to its width.

With Meera ahead of him, Colin knew there was only one way they would bring down their quarry. A tap on her shoulder was the signal; as Colin dropped to one knee she placed a boot into his hands and let him lift her high like a shot-putter, sending her into the air. She landed squarely on the running man's back, bringing him down. With a shocked yell he slammed on to the gravel path. She turned him over and shone a light into his face.

They found themselves looking into the frightened features of a sixteen-year-old boy. 'He's a kid,' said Meera. 'What are you doing in here, mate? What's in the bag?'

In one raised hand he held a white plastic Tesco bag. While Meera sat on him, Colin reached over and disentangled it from the boy's fingers. Carefully he opened the top and looked inside.

'What is this?' he asked again.

'Can't breathe—' wheezed the boy.

'Meera, get off his chest for a second.'

'If you try to go anywhere I'll stamp on your spine,' warned Meera, climbing off. The boy rose and coughed. He said something that sounded like 'It's Muddabay.'

'What's he saying? Where are you from?'

'Trakai. Trakai.'

'What's that?' Meera looked at Colin.

'It's a town near Vilnius, in Lithuania,' said Colin. 'He's Lithuanian.'

'What's Muddabay?' Meera patted him down and removed a pen from the pocket of his jeans. 'What's this?'

'It's a laser pen.' Colin held it up and flicked on the red beam. 'The smart little sod. Kids put out the CCTVs with them by overloading the imaging sensors.'

'What did he take from the site?'

Colin pushed a hand into the bag and drew up gravel in his fingers. 'Where'd you get this from? Show us.'

The boy led them along the alley while Meera hung on to the back of his blue nylon jacket. When they reached the area that the crime scene manager had roped off, the boy dipped beneath the ribbon and brought them to the edge of the path, pointing to a shallow dip in the shale.

'He dug it out of there. What did you do this for, mate?'

The boy indicated that he wanted to take something from his pocket, but was understandably wary. Removing his phone (which, Colin noted, was a newer and better model than his own) he thumbed through the web pages and turned the screen towards them.

'Jeez, the little bugger's putting souvenirs from the murder sites online,' said Meera, amazed.

The screen showed clumps of earth, stones and pieces of slate taken from the gardens where the bodies had been found. A collection of stones from Russell Square Gardens was accompanied by photographs of provenance showing them *in situ*. 'You're going to love this, Colin. "MurderBay, the Crime Scene Collectors' Site", based in Arizona. Money for old rope – literally. Who do we know who works in a park and owns a professional camera?' She turned to the cowering boy. 'Do you know Ritchie Jackson? Did he put you up to this?'

The boy stared at her blankly. 'Damn,' said Colin. 'I guess that would have been a little too neat. Show me exactly where you took this from.'

The boy accepted the bag from him and emptied it over the small ditch he had dug, perfectly filling the hole. As Colin shone his torch over it he spotted something glittering. Reaching forward, he extracted several small grey seamed pellets, rolling them in his broad palm. 'Were these here?'

Anxious to be let off, the boy nodded vigorously.

Colin raised his hand to show Meera. 'What are they?' she asked.

'It's lead shot,' said Colin. 'She was strangled, just like the others. But it looks like someone fired at her first. Why would they have done that?'

'Maybe it was hers and she dropped it,' said Meera. 'What's it used for?'

'I don't know – hunting geese, fishing, putting into belts.'

'So we're after a frustrated duck hunter?' asked Meera.

'Shot towers,' said Colin. 'That's the only other thing I know. They make it by dripping molten lead in tall towers. The metal becomes spherical as it falls, and there's water at the bottom so it hardens at once. There are still a few towers left in London but I don't suppose they're operational any more.'

'Why not?'

'Because lead was reclassed as highly toxic and can't be used for hunting birds. So they have to use non-lead alternatives.'

He shook the mix of gravel and shot at the frightened lad: 'What is this?'

'They pay me money,' was all he said.

'How? How do they get in touch with you?'

'Online, man – what you think?'

They let the boy go. 'Blimey, he's got some front, hasn't he?' said Meera, watching him run off. 'A right little entrepreneur.'

'These are tough times to be young.' There was an odd catch in Colin's voice, as if he was thinking about someone in particular.

They headed back to Meera's Kawasaki. 'It's weird.' Colin glanced up at the darkened church. 'We find rifle ammunition and daggers, everything but the actual murder weapon. It's like Cluedo. I was in Chiswick Park with my mum once when I was a nipper – an amazing place, a bit of Palladian Italy in West London, statues, follies and this thing called an Exedra, a semicircular yew hedge with a lawn and cypresses and white stone urns, dead posh, and I was walking around and found a loaded gun, a Glock revolver, lying right in the middle of the lawn. I took it back to my old man – 'cause you know he was a copper – and he told me it had been fired three times. D'you know what he said? "There's probably a body buried under one of those trees, but unless someone cares enough to make a fuss it'll probably stay there for ever."'

'And is there some kind of life lesson you want me to draw from that?'

'We're the ones who have to care,' Colin told Meera. 'Don't you see that? Everyone else is out for themselves.' He looked at the bike. 'No, don't give me a lift. This is getting to me. I think I want to walk by myself for a while.'

She watched as he walked away into the wet night with his

head down and his hands in his pockets, and could not stop herself from feeling that she had in some way disappointed him.

THE FIFTH DAY

32

'THERE ARE NO UNANSWERED QUESTIONS LEFT'

At seven thirty on Friday morning the passengers on the top decks of the buses passing Clement Crescent caught brief glimpses of what appeared to be a film shoot taking place beyond the plane trees.

As Steffi Vesta was the only woman in the unit who could remotely pass for the deceased (although she was nearly six inches too tall), she had been enrolled to play the part of Helen Forester in the re-enactment of Monday's murder.

Having been against the idea from the start, the detectives were staying back at the PCU, but Raymond Land insisted that the replay should go ahead with himself as the director.

Every detail had been checked for veracity. Beauchamp the terrier had now been adopted by Margo Farrier and was on hand for the occasion, Colin Bimsley had been wedged into the bushes as a replacement for Jeremy Forester, and in an interesting bit of colour-blind casting Jack Renfield had been awarded the part of the gardener. Ritchie Jackson stood to one side making sure that everyone was in the right place. With Banbury recording and Land watching from a safe distance, the scene was set.

'We need to start now,' said Land, checking his watch. 'Steffi, if you would?'

She peered over the gate. 'You are ready for me?'

'Yes – action.'

Vesta had trouble twisting the key in the lock.

'Stop, stop,' called Land.

'You're supposed to say "Cut",' Colin told him.

Land shot him a filthy look. 'Start again.'

Steffi didn't move.

'Now what's wrong?' Land asked.

'Sorry, I was waiting for you to call "Action",' said Vesta.

'Oh, for God's sake. Action.'

She let herself into the garden. Renfield crouched down with his camera and Bimsley peered out of the bushes. Ritchie Jackson stayed low beside Renfield, offering advice. 'That can't be right,' he said. 'I can see Colin from here.'

'Oi,' called Bimsley, 'you don't get to be on first-name terms with us while you're a suspect.'

'I thought I wasn't a suspect any more,' Jackson called back.

'Can everyone be quiet?' Land called through a rolled-up magazine. 'Steffi, where are you?'

'I am sorry,' called Vesta. 'The little dog has stopped to do his business.'

'Well, can you hurry him up?'

'Has anybody got a plastic bag?' Vesta tried to untangle the dog's new leash and inadvertently released it. Beauchamp took off into the foliage like a prisoner of war timing an escape. There was a yelp and a crash as Bimsley fell backward into a holly bush.

'Keep going, everyone!' Land shouted. 'This is a take. Steffi, where are you?'

'I have trodden in something,' called Vesta. 'I've lost my shoe.'

'Am I supposed to be filming this part or would you like me to start when everyone behaves professionally?' asked Banbury unhelpfully.

Jackson tapped Renfield on the shoulder. 'This is when I took the photos.'

'Yes, but she's not here yet, is she?' said Renfield. They both looked around.

'You're supposed to come out now,' Land told Bimsley.

'I can't,' called Colin, 'the dog's on my leg.'

'Well, get him off.'

'I think he's getting himself off.'

Vesta hobbled into the shot on one heel. 'I am sorry, I had to leave the shoe there,' she apologized. 'Where do I go now?'

'You missed your entrance, you have to go back,' said Land. 'Colin, you're supposed to have made yourself scarce by this time.'

'Hang on. Bollocks.' There was a yelp and the dog shot out. 'I can't stand up, I've got cramp.'

Margo Farrier wandered into Banbury's sightline. 'Have you finished your little film show yet?' she asked. 'I need to take Beauchamp to the vet, he's got an upset tummy.'

'For God's sake,' cried Land. 'This is where Mrs Forester's killer is meant to enter.'

'You didn't cast anyone to be the killer,' said Banbury wearily.

'Bugger.' Land thought for a moment. 'Can you stand in for him?'

Banbury was affronted. 'Who's going to shoot the scene? I don't want anyone else touching my equipment.'

'Wait a minute,' said Colin, hopping out of the bush, 'if it was Forester or Jackson – no offence, mate – one of us should play the killer, otherwise we end up with three blokes at the scene.'

'Well, I'm not going to play him, am I?' said Jackson. 'How would that look? Can I just say that this is a really rubbish way to conduct a murder investigation?'

'I'll bloody do it,' said Bimsley, massaging his calf. 'Where's the murder weapon?'

'We don't know what it is, do we?' cried Land, exasperated. 'You'll have to improvise.'

'What with?'

'I don't know, use your initiative.'

Colin looked about just as the terrier raced past. Flinging himself on it, he grabbed the leash and released it from Beauchamp's collar, threw it around Vesta's neck and pulled. Caught by surprise, Vesta screamed and they both toppled back into the bushes.

'He's very good, isn't he?' said Renfield admiringly.

'Don't ask me,' said Jackson. 'I'm a suspect, apparently. Show some respect.'

'And cut, and print,' shouted Land.

'It's digital, you berk,' said Banbury.

'He's not exactly Steven Spielberg, is he?' Jackson decided.

'You've squashed the poor little thing!' cried Mrs Farrier, horrified. Unhappy at being left out, Beauchamp darted into the bushes to join the others.

'I don't want any members of the public to see this until we're ready to air the piece,' said Land, looking around.

'Perhaps you'd like to take it to the Cannes Film Festival first,' Banbury muttered.

Beyond the railings half a dozen Chinese tourists were watching them and taking photographs.

Steffi crawled out on her hands and knees, covered in mud, minus a shoe. 'A little overenthusiastic, Colin, I am thinking,' she said, trying to rise and collapsing. The Chinese tourists laughed and applauded.

'There's no point putting emotion into it now that I've stopped filming,' said Land, bending over her. 'Good God.'

Imprinted around Vesta's neck were the braided markings of the dog leash.

Back at the PCU, Arthur Bryant wandered into Longbright's office eating a *Thunderbirds* ice lolly. When he wasn't directly engaged in investigation, he had a tendency to drift about disrupting everyone else.

'I wonder how it's going in Clement Crescent?' Longbright asked. 'Your tongue's blue.'

'I don't know why Raymondo had to do it,' Bryant said. 'A re-enactment involving a suspect?'

May ducked in, reading his phone. 'Dan just texted. He says: "Raymond shouldn't give up his day job but we may have an idea about the murder weapon."'

'How is that possible? I thought Dan conducted a finger-search of the area.' Bryant flicked his lolly stick into the bin and missed. 'Raymondo's not going to try to get the re-enactment televised, is he?'

The DS pointed over her shoulder with a pen. 'Ask him yourself. He wants to hold a meeting with at least six members of staff to discuss it in detail.'

'I'll leave that one to you,' said Bryant. 'I'm seeing steamed prawns with chilli.'

'You can't be thinking about lunch already.' She checked her watch.

'Sun Dark owns one of the largest restaurants in China-town,' Bryant explained. 'He's celebrating there right now. In case you haven't noticed, preparations are already under way for the Chinese New Year. I think John and I should pop down, grab some dim sum and surprise him. That way he won't have time to bring his lawyers in.'

The detectives arrived at the Lucky Dragon before the lunch-time rush had started, and found themselves in an overlit barn of a restaurant hung with gold and red tinsel. A carp stream cut across the ground floor, crossed by a humped wooden bridge finished in fierce red lacquer. Four very thin waiters who looked as if they hadn't slept since Bruce Lee's death listlessly folded napkins behind the counter.

'Two of you?' asked the maître d', already turning to walk them to a table.

'We're joining Sun Dark, over there,' said Bryant, pointing to a booth at the rear. At the mention of Dark's name the waiters evaporated.

'Try to rid your mind of any preconceptions,' Bryant told his partner as they headed for the table. 'We don't know what we're dealing with yet.'

'You're late. We've nearly finished. I'd offer you some but it's cold now.' The man who spoke waved away his three companions and waited for the detectives to seat themselves.

Sun Dark was small and neat, in his mid-forties, smoothly handsome, his hair brilliantined and shaved at the sides. He wore a black Turnbull & Asser suit and rimless glasses, and looked as if he might eat your heart raw from a silver tray. He pointed to a partially demolished plate of Quattro Stagioni in the middle of the table. 'I hate Chinese food,' he said. 'Give me a pizza any day. My family is horrified by my unsophisticated tastes. I suppose you want to know why one of my employees chased your suspect across a North London street brandishing a knife.'

'I'm glad you have the grace not to deny it.' Bryant seated himself and flicked open a menu.

'Why would I do that? You have the evidence. By now you must know where the knives came from.'

'Were they thrown by one of the gentlemen who just left?' asked May.

'No, they don't stab people in the back, Mr May, they're lawyers.' Sun Dark called one of the waiters over. 'Let me order for you, at least. That menu is for *lao wai*. Tell me, what do you call a man who takes a lot of money from you and does not return it?'

'The Chancellor of the Exchequer,' said Bryant.

'How about someone who makes a promise in a contract, then breaks it? Mr Forester leased some very valuable land from us via a third-party company which he then deliberately bankrupted.'

'This is all fascinating, really, and you simply must tell me more sometime,' said Bryant, 'but my job is to keep your hired thugs from sending British citizens plummeting off bridges. You have no jurisdiction here.'

'I appreciate the implication,' said Sun Dark. 'I don't understand your laws, or worse, I understand them and deliberately flout them. If you'd done your homework you'd have discovered that Mr Forester's companies are registered to his home address here.' He sat back with a sigh, resting his hands on his flat stomach. 'What do you see when you look at me, Mr Bryant? A Chinese movie villain? I didn't grow up in the street. I was schooled in Geneva and graduated from King's College, Cambridge. I speak seven languages. My family funds some of the biggest arts festivals in Germany and Austria. My wife is a Veronese opera singer. My daughter runs a sanctuary for marshland fowl in Norfolk, and my sons, in the time-honoured western tradition of wealthy families, are quite useless. I now amuse myself by selling land to developers. Do you honestly think I would hire a *knife-thrower* to take care of my debtors?'

'So when you seek justice, you operate through purely legal channels.' May was unable to keep the scepticism from his voice.

'There are other ways.' Dark removed a silky black cigarette from his case and lit it. 'Where I come from, the survival of the family is the only thing that's important. Breaking the law would bring members of my family into contact with your draconian immigration laws, and would also ensure that I'd never see a return on my investment.'

'Then you didn't arrange for Mr Forester to be attacked?'

'Attacked, no – persuaded, within reason. I asked one of my employees to negotiate the return of our investment, nothing more.'

'And you trusted him to do your bidding,' said May.

'A good businessman knows who to promote and who to cut loose. We have a saying: If you want one year of prosperity, grow grain. If you want ten years of prosperity, grow trees.

If you want one hundred years of prosperity, grow people.'

A plate of steaming tangerine beef arrived, along with two halves of a crisped golden duck, severed with expertise. 'If you think I would jeopardize my family's future affluence for the sake of one debtor, you are less experienced than you appear.'

'Fair enough,' said Bryant. 'I'll have to take your word for it when you say you only ordered your man to threaten Mr Forester. I'm always over-ordering Chinese myself.'

Dark looked at Bryant pityingly. 'It's so hard for you seniors to let go of those old empire stereotypes, isn't it? Funny foreigners, we're still good for a laugh, aren't we? Do you ever stop and look at where you are in the world these days? The South Koreans are better educated than the English. The Swedish are happier. The Germans are more compassionate. The Azerbaijanis are more literate. Brunei has cleaner air. Latvia has faster broadband. *Everywhere* has a better climate. And yet for some astonishing reason you still act as if you matter. Why is that, do you suppose? Ah, yes, *empire*. You lost yours over a century ago. The Americans are only just losing theirs and that's not going down so well, either.'

'We have a saying, too,' said Bryant. 'It's safer to live in a country that doesn't want to be a world power. Your employee threw knives at a man who owed you money.'

'Do you think they would have missed their target if my employee had intended to kill him?' Dark pulled a Mont Blanc pen from his top pocket and scribbled on a napkin. 'These are the contact details of the man I hired to deal with Forester. Arrest him, deport him, hang him upside down and beat the soles of his feet for all I care. He's a monkey who disobeyed orders. I've already terminated his contract. I'm sorry we didn't get to eat together. Perhaps I can arrange a doggy bag before you go.'

'I thought that went rather well,' said Bryant, leaving the restaurant with a large carrier bag in one hand. 'We got a free lunch out of it. And I managed to get right up his nose.'

'Yes, but you manage to get up everyone's—' May began, and thought better of it.

'When you upset someone they speak with honesty,' Bryant explained. 'Dark commissioned Forester's shakedown, that's all, but we can't rule him out of the investigation. Let's keep an eye on him.'

'He's handed his debt collector over to us,' said May. 'If he'd really wanted to hurt Forester I can see why he would send someone after his wife – but the nanny?'

'This is about the death of little Charlie Forester, not his father's debts.' Bryant held up a hand and stepped out in front of a startled taxi driver. 'So where are we? Dan's already had a look at Lauren Posner's suicide note and says it backs up what Aston told us. She'd been drinking and was over the limit, which is why she left the scene. Her reactions were off; the boy's death could have been avoided. She apologizes for her life. No parent should have to read that.'

When the detectives arrived back at the unit, Dan Banbury caught up with them. 'Listen to this,' he said anxiously. 'Back in February the traffic detail found a snippet of blurry camera footage that they thought might show Posner's car weaving across the central divide in heavy rain, just south of Bermondsey Street. She didn't have a driving licence – she'd never passed her test. They were meant to follow up the case but for some reason never got around to it. While it was going back and forth between the Met and the Transport Operational Command Unit, the coroner filed a verdict of accidental death.'

'Then there are no unanswered questions left,' said May. 'I still don't see how the events of almost a year ago can be connected to those of this week.'

'What do you get if you let your imagination run a little wilder?' Bryant wondered. 'Sharyn Buckland used the accident to stab her charge in the eye and leave the way open for Jeremy Forester to divorce his wife. You'd have to admit that as a dating stratagem it leaves something to be desired.

Forester divorces but doesn't get together with the nanny after all. He loses his job and goes broke, so he decides to kill the women who brought him low. It's trying a bit too hard, don't you think?'

'Stranger things have happened,' said May.

33

'A SYLVAN SETTING THAT'S POISONED SOMEHOW'

'I say, will you indulge me a little tonight?' asked Bryant. 'I need to explore one last avenue before conceding to you. I'll buy you a pint after.'

'What did you have in mind?' asked May, who was by now willing to try almost anything that could unblock the investigation.

'You'll see.' Bryant rewound his scarf around his throat and filled his pockets with peppermints. 'As much as I hate to expose my lungs to the King's Cross traffic, we'll never solve anything at our desks. Get your coat on.'

Bryant had noticed that the eight o'clock performance at Leicester Square's Prince Charles Cinema that evening was Antonioni's *Blow-Up*, and knew that his contact would be there. The cinema had discovered the popularity of inter-active film events, from *Singalong-a-Grease* to *The Wicker Man*, where the audience were handed, with their admission tickets, party bags containing fox-shaped masks, sparklers, song sheets and maypole streamers.

Like Ray Kirkpatrick, Nathan Buff had a portfolio career. During weekdays he was on call, freelancing for the

Metropolitan Police Film Unit, London's fifteen-strong team that provided police services for filming. At the weekends he worked at the Cinema Museum in the Elephant and Castle, running the projectors for silent film shows. He was also the resident film critic for the Saturday arts magazine at *Hard News*.

He often wished his love life was as busy. As most of the girls he knew were not prepared to have in-depth conversations about the pros and cons of Peter Jackson's extended cuts for the *Lord of the Rings* films (he was generally in favour of them all with two exceptions, the farewell scene from *The Return of the King* and the opening scenes of *An Unexpected Journey*), he was attending tonight's screening unaccompanied.

Buff ritualized his cinema-going because the experience always left him with a profound sense of security and stability. Cinemas were palaces of promise, wherein he was offered everything the world might deny. He was always the first to arrive in an auditorium for the next show because he enjoyed the pristine calm of an empty cinema, and always sat in the same seat, B12, because it afforded him the correct amount of peripheral vision and let him rest his knees in the curved indentation between seats A12 and A13. He knew tonight's film by heart, and was excited by the prospect of watching a version that incorporated newly discovered footage. He was so excited that as he lowered his ample rump on to the velour dome of his fold-down seat, he failed to spot the detectives entering the auditorium.

May pushed aside the red door curtain and took a look around. 'I assume that's the man we're looking for,' he said from the side of his mouth.

'Where?' Bryant peered into the gloom of the auditorium. In half-light he had the eyesight of a mole with cataracts.

'Over there. The one who looks like a character from a fruity Victorian novel. You can't miss him – in the middle of the second row with the handlebar moustache, cravat and waistcoat.'

'Yup, that's him all right,' said Bryant. 'He's the greatest film expert in the country. When he was a child he became obsessed with James Bond movies. Got into terrible trouble for shaving his cat and painting it gold.'

A moment later, just as the film's certificate appeared on the screen, Buff felt a tap on his shoulder. It was unthinkable that anyone should interrupt him during his viewing experience. The staff had long ago learned to stay away until after the lights had come up.

'We need to talk to you,' said Bryant in his worst stage whisper. 'Police business.'

Buff was unable to tear his eyes from the credits. 'Can't it wait until the end of the film?'

'Come on, up,' said May, leading the reluctant Buff upstairs. He was not prepared to tolerate any nonsense. 'What's so special about that film anyway?'

To Buff, all films were special, even the really bad ones starring Keanu Reeves. 'It's a British art-house classic.'

'Oh, one of those where the actors leave five-minute pauses between lines and the rest is tinkling piano music and a lot of staring out of windows. My colleague wants your advice on a police matter, heaven knows why. Is there somewhere quiet where we can go?'

The Phoenix Artist Club was the last surviving bastion of old Soho, even though it was not technically situated in Soho itself but on the other side of Charing Cross Road, which divided Soho from – what exactly? An odd wedge of no man's land once known as St Giles, some rain-blackened houses, an unkempt square, several pungent alleyways and a dilapidated church. For centuries it had acted as the connective tissue to more vital organs. Now it looked as if a bomb had been dropped on the neighbourhood. An insalubrious past had been cleared to make way for a bright, bland future.

On the corner of one alley stood a lone survivor, the Phoenix Theatre, a curved and colonnaded playhouse constructed in restrained Italianate style. Underneath the building was something odder: the clubhouse, open to members and those who could answer an assortment of whimsical theatre-related questions.

The detectives made their way down its winding staircase. In the light of the gleaming brass bar Nathan Buff appeared much younger. 'I thought it had to be you, Mr Bryant,' he said with a theatrical exhalation. 'The way you turned up at the door, like Rick Blaine surveying his nightclub in *Casablanca*. Well, you've ruined my evening's entertainment. How can I help you?'

'Pictures in the Park,' said Bryant. 'What do you know about it?'

'I set it up.' Buff flagged down a barman and magnanimously ordered pints. He seemed pent-up with a tremendous energy that could be unleashed by any discussion of films. 'A fortnightly event sponsored by my paymasters, the philistines at *Hard News*. Cult cinema attracts an urban audience, solvent and youthful. Our outdoor screenings of *The Wicker Man* had a positively pagan impact.' His pint of Guinness had left a foamy stripe across his moustache that Bryant longed to flick away.

'Weren't you invaded by anti-capitalist rioters?' said May, looking around at the motley theatricals inhabiting the red velvet bar stools.

'A disruption coordinated by a rival critic,' Buff explained, wincing at the thought. 'Just a blogger, of course, not a *real* writer. We professional critics are losing readers to unpaid amateurs. I was J. J. Hunsecker to his Sidney Falco.'

'That analogy doesn't run true, though, does it?' said Bryant. 'You're more Sheridan Whiteside to his Hildy Johnson.'

May had no idea that his partner ever went to the cinema. Just when he thought he knew everything about Bryant that there was to know, the old curmudgeon still had the capacity to surprise him. 'Once you two have finished out-geeking each other,' he intervened, 'could we perhaps get back to the matter in hand?'

Bryant felt inside his jacket. 'Do you have a club membership list?'

'Why do you want to know?'

'Our investigator turned up this at the crime scene. Unfortunately it was torn in half and has no date.' He handed over a clear plastic packet. 'This is a ticket stub to Pictures in the Park, isn't it?'

Buff held it to the light and examined it. 'Yes, but it could be for any performance. We don't print individual tickets; it's too expensive. What else did you find?'

'Those interactive screenings where people throw things. Is there any reason why they'd throw lead shot?'

'No, they mostly chuck toilet rolls and confetti, but we stopped them from doing it because it was too expensive to clear up. Now I don't suppose we'll ever have another screening in a park, seeing as they're all shut.'

'Can we see the membership list?' asked May.

'I always have it with me,' said Buff, flourishing his phone, only to withhold it. 'There are over four hundred names and addresses here. I can't just give you their details. Why do you ask, anyway?'

'Because three women have been murdered in public locations and I suspect their killer chose the spots because he knows them well. Two of the three are sites you use for your Pictures in the Park events. Surely, given your connection with the Metropolitan Film Unit, you'd be keen to help us.'

'I am, and don't call me Shirley,' said Buff, who was incapable of leaving a film reference unacknowledged. He saw the world not through the pleasures and pitfalls of grubby-palmed experience, but through the pristine prism of an anamorphic lens flicking light on to a screen. Life became more manageable when it was viewed at a distance.

May accepted the phone and searched the list, but no names jumped out at him.

There had to be something else. 'Strangulation,' Bryant

caught himself saying aloud. 'How many films are there that feature such a murder method?'

Back on safe ground, Buff perked up. 'Well, the obvious one is Hitchcock's *Frenzy*, about the Covent Garden necktie murderer, but there are countless others before the 1960s because it's a bloodless method of killing. Prior to the arrival of *Psycho* the censors were far more squeamish about showing murders, but they allowed strangulation. *No Way to Treat a Lady*, *The Stranglers of Bombay* and *The Haunted Strangler* are specifically about killers using that method. The trouble is that death occurs in just about every story ever told. We prefer darkness to light. Even *Jane Eyre* and *Rebecca* have houses on fire in the final reel.'

May looked over at his partner and knew he was about to indignantly point out that *Jane Eyre* and *Rebecca* were novels, but for once Bryant spotted his look and stayed quiet. 'Do you personally know all your members?'

'We have some spare time between features so I talk to them, and I guess they're on nodding acquaintance with each other, but only in the way that men are when they find themselves accidentally sharing the same space,' said Buff. 'When we showed *Gravity*, the bar was crowded with chaps arguing about the impossibility of opening an airlock with a spanner.' He sighed. 'We don't have as many women in the club as we'd like.'

'According to your schedule you repeat a lot of the films,' said Bryant. 'Do people come to see them more than once?'

'Are you kidding?' Buff looked from one to the other. 'The same people come again and again. When we ran *The Wicker Man* we had incredible repeat audiences. Not for the Nicolas Cage version, obviously, but for the extended cut of Robin Hardy's original masterpiece.'

'Do you get people with, shall we say, *special interests* at your screenings?' Bryant asked.

'It depends on what you mean,' said the film critic. 'There's a group that usually takes a whole row of seats.'

'Can you point out their names?'

Buff gave him a look of genuine apology. 'I happen to know that one of them is currently under investigation. Flashing in the park.'

'Not at an event of yours, I hope.' Bryant pulled a piece of paper from his pocket and flattened it out on the bar. 'There may be a licence problem with your cinema club. Westminster Council has very precise rules about health and safety.'

'Really? Are you threatening me?' Buff assumed a look of outrage. 'What are you now, *Bad Lieutenant*?'

'Which version?' asked Bryant. 'Harvey Keitel or Nicolas Cage?'

'Maybe you should recast yourself as Lieutenant Kinderman in *The Exorcist*,' sniped Buff loftily. 'He considered himself a movie fan.'

'You'd be better off thinking of me as Richard Attenborough playing Inspector Truscott in *Loot*,' Bryant countered. 'Above the law and liable to lash out when you least expect it. What about film seasons that could appeal to people of an unstable nature?'

'Well, we have our Cold-Blooded Killers season at the Prince Charles. And membership for Pictures in the Park gets you into several other clubs. I can give you some contacts.'

'I want a list of all attendees,' said Bryant. 'There may be something we've missed.'

'In that case I'll need to cross-reference them,' said Buff. 'I'll leave you to look under that particular rock because some pretty strange people attend. There is one thing, though. Whenever we show movies with sequences set in parkland we get a slightly different type of audience.'

Bryant's ears pricked up. 'Really? Different in what way?'

'I suppose they're more romantically inclined. There's something sensual about grass and trees with a breeze blowing through them, especially on film. Have you ever noticed how Fellini's movies all use the sound of the wind to indicate sensuality?'

'I can't say I have,' said Bryant.

'And there's often a slightly sinister mysticism. I suppose an obvious example would be *Picnic at Hanging Rock*, in which three virginal schoolgirls dressed in white simply vanish into thin air in an idyllic pastoral setting. *Blow-Up* has a famous scene featuring a murder filmed in South London's Maryon Park. David Hemmings plays a photographer who witnesses the killer and his victim struggling in the distance. He takes photographs, but when he looks at the pictures he can't be sure if they show a murder. The mood of the film is strangely sensual. There's a mimed game of tennis, and the trees keep rustling – it's a sylvan setting that's poisoned somehow, and maybe someone dies or makes love, it's hard to tell.'

'Have you ever screened that in Russell Square?' asked Bryant.

Buff did not need to check his phone. 'Just last week, last of the season,' he answered. 'The location is so perfect that in some scenes it was hard to tell where the screen ended and the park began.'

34

'PLACES HAVE THE POWER TO HAUNT AND DISTURB'

'What is wrong with you?' asked May as they left the club and headed out into the crowds of Leicester Square. 'We're running out of time to uncover a link between the victims and you're arguing about obscure films.'

'It's the only way to get anything out of Buff,' said Bryant. 'He wants to believe he's in the movie of his life, but he loves being involved in real-life crimes. I need him to give me a name.'

'It's a lot to hang on a torn cinema ticket.' May pushed through a group of capering silver-clad jugglers tossing burning clubs to each other.

'It's a long shot, I'll give you that.' Bryant parted the buskers with his walking stick, causing them to scatter fiery skittles everywhere. One of them called him a wanker.

'You think someone was corrupted by watching a few weird movies? The idea that films are linked to antisocial behaviour was discredited years ago.'

They turned into Charing Cross Road. 'John, there are a huge number of documented cases in which killers have obsessively watched films replicating their crimes,' said

Bryant. 'Could you slow down a little? I'm still in recovery. Maybe we'll get lucky. Right now we don't have much else to go on.' He looked about at the milling crowds. 'I'm not ready to go home yet. That last beer cleared my head.'

'I doubt that very much, Arthur.'

'Rubbish, it's a brain sharpener. They used to give it to children.'

'Only because London water was too disgusting to drink.' May sighed. 'Well, I officially have no home life any more so I might as well carry on discussing the case with you over another pint.'

'That's the spirit,' said Bryant. 'What could be more satisfying than your work? Everything else is just marking time until you peg out.'

They made their way down to the Coal Hole pub on the Strand, thence to the Wolf Parlour, the gloomy Gothic room at its rear which had been christened by the great tragedian Edmund Keane. Since the conversion of the Nun and Broken Compass into luxury flats, the Coal Hole had returned to being Bryant's favourite old pub.

'I hear Land's reconstruction footage isn't usable. He's probably unhappy with the performances.' May summoned the barman and ordered two pints of Farmer's Arse Best Bitter. 'If the killer used Beauchamp's leash to strangle Helen Forester, surely he wouldn't have reattached it to the dog afterwards.'

'But that's precisely why he would have done so,' said Bryant. 'The dog then takes away the evidence. What happened to it, do we know?'

'I tried to find out. The leash was still joined to his collar when Meera found him in Green Park but it went missing some time after.'

Bryant was appalled. 'You mean to say we lost the murder weapon? There could be DNA evidence on it.'

'We didn't know it was the weapon. I asked Meera if she remembered what happened to it, and she thinks it was still on the dog when we took him to Mrs Farrier. The old lady insists there was no leash. Dan got her to search for it but she didn't find anything.'

'For God's sake, don't tell Raymond or he'll inform Faraday and we'll be crucified.'

May rubbed a fist across his aching temples. 'Of all the cock-ups we've made, this has to be one of the worst. Dark was right when he talked about other countries being ahead of us. Why are we still conducting investigations without funds or equipment? I read yesterday that everyone in Estonia has a digital identity. They can use hundreds of state services online, access medical records and prescriptions, file taxes, register businesses, manage their education. The system can't be abused, either, because everyone has equal access.'

'We don't need to trace electronic footprints,' said Bryant. 'You and I should be able to solve this together with the judicious application of logic, an innate understanding of human nature and at least three more of these.' He peered into his empty glass. 'And some pork scratchings.'

'Why parks, though? Why does he feel the compulsion to attack them there? That's what I can't fathom. There are plenty of other areas not covered by CCTV. It can't just be that.'

'The deaths have a specific purpose,' Bryant stated. 'To bury the truth.'

'Isn't this the point in the investigation where you drag out some potty academic and go off dowsing for ley lines?' asked May. 'We could really use a little help from someone right now.'

'Ah, I thought I'd find you here,' called a familiar voice. 'I had to go to Marabelle and Dimmock to get an ectoplasmic shield and thought, *I bet they've popped into the Coal Hole.*'

Maggie Armitage, the good-natured Grand Order Grade IV White Witch who ran the Coven of St James the Elder in Kentish Town, barely came up above the height of the bar. 'I say, could I have a milk stout and blackcurrant?' She dug into her purse and laid out several unfamiliar coins, what appeared to be a dehydrated bat and a receipt for two candles purchased from Our Lady of the Pointless Miracle, Walthamstow. Her fingerless gloves were knitted from rainbow lace and her sparkled nails were chipped to reveal multiple layers of paint, like old doors. May watched her with ill-concealed disgust. 'All of my small change appears to be Egyptian. Would you stand me a drink, old sock?'

'Of course, Maggie. It would be my utmost pleasure.' Bryant emptied his coat pocket on to the bar counter and spread out seventeen and sixpence three farthings in pre-1973 money, two tram tickets and a Benwell's Aerial Bombshell left over from a long-past Guy Fawkes night. 'Why do you need an ectoplasmic shield?'

'Oh, Dame Maude's been suppurating again. Her familiar is on the blink. General Fortissimo hasn't been the same since we got rid of the storage heaters. It's too damp for him. When we hold a séance I usually put a dust sheet down for spillages but last night he materialized a psychokinetic membrane that realigned our Sky dish and set off Maude's car alarm. I miss Rothschild. He was a lovely cat when he was alive, but a brilliant medium after he passed beyond. Of course he was never the same once he got the moth.' She looked up at the barman, who was still waiting to be paid. 'I think we may need another sixpence.'

'You're as bad as each other.' May surveyed the mess of pocket contents on the bar counter. 'Let me.' He swiped his contactless credit card over the machine on the counter.

'There,' said Bryant, 'you've just sent your electronic fingerprint to China. If you want to evade detection you should stick to hard cash.'

'But I don't want to evade detection, do I?' said May, suddenly feeling outnumbered by lunatics. 'You haven't been able to use old money for over forty years, and that firework is dangerous.'

'I'm only doing what Jeremy Forester was doing,' Bryant insisted. 'He couldn't use his cards, so he made himself untraceable. But he couldn't avoid returning to his old haunts. He needed to visit his wife and his assistant in person. Dark knew he'd turn up at one of the addresses as soon as he ran out of money.'

'Is this about catching the park strangler?' asked Maggie. 'What larks! Is there anything I can do to help?'

May considered the proposal. This diminutive smiling lady of an uncertain age, her eyes shining and ever-hopeful, her raspberry-shaded hair sprinkled with gold glitter, her throat and bosom festooned with cheap gilt ropes like chain mail on one of King Arthur's camper knights, was honestly and wholeheartedly offering her services. 'What could you do, Maggie?' he asked as kindly as possible.

'I may not know what drives these people to commit such awful crimes,' she said, 'but I do know a lot about the human spirit. The walls between life and death are very thin. I can see them, all of the lost ones. And I know that much ritualized behaviour is associated with green spaces.'

Bryant gave his partner a look that said, *See, you've set her off now.*

'You're not going to tell me about druids,' said May, pleadingly.

'Not at all.' Maggie waved the thought aside. 'We know nothing about real druids. They left behind not a single artefact or image. But there is one thing that connects them to your victims – the idea of sacrifice. Pliny the Elder described a ritual in which druids cut down mistletoe growing on a sacred oak, killed two white bulls and created a potion to cure infertility. There were rituals to suit every occasion. Sacrificial points were constructed in elevated spots where sunrise could be observed – and every single one was in a park.'

'So you think he's carrying out sacrifices?' asked Bryant. 'He uses the same method each time, so it's not simply about the disposal of some perceived enemy. He's following a ritual.'

'Wait, I'm not sure I believe that,' said May uncertainly.

'Many repeat kills have ritualized elements.' Bryant drained his pint. 'His happens to involve women and trees.'

'Trees have great symbolic value,' said the white witch. 'They're rooted in the earth with their heads in the air, but they need water and sun to grow, so all four elements are represented. They offer protection and are symbols of eternal life. The Vedic school of thought is that trees are a sacred, primal form of humanity that has accumulated great wisdom.'

'I'm sorry,' protested May, 'this is getting a bit too *Lord of the Rings* for me.'

Maggie would not be swayed. 'Individual trees have different meanings,' she explained. 'The ash tree symbolizes sacrifice, the oak means power, the fig and willow suggest perception and dreaming, the lime and magnolia, intimacy. Do you know which trees your victims fell beside?'

May's patience was wearing thin. 'I haven't a clue, Maggie. And somehow I don't think it's likely to have any relevance to our case.'

'Then I suggest you study the locations more carefully.' The white witch took a sip of her bilious-looking concoction. 'Places have the power to haunt and disturb. Killers return to crime scenes in order to relive their experiences. He may be doing it because he has to, but he's choosing parks because he needs to *feel* something very specific.'

Bryant took the plastic bag from his pocket and removed the torn cinema ticket, pressing it into Maggie's hand. 'Tell me what you feel,' he instructed. He wanted the white witch to prove her relevance to his sceptical partner.

'You've just contaminated our only piece of evidence,' said May, appalled.

She stayed still with her eyes closed, slowly rubbing her palms in a circular motion. 'He likes the trees,' she said softly. 'They make him feel safe. They prepare his victims.'

'How do they do that?' asked May.

Maggie suddenly opened her eyes. 'By absolving their sins,' she said, 'and preparing them for death. You should be looking for someone who idolizes women in their most natural and pure surroundings. Or one woman, perhaps. A defining experience that left its mark.'

May was determined not to let his partner admit pseudo-science into the case. 'Then here's my problem,' he said. 'The suspects we're looking at don't have the kind of mindset you're describing. One's a gardener; the other's a business-man. They have problems but they also have friends and lovers and jobs. They're not lonely weirdos.'

Maggie answered with the simple logic of a child. 'Then they weren't the only two people in the garden with Mrs Forester that morning. The owner of this cinema ticket was there. You need to start looking for the third person.'

35

'MISERY MAKES MONEY'

They drank until ten p.m., after which Maggie Armitage wandered off on the arm of a complete stranger, a wild-haired creative consultant from Norway whom she decided had a healthy enough aura to conduct her to the tube station. More important, he had an umbrella, and it was bucketing down outside.

'I'm afraid I can't share a taxi with you,' said May. 'I'm heading over the river.'

'Not a problem, got a brolly.' Bryant tapped his furled Smith & Sons on the tiled floor. 'You be off. I may have a pipe before I head back. Alma's banned me from smoking in the flat.'

He dug out his tobacco pouch and watched as May hailed a taxi. Stuffing his pipe with Dick Deadeye Old Salt Marine Tobacco and tamping it down, he slipped into the alleyway beneath the pub awning and lit up.

Bryant raised his nose and sniffed the air. Instead of smelling the sweet reek of seasoned tobacco leaf he picked up a different scent: aniseed and cloves, Parma violets and horse manure, old flavours recalled from childhood.

'I saw a man stealing dogs here,' said a low, lugubrious

voice. 'Short, reddish whiskers. Had a sack full of 'em kept at the alley. Long ago, of course. Always wondered what he did with 'em.'

Bryant turned to see a tall, heavy figure calve itself from the shadows and loom towards him. Greying mutton-chop whiskers extended from a hatless head, almost to the start of a fulsome double chin. The eyes were surprisingly small but bright with life and curiosity, although his whole demeanour could easily be turned to wrath.

'Are you waiting for the curtain?' Bryant asked, awed.

'Me? No, no.' William Schwenck Gilbert tipped back his great square head and jetted cigar smoke into the rainy night. 'My days for that have passed. I could hardly stand it inside the Savoy tonight, listening to them rustling their librettos like leaves in an autumn forest. The band is two violins short and of a very indifferent quality. They need to engage better string players. And the ladies are banging their fairy wands all over the stage, so that the diamonds in the heads keep dropping out. It's less a revival, I feel, than a resuscitation.'

Bryant looked back at the speaker's grey sagging features and understood. His smoking companion was one half of British theatre's most celebrated duo, but late in his life, and world-weary. Gilbert and Sullivan had fallen from fashion. Sadder still, Gilbert was now alone. *Iolanthe* had first been performed at the Savoy in 1882, but had been revived after Arthur Sullivan's death. The great theatre was in its dying days. The impresario Richard D'Oyly Carte had quickly followed Sullivan to his grave, and his wife was overseeing the final few productions.

Times were changing. From out in the Strand the hoot of automobile horns mingled with the clop of horses' hooves. Gilbert had learned to drive, and had already been in an accident.

'Yes, I spoilt a parson,' Gilbert said, reading his mind, for he was but a figment of it. 'He came off his bicycle. I went over the dashboard and my wife was pitched very comfortably into a hedge, where she looked like a large and quite unaccountable bird's nest.' He barked out a laugh.

'May I just say that *Iolanthe* is one of my—' Bryant began, but Gilbert raised his hand.

'Please don't tell me how you thought the music superior to the libretto. I sometimes think the audiences only came to see the new electric light.' Gilbert drew on his cigar, making it glow and crackle. 'I do miss him, you know. Nothing was ever as good again. People think Sullivan and I could no longer speak, but we were about to be reunited when he had the confounded temerity to die. He passed on the day of St Cecilia – the patroness of music. No topsy-turvydom there, just plain propriety. I suppose they let him into Paradise because he wrote "Onward, Christian Soldiers". How typically Sullivan! Of course, I took the blame for our falling-out. How everybody loved Sullivan, so kind, so patient, so melodious. They saw me as a bitter, selfish creature. It was because I cared about the words. Was that so terrible? Genius exacts its price. Is it wrong to be demanding when one's livelihood is at stake? You're a detective, would you settle for less than best?'

'You know me?' Bryant's blue eyes widened.

'Well, I'm dead and you're imagining me, so I should know you.' Gilbert tapped the ash from his cigar over the alley grate. 'I assume I've been returned for a purpose, so ask away and let's get it over with. What don't you know about me? I kept lemurs in my garden. I've been to the cinema. I watched Crippen's trial. I purchased the axe and block from *The Yeomen of the Guard*. I am six foot four inches tall. You know all this. Come then, ask away.'

'Women,' said Bryant.

'Ah. And there you have me.'

'Is it true that after dinner you used to send the men off and stay with the ladies?'

'Not always, but often. The younger ones, anyway. My wife, my kitten, paid no heed. When everything you do and say is based upon the idea of paradox, you may behave as you wish.'

'You drowned saving a young woman's life.'

'Yes, well. Folly was my foe and wit my weapon. Unfortunately pond water was my downfall.'

Bryant knew all about his hero's ingenious paradoxes, his balancing of warmth, comedy and darkness, an application that existed as much in his private life as on the page. 'The older women,' he said. 'Katisha in *The Mikado*, Ruth in *The Pirates of Penzance*, Lady Jane in *Patience*. Why did you always make fun of them?'

'Oh, *that*. I needed contraltos to balance my comic baritones,' replied Gilbert. 'And they weren't so hard done by. I always married them off. Is that all you wanted to ask?'

'Your relationship to women—'

'Your impertinence is second only to your perseverance, sir, so let me answer thus. I made fun of them because I loved them; does that seem strange to you? Men are made by women, so we are right to question them. But we know women are superior, despite their tendency to be over-absorbed by their ideals, so we listen and learn from them. We place them on pedestals, set them in pastoral surroundings and idolize them, but when we have finished learning and they cease to be novel we allow our love to turn to dust. And that, my dear fellow, is the paradox of man.'

'It won't help me catch a murderer,' groused Bryant.

'I'm a librettist, not a consulting detective,' said Gilbert tartly. 'Might I suggest you employ the principle of paradox in your investigation? Why are you at odds with your partner? Surely you may both be right about these terrible acts, committed with both passion and purpose. What if the killer attacked with reason and discovered pleasure?'

'That hadn't occurred to me,' Bryant admitted, puffing his pipe.

'Then before I leave you I'll trade you a question,' said Gilbert, putting out his hand to see if the rain had ceased.

'My theory of topsy-turvydom dictates that in British society no political measures can endure because one party will assuredly undo all that the other party has done. No social reforms will be attempted if there is no capital to be made. And while grouse can be shot and foxes worried to death, the legislative action of the country will remain at a standstill. In short, if you empty the buildings and fill the jails there will be general and unexampled prosperity. Misery makes money. Has all that come to pass?'

'That and more,' said Bryant. 'The only difference is that we are powerless to do anything about it.'

'Then I'm glad I had a voice and used it,' Gilbert replied, withdrawing something shiny from his pocket. 'This is a new invention. It's called a reservoir pen. I was presented with it during the run of *The Mikado*. I have no use for it any more.'

He handed the silver and tortoiseshell fountain pen to Bryant, then stepped out into the alley's chill air. Turning in the direction of the Savoy Theatre, he released a baritone sigh. 'We were as much an institution as Westminster Abbey,' he said. 'I am unmoored without him. There is no Gilbert without a Sullivan. Treasure your partnership with Mr May, and remember how lost he will feel when *you* are turned to dust.'

'I'm only three years older than him!' cried Bryant indignantly. 'Bloody cheek. He might go first – he's like you, he's got a dodgy ticker!' Gilbert was striding slowly away into the misted street. 'You should never have argued over a bit of bloody carpet!' he called. 'And your last two operas were rubbish!' No reply came from the empty swirl of mist.

Bryant pocketed the fountain pen anyway.

THE SIXTH DAY

36

'WE'VE COME FULL CIRCLE'

Saturday morning saw the appearance of what Janice Longbright's mother used to call 'a continental sun', as fierce blue skies sharpened the city's bristling skyline.

The headmaster of the Royal Order of St John in Blackheath answered Longbright's call. 'Nathan Buff, you say? I'm afraid we don't allow the film club to be held here at the school any more.' There was a cool edge to his voice. 'Some of the audiences were rather too *outré* for us. Let me put you in touch with Fergus Carrington. He's the art teacher who ran the cinema club here until I discovered the sort of things they were showing and asked him to find an alternative venue.'

Longbright tried another number. On her fourth try she struck lucky. As it was Saturday, Carrington could be found at the National Film Theatre, so she headed for the South Bank.

It felt appropriate that a nation whose film industry had passed from being on permanent life support to a state of assisted death should have its pantheon shoved beneath a railway bridge. The National Film Theatre was a building designed to punish people for enjoying movies, and proved there was such a thing as feng shui, if only because you knew when it wasn't there.

It was fair to say that Fergus Carrington was in touch with his inner film freak. On a freezing winter morning he was wearing an XXL *Matrix Revolutions* T-shirt advertising one of the least loved SF movies of the past fifty years, and smelled as if he'd been lifting bricks on a hot day. The Gandalf-bearded art master gazed upon Longbright as if she was being delivered to him gift-wrapped on a conveyor belt, a look that crossed the line from inappropriate to creepy in a matter of seconds.

'What have I done to attract the attentions of such a lovely WPC?' he asked, seating himself a little too far within the circumference of Longbright's personal space in the NFT's depressing coffee shop.

'We don't say WPC any more,' said Longbright briskly, accepting the membership list she had requested from him.

'These were all I could find,' he explained. 'Members are allowed to bring one guest, and we don't keep records of those names.'

Unfolding the page listing members from the Pictures in the Park subscription list, she compared the two. Four names fell into both groups. 'Do you know any of these people?' she asked.

'Not personally but they may be on our website.' He pecked at his phone and squinted. 'Yes, they're all paid-up members.'

'And they're all still active in your club?'

'I only have their names, not their attendance details.'

'What kind of films do you show?'

Carrington looked suddenly wary. 'We operate under club conditions, so we're not governed by general exhibition certificates.'

'What does that mean?'

'It means we have a special licence to show films that have not been passed by the BBFC.'

'You're talking about pornography?'

Carrington looked at her pityingly. 'There's no such thing, my love. We show countercultural art films, experimental shorts and cult rarities. Sometimes the members contribute works they've made themselves.'

'A man called Nathan Buff told us that your club has some unusual guests and members.'

'Oh, *Nathan*. That's what you get for talking to someone in the pay of Hollywood. It's true that we've hosted artists from the American adult film scene and have covered a number of transgressive subjects. But what our members watch and what they do in their private lives are entirely separate. It's an academic forum.'

'I appreciate that, Mr Carrington, but we're looking for a man who follows women into public parks and chokes them to death.'

Carrington shifted uncomfortably.

'So it's possible that he may be interested in watching others perform similar acts, even if it's only make-believe. Is there anyone on that shortlist who you think is capable of causing harm?'

Carrington hesitated, and then appeared to reach an uncomfortable decision. 'There's one, but the name isn't here.'

'I don't understand,' said Longbright.

'We had someone who did rather bother me. There was a season back in the spring – films and documentaries about aberrant psychopathy, sadism, masochism, victim status and so on. Such events are intended to encourage legitimate dialogue around taboo subjects. Many of the people who come along have a professional interest in the issue under discussion. But I must admit I've wondered about some of the attendees.'

'Can you recall any particular instances?'

'There was one after-film conversation that especially disturbed me, partly because I remembered what happened

303

later. We'd shown an uncertificated documentary called *Narratives of Guilt and Conscience* by a renowned American neuroscientist.'

Someone dropped a tray of cups behind them. Longbright flinched, her concentration momentarily lost. 'What was the film about?'

'It used explicit documentary footage to explore the idea that the brain imposes a narrative on harmful events, which the individual must then decide whether or not to act upon. This person became very agitated and disrupted the discussion group so much that we had to call a halt to it.'

'Do you remember his name?'

'Yes, but – well, rather unusually, it was a woman. And she wasn't interested in killing. She wanted to die. Her name was Lauren Posner.'

'Posner,' said Longbright. 'She saw half a dozen films about victims, self-harmers and masochists, mostly academic documentaries, and subsequently took her own life.'

'So we've come full circle,' said Bryant. 'All this time we've been following the wrong case. It didn't begin with Helen Forester's death, it started with her son's killer. Hell's teeth, I should have seen this.'

'If the ticket stub was hers,' said May, 'then Maggie is wrong and there was no third man at Clement Crescent. So how did the ticket end up in Russell Square?'

The question hung in the air as Raymond Land appeared in the operations room with the morning papers. 'Look at this. *"Experimental Police Unit"* – that's this dump, apparently – *"forced illegal closure of London parks"*. Faraday's hung us out to dry. Darren Link's taking the bloody case away! We have to hand over all our files this weekend so that the CID can start afresh first thing on Monday morning.'

'Then we've still got a bit of time,' said Bryant. 'If we delay giving them the documentation until Sunday night we could be in with a chance.'

'How would we do that?' asked May.

Bryant gave a shrug. 'I don't know – tell them our computers are down or something. Surely Dan can help us make up some rubbish about the operating system being upgraded or our passwords being mislaid. He could say we've caught an infection.'

'You mean a virus,' said Land.

'Yes, that's it, or we could simply barricade the doors.'

Land studied his most senior detective as if examining an unknown biological specimen. 'What is it with you? Why don't you ever give up?'

'For the same reason that you give up so easily; it's in my nature,' Bryant countered. '"Accept finite disappointment but never lose infinite hope" – Martin Luther King, Jr.'

'You don't understand, Raymond,' said May. 'Darren Link thinks we're responsible for getting the parks closed, but it's Faraday following his own agenda. We need to set the record straight.'

'So you have to help us by keeping Link off our backs,' Bryant pleaded. 'He's not a bad chap, just rule-bound and prone to outbursts of violence. It's probably best not to tell him the absolute truth. Say the two Daves went through a cable and it'll take us until Monday morning to get everything running again.'

'I will not be complicit in this!' Land protested. 'My pension is on the line. You two don't have to worry about retirement because you're going to be carried out of this office feet first, but I have a caravan on the Isle of Wight to pay for. I want my time in the sun, doing what every other retired copper does, reading and drinking until my liver packs up. I've earned it.'

'Thank you for that, *mon petit crapaud*. Your role in this is easy: call Link and lie through your dental crockery. Make him believe we're contrite and that we've already closed up the case all nice and ready for him, the problem being that we can't access it for forty-eight hours.'

Land looked as if he was about to have a heart attack. 'And what if you fail? What happens then?'

'We hand over the files, just as we promised. What could possibly go wrong?'

'I hate it when you say that. What if he wants to come around here?'

'Tell him the two Daves are having the place fumigated because they're concerned that the coffin in the basement is part of a medieval plague pit and there could be micro-organic pathogens harbouring Black Death bacilli.'

Land's eyes narrowed. 'Have you ever lied to me like this?'

'To be honest, I can't actually recall the last time I told you the truth,' said Bryant placidly. 'Except just then.' He leaned back, studying the operations room whiteboard. Upon it had been drawn every link and interview, arranged in a messy timeline covered in arrows, dotted lines, scribbles, pieces of coloured wool, question marks, photographs, Post-it notes, taped scraps of paper and, for some reason, the lid from a packet of wine gums.

'I don't know why you keep staring at that,' said Land, mystified. 'It looks like an ordnance survey map of the Himalayas.'

'Yes, but somewhere in that mountain lies the answer,' said Bryant, brushing his fingertips over the connections and dead ends. 'It's right here in front of us, waiting to be picked out. The CID sometimes coordinate as many as thirty thousand interviews in their own murder cases. They'll take maybe three thousand statements and list hundreds of suspects. We make do with a staff of ten and a cat.'

'For God's sake, be honest and admit for once that you haven't the faintest idea what you're looking for,' said Land, irritated.

'Oh, but I do know what I'm looking for.' Bryant widened his cornflower-blue eyes. 'Proof that my instincts are correct. John and I may disagree on the purpose of the deaths but in a way I think we're both right.'

'I hate it when you talk in riddles,' Land complained. 'If I find out you're withholding information—'

'But I'm not.' Bryant waved his hand across the anarchy of the whiteboard. 'It's all here. The trick is seeing a simple pattern in all this chaos. We don't have the resources to track five hundred suspects so we have to make something else work in our favour, and you know what that is? A perspective so perversely eccentric that no one in their right mind would think of using it.'

'What?' Land had the look of a man in a nose-diving plane who'd just realized he hadn't paid attention to the safety demonstration. 'That's your big idea for making an arrest this weekend, is it? Along with sabotaging the computers? Well, heaven help us. I needn't have worried; it's obviously all in hand. I'll go ahead and book my Isle of Wight watercolour course for next week, then.'

'I wouldn't do that just yet,' cautioned Bryant. 'I may have to break the law first. I need to see the two Daves about borrowing a pickaxe.'

37

'HE'S IDEALIZING THE FEMALE FORM'

'And so the mighty machinery of the criminal investigation unit moves into high gear once more,' said Colin Bimsley, dangling himself over the end of a steel rubbish container. 'The old man declares we'll have one final mad dash at the case before losing it, and what do we uncover? The remains of a dinner party, a deflated exercise ball and a dead cat.'

'How come Heidi hasn't got her hands dirty yet?' asked Meera, sorting through the reeking yellow Lidl bags that had been stacked beside the bin. '"Welcome to London, get some rubber gloves on, you'll be poking through dirty nappies this weekend." Why is it always *us*?'

'We make too good a job of it.' Colin fished out a perfume bottle and uncorked the top to sniff it. 'There's still some left in this. What do you think?'

Meera was disgusted. 'I'm not dabbing that on my skin. You don't know where it's been.'

'It's a knock-off, anyway. Chanel only has one N.' Colin dropped the bottle back in the container. 'You wouldn't last long as one of those recyclers who take comestibles past their sell-by dates from bins.'

'Have you ever been to India?' said Meera.

'No, have you?'

'That's not the point. My grandparents came from a city they still can't stop calling Bombay, and once they got here the first thing they did was buy a vacuum cleaner. They spent years trying to get away from mess and dirt. Thank God they can't see me now. They wouldn't think we'd progressed very far.' Rocking back on her heels, she snapped her gloves off. 'I'm done. We're not going to find anything useful here.'

They had searched through detritus from a number of households this week. Last night they'd checked waste bins used by Ritchie Jackson (disinfected, eerily neat) and Sun Dark's restaurant (tangy, noodle-heavy). This morning the last search on their list smacked of desperation. As Jackson's former crush, Sofia Anzelmo was only tangentially connected with the case, but they were running out of leads.

'There's a big stack of magazines that look like they came from her flat,' said Colin, pulling out some food-sticky copies of *OK!* magazine and *Education Today*. 'She was a primary school teacher for a time, wasn't she?'

'Yeah, somewhere over Leytonstone way. Now she works in a recruitment agency off Baker Street. Go on then, chuck me half of that pile, we'll get through it quicker.' Meera dropped beside Colin on the concrete platform by the bins, riffling through magazines. '"*Most women wear the wrong bra size*". We're not going to bring this bloke in under forty-eight hours without any fresh leads, are we?'

Colin checked inside a pizza box, but Meera slapped him. 'Let's say, for the sake of argument,' he said, 'that Jeremy Forester knocked off his nanny and his wife. He could be using the whole hiding-from-debtors alibi as a double bluff. Most murders are committed by the marital partner. I could see you murdering someone.'

'I wouldn't murder a husband, I'd make him suffer by never leaving. "*How to get buttocks like Kim Kardashian*". God, I could be at home doing laundry instead of this.' Meera straightened out her legs. 'I've got bacon rind all over my boots. My flat looks like an Ikea storage facility. I'm starting to smell like a bin bag. I'm so rarely at my flat that the council doesn't even call round to see if I'm dead.'

'You could have got married to that doctor bloke,' Colin reminded her.

'What, that's my choice, is it? Someone my mother picked out for me or bin duty with you?'

Colin Bimsley had never been good at disguising his feelings. Right now he looked like a slapped puppy.

'Sorry, Colin. Being with you isn't the bad part. I'd rather look at you than look at a bin.' She set about pulling apart copies of *Empire* film magazine. 'What have we here? Cult Cinema Club – isn't that the place Lauren Posner went to?' She turned the page. 'There's a special offer for an event, underlined – *Narratives of Guilt and Conscience*. You don't think she knew Posner, do you? That would be a real lead.'

'Let's ask her,' said Colin.

Bryant found himself in the vast colour-plate restoration room of the British Library, this time with art history lecturer Peregrine Summerfield, the self-styled Ozymandias of Stoke Newington, who had abandoned a promising career as a painter in order to teach. It had not surprised the detective to discover that Summerfield and Kirkpatrick were half-brothers. They might have been twins, but for the fact that Summerfield appeared more benign. He favoured suits and ties (not that much of a tie could be seen beneath his immense ginger beard), and didn't look as if he wanted to beat people up for making grammatical errors.

'All hail, *senex investigator*,' said Peregrine, setting aside some kind of arcane wooden calligraphy tool and pumping Bryant's hand vigorously. 'I heard you'd been in. If you're after our Mr Kirkpatrick, he's away attending a course on cryptographic semantics. I'm covering for him.'

'Actually it's you I wanted to see,' Bryant replied. 'You may remember we talked in the past about symbolism in paintings. You were most helpful in a couple of our investigations.'

'Yes, you promised to buy me a beer after and never did,' said Summerfield. 'Apparently you do that to everyone.'

'Well, I'm about to do it again,' said Bryant.

'Ask away, why not?' Summerfield sighed. 'I've nothing better to do. I've given up trying to get schoolkids to look at art. What they really want to do is go to M&M World. I'd only take a child there if I hated it enough to want its teeth to fall out. What's wrong with the National Gallery? Since when did Hans Holbein's *The Ambassadors* become less enlightening than a dancing chocolate?'

'I forgot, you don't like the modern world much, do you?'

Summerfield looked mystified. 'What's to like? In my world it's still 1752, but I have to stick my head out into the rain occasionally to buy a prawn sarnie. I can't tell a compote from a compost but I know I don't need three hundred branches of the same coffee shop in one city. Nothing gets better. We're all treated like babies. We're told that doors open outward and escalators stop moving at the end. Next they'll be reminding us to breathe in and out. Strewth, the rich panoply of life from Primark cradle to Co-op grave laid out in all its artery-hardening glory. No wonder the bloody suicide rate has gone up.'

'I take it you don't get out much these days,' said Bryant, noting that Summerfield used his desk as a dining table and possibly a bedroom.

'No, and I'm staying where no one who's interested in baking shows or singing competitions will ever venture. I pray that when we find life on another planet it turns out to be a lot more fun than ours and that they have relaxed immigration laws. I really do prefer 1752. If we'd had the internet back then people would have spent their days looking at Rembrandt's *Storm on the Sea of Galilee*, not shots of Justin Bieber's dick. What can I do you for?'

'It's about women being strangled in parks.'

'Actually, I did see that in this morning's *Metro*. You got all the parks shut. Well done you. What're you going to do next, get Admiralty Arch turned into a Jamie's Italian?'

'We've been set up, Peregrine.'

'Hey, I read it in a commuter free sheet so it must be true.'

'I need to understand the killer's motives.'

'Shouldn't you be trying to figure out who it is first?'

'That's not how it works with me,' said Bryant. 'I'm drawing a blank with traditional methods, and thought it might be helpful to look at the lessons we can draw from art.'

Summerfield had a scratch at his beard. 'That's a bit like deciding what crops to plant by checking a bus timetable, but go on.'

'I was thinking about scandals involving nude women in paintings. Strangulation, you see. The victims weren't disfigured or even – *disrespected*. I know that's a bizarre thing to say, considering they were murdered. Their bodies weren't found as they fell.'

'You mean he arranges them?'

'Not exactly. He tidies them up a little, moving the limbs, and gives them some grace in death.'

'Do their eyes remain open?'

'Yes. Why?'

'I think I can help you. Come with me.' Summerfield led the way to an immense metal bookcase in the corner of the floor and pulled down a large volume of art prints. 'Broadly speaking, there are two kinds of female nude, the virgin and the whore. In the former grouping you get the Nereids, nymphs, goddesses, the Madonna. So without the benefit of clothing to denote class, what distinguishes the latter? The gaze.' He tapped a colour plate. 'Goya's *La maja desnuda* was commissioned to be hung in a private cabinet filled with nude paintings, the late-eighteenth-century equivalent of a porn stash. It wasn't her body that caused outrage, but her eyes. She's looking directly at you without any shame. Goya repainted her with clothing but the effect is still the same, almost more so because she's in modern attire. Goya was charged with moral depravity but escaped prosecution. The two versions hang side by side at the Prado in Madrid.' He flipped a page to reveal another nude. '*The Rokeby Venus* by Velázquez features a naked woman with her back to you, but she's looking directly at the viewer in a hand-mirror. The gaze is pure when downcast, offensive when direct. Women must show guilt, especially if they're supine and indoors. Move them outside and even the most brazen automatically become virginal. Pastoral surroundings always restore virginity – with one exception.'

'Manet's *Le Déjeuner sur l'herbe*,' said Bryant.

'Exactly. Two men – Manet's brother and brother-in-law – enjoy a picnic fully clothed while a naked woman smiles and blatantly stares at the viewer. The woods of Paris were filled with prostitutes but nobody ever mentioned it, and suddenly here was this disgusting painting that confronted the truth and normalized it, exposing the hypocrisy surrounding female sexuality.'

'You think he kills them in parks because it will reveal the truth about them?'

Summerfield closed the book and replaced it. 'What are parks but pieces of earthly paradise in the city? He's not just restoring their purity, he's preparing them for heaven.'

'So he's idealizing the female form.'

Summerfield shrugged. 'Dunno, mate, you're the cop.'

While he was there, Bryant decided to look in on Duncan Aston. He found the map restorer hard at work on an immense diagram of Joseph Bazalgette's great water main for London. 'I was passing and wondered if I might pick your brains?' asked Bryant.

'I'm not sure I have any left after staring at this thing all day,' said Aston, pushing back the sleeves of his sweater.

Bryant peered at the map with and without various layers of focal lenses. 'What are you doing to it?'

Aston rubbed his eyes. 'It was originally hand-coloured but the inks have faded, which means the finer lines can't be easily interpreted. The question is how much do we put back before the original becomes debased? Some of the colours can no longer be accurately reproduced.'

'And do you have an answer?'

'We add just enough original pigment to make the diagram readable again, no more.'

'I wish you could do that with London,' said Bryant sadly. 'Just put back enough of the buildings we destroyed to restore some of the city's unique atmosphere.'

'Then you'd have to spray all the buildings black.' Aston sat back to examine his work. 'Wars and fires left their marks on every stone. Nothing remains in its pristine state for long. What did you want to ask me about?'

Bryant's reverie was broken. 'Last spring, after the accident in the tunnel, did Lauren Posner say anything else to you about it?'

Aston was visibly disappointed by the turn in the conversation. 'In what way?'

'Did she mention the reaction of the boy's nanny, Sharyn Buckland?'

'Not that I recall. I don't think either of them reacted strongly at the time because they didn't realize what had happened. The boy was fine when she left. He died quite unexpectedly in hospital.'

'And only the nanny was with him in the ambulance on the way there?'

'I think the others went directly to the hospital. A lorry driver, and perhaps the traffic officer.'

'When did Ms Posner start to blame herself for what had happened?'

'Right from the moment she heard he'd died, but she quickly got worse. I went to church with her sometimes. I'm also a Catholic. I've learned to stop apologizing about my faith.'

Bryant decided to keep his counsel on that score. 'Ms

Posner attended a cinema club which held discussion groups about various states of neurosis and anxiety.'

'She was drawn to self-examination. I tried to stop her. The films upset her.'

'Did she ever take you?'

'She usually went with a girlfriend.'

'Do you remember her name?'

'No, we never met.'

'Does the name Sofia Anzelmo ring a bell?'

'I don't think so. Lauren kept her friends separate. She didn't talk about them much.'

Bryant studied the Bazalgette diagram once more. The system of pipes and floodgates seemed as complex and confusing as the case map on the PCU's office wall.

'A man of great foresight,' he mused. 'When Bazalgette planned London's sewage network his calculations allowed a generous level of sewage production for every Londoner. At the last minute he realized he'd only ever do the job once and doubled the figures. If he hadn't, London's sewage system would have burst soon after the mass construction of tower blocks in the 1960s. I'd like to think that something I did would be of use 150 years later.' He tapped his hand on the table in admonition. 'Forgive me, I'm a foolish old man much given to fancies. I'll be in touch if I hear anything more.'

Aston watched as the shambling figure donned his hat and searched for the clearly marked exit door, repeatedly walking right past it. He wondered how such a fellow could have ever ended up in a police unit.

38

'WHY WOULD ANYONE WANT A SEVEN-YEAR-OLD BOY DEAD?'

'Where is she going?' Meera asked, trying to see over the heads of the tourists leaving Camden Town tube station.

'Give me your hand,' said Colin. 'I'm not trying to touch you – look, just give me your hand.'

When she realized why Colin was offering, Meera gave in. She was too short for the crowds of Camden, especially in the rain and poor light of late afternoon, when everyone slowed down. The area that had once been the home of hippies and antique dealers now housed seven markets owned by a single corporation. What the borough had gained in tourist currency the residents had lost in every other respect.

It started to rain harder, and the giant statues of boots, skulls, snakes, jets and playing cards that hung from the low brick buildings were dripping sooty water on to the heads of Chinese coach parties. Camden's markets were in thrall to images of old Las Vegas, tattoos and disco-era lighting.

Colin dragged his colleague through a knot of selfie-snapping French students and out into Bayham Street. 'She's just ahead,' he called back. 'Stay with me.'

They had arrived outside Sofia Anzelmo's flat just as she

was leaving it, and were not so much following as trying to keep up with her.

'Now I remember why I never come up here any more,' said Meera, forcing herself through a rat king of drunken neopunks. 'Look at all this crap.' She pointed to a plastic Alice band of fibre-optic LED punk rock hair spikes labelled 'Crazy! Anarchic!' and grimaced. 'Made in China, £14.99. Bloody hell.'

'Hang on, she's crossing the road,' warned Bimsley.

'Why don't we just confront her?'

'Because Janice doesn't want us to. Anzelmo's not considered a part of the main investigation. If we're going to build a case by tomorrow, we have to justify every step.'

'She thinks we're going to screw up, doesn't she?'

'She's just watching out for us, Meera. Darren Link is checking every move the unit makes. She's heading towards Regent's Park. Come on.'

The crowds were thinning. The tourists stayed on the narrow strips of pavement that led to and from the markets.

Sofia Anzelmo was wearing a leopard-pattern raincoat and carrying several bright red shopping bags that made her stand out. Darting through the stalled, steaming traffic, she slipped into the park as Colin and Meera broke into a run behind her.

Regent's Park was the largest of central London's royal parks. Bordered by Marylebone, Camden and the Grand Union Canal, it was overlooked by the city's most elite terraces. From its tree-shrouded theatre and Victorian zoological gardens to its Nursemaids' Tunnel, built to let nannies take their charges to the park without having to cross the road, it retained a sanctified, affluent air. Formally landscaped with fountains and lakes, it was a country park in the heart of the city.

Sofia Anzelmo left the footbridge over the green canal and turned on to a long diagonal path. 'She's cutting across the park,' said Colin. 'I think she's heading for her office in Baker

Street.' He had been playing football here since he was five, and had brought his first date to the boating lake. In the zoological gardens the chimps had stopped having tea parties and the camels no longer gave rides, but occasional roars could be heard from creatures kept far from their natural habitats.

'You can let go of my hand now, Colin.' Meera's fingers were going numb.

'Yeah. Right. Sorry. We can catch her.'

As this part of the park had no gates, Anzelmo was able to pass swiftly and easily through the grasslands. For a moment they lost sight of her beneath the street lamps, but as she reappeared it was clear that someone else was following her. As the figure lurched into the long grass and made to cut her off, Meera ran forward and threw herself on to his back. The pair went over into a mud puddle as Anzelmo screamed.

'Get off me – I was just going to talk to her,' said the Latin-accented young man.

'Why?' Meera demanded to know as she helped him to his feet. 'What were you going to talk to her about?'

'Why?' He looked at her as if she was insane. '*Why?* She's a pretty girl. Is that a crime?'

'See, this is why Janice doesn't like us acting alone,' said Colin, breaking off from explaining to Sofia why they were there. 'That's the second time you've done that.'

'You've ruined my jeans,' said the young Spaniard. 'You can pay to have them cleaned.'

'Piss off before I run you in,' warned Meera.

'Here you go, mate,' said Colin, handing him a tenner. The man took it without another word and limped off.

'God, you're a soft touch.' She turned to Anzelmo. 'We're police officers, Miss Anzelmo. Are you all right?'

'You nearly gave me a heart attack.' She looked about herself to make sure that she hadn't dropped anything. 'Were you following me?'

Meera felt a fool. 'It's part of our ongoing surveillance. We understand you knew Lauren Posner? You attended the cinema club she went to?'

Anzelmo brushed herself down. 'No, she told me about one of the films, though. She gave me a flyer for it.'

'Yeah, we found it in your bin.'

'You've been going through my rubbish? Wouldn't it have been simpler to ask me?'

'How did you know her?'

'We had a friend in common, Ritchie Jackson,' she explained.

'How did *he* know her?'

Sofia rolled her eyes. 'They'd both been involved in the same accident. They talked about it online. I think she found him on Facebook from the name on his truck. The three of us went for a drink together one time. Didn't Ritchie tell you that? You lot don't communicate very well, do you?'

'What was Lauren Posner like?' asked Meera, wiping the mud from her jeans.

'She seemed like she had a lot of problems.'

'What kind of problems?'

'She was very nervous, drinking fast, talking about how terrible her life was. I asked her if she'd ever considered therapy but she said she wouldn't be able to handle it. I promised to go to the movies with her but then Ritchie started getting serious with me and – well, you don't stay in touch with everyone when you split up with a partner, do you?'

'Do you remember anything specific about the meeting, anything that could help us?' Colin asked.

'There was one thing,' said Anzelmo. 'Lauren said she could have prevented what happened to that little boy. I thought it was an odd thing to say. I don't know, she didn't talk a lot of sense. But she kind of implied that it wasn't an accident.'

'OK, we've turned up samples from the site in London Bridge where the traffic accident occurred,' said Dan Banbury, turning his laptop so that everyone in the operations room could see. 'An enterprising member of the EMT snapped them on his phone before the street was cleared, and tried to match them to the glass sliver that was taken from Charlie Forester's head.'

He tapped the first shot. 'This is a splinter from the wine bottle that broke when Posner's car mounted the kerb. As you can see, it's green and jagged. The cheaper the glass the more likely it is to fracture, and this burst into many tiny fragments. The second shot shows some of the debris on the ground. There have been a number of accidents at this spot before. We can exclude windscreen glass because it's laminated to break into smooth-edged globules. This third shot shows a sliver of glass from a wing mirror, which is toughened and hard to shatter. Finally, we have the fragment that was extracted from the back of Charlie Forester's eye.'

John May leaned forward, squinting at the screen. 'But that doesn't look like any of the pieces you've shown us.'

'It's small, less than half a centimetre, but unfortunately lodged in the corner of the eye where it was able to pass to the back of the socket, into the artery containing the optic nerve and then to the brain. The hospital didn't keep the piece so we only have this photograph to go by. The sliver doesn't appear to have come from any of the known sources.'

'Then how did it get into his eye?' asked May. 'Could somebody have fired it from a home-made device?'

'That's a rather fanciful idea,' said Banbury, although the same thought had briefly crossed his mind. 'The theory poses more questions than it answers, because the chances of it entering at that exact point and passing into the artery are small. But there are precedents. I found a case of a child losing her eye from a sliver of foil on a chocolate bar wrapper, and another in which a woman passed a breadcrumb from her thumb to her eye. She died of septicaemia after the crumb was introduced into her tear duct. Anyone can die from anything if luck is against them.'

'So where did this piece come from?' May persisted.

'I don't suppose we'll ever know the answer to that.' Banbury shook his head. 'I went down to the site this morning and found over a dozen different fragments of glass that had missed the mechanical sweepers. Most of them are so small that they would have to be identified at a microscopic level.'

'The traffic cop, Sergeant Samuel Kemp-Bird,' said Longbright, scanning her tablet, 'he gave a press interview about the incident and was very clear about where he felt the blame lay. He'd understood there was to be another traffic control officer at the mouth of the tunnel directing pedestrians away from the vehicles, but this position was never assigned. Kemp-Bird saw the boy bend low, then stand and rub his eye.'

'Can we talk to him?'

'Unfortunately Kemp-Bird died of cancer two months ago.'

'I have to say it *feels* like an accident. There's no evidence to assume it's anything but.' Banbury closed his laptop with an air of finality. 'That's where our real problem lies. It's hard to impose a narrative structure on what was simply a series of bad decisions.'

'So Posner blamed herself for Charlie Forester's death,' said May, 'and Helen Forester was strangled nearly a year after losing her son – why the gap? And if the intention was to kill the nanny as well, why not take care of her first? The mother wasn't in the tunnel when the accident occurred but she *did* get to the hospital, along with Ritchie Jackson, who lost his job for showing compassion, and Sharyn Buckland, who also felt responsible. But none of them has a motive. Why would anyone want a seven-year-old boy dead?'

Before anyone could react to the question, Steffi Vesta appeared in the doorway. 'Mr Forester has checked himself out of the University College Hospital without his doctor's permission. He stole another patient's clothes along with some money and a phone. Nobody knows where he has gone. I have the duty nurse on the line right now.'

May's partner had been silent for an inordinately long time. 'Arthur, do you have any idea where he might go?' May asked, and then looked around. His partner had disappeared.

39

'IT'S AN URBAN EPIDEMIC'

Leticia Claxon had been writing murder mysteries for forty years. Clearly she could not use her family name (which was actually worse, as her middle name was Merriwether, apparently pronounced Midditch, in memory of her titled grandmother) so she went under the pseudonym of Alice Sharp.

Now so desperate that he was prepared to take theories from a crime writer, Bryant had lured Ms Claxon to the Lighterman pub on Regent's Canal with the intention of picking her brain. The idea had precedent: Winston Churchill had once hired the supernatural writer Dennis Wheatley to advance theories about how Germany would set about invading England from the shores of France, so why shouldn't a policeman talk to a novelist?

Claxon was a writer of considerable ingenuity and surprising intellect. She was, however, no prose stylist. In the literary landscape, her words landed like a series of house bricks upon which unwary readers stubbed their toes. Claxon herself had an air of breeding and distinction so carefully cultivated that no one would guess she had once been a housemaid in a Hampstead mausoleum belonging to a wealthy Chinese family – a house she had since been able to purchase with the profits from *A Killer's Eyes*, a novel filmed with two Hollywood stars who possessed such little on-screen chemistry that they had, with grim inevitability, married in real life, their names amalgamating into a single word, much as seaside villas once bore the names of their owners.

Short and slender and expensively turned out, she brushed at the hem of her floral Dries Van Noten frock, folded herself into a corner chair and waited for her white Rioja to be delivered. She had come to enjoy being waited upon.

'A murder mystery', she told Bryant as he accepted a cloudy pint of Camden Liver Damage, 'is an intellectual exercise, a game between reader and writer in which a problem is precisely stated, elaborately described and surprisingly solved. The traditional rules of fair play demand that the criminal must be someone we've met. There can be no supernatural elements, no secret passages, no imaginary poisons, no Chinamen, no twins, no mystical intuitive powers, and the detective himself can't have done it. To them I would add several further moratoria: no more alcoholic policemen with dead wives, no autistic idiot-savant crime scene specialists, no oppressed female detectives derided by sexist colleagues, no overweight computer nerds in dimly lit rooms, no erudite killers arranging corpses in tableaux reminiscent of medieval paintings, no renegade detectives sharing a psychic bond with the killer, no cryptic messages hidden in museums by victims, no opera-loving loners who solve crimes because without them their lives would have no meaning, and absolutely no more reinventions of Sherlock Bloody Holmes.' She seized her wine gratefully and took a swig.

'Do you think you'd make a good murderer?' asked Bryant, intrigued.

'Heavens, no, the real thing is far too messy.'

'What do you mean?'

'Murder hardly ever goes according to plan in real life.'

'But does crime fiction ever inform fact? Are people influenced by what they read and watch?'

'It's a two-way street.' Claxon tore open a packet of nuts and necked a fistful. 'The idea that fatal doses of poison can be built up over time goes back to Charles Bravo and Dr Crippen. Strange gadgets and unusual alibis are found in police manuals as well as novels. Look at Charlie Peace's collapsible burglary ladder in the Crime Museum if you don't believe me. A few of Conan Doyle's observational ideas made it into police procedure – ballistics, toxicology, footprints and so on – but fictional killers are usually more intelligent and organized than their real-life counterparts. However, the two can cross over from time to time, so that murderers emulate characters and vice versa. What you've described to me doesn't sound as if someone copied it from a book. The deaths aren't gory enough, for a start. There are no decent car chases or violent internal conflicts, and none of the traditional tropes are present – except one.'

'What's that?' Bryant cut a Scotch egg in half and smeared it with mustard pickle.

Claxon brushed nuts from her cleavage. 'You've got your own version of a locked-room mystery, a strangler who appears and vanishes unseen from a private park. Forgive me for sounding callous, but it's the sort of creaky melodramatic idea that would have seemed old hat in the 1930s.'

'Then I shouldn't be looking for a clever killer with an elaborate plan,' said Bryant. 'I should be forming a much simpler and more obvious conclusion.'

'I'm afraid that's so,' Claxon agreed. 'You'll probably find out that the murderer followed your victim into the park because she didn't shut the gate properly. It's a more realistic solution, just not as satisfying. Of course, you're asking the wrong person about such things. I'm only good at doctored cocktails and electric cables hidden inside bedsprings.' She shook her pixie cut sadly. 'When it comes to real-life murder, I simply don't have the lack of imagination for it.'

The pair ordered again, surprised to be relaxing in each other's company. Bryant took a sip of his Hoxton Spleen Cleaver and set it aside at the far edge of the table. 'We've got a couple of obvious suspects. The obsessive gardener, Ritchie Jackson, and the bankrupt husband, Jeremy Forester. The other two, the ambitious wife and the loving nanny, are both dead, but that doesn't mean they weren't involved.'

'Can't you sort out this kind of thing with DNA testing?'

'The idea that all crimes leave a trace only works in controlled environments,' said Bryant. 'In a rainy park all bets are off. That's the other element I'm having trouble with – the crime scenes. At first I thought he picked green spaces because there was no CCTV, but now I believe they simply provide the right setting.'

'I don't envy you your task, Mr Bryant,' said Claxon, perusing the wine list for another assault. 'In my world all murders have tidy solutions. You have to face the idea that yours may never be solved.'

'So you've never used a park as the setting for a murder?'

'Certainly, but that's because of their wildness.'

'Explain, please.'

Claxon sucked nuts from her teeth. 'The city is built up and built over. We no longer connect to the earth. We can draw no sense of magic from concrete and steel, so we need parks to remind us of the beasts we once were.'

The search for Jeremy Forester continued into the night. The detectives pulled in favours from the Met's surveillance teams and the City of London's electronic fraud department, but no fresh information came in. May called GPS, who ran another check with the Rough Sleepers Community, and Bryant checked with the Haphazards, a loosely knit group of drifters, grifters and petty criminals who acted as the city's eyes and ears if the money was right.

For good measure Bryant also put in calls to the National Warlocks' Confederacy, the Dracula Society, the Camden

Passage Druids and the Mystic Order of the Mandrill, all of whom were meeting over the weekend in central London pubs. He needed people who were out on the streets, in bars and cafés, on tubes and buses, who might have seen a limping, desperate man with nowhere to go.

An hour later, Bryant noticed a light under the door of Raymond Land's office and wandered in to find the unit chief leaning out of his window with a cricket bat. 'I'm trying to get rid of a pest,' he explained. 'I did what you asked.'

'You spoke to Link?'

'Not exactly. He wasn't in, so I emailed him.'

'You cowardly toad,' said Bryant. 'Why didn't you call his mobile?'

'I thought he might shout at me. It was easier to gather my thoughts in an email.'

'Thoughts plural, that's a start. You'd better call him first thing in the morning or he'll come around here trying to catch us out.' Bryant unstuck a lemon drop from a paper bag and popped it in his mouth.

Land gave up with the bat but left the window open, shaking raindrops from his sleeve. 'Have you had any luck with Forester?'

'Not yet, but we have calls out all over the city. He has no money and nowhere to go. I hope we get to him before Sun Dark does. We picked up the knife-chucking minion and got the "I know nothing" speech.'

'Do you think Forester's behind all this?'

Bryant sucked the lemon drop through his false teeth, thinking. The sound, not unreminiscent of vegetable soup being strained into a pot from a great height, was unappealing. 'I don't see how he can be. The loss of his son was the start of his downfall. Unless . . .'

'Yes, unless?' Land had a look of desperate hopefulness.

'Unless his wife was somehow involved in the boy's death, in which case several possibilities present themselves. Either

Sharyn Buckland killed him and blamed the wife, or Helen Forester found some way to engineer the whole thing, and in both cases her husband found out, which makes about as much sense as you attempting to organize this gin dive with the aid of a business manual.'

Land guiltily slid the book into his desk drawer. 'Isn't your partner supposed to be helping you?'

'He's keeping me focused and providing me with all the data I need. My brain's not working fast enough. I feel like you must feel all the time. Tomorrow's our final day, and I can see no sign of a making an arrest unless—'

'What if it's just some lone nutter?' said Land. 'You know, like what Link was suggesting?'

'Oh, to have your linguistic dexterity. I do wish you'd attempt to use grammatical English,' said Bryant testily. 'Talking to you is like watching a dubbed film.' He descended into an armchair. 'You mean in a city of eight and a half million people he just happened to pick three people who all knew each other? It's as my author Leticia Claxon said: for a murder to be believable there can be no unlikely coincidences.'

'What are you talking about?' Land ran his hands over the spot where his hair used to be. 'Unlikely deaths happen all the bloody time. God knows we've had our fair share of them here.'

'That's true,' Bryant agreed. 'Did you know the ninth-century Earl of Orkney was killed by an enemy he'd beheaded several hours earlier?'

Land knew he shouldn't be diverted, but took the bait anyway. 'How is that possible?'

'He'd tied the man's head to his horse's saddle, but while he was riding home one of the skull's protruding teeth grazed his leg and infected him.'

'I suppose that was one of your early cases.' Land sighed. 'What are we going to do? Link will take the case away, Faraday will start flogging off bits of prime parkland, the unit will take all the blame, Steffi will go back to Cologne and make fun of us and that damned pigeon will keep dropping its guts on my windowsill.'

Bryant placed a sherbet lemon on Land's desk like a votive offering. 'I think you're forgetting the most important thing, *mon petit Pétomane*. Three people will have died without anyone knowing how or why. But perhaps the killer hasn't finished. Perhaps he's not achieved what he set out to do. How can you take the life of someone like Helen Forester and not get caught? She seemed like a successful member of London society, but was actually very isolated. She had no real friends, not the kind you can call in the middle of the night and tell everything to. She was part of a new generation who don't know who their neighbours are or what to do in an emergency. Loneliness: it's an urban epidemic that impoverishes us all. At its core is the desperate desire to be reunited with your lost self. And now more victims must be added to that sad roll call because of a situation *we* caused.' He stabbed a finger in Land's direction. 'Well, let me warn you, if we can't close the case tomorrow we shouldn't wait for someone to disband us, we should admit defeat and close the unit down ourselves, because we're not worthy of the title. "Peculiar Crimes", it says on that board outside. Remember why? "Crimes peculiar to the City of London", according to the handbook. These are our people, Raymond, and we're failing them. So now we have to continue for their sake, until we have nothing left to give.'

Land rested his fists on his hips. 'Finished? I did enjoy that. The next time you feel like delivering a lecture on the duties of this unit, perhaps you can give Leslie Faraday a PowerPoint presentation instead of attacking me. I will not be your whipping boy any longer!'

'You're hardly a boy,' said Bryant.

'It's all very well for you and John – and Janice, come to that – whispering and conspiring together like – like a pair of superannuated schoolboys and their sister—'

'—and Jack,' said Bryant, checking his sweet bag.

'Yes, and Jack—'

'—and Dan.'

'Yes, he's just as bad—'

'—and Colin.'

'Yes, yes—'

'And the rest of us, all except you, Raymond. I can imagine how awful your school years must have been, the first to go down with measles, the last to be picked for the badminton team—'

'I went to a boys' school,' Land pointed out.

'Whatever, the point is that you're a natural target because you're incapable of making up your mind about anything. You're crippled by indecision because you're basically nice. You're English, you're lukewarm and drippy and reasonable and – *nice*. You've even let a pigeon beat you. A one-legged one.'

'And how easy it must have been for you,' Land snapped back, 'the smart kids who always got the weak ones to do whatever they wanted, making us run your errands, taking the blame for you, not being given a fag when you all had one, making me pay an extra shilling to park in your bloody bike racks.'

'Hey, what's going on in here?' asked John May, coming in. 'I could hear you in the street.'

'Raymond wants a bike rack or something,' said Bryant. 'What were you doing in the street?'

'I went to get a crayfish and rocket sandwich.'

'Did you get me one? John, reassure Raymondo that we'll close the case tomorrow or go down trying, will you?'

'I don't know, will we?'

'Yes, we will,' Bryant replied, gritting his teeth, or rather the teeth he currently owned. 'We will find the killer and save the day, or I will leave this building tomorrow night and never come back.'

'You say that like it's a threat,' muttered Land,

disconsolately blowing his nose. 'If you leave and don't come back it'll only be because you've forgotten the address.'

'Try me,' warned Bryant. 'It's going to be us against them, and this time you have to pick a side.'

40

'IT'S THE PERFECT SPOT FOR A CONFRONTATION'

It was a bad night for all concerned.

While Jeremy Forester remained at large, hiding in the city's unvisited corners, a sense of impending doom saturated the unit like a rising river. As Colin Bimsley and Meera Mangeshkar had only managed to assault a Spaniard in Regent's Park, they stayed late to re-examine all the files they had collated. Infuriated by his inability to pinpoint the origin of the glass sample, Dan Banbury was also still at the unit far past midnight.

The detectives' office was a mess. John May paced about, frustrated by the wealth of information that led nowhere, but Bryant was worse. Although his eyes burned with a bright intensity, he was leaden-limbed with exhaustion. Unable to settle, he roved between his desk and his bookshelves, searching for something he could not define. His hands hovered over yellowed pages, pawing at dust-covered history books, but for once these esoteric avenues of exploration failed to take him anywhere. Volumes on parks, gardens and squares had been pinned open with pieces of tape and were scattered about the room. It was enough to give a librarian a heart attack.

'I tried tracing the transport police who were working the night Charlie Forester died,' said May. 'Sergeant Kemp-Bird didn't know it but there were actually two other officers keeping an eye on the traffic. One took early retirement because of an old back injury and now lives in Spain. The other one died of liver failure in May after years of struggling with alcoholism. There was a constable on point duty, but she was away from the tunnel on Borough High Street and didn't see anything. So there are no other witnesses to any conversation that took place between Lauren Posner and Sharyn Buckland that night.'

'What about the ambulance crew?' said Bryant. 'Did you have any luck with them?'

'One, the driver. She says Buckland went with the boy but wasn't allowed to ride in the back of the vehicle because they'd started emergency treatment. She doesn't remember details, but I pulled the duty log. They'd realized the boy was in trouble but couldn't isolate the source of the problem. He was given a diluted bronchodilator in the form of a nebulizer to help him breathe. The driver was concentrating on getting them through the traffic in one piece. The EMTs burn out fast. You can't expect them to remember everything. She said Ritchie Jackson followed them. The boy went straight into surgery and both Jackson and Buckland gave statements to the Admissions Nurse, neither of which we can find because the NHS computer system wasn't backing up properly. There was a nurse present, but we're still trying to find her. Both Jackson and Buckland thought that the girl in the red car should be brought in, but the officer didn't deem it necessary.'

'Was any effort made to trace her after?'

'Not initially. Jackson complained a second time, and a fortnight later Sharyn Buckland was interviewed. We don't have that statement, but it's understood she didn't add anything significant to what had already been reported.'

'I thought I'd find the answer here,' said Bryant wearily,

waving his hand across the volumes spread before him. 'It had to be someone living or spending a lot of time in the parks, to gain access, to know the secluded corners, to escape easily. Nearly half of this city's residents were born abroad, five per cent don't legally exist, fewer and fewer own their own homes. It's not the city of my youth. I'm having trouble understanding it.'

'Come on, has it ever really been different?' asked May. 'The migrants arrive because their harvests die and they'd rather be penniless in a foreign land than face starvation. It's human nature to go where you think you'll survive. And you still know more about this city than anyone.'

Bryant angrily slapped at the covers of his books, barely hearing his partner. 'The parks are the answer. They're here as a calming measure, like arboreal speed bumps. The modern world is an equation: time plus people equals productivity. You're as bad as everyone else. You ask your barber to speed up your haircut, eat at your keyboard and stand in a window-less kitchen squeezing a teabag against the side of a mug because you don't have time to let it brew.'

'Arthur, you're not making sense,' said May gently. 'Why don't you go home? It's Sunday now, there's nothing more we can do. Go and put your feet up.'

'It's not just that I'm tired, I'm bloody furious. Three women are dead who should be alive. He killed first to survive and then because he grew to like it. Something made him this way, don't you see? And we will never find out what that thing is because it's simply not possible to sift through the formative experiences of everyone we've interviewed. Remember what I told you at the start of the week about the parks, how they represented the countryside but came to be enclosed? We have to keep them safe or we'll have nothing left. People are living in tower blocks behind electronic gates, tricking themselves into thinking everything's fine, but life is slipping out of kilter. And there's nobody left now to remember how it once was. I wish . . .'

'Hey,' said May, 'hey, come on.'

'I wish I could go back. Just reset everything to the 1950s, when we thought we could rebuild the world. I never thought I'd say that, John. I want it back the way it was. I'm worn out. I wish I was young and fresh again. I wish—'

Opening his fist, he set a folded piece of postcard upon his desk.

May rubbed his partner's back and waited while he wiped his eyes on his sleeve. 'You don't want it back, Arthur, not really. Everyone thinks they do but they don't. When you weigh it all up, now is better. We do progress, even though it doesn't always seem that way. Do you want to stay here tonight? Tell you what, we'll go and talk to Ritchie Jackson first thing. We'll try to get this sorted out.'

Bryant sat up and briskly straightened his jacket. 'I didn't mean to get maudlin. The treatment took a lot out of me. I get overwhelmed sometimes.'

'I'll make us some tea,' said May.

'No, it's all right, I'll make it – your tea always makes me think Crippen got caught short near the pot.'

As Bryant headed out to the kitchen, May picked up the postcard and opened it out. The girl was dressed in pale lace, with a makeshift tiara of little white flowers. She was standing by a small tree blooming with saucer-petal flowers, a pearl bush commonly known as the Bride. Head tilted down, she had been coaxed to give a shy smile for the camera. He instinctively knew who she was; it was the only photograph he had ever seen of Nathalie, the woman Arthur would have married. It must have been taken soon after their engagement. Neither of them could have foreseen the coming tragedy.

May placed the photograph back inside his partner's desk and was about to call Ritchie Jackson when Bimsley swung into the room with more than his usual lack of coordination. 'We've got another one,' he said breathlessly. 'St James's Park, near the lake, Dan's going there right now.'

*

When John May last took his BMW in for an MOT the mechanic was shocked by the state of his tyres. 'It looks like you've been in a high-speed pursuit,' he said, chuckling. Recalling that he had actually been in several since his last service, May had said nothing.

'I don't know why we can't have one of those magnetic blue lights they place on the roofs of cars in American films,' Bryant complained, recovered to his old self. If there was one thing you could always rely on, it was his ability to bounce back. 'Doesn't this thing go any faster?'

'It's London,' said May. 'We're in a twenty-miles-per-hour zone.'

'What's the point of being a cop if you can't wing the odd dustbin?'

'The last time you drove to get to a crime scene you didn't "wing the odd dustbin" as you put it. You drove through a garden fete. We arrived covered in bunting.'

'Those cakes were dry,' said Bryant. 'I'm glad I didn't have to eat them.'

'You couldn't have, seeing as they were all over the windscreen,' said May. 'Hang on.' They cut through the red lights at Shaftesbury Avenue amid the blasting of horns and swung down towards Trafalgar Square.

The view from the Blue Bridge in St James's Park was one of the most beautiful in London. At one end Buckingham Palace sat framed by trees. At the other, the Horse Guards parade ground was backed by the vaguely Arabian turrets of Whitehall. In the summer deckchairs were set out by the bandstand, but now the trees were bare and brittle in the spiky winter night.

They found Dan Banbury surrounded by tripod lights and a handful of sleepy pelicans who would not be moved from their spot beside the lake.

'The bird-keeper saw something floating between the nesting sites.' He led them past the medics, who were removing their body net from the lake edge. 'Take a look. Eight stab wounds to the throat, thorax and stomach, and a deep, vicious defence slash across his right hand. It's completely different methodology but – well, it would be pretty weird if it wasn't connected.' He pulled open the top of the net and revealed the staring face of Ritchie Jackson.

'The poor devil,' said May. 'He was a nice bloke.'

'His attacker's going to be covered in blood right now,' said Bryant. 'Someone's bound to notice him. I assume you've put out the call, Dan?'

'Before I got here,' said Banbury. 'Jackson's last phone call came from a blocked number at ten sixteen p.m. It suggests to me that he was meeting someone because the call pinged at the Birdcage Walk telecom tower, so it was made locally. Adding the time he took to walk here from Charing Cross Station, where his travel card flagged, I'd estimate he died between eleven and eleven fifteen p.m. What I don't understand is why he took the chance of coming alone. He could have armed himself, but there's nothing on his body except his phone, wallet and flat keys, so we'll have to dredge the lake. Unfortunately, to do that we need to get permission from the landlady.'

'The landlady?' asked May.

'Her Majesty is in residence at the moment,' said Dan, pointing in the direction of Buckingham Palace, 'and it's her lake. This whole park functions as her front garden. She's already had an intruder sit on the end of her bed in the middle of the night. I'd rather it didn't get out that someone was murdered in her flowerbeds and chucked into her duck pond.'

'Do you know exactly where he was attacked?' asked Bryant.

'I've a pretty clear idea. He certainly wasn't drowned. There's some mud and disturbed gravel on the path, just over here.'

Banbury walked them to a taped-off patch of track leading

to the lakeside. May knelt and ran a torch over the bloody striations. 'No air-rifle pellets this time. Whoever did this will need to change his clothes fast.'

'What if someone close to one of the victims knew that Jackson was the killer and decided to take matters into their own hands?'

Dan rubbed his nose, unhappy at the idea. 'It would explain the different method and the aggression of the assault, Mr B., but it offends my sense of order to think we might have two murderers on our hands.'

May called Sofia Anzelmo and asked if she'd heard from Jackson. She sounded sleepy, and explained that she was in Birmingham helping to prepare for a company convention on Monday morning.

Bryant stood at the edge of the lake looking down into the ice-green water. 'What would have made him risk coming here?' A fat white pelican lazily raised its head and eyed him suspiciously. 'It's the perfect spot for a confrontation: poorly lit, underpopulated, unenclosed. One of the only parks that haven't been sealed.'

'People feel safe because of where we're situated, Arthur. Maybe there was a witness.'

May looked towards the illuminated windows of Buckingham Palace.

41

'NOT THE MOST SALUBRIOUS AREA'

As soon as Ritchie Jackson's death was registered and his body headed to the St Pancras Mortuary, the detectives went home to grab a few hours' sleep; there was nothing to be gained by returning to the unit until daylight. If anyone was picked up with blood on his clothes the PCU would be called at once.

Arthur Bryant decided to make the short walk from Euston Road to Harrison Street as it saved his partner having to go out of his way. He stopped on the corner of the pavement and sniffed the air: coffee, burned wood, varnish.

Warning signs. He picked up the pace, reaching the gates of his building.

The scene before him tipped slightly and righted itself. He closed his eyes for a moment, saw something jewel-like shimmering, lost track of time, closed and opened them wide once more.

Her Royal Highness, Queen Elizabeth II, dressed in the black velvet robes and white silk ribbons of her famous Annigoni portrait, sat before him in the cluttered front parlour of his mother's old house in Bethnal Green, perched on the edge of a floral settee.

'You must forgive us,' said Her Majesty, looking at the sideboard lined with silver-framed pictures of royalty purchased down Petticoat Lane. 'One is more used to going to a friend's home and finding photographs of their family rather than of one's own.'

'My mother was a great royalist,' Bryant explained. 'She collected the set. The Duke of Bedford's eyes tend to follow you around the room.'

'As indeed they did in life.' The queen sniffed faintly. 'I fancy we came here to open a homeopathic centre, which of course one now regrets. Have you lived here long?'

'This is my mum's old gaff,' said Bryant. 'I'd offer you a port and lemon but it's been in the sideboard a long time and is probably past its zenith. The women used to drink while their husbands were away at sea.'

'So you could say there was a port in every wife.' Her Majesty's eyes betrayed a sense of mischief.

'Indeed, Your Majesty,' said Bryant, moving the best china between them and pouring tea. 'This house must seem very cramped to you.'

'Not really. We have 775 rooms but live in about six of them. As you can imagine, the Throne Room doesn't get much use. It's terribly inefficient to heat. Thanks to Balmoral, we have quite a lot of blankets. Are these Bourbons?'

'Please feel free to load up, Your Majesty. Stick one behind your ear for later, I won't be offended.'

'It was you who summoned me, was it not?' said Queen Elizabeth, dunking her Bourbon in builder's tea. 'Time is rather pressing.'

'I beg your pardon, ma'am,' Bryant apologized. 'I wondered if you saw anything untoward occurring in your front garden last night.'

'One so rarely looks from the front windows,' sighed the queen. 'It doesn't do to be seen peering around the curtains, and there are always so many people waiting outside to catch a glimpse. One doesn't dare put one's own milk bottles out.'

'There aren't many milkmen left now, ma'am.'

A look of surprise crossed Her Majesty's delicately powdered features. 'Are there not? What a shame. Next you'll be telling us the telephone boxes have gone.'

'So you didn't clock anything odd earlier tonight?'

'Actually, we did have a small peek but saw nothing untoward. You should ask Philip, he often gets out his binoculars and has a good shufti.'

'If I need to get in touch with you—' Bryant began.

'We imagine you know the address,' said Queen Elizabeth. 'We're in Victoria, near the station. Not the most salubrious area, but there's a bit of a garden.'

'Could you have one last really hard think for me, Your Majesty?' He tipped some custard creams on to the plate by way of enticement, seeing as she had wolfed the Bourbons. 'Did you really not see anything happening in the park?'

Queen Elizabeth's intelligent eyes narrowed as she tried to recall the landscaped gardens beneath the cold night moon. 'Well, there were the usual young men strolling about – one tends to get that a lot when you've a household full of male servants with too much time on their hands – but we do remember seeing a chap by the lake greeting a friend.'

'How do you know it was a friend?' asked Bryant, leaning forward to make sure he heard the answer clearly.

'I'm putting a bacon butty on your nightstand,' said the queen. 'Don't get brown sauce all over the duvet this time.'

Her Majesty dissolved into Alma Sorrowbridge, who was standing beside his bed with an immense pork-filled doorstop and a mug of tea. He was tucked up to his nose in his brass bedstead at number 17, Albion House, Harrison Street, and it was morning.

'You stupid woman, you woke me up just as Her Majesty was about to tell me something important,' said Bryant, sitting up and reaching for his spectacles.

'Your knighthood still hasn't come through, if that's what

you were wondering.' Alma sniffed, heading out. 'The thanks I get.'

He tried to imagine where their conversation had been going, but the dream had become spider threads dissolving in watery sunlight. Then he remembered: Queen Elizabeth knew that Jackson had thought he was meeting a friend because he was walking towards him with his right hand outstretched. Unable to contain his anger a moment longer, the 'friend' had slashed at the outstretched hand with a knife. Defence cuts were usually on both hands and forearms. Jackson's was on the right only.

His defences were lowered because he knew and trusted his killer.

THE SEVENTH DAY

42

'YOU KNOW THE WHOLE THING'S A BLUFF'

Leslie Faraday had a wife who had promised to stand by him in sickness and in health but not on the witness stand, and when the Home Office liaison officer was caught lying in the most recent civil service expenses scandal, he had a terrible time persuading her to support his story.

Sandra Faraday decided to testify against her husband, but he escaped censure after his lawyer spotted a loophole in the reams of legal semantics that forced the Crown to drop the case. Once a respectable period of time had elapsed, his wife filed for divorce and departed to set up a company that designed cheap electronic equipment for African school-children. Faraday told his colleagues he harboured no ill will towards her, then used a private security firm to find health and safety infringements on her company premises which got her shut down long enough to wreck most of her contracts.

Leslie Faraday saw nothing wrong in this. His lack of moral discernment meant that he recognized no difference between altruism and profiteering. Money was money. Civil servants were required to possess objectivity and impartiality, unencumbered by political affiliations or alliances. They could, however, be bastards.

All of which is a rather roundabout way of illustrating that as he made his case for the closure of the PCU, Faraday did so entirely without malice. Bryant and May were an untidy obstacle more than anything else, like a stack of obsolete magazines that had piled up in a corner and needed to be thrown out.

The park privatization scheme was coming along nicely. When the PCU's investigation failed it would be handed over to the CID, and it would take them a while to get up to speed, and the longer everything took the longer the parks could remain shut, and the more people would get used to the idea of not taking them for granted. Even the protests had started to die down, although many kept lonely vigils by the railings.

The only thing Faraday had going against him was his own ineptitude. He had recently sent Darren Link a screen grab from his computer showing protestors outside the locked gates of Battersea Park, but had forgotten to erase his NSFW browsing history, which appeared in a bar above the photograph. What a field day the press had enjoyed with that!

So when he picked up intelligence about another corpse being found in a park, and this time virtually on Her Majesty's front lawn, he knew he had finally sealed the unit's fate. There was no way that they could conclude their investigation by the end of Sunday.

When Darren Link called to inform him of the latest development in the case, Faraday was at home in Chipping Norton, getting ready for the day's golf game. Link considered Faraday to be a pusillanimous little weasel with the morals of a maggot, especially since the situation with the parks had created antipathy towards the police, but he recognized his usefulness as a snitch.

FARADAY: A corpse bearing multiple stab wounds, dragged out of the St James's Park lake in full view of Buckingham Palace? I'm surprised they didn't think to mention it.

LINK: Raymond Land just fed me some cock-and-bull story about their computer system being down. I've run a check from here and it seems to be working perfectly. He says he can't access any of their case records until tomorrow morning at the earliest.

FARADAY: I know how he feels, I'm hopeless with email. [*Aside*] Just set it down there, Deirdre, and see if there are any Garibaldis. Or wafers, but not the pink ones. [*To Link*] It's Sunday, there won't be much happening there today, surely.

LINK: Why is your secretary at home with you?

FARADAY: She's polishing my clubs. So you think they're all at their King's Cross headquarters, up to something?

LINK: Of course I bloody do! They're busy clearing out files, getting ready to cart them off-premises and bury every sign of their incompetence.

FARADAY: Then why don't you send your men around to stop them?

LINK: Because Bryant and May will feed them a load of nonsense and pack them off until they've finished. My men aren't devious enough to keep up. You could distract most of them by waving a piece of coloured cloth.

FARADAY: Then *you* should go round.

LINK: Land warned me not to come over because the workmen are having the place fumigated today. They reckon the coffin they found in the basement could be part of a medieval plague pit.

FARADAY: And they're all still inside?

LINK: I know they're up to something. I rang a few of them from different numbers and all of their phones are on voicemail.

FARADAY: Then that's your answer. You think they're planning to move the hard evidence off-site? Give them

347

exactly what they'd like you to believe they want. Go with the idea that the building is a contamination zone. Check that everyone's inside, cordon it off and lock it down until tomorrow morning. Under the quarantine laws put in place by the Francis Crick Institute they'll have to remain isolated. They daren't take the risk of destroying electronic police files without obstructing the case, and they won't be able to smuggle hard copies out. Seal them up and reopen the building after the deadline has passed. I can push the order through right this minute.

LINK: You can do that?

FARADAY: With one phone call. You know the whole thing's a bluff.

LINK: Is it, though? The CoL really did find plague victims in Houndsditch a few weeks ago when they were excavating the lower floors of a new office block. And the unit officially reported finding something in their own basement during the renovations.

FARADAY: For Christ's sake – they're using you, Mr Link, so play along. Shut them today and I'll make sure they stay shut for good.

Link was amazed. As much as he disliked Faraday, he had to admit that the weasel had finally come up with a foolproof method of destroying the PCU's credibility once and for all.

The problem was, he suddenly felt uncomfortable with the plan.

43

'THIS IS NOT NORMAL PROCEDURE, I THINK?'

Rosa Lysandrou peered through the mullioned window of the St Pancras Coroner's Office and saw the pudgy scarf-cocooned face of her nemesis peering in. With a heavy sigh she unlatched the front door.

'Ah, you *are* there, I've been ringing the bell for ages,' said Bryant, stepping inside. 'I suppose it takes you a while to get up from the cellar.'

'We don't have a cellar,' retorted Rosa, her eyes hooded, her face immobile. 'Wipe your feet.'

Bryant stamped his wet boots on the mat. 'Really? I thought you slept here. I'm sure Giles said something about having to fix a new lid on your bed.'

'I don't listen to you, Mr Bryant. There is no room for levity here.'

'Oh, come now. I know Christian doctrine wants us to believe that life is simply a *vallis lacrimarum*, but you must think there's more to it than a vale of tears.'

'Yes,' said Rosa, 'there is heaven for those who meet the conditions.'

'That's me out, then,' rejoined Bryant cheerfully. 'You

should meet my landlady; she imagines paradise as a sort of golden nightclub with bouncers. You two would get on like a church on fire. Don't bother to announce me, I'm going in.'

He found Kershaw bent over the body of the late Ritchie Jackson. 'I thought I heard you,' said Giles, rising and removing his gloves. 'I was thinking about what you told me on the phone, and you could be right. Here, hold out your right hand as if to shake mine.'

Bryant did as he was told. Gripping his telescopic indicator like a knife, Kershaw slid it across the detective's palm, then continued the movement, ending it at the point where the indicator touched Bryant's stomach.

'Jackson strides towards his attacker, anxious to see him, his arm extended, and is caught by surprise. After the stomach wound he bends over so that his body lowers, which is why the next penetrations are in the thorax and finally, as he falls, in the throat. He lands face down on the path as the killer steps back – I found some specks of gravel stuck to the front of his jacket – and is hauled by his collar into the lake, which is no more than a couple of metres away. All over in a moment.'

'So as Jackson approached all he saw was someone standing looking out over the lake,' said Bryant.

'It appears that way.'

'Someone he knew and trusted.'

'Not necessarily,' Kershaw replied. 'You do know that St James's Park once had a reputation as a cruising ground?'

'Not any more, though, surely? It wasn't an assignation, he was summoned there by a phone call.'

'Just working through all of the possibilities, Mr B. There's something else, a bruise across his face, a thin stripe, like a braided whip.'

'You mean like the ligatures on the other victims. Any ideas about the knife?'

'It's smooth-edged, not serrated, with a two-and-a-half-inch blade, very sharp. Nothing like the ones your knife-thrower used.'

'Jackson owned a Swiss army knife, a Victorinox Pioneer. We gave it back to him. He could have had it at the meeting for protection.'

'In which case Jackson holds out his hand with the knife in it, is lashed on the face, drops the blade and is then stabbed with it.'

'Now, that makes more sense. And he was killed because he was the last one there at the scene of Charlie Forester's accident. I like my loose ends neatly tied.' Bryant unwrapped a tube of Army & Navy lozenges, adding liquorice to the room's chemical odour.

'I've a feeling you're not going to get them tied this time.'

'Oh? Why not?'

'Our only remaining suspect is missing and we still have no motive. And this death is different, obviously, so we're starting afresh.'

'It's only different because of his gender,' argued Bryant. 'Rosa said something about entering paradise—'

Giles knew his detective too well to be thrown by the sudden change of subject. 'Yes, she tends to do that a lot.'

'She's right. The killer chose to despatch his first victim in idyllic surroundings, but the others were killed for expedience.'

'And what makes you think that?'

'The first time he had to do it, *and* he wanted to. Ritchie Jackson is an afterthought. The phone call was made to confirm a suspicion that Jackson knew the truth.'

'What, so Jackson goes trotting along to a deserted park after dark to meet his murderer? Why would he do that?'

'Because he still didn't think he was in any danger. An attacker of women, a strangler? Jackson's a big lad who owns a knife. He underestimated his opponent. And I think that's what we've been doing all this time.'

'You sound like you've decided who you're looking for, Mr Bryant.'

'I'm beginning to think I have. But by the end of the day I need to prove it. I know how our killer gained access to Clement Crescent. I've known ever since I found out that Mrs Farrier keeps a budgerigar.'

'Don't tell me any more,' warned Kershaw. 'I've been told to stop sharing information with you.'

'Really? Why?' Bryant's eyes widened in a display of innocence that could have been seen from the rear of the stalls.

Kershaw looked embarrassed. 'Because the case is technically no longer yours.'

'Who told you that?'

'I had the Missing Link on the blower just before you got here. Amazingly, he doesn't buy the pack of outrageous lies your boss fed him about crashing computers and plague germs.'

Bryant waved the idea aside. 'I'm not worried about him. He's not the brightest bulb in the candelabrum but he usually plays fair.'

'Not this time,' Giles warned. 'He told me that if I saw you, I was to make sure you headed straight back to the unit as quickly as possible. He checked to see if anyone else was here. If they were, I was to tell them the same thing.'

'Interesting,' said Bryant. 'It sounds as if he wants us all in one place. Thanks for the alert. I think I know what he's up to. If I'm right, two can play at that game.' He tightened his scarf. 'One other thing. What do you know about Shakespeare's Titania?'

Unfazed, Kershaw went to his computer. 'English archetype, queen of the fairies, kissed a donkey in the woods. I know someone who lectures on the subject. Shall I ping the contact to your phone?'

'You can if you like. I won't see it as I have no idea what to do if my phone pings. Try writing it on a bit of paper. That often works.'

With the number tucked into his top pocket Bryant headed off, tramping disrespectfully over the gravestones in the churchyard.

When he reached the corner of the Caledonian Road, he ducked behind a traffic sign and peered over at the headquarters of the PCU, where two constables were supervising a group of council workers. Beside them two men in yellow hi-vis jackets were unloading corrugated steel barriers from the back of a lorry.

With his worst fears confirmed, Bryant turned up his collar and hastily diverted away from the unit, hoping that no one had had time to spot him.

'Someone's putting bloody huge stickers over the ground-floor windows,' announced Meera Mangeshkar, running up the stairs to find Raymond Land. 'Look at this.' She slapped a red roundel that read 'CONTAMINATION ZONE' on to his desk. 'And they're heat-sealing cordons around the building.'

She found the unit chief staring at his phone in disbelief. 'We've been declared a biohazard,' Land told her. 'Leslie Faraday has ordered the Temple of Doom to place the building under quarantine.'

The mission of the Francis Crick Institute was to help understand why diseases develop and to find new ways to treat them. It was housed in a spectacular new biomedical research centre of steel and glass built beside St Pancras Station, and was locally known as the Temple of Doom because it had teams of biologists working there around the clock in the middle of a residential neighbourhood. The area had long been associated with tropical disease hospitals, but nobody liked having a biohazard centre on their doorstep.

Land and Mangeshkar went to the windows and looked down. Yellow plastic ribbons could be seen crisscrossing the brickwork. Pinholed metal panels had been erected to hide the ground floor from public view. The surrounding pavements had been blocked, and a workman was screwing a wide steel belt over the front door.

Land pulled up the window and yelled down, 'What the hell do you think you're doing?'

'We need you to get back inside, mate,' the workman shouted back up. 'Otherwise we'll have to seal those as well.'

'You can't do that! And I'm not your mate! I'm the head of this unit and I absolutely forbid you to shut us in like this!' Land's plea was met with deafening indifference. He scooted to the detectives' office, where he found John May on the phone.

'I know,' said May, taking one look at Land's panicked face. 'They're saying we have to stay here until the Crick's health and safety officers can give us the all-clear. I'm trying to sort it out.'

'Well, how long is it going to take?'

'They'll probably be over tomorrow morning.'

'Of course they will. I knew something like this was going to happen. I should never have listened to you! I can't stay here all night – I don't have pyjamas. It's hot in here. I can't breathe.' Land looked like a hypoglycaemic runner about to drop in his tracks after a marathon.

'We didn't have a choice, Raymond,' said May. 'We had to tell them something.'

Land fanned himself. 'This is Link's doing. This is his revenge for us fighting back. He can't simply imprison us. God knows it's bad enough having to come here every day without locking us in overnight. He's blocked our access to all the Met databases, too, including HOLMES. How could he even do that? I thought we had control over our own computer system. They can't get away with this.'

The anguished unit chief was turning a strange shade of heliotrope. 'Take a few deep breaths,' May suggested. 'We fight to stay operational in order to provide safekeeping and protection to all. We'll do that by catching all those who would undermine the process. We'll get him, all right?'

Land loosened his collar and sucked in air, breathing out through his nose. 'All right.'

'Good. Just to warn you, we're not all here.'

'Who's missing?'

'Arthur. He's still outside somewhere.'

Land threw himself down into a chair. 'Are you saying our fate now hinges on the findings of a delusional pensioner?'

'I won't tell him you said that.' May poured some brandy into a strong tea. 'All we can do now is sit tight and wait.'

'What is happening?' asked Steffi Vesta, coming in. 'I could not open the front door. When I asked to be let out a man shouted something most vulgar through the letter box.'

'It's nothing, Steffi. We've been locked in until tomorrow morning,' said May.

Vesta looked confused. 'This is not normal procedure, I think?'

'It's not normal even for us,' answered May. 'We have something they need.'

'And you do not wish to give this something to them?'

'No, Steffi, it's the case. If we surrender it now, we get closed down. The expense of running the investigation and then handing it over unsolved will finish us off.'

'Oh. Then we must close it, yes?'

'Well, it's going to be difficult. My partner is stuck on the outside and we can't leave the building, so I'm open to any suggestions you might have.'

Steffi set down her shoulder bag and opened it. 'Mr Banbury found this in the sample he took from St James's Park. It was about a metre from Mr Jackson's body.' She handed May a small plastic bag containing a single tiny lead ball. 'There was only one this time, but it is identical to those found in the St Olave churchyard. You thought it was from a type of air gun designed to fire projectiles called pellets, yes? But in your country all air pistols powerful enough to cause injury require a licence. So I ran a check, and this little thing does not match any known pellet made for such a gun. And there is something else. It is pressed, not dropped, which is why it has a seam. This type is commonly used by clothing designers. I called the wholesale fashion shops behind Oxford

Street and had better luck. It is used to weigh things down, like the hem of a gown or dress.'

'Are you telling me we're looking for a *woman*?' asked May.

44

'IT WAS QUITE A RIDE'

Jeremy Forester sent one final email, closed the phone and dumped it in a litter bin outside the coffee shop.

The pain in his leg had become unbearable. He sank on to the bench in Postman's Park, one of the few to escape being locked in London's Square Mile, not far from where he had worked for so many years. *We think we escape,* he thought bitterly, *but we never get far.* The cutting wind had finally dropped, and the day was settling into a dismal run of rain. He watched cascades of needles falling beyond the edge of the loggia. The last time he was here was on a hot summer's day when he still had a career. He had brought his son to read the tiled inscriptions of brave self-sacrifice, more than fifty ceramic plaques dedicated to those who had died saving the lives of others. It seemed like a lifetime ago.

Rolling up the left leg of his jeans, he saw that blood had soaked through the dressing and around the grey plastic splint that was setting his fibula. He needed medical attention, but somewhere out there Sun Dark's men were still looking for him. He was fairly certain that by now the police would have upgraded his status to that of prime suspect.

How the hell did he drop, Icarus-like, from the aureole of

the sun? He knew the exact moment when things started to break apart. It had begun with that damned woman in the tunnel and the death of his boy. If Charlie had lived everything would have been different. He would never have got into debt and lost his job. Perhaps the marriage would still have ended, but Helen and his boy would still be alive. And the nanny, gone as well, as if someone was erasing each phase of his life.

Before any of this happened, he had hardly ever visited a London park. Now he kept returning to them. They calmed him and let his thoughts fly free. You only had to walk a few feet in from the hedgerows and the noise of traffic dissipated to be replaced by birdsong, even in midwinter. The birds never quite left the city any more. It was too warm here now, and there was too much for them to eat. They were better at survival than the human residents.

He watched an old man meticulously emptying a litter bin, looking for bottles and unfinished sandwiches. Where once he would have felt a kind of pitying revulsion he now saw stubborn endurance. Where was the shame in wanting to live? He watched a woman in a black business suit pointedly looking the other way as she passed, using her umbrella to shield herself from the offending sight. Once he would have done the same thing, fearful that he might see a reflection of his own possible fate. Now he felt a strange kind of kinship.

I've changed, he thought. *The parks have made me change. They've taught me not to be afraid any more. When your worst fears come true there's nothing beyond them except peace.*

It had taken a little less than a year for his world to collapse. He accepted that he would never get to live out his dreams in Hong Kong. By now the police would have found the note he had mailed, explaining exactly what he had done for Washbourne Hollis and why. He wished he could see the look on Larry Vance's face when that came out. The City of

London Fraud and Economic Crime Squad would have been called in, and both he and Vance would face considerable jail sentences. Even that wasn't a problem; it was the idea of existing afterwards with a criminal record and no money, no home, no love. Right at this moment the old man at the litter bin possessed more useful survival skills.

As Forester rose from the bench and stepped back into the rain, the old man lifted his head and their eyes met. In that brief but infinite moment, he felt that he would be more than happy to change places.

That settled it. He reached a decision.

Number One, Poultry was so old that it had been nicknamed the Heart of the City. It stood in the centre of the Square Mile, covering what had once been the Walbrook, the stream that had fed the ancient Roman town of Londinium, part of the ghost map that existed beneath the pavement's surface. On its third and fourth floors, Washbourne Hollis had provided a different kind of stream, a steady flow of money that allowed properties around the world to flourish.

Forester looked up at the rooftop, feeling the cool rain on his face.

The building had another, less desirable reputation: the flying buttresses of its roof garden provided diving boards for anguished bankers. During the past decade at least half a dozen had hurled themselves from its terrace into the distant street.

He had almost fulfilled his death wish once. It seemed like a trial run for this moment.

'Well,' Forester told the darkened windows, 'it was quite a ride, and I've already outstayed my welcome.'

On this Sunday morning, armed with the only card he had managed to save, the private members' pass that allowed him access to the suicides' launch pad, Forester rode the lift and walked past the kitchen staff, who nodded to him in vague recognition. Then he slipped into the meticulously planted garden, climbed the concrete buttress and entered London's history as one of those who fell short of the sun.

Steffi Vesta was puzzled. She studied the screen again and did the maths, tapping her pen against perfect white teeth. Before her was the spreadsheet detailing Jeremy Forester's finances.

It had been mailed to her via an apparently defunct email account from a Costa Coffee shop near St Paul's. That meant Jeremy Forester was less than two miles away from the unit, but now there was no way they could send anyone after him.

He had sent it to the PCU's only public address, *info@pcu. org*, but why? Was he trying to turn himself in? Or was he up to something more?

At first glance the spreadsheet made no sense. It detailed his bank withdrawals and transfers together with his flight schedule. It was a document he had created to keep track of his financial dealings, and was difficult to interpret. But Vesta had the kind of mind that instantly registered anomalies, and it didn't take her long to spot what Forester had intended her to see.

The only person on the outside now was Mr Bryant. Steffi called him at once, but there was no answer, so she texted.

'I have something for you,' she wrote. 'Please call me as soon as you get this.'

45

'I'LL HAVE TO GO IT ALONE, UNLESS . . .'

'Where the hell is he?' Raymond Land stormed about the operations room, sending paperwork flying. 'Bryant knows every ranting nutcase and lunatic in London. I've called the only ones I can find numbers for. One of them told me there was a government conspiracy behind the fact that you never get green crisps any more, then tried to sell me some herbal tea. Another one warned me that the coming apocalypse will be caused by penguins. They're full of ideas to save the world but just when we need them to do something useful they let us down. Somebody sane must have seen him.'

'Unfortunately, Arthur keeps the names and addresses of all his academic contacts in his little black book,' said May, 'and that's in his jacket pocket. Why penguins?'

'Oh, something to do with magnetic radiation and fish,' said Land vaguely. 'Do you really mean to say you can't do anything?' He felt like tearing his hair out, except that he was newly single and needed every strand he had left.

May shrugged. 'You know the situation. We can't leave the building. By the way, our computer system really doesn't work. Someone's put a pickaxe through the electrics.'

'It's *him*,' raged Land. 'He went off to borrow one from the two Daves. He did it to stop us from giving in. Call them and get this ended, can't you?'

'Link's not answering his phone, Faraday's number goes straight to voicemail and the council lines are shut until tomorrow morning.'

'Oh, I've heard from Link,' frothed Land, still pacing about madly. 'I swear that man has a sixth sense. He knows Bryant's not in here with us. I lied, of course, said he was in the toilet, but he wants me to bring him to the window as proof. He's standing outside right now. What am I going to do? Somebody must have some bright ideas. Get everyone in here *right now*.'

Land charged back to his office. Somewhere in his business manual there had to be a chapter on restoring order and staying calm in the face of an enemy siege.

'Do you think he might be heading for a heart attack?' asked Janice, tilting her head to watch him go. She hadn't seen Land this furious since the cold lasagne he'd tried to eat from the unit fridge had turned out to be a part of a sheep's stomach on which Bryant was conducting experiments. 'Has anybody tried the basement?'

'What do you mean?' asked Renfield.

'We're attached to the building next door. Isn't there supposed to be a door down there that still opens?'

There was an instant murmur of agreement. 'Wait, Mr Land has just called a meeting!' Steffi cried, but the room was already emptying out as everyone headed downstairs.

'I cannot believe this,' Land muttered to himself, riffling the pages of his management manual. 'You didn't bother to cover failure? Don't any of your readers ever screw up? What kind of a name is Osbert Desanex anyway?' The author photograph showed a man in a bomber jacket and mirrored aviator glasses who looked like a Lithuanian pimp. Land searched the index – 'bankruptcy', 'loss', 'debt', 'humiliation' – nothing about quarantines or biochemical hazards.

Heading over to the window, he looked down into the road. The black BMW opposite was an unmarked police vehicle; it sat too low in the rear and there was too much kit on the dashboard. As he watched, Darren Link lumbered out from the driver's side and looked up at the unit's windows.

Land fell back against the wall, hoping he hadn't been seen. He would have to warn the others to stay away from the windows and the phones. If Link was going to cut them off from the outside world, they could cut themselves off from Link. *God knows life here hasn't been easy,* he thought. *The pay is lousy, the targets are impossible and my detectives ridicule me, but at least . . .* He couldn't think of a way to complete the thought. *What have our bosses ever done for us except try to shut us down and make our lives hell? Well, it's time to pick a side and make a stand. They may not be much, but the PCU staff are all the family I have, and families should stick together.*

Thus fortified, he went to the operations room. And found nobody there.

Janice Longbright reached the bottom of the basement's scaffolded staircase and pushed at the riveted iron door that stood before her. 'Has anyone else been down here recently?' she asked over her shoulder.

'Arthur told the two Daves not to allow anyone to use the steps,' said May. 'They're only held together with nails.'

Renfield tried the torch on his phone. 'Where are the lights? I thought they were supposed to finish the electrics ages ago.'

'They haven't been put in yet,' May explained. 'The old wires went under the floor and were corroded because of the damp down here. We're built over a tributary of the River Fleet.'

Janice put her shoulder to the door and screeched it back a couple of feet. Colin tried the switch to a single overhead bulb. Dead.

'God, what's that awful smell?' Janice covered her nose and mouth. 'It's like rotting fish!'

'Let me go first,' said Meera. 'I'm used to bin duty and Colin. Weird smells don't bother me.'

The basement covered almost the entire footprint of the building, but the air was so dust-filled that their torchlights failed to reach the far walls. 'It smells like death,' said Dan Banbury, who knew exactly what death smelled like.

Their lights delineated the grey concrete sarcophagus that rose from the far end of the floor. 'That's not very old,' Banbury remarked. 'You can see the striations where cement was poured into a planked mould. Concrete's only been around since 1824.'

'Hey, the body's still in here.' Renfield reached the edge and shone his torch inside. 'I thought someone said it had gone to Giles's mortuary?'

'So did I.' Joining him, Longbright ran her light over its length to reveal a human form beneath rotted grey rags. 'He's well preserved. I thought the air down here was too damp to do that.'

Suddenly the corpse sat up. Everybody yelled. The corpse yelled back. For a moment the unit's basement turned into the set of a Hammer horror film.

'Jesus, you just took a year off my life,' said the corpse. 'What's the matter with you?'

'It's a bloody Terence!' said Meera.

'I'm not a tramp, I'm a gentleman of the road. I'd shake your hand but it's not very clean. Harry Prayer,' said Harry Prayer. 'I'm a friend of Mr Bryant's.'

'Of course you are. What are you doing here?' Longbright asked, backing off.

'Mr Bryant said I could doss down here if I got into a situation.'

'What kind of situation?'

'One involving a rare edition of the King James Bible, a boxing priest and the likelihood of me getting my face punched off.'

'Fair enough. How did you get in?'

'The café next door,' he said, which explained everything. The Ladykillers Café was a perfectly respectable cake shop on the ground floor but had a sex shop in the basement, and their fire escape door connected to the basement of the PCU.

Renfield rolled his eyes. 'So much for being a secure unit.'

'At least we can get out,' said Longbright.

'No,' said Harry. 'I came in here for a kip last night but when I got up this morning and went to find some gentleman's reading matter to peruse while performing my ablutions I found that someone had barred the door from the other side.'

'How do you know Mr Bryant?' asked Bimsley.

'I've many strings to my bow,' Harry explained. 'I'm a theologian and a cobbler.'

'Great,' said Meera. 'If we need someone to dispute the existence of God with a mouthful of tin tacks we'll let you know. Can you just get out of our unit?'

'He can't leave, Meera,' said Longbright. 'We're stuck with him.'

'I'm right here, I do have feelings,' said Harry, pulling the lapels of his ragged overcoat about him like an affronted landlady tightening a dressing gown.

'He's right,' said Renfield, 'and he might be able to help us. Harry, if we disguised you, do you think you could pass for Mr Bryant?'

'He doesn't need a disguise,' said Meera disgustedly.

They took Harry Prayer upstairs. With the addition of a striped scarf and a homburg, Prayer made a more than passable Arthur Bryant, although he could also have passed for a particularly disreputable greyhound trainer.

'Thank God you're back,' exclaimed Land as they all trooped in. 'Good Lord, what on earth is that awful smell?'

'That would be me,' said Harry cheerfully. 'My socks have passed peak cleanliness. Harry Prayer. You must be Raymond Land. I've heard a lot about you, you poor devil.'

Land looked in horror at Prayer's proffered hand. 'Who is this revolting-looking creature and what is he doing here?'

'I'd like to know what it is that encourages everyone to refer to me in the third person,' Harry complained.

'We need you to walk back and forth in front of this window, maybe open it and look out a couple of times,' said Renfield. 'Actually, let's open it now. Do you think you can do that?'

'I have a master's degree in theology and honours in hermeneutics, Greek and Hebrew,' replied Harry. 'I should be able to open a window.'

'Not necessarily,' said John May. 'My partner is the smartest man I've ever met and I've watched him shoving at a door marked "PULL" for at least five minutes.'

After setting Harry Prayer to work and leaving Meera to oversee his movements, they headed to the operations room. 'Right,' said Land, 'we can't wait any longer for Bryant to appear with some miracle breakthrough, so we'll have to come up with something ourselves.'

May's phone rang. 'It's him!' he told the room. 'Arthur, where are you?'

'I know what's going on,' Bryant shouted above the noise of traffic, 'I just need to check one more thing, but I'm not sure if it's safe to try it alone. Could somebody come with me?'

'You never usually ask for help,' May reminded him. 'Unfortunately this is the one time we can't give it to you. Link is using your excuse about the plague body to quarantine us. Nobody's coming in or getting out until after the health and safety officers from the Crick Institute have given the building the all-clear.'

'That's a bit of a nuisance,' said Bryant. 'I'll have to go it alone, unless . . .' And he hung up.

46

'SOMETIMES WHAT LOOKS LIKE CRUELTY IS ACTUALLY KINDNESS'

Arthur Bryant was sitting in Nino's, the scruffy Italian café that stood diagonally opposite the headquarters of the PCU. 'Is that supposed to be me?' he asked Maggie Armitage, watching as Harry Prayer marched theatrically back and forth past the first-floor window. 'I don't look like a Terence, do I?'

Maggie considered the idea. 'Not a tramp exactly, but he's wearing one of your overcoats. Wherever did you get that belt?'

'I shut my old one in the doors of a Piccadilly line tube train,' Bryant explained. 'That's a curtain sash I liberated from one of the windows at Somerset House. I design my own clothes, you know. But enough about *haute couture*, I need your help. There's no one else who can do this. The staff have been barricaded into the building and I'm shut out. Would you be able to accompany me somewhere?'

'I don't see why not,' said Maggie. 'Dame Maude Hackshaw and I were supposed to hold a spirit-raising at the Quakers' Society later today but the meeting was cancelled. You need thirty-two knives to materialize Asmodeus, and that's a lot of cutlery to smuggle through a metal detector. Plus he's the Lord of Conjugal Discord and the organizer is trying for a baby, so it wasn't advisable. What do you need?'

'I've lost my primary suspect. I told you about Jeremy Forester, didn't I?'

'The businessman who was in the park when his wife was killed.'

'Yes. I was thinking about that M. R. James story "Casting the Runes". You know the one: a man is slipped a piece of paper with a spell on it, and if he isn't able to pass it on to somebody else before a certain length of time elapses, a demon comes to kill him.'

'I'm sorry, chum, I'm not entirely sure where you're going with this.' It was a familiar feeling among those whom Bryant counted as friends: the sense that she'd missed some crucial link in his logic.

'Let me see if I can explain it a bit better. I'd assumed Forester was trying to get out of the country because he was wanted for fraud and deeply in debt – heaven knows those are good enough reasons for needing to leave in a hurry. But Steffi Vesta thinks there's another reason. His fraud case concerns the hiding of assets in a free port storage facility. We know about one in Luxembourg but she says there's a second registered account number. He was spending a lot of time in Hong Kong, so it's likely the other one is there. He just can't get to it.'

'How is it accessed?'

'By a lengthy code that only Forester knew, and it has to be entered in person at the site. Obviously, he couldn't do that. This morning he let himself into the private members' entrance of Number One, Poultry, where his office was based. The club on the roof hadn't opened yet but he gained access via his old swipe card and was able to get out into the garden. He climbed over the guardrail, on to the left-side buttress that hangs out over the road, and jumped.'

'He's dead, I take it?'

'A bit more than dead. He dispersed himself over a fairly wide area. Link thinks that's the end of the case.'

'But you don't.'

'I agree that on the surface Forester *looks* culpable. He was there when his wife died, and had good reason to wish her dead because she was about to take him for everything he had left. We don't know if she had knowledge of his hidden assets, but considering he never even told her he'd lost his job it seems unlikely that she knew the full extent of his dealings. But I never really suspected Mr Forester. He just seemed to be in the wrong place at the wrong time. If you had a fortune stashed away in a spot where you couldn't get at it, what would you do?'

Maggie twisted a length of iridescent funfair beads around her fingers, thinking. 'I suppose I'd try to find someone else to get it for me. Somebody I could trust completely.'

'Except that he was a loner, and there was no one to whom he could turn.'

'You're telling me that a rich, successful businessman like Forester had *no* friends?'

'Think about it, Maggie. His colleagues could no longer speak to him, and his wife and child were gone. What do you see when you head down the City Road? Rows and rows of secure apartment buildings filled with people just like him. They work and sleep, and barely interact with anyone else. Whom could he rely on to dispose of his assets? Plus, there was another problem. If Steffi is able to work out that he had a second account in Hong Kong, the City of London Fraud and Economic Crime Squad can, too. So you see the code is no longer the key to untold riches – it's the proof of guilt. That innocuous slip of paper is like the curse in "Casting the Runes". Forester couldn't access the money and he couldn't trust anyone else with the code. The thing was a millstone around his neck. But of course there *was* one person to whom he could give it.'

'I'm sorry, Arthur, I feel like I've wandered into the middle of a particularly confusing film.' Maggie shook her head and rattled her many Incan beaded earrings. 'Who did he give this code to, and why do you need me?'

'Good Lord, woman, do try to pay attention, it's very simple,' snapped Bryant, exasperated. 'There was one person in Forester's life whom he still loved and cared about in spite of everything that had happened. His wife. That was why he went to Clement Crescent that morning – to catch her and tell her that he was sorry, and to give her the code. He'd jotted it on the back of the piece of card he used to find the gardens recommended by the Rough Sleepers Community. That was why it was under his shoe – it had been in his hand, and he dropped it when he saw her killed. It happened so fast that he didn't even have time to react. He watched and then fled. But here's the other thing – *he couldn't have recognized her murderer.* It would have been the first thing he'd have told us.'

'I don't really have the faintest idea what you're talking about, Arthur. You still haven't answered my question.' She laid a bangled hand on his, speaking slowly and loudly. 'Are. You. Having. A. Relapse?'

'Certainly not.' He pushed back his chair and gathered his hat and scarf. 'But I need you to come with me.'

'Where are we going?'

'I have to look at something. It's not very far.'

'What, exactly?' she asked, pulling on her raincoat.

'Drains,' said Bryant. 'My fault. Easily distracted, I can see that now. It would help to know what Lauren Posner was wearing on the day she killed herself. Also, she was short-sighted. Was she wearing her glasses when she died? Let me call John and ask him. Then there's the matter of the budgerigar. It all fits. Come along.'

He's telling me the case hinges on drains, clothes, glasses and a budgie? thought Maggie as they stepped back into the street. 'Shouldn't we tell John and the others where we're going?' she suggested gently, not entirely convinced that her old friend hadn't mentally left the building.

'They can't help us now and nobody else would believe me. Hurry up, there's no time to lose.'

'I'm not sure I'm going to be of any use to you,' she warned, impeding the traffic with a stab of her umbrella. 'I'm not terribly brave.'

'Oh, I think you are,' said Bryant. 'You stopped the Arsenal Electrocutor from making an escape, remember? You chased him into your garden.'

'Strictly speaking, he fell over my lawnmower cord.'

'Still counts.'

On the other side of the road, Darren Link watched and told his men to stand down. 'No, let them go,' he told them. 'What are those two going to do? It's over. A hallucinating old man and a crazy white witch? I almost feel sorry for them. We'll miss them when they've gone, but I think their time has finally passed.'

He stared after the scruffy old fellow in the striped green scarf and crumpled hat as he linked arms with his tiny rainbow-cloaked companion, trying to find a way across the traffic-choked road.

Link looked at his impassive sergeant, Bassett, then back at the retreating pair. 'You know, after my old mum died we wondered whether my father could cope, living by himself out in the middle of Kent. He swore he was fine, preparing his own meals, going for walks, staying well. He didn't need to go into care. But I was worried, so one day I told him I was going to watch him all day long, from when he got up to when he went to bed, and all he had to do was go about his usual daily routine. Old people can be really crafty. By mid-afternoon he still hadn't eaten anything hot. He didn't have the strength to get the freezer open; he'd been living on bread and jam. At the end of the day I asked him: How do you think you did? And he started crying. Finally he said, "Perhaps I do need help. Perhaps it's time."'

He glanced over at his sergeant, who was not even

bothering to pretend he was listening. 'That's what this is, Bassett. An intervention. We had to let them see for themselves that they can't handle crimes of this magnitude any more. It's better to let them fail and understand why I'm doing it than to just close down the unit without their approval. Sometimes what looks like cruelty is actually kindness.'

'Whatever,' said Bassett. 'How much longer do you want to hold off?'

'Faraday's found a health and safety officer from the Crick Institute who's prepared to sign the order for sealing off the unit,' said Link. 'She doesn't even have to view the property first if there's a reasonable suspicion that it's a risk to the public. It looks like we won't have to wait until tomorrow morning. As soon as we have a verbal verification of the order we can enter the property by force, evacuate it and sequester all the files.'

'It's a bloody embarrassment,' said the sergeant angrily. 'Bryant and May should have been packed off into an old folks' home decades ago. They're just holding everything up for the rest of us.'

Link bristled. 'You haven't earned the right to say that! Those two have done more good for this city than you or I could ever do. The same thing'll happen to us when the next lot comes in, did you ever think about that? Show some bloody respect.'

All tenures come to a close eventually, he thought. *So long, lads, you had a good innings.*

47

'HE'LL ONLY SOUND LIKE CASSANDRA IF HE TRIES TO EXPLAIN'

Even at the best of times the offices of the Peculiar Crimes Unit resembled student accommodation, not the kind that consisted of elegant Oxford rooms filled with tidy hard-working pupils quietly tapping at laptops, more like an off-campus overspill where someone was likely to leave a motorcycle in the common room. On Sunday afternoon the PCU offices reached a new level of chaos.

Without the sternly benign ghost of Arthur Bryant stalking the corridors issuing admonitions around a clenched pipe, the wheels of this particular investigatory vehicle had come off in spectacular fashion. Steffi Vesta watched in ill-concealed amazement as the arguments raged from room to room, Longbright dropped another great stack of witness reports on to her desk and Raymond Land repeatedly fell over the cat. Nothing like this ever occurred in the Cologne Bundeskriminalamt.

'It's all right, you know,' May reassured her. 'They're not having a go at each other; they're trying to find a solution. They just get a bit shouty sometimes.'

'I do not understand how anyone can work productively in

such an environment,' said Vesta, watching as Land threatened to have the operations room cleared for the third time in an hour.

'You seem to be managing,' May told her. 'Look at the information you were able to dig up on Forester's secret investments.'

'Yes, but this is not important for the case, I think,' said Steffi.

'Of course it's important. Can we find out what's in the Hong Kong free port consignment?'

'That is privileged information. But if the goods were imported from the EU there may be a way.' She headed for one of the unused laptops. 'Give me a few minutes. I will see if I can find someone in Customs and Excise.'

May went to the window and looked out at the officers massing on the pavement. They looked like a chorus waiting to go onstage and perform 'A Policeman's Lot Is Not a Happy One'. 'I think we're about to run out of time,' he warned. 'Dan, do you have anything that can pick up what they're saying?'

'That's easy,' said Banbury. 'Give me a mo.' He returned with an electronic cone covered in black wires. 'This little bugger increases ambient sound gain by more than fifty-five decibels and picks up sounds more than one hundred yards away using a multi-element, high-sensitivity, ninety-degree swivelling microphone.'

'Point it at Link,' May instructed.

Banbury raised the window six inches, put on his headset and aimed the cone.

'He's telling his men they've found a health and safety officer who's prepared to approve the closure. They're just waiting for her to say that the order's been filed, and then they're coming in.'

'How long?'

'Hang on.' Banbury listened. 'Five to ten minutes,' he reported.

'OK, listen up, everybody.' May turned to the others, who all stopped talking except for Meera, whose last words were '—and that's why Raymond's wife left him', before lapsing into awkward silence.

'Link is getting ready to clear the building,' May said. 'We could still make it difficult for them to gain access.'

'This isn't a St Trinian's film,' said Banbury. 'I'm not going to stand on the battlements throwing bags of flour at them.'

'There are London bolts on the front and back doors,' Colin pointed out. 'The two Daves are supposed to have put in an electronic operating system so that we can control them from up here, but I don't think they finished installing the junction box.'

'Link doesn't know that,' said May. 'Go and lock them manually. If Arthur reckons he has a lead, we're just going to have to trust him.'

The phone in his hand rang. Everybody froze and listened.

'It's Giles,' May told them. 'He says the cadaver they removed from our basement isn't infected. He's just texting Link now to warn him that there's no legal reason to quarantine the building.'

'But that's great news!' said Land. 'We'll be able to stay here.'

'Too late.' Banbury pulled off his headset. 'The order's just been approved. They're coming in.'

'Hang on.' May raised a hand for quiet and listened. 'Thanks for the warning.' He put down his phone. 'We're going to be investigated by America's Central Intelligence Agency.'

'The CIA? Are you crazy?' said Renfield. 'What for?'

'Giles has some further information on the body. It seems that seven years ago, the US ambassador to Britain lost his son. Well, he just turned up.'

'In our basement?' Land was beside himself. 'The government purchased this property – it has nothing to do with us!'

'Let's not worry about it right now,' said May. 'We've got other problems.'

Land's phone was the next to ring, making him jump.

'Mr Land, there appears to be a tramp marching up and down past Mr Bryant's window like a goose-stepping soldier,' said Darren Link with exaggerated politeness. 'If he's meant to be stunt-doubling for your detective, I have to say his performance isn't likely to bag him a BAFTA. My uncle Wilfred could have done a better impersonation and he was in an iron lung. By the way, we've got the closure order, but my men appear to be having some trouble gaining access to your building. Can you come down and let them in?'

'Ah, I'd love to be able to help you,' said Land, trying to sound casual, 'but we're having a few teething problems with our new electronic operating system. There's a faulty junction box. We've called out the engineers and they should be here within the next hour.' May nudged him. 'Two hours. Three to be on the safe side.'

'Not good enough,' insisted Link. 'We can't wait out here that long. Just open the bloody door. I can almost hear you lot thinking – it's like watching a baby giraffe trying to stand up. It's just too painful. The Crick Institute is sending over its team, and we need to allow them access. Failure to comply will mean—'

May interrupted. 'Darren, come on, you know me, we've worked together often enough in the past. I'll be honest with you, really honest this time. Arthur has a fresh lead on the case. He won't tell me what it is or how he got it, but it won't take him long to find out if he's on the right track, possibly only a few more minutes. That's why we're stalling you. If I let you in now it'll be the end of us, you know that.'

May pressed his ear close to the phone. Link was thinking. He pushed the point. 'We've helped you immeasurably in the past, Darren. Our strike rate pulled up your own aggregate at the City of London and helped to secure your funding. Faraday's your enemy, not us. He's planning to push privatization on to the parks, and doesn't care how bad it makes you look. We don't need the Crick sending a team; there are no infectious diseases here. Please, keep this line open for me, just for one more hour.' He checked his watch. 'It's three p.m. now. If I haven't heard back from Arthur by four o'clock I swear I'll open the doors to you. And if he calls me before that to admit that his lead is a dead end, I'll let you in immediately.'

The line fell silent again. May could feel the seconds ticking by.

'No deal,' decided Link. 'My neck's on the line, too.'

'All right,' said May. 'Half an hour. You get in at three thirty. Darren, I have never asked you for a favour.'

'I'll hold them off until I hear from you.' Link hung up.

May turned to the group. 'OK, let's see if we can help Arthur. I've got a text from him asking if Lauren Posner committed suicide in a summer dress. Is there some way we can check that out?'

'Easy,' said Longbright. 'I've got the coroner's file. Give me a minute.'

'Why would Mr Bryant want to know something like that?' asked Colin.

Longbright searched her laptop. 'You know Arthur, he'll only sound like Cassandra if he tries to explain.'

'Blimey, have we got another suspect?' asked Meera.

'No, Meera, in Greek mythology snakes licked Cassandra's ears and gave her the ability to hear the future, but Apollo cursed her by spitting in her mouth so that no one would ever believe her prophecies, even though they were truthful.'

Mangeshkar pulled a face. 'That's gross. I don't understand Mr Bryant's reasoning. If he knows what Posner was wearing when she topped herself, does that mean he'll know who the killer is?'

May sighed. 'Your guess is as good as mine.'

Longbright scrolled through her screen. 'Here we go – a white cotton skirt and white blouse. That's odd.'

'Why?'

'It was the end of April and unseasonably cold. Why was she dressed for mid-July?'

48

'YOU SAW THE LIGHT DIE IN HER EYES'

'Arthur, I can't walk any faster.'

'We're running out of time,' Bryant warned, hurrying his companion along Euston Road. 'We can't afford any further delays. Turn in here.' They passed Paolozzi's huge bronze statue of Isaac Newton and headed into the rain-slick courtyard of the British Library.

'I'm sorry, sir, I need to see inside your bag,' said the security guard as they stepped inside the entrance to the building's immense atrium. 'And you, too, madam.'

'I wonder if you could just let us through?' asked Bryant, sounding far more suspect than he'd intended. 'I'm afraid we're in a bit of a hurry.'

The British Library was not used to dealing with rush demands. The guard took Bryant's satchel from him with slow deliberation and put his hand inside it.

'I wouldn't do that—' Bryant began, just as the trap went off and the guard yelped. 'I'm most awfully sorry.' The grimacing guard withdrew his hand, encased in steel mesh. 'I adapted a Victorian model originally designed to trap badgers. I thought it would deter thieves. We live in King's Cross,' he added by way of explanation. 'Here, let me.'

Together, they wrested it off the guard's bruised hand.

'Perhaps you'd care to show me what else you've got,' suggested the guard. 'Save me losing any more fingers.'

Bryant emptied out a pound of liquorice allsorts, a volume by C. C. Stanley entitled *Highlights in the History of Concrete* that he had borrowed from Banbury, a weather station barometer – 'I'm taking it in to be repaired,' Bryant explained – his address book, two notepads, various assorted pens, pencils, bits of string, magnets, coins and a gun.

'You really can't bring that in here.' The guard pointed to the Walther PPK with an air of apology.

'Oh, I wasn't planning to fire it, although it is loaded,' Bryant assured him. 'I was using it in a demonstration the other day and thought it might be useful.'

'I'll just set this on one side for now,' said the guard, lifting it by poking a pencil down the barrel.

'He's a police officer,' interposed Maggie. 'Tell him, Arthur.'

'Oh, didn't I mention that?' said Bryant, surprised.

'No, sir, you didn't,' replied the guard. 'Madam, what have you got?'

Maggie upturned her bag on to the guard's counter. This time the haul included dowsing rods, a Ouija planchette, playing cards, a hammer, various purses and a bugle, the latter for use in séances. Some kind of insect fell out and ran out across the floor. The guard raised the hammer and one eyebrow.

'You never know around here,' said Maggie. 'A lady must feel safe.'

'Are these drugs?' the guard asked, raising several packets of amber, cobalt and saffron powders.

'It rather depends on your belief system, I suppose,' answered Maggie. 'I mean separately they're not illegal – except that one – but in the right combination they can be absolutely lethal. If you mix this one with cayenne pepper, sulphur, gunpowder, willow bark and dill you can give your enemy the most appalling diarrhoea.'

'I think you'd better leave all of these items with us,' said the guard. 'I think I need to call my boss.'

'This is really most inconvenient,' said Bryant, checking the single working hand on his watch. As the guard turned to look for his superior, Bryant grabbed Maggie's hand and pulled her around the counter. They set off at a half-run and disappeared under the central staircase before anyone realized they'd gone. The guards weren't used to senior citizens operating at speed on highly polished floors.

'I need you to meet me in ten minutes,' Bryant told the white witch. 'Do you think you'll be able to find room B230?'

'Darling, I know this building like the back of my hand,' she retorted. 'I could find my way around the occult history section in a power cut. It's over there, isn't it?'

'No, those are the wheelchair toilets. Never mind. Perhaps it's best if you stay here.' He patted her on the head and set off for the lifts.

They had lost valuable time having to explain themselves to the security guard, and now, without Ray Kirkpatrick to guide him, Bryant had trouble locating the antique maps room. Finally he chanced upon the door and entered. The floor was deserted, but he remembered where to go.

Heading over to Duncan Aston's desk, he saw that the huge map book detailing Bazalgette's drains was still here, although now it was closed. It was the sight of this open book that had fascinated him on his last visit.

'So easily distracted,' he muttered, looking away from it to the Impressionist prints and old photographs that lined the walls.

One particularly drew his attention. The monochrome stage portrait showed a young woman in a bower of small white flowers. She wore a headdress and a diaphanous flowing gown. From the faraway look in her eyes, it was obvious that the photographer was attempting to suggest a dreamlike quality, but as in so many old theatre photographs she looked rather lumpen and earthbound. Bryant had been reminded of it when he had looked at the photograph of Nathalie. He had seen it from the corner of his eye but not spotted its meaning. *What can I do?* he thought. *How can I bring this to a quick end?*

The entrance door swung open and shut. If Duncan Aston was surprised to find the elderly detective standing over his desk, he didn't show it. 'Can I help you, inspector?' he asked.

'Oh, I'm not an inspector,' Bryant replied. 'I don't even have a title any more. They're taking them all away from us. Plain old Mr Bryant will do.' He pointed at the picture. 'I rather like this portrait, for all its theatricality.' He waved a hand across it. 'Do you know who's in it?'

'That's my grandmother.' Aston seemed harassed, and ran his hand through his cropped russet hair with impatience. 'I have a lot of work to get through this afternoon. We're preparing for a major exhibition of rare London maps.'

Bryant held up his hands. 'Sorry, I only popped by for a chat. I don't want to hold you up. You said your mother was an actress as well, didn't you? It's funny how often theatre runs in the family.'

'In my case only the women.'

'Quite so.' Bryant pulled out his trifocals, leaned forward and squinted at the caption. '*Sleeping Titania in Her Faerie Bower.* You've been in this room a long time, haven't you?'

'Far too long.' Aston advanced on him. 'Why do you ask?'

'And you chose the pictures?'

'I found that one in the archive. We have an extensive collection of theatre photography.'

Bryant chewed his lip, thinking. 'It's just that after remembering this photograph, something stuck in my brain. I tried to decide – and I know you'll think this sounds silly – what parks and gardens are actually for. They're to provide tranquillity. To show you perhaps, and I hope you won't think this too fanciful, what Eden or heaven looks like. If it was the last thing you saw before you passed away, wouldn't you die happier?'

'If this is about my girlfriend, Mr Bryant, it's in rather poor taste.'

'I suppose it is about your girlfriend.' Bryant tapped his pockets for his pipe. 'But first, tell me about your mother.'

'Mr Bryant, I really don't have time for this.' Aston irritably tapped his foot on the parquet.

'I'm sure you can make time. You see, I made a number of mistakes. Helen Forester came to our attention first, so we assumed that our investigation started there, but it went back earlier, didn't it? Right back to when Lauren Posner killed herself. It was a raw April morning, bitterly cold, but she went to sit in the park dressed in white like the woman in the photograph. She didn't even have a coat.'

'She wasn't herself,' said Aston.

'So you told me.' Bryant folded his glasses away. 'So you told everyone. And you'd know, because you were there with her, weren't you?' Bryant's wide cornflower-blue eyes could not be avoided. 'There were no cameras to see you, of course, but there was a witness. An old man with a dog said he remembered you, but he thought he saw you leaving while the girl stayed behind sitting on the bench, so his witness statement was filed and forgotten. Until I unearthed it.'

'It's no secret,' said Aston tetchily. 'I sat with Lauren for a while. She was drunk and tearful. I didn't know she had pills on her. She'd hardly stopped crying since—'

'*The accident.* Ah, yes.' Bryant touched a forefinger to his temple. 'I couldn't help thinking that you rather over-egged the pudding, telling me her alcoholism was in her medical records. What gave me more trouble was the suicide note. She handwrote it, didn't she, posting it to her parents earlier that day? All rather formal, but not beyond the bounds of possibility. Funny that she didn't leave one for you.'

'I suppose I saw more of her.'

'And as you say, she was not herself. Luckily her parents kept theirs, although they threw away the envelope, which was a pity.' Bryant looked around the room. 'I love it up here. Maps, books, pens – calligraphy pens. How are your handwriting skills?'

Aston shrugged. 'Part of my job is retouching map panels as well as restoring them, so my handwriting has to be perfect. I'm a trained calligrapher.'

'It's funny, Duncan – can I call you Duncan? Probably best to, because Aston isn't your real name, is it? You see, the last time I saw you I still had Bazalgette's drawing of the London drains in my head. And as I walked out into the street, looking down at the pavement, what did I see? "Aston's New Warrior". That's what it says on the drain panel outside. They're all over London. A silly connection, but I couldn't resist running a search. And what did I find? You changed your name when you came to work here. Your real surname is Richmond, isn't that right?'

'I changed it,' said Aston flatly. 'The name had bad memories for me. That's not a crime.'

'I suppose it's not,' Bryant agreed happily. 'But having the right name helped to sort everything out in my head. Your mother was Julia Richmond, critically acclaimed for her fiery portrayal of Titania. You saw her perform in the same role many times, didn't you?'

Aston remained still and silent.

'She kissed an awful lot of donkeys, by all accounts. She even got a criminal record for doing so. "Running a disorderly house", I think they still called it then. And you were there all the time, showing the punters in. Which is why you were put into care.'

'My past has nothing to do with you,' Aston said with low menace.

'Oh, I think it does. I wondered what kind of effect it would have had on a young boy.'

'I still loved her,' he said softly, staring at the photograph.

'I have a picture of her in the exact same pose. In her mother's pose.'

'The same pose Lauren Posner was in when they found her,' said Bryant. 'One of the hardest parts of being a policeman is knowing when to pursue something and when to leave it alone. They go to a house, the girlfriend's been hit, she called the cops earlier but now she doesn't want to press charges, that sort of thing. The Met's busy, they're not being paid to watch everyone; people have to be trusted to lead their own lives. *Five* call-outs to the flat of one Duncan Richmond, and nobody ever questioned it?'

Aston rose and put on one of his white cotton gloves. He slowly circled the map desk, watching Bryant. 'Lauren could be difficult sometimes. Tempers became overheated.'

'Would you say Ms Posner was in an abusive relationship? Would you call yourself a latent sadist? Forgive me, I don't suppose you knew back then, did you? Thought you just lost your temper because she was being annoying, not because you were enjoying it. You couldn't see it until after the accident in the tunnel. And it *was* an accident, coming back from the party that rainy, chaotic night in the pretty red car, the Chevrolet Cruze, a bit over the limit, then getting diverted under the station. You must remember. After all, you were driving.'

Aston looked at him blankly. 'I don't know what you're talking about.'

'For of course the car was an American import and the steering wheel was on the other side, wasn't it? So when you pulled up it was *Lauren* who spoke to poor old Sergeant Kemp-Bird, not you. Because he was standing in the middle of the road. An unwell traffic cop in steamed-over glasses with a babbling headset and honking vehicles trying to squeeze past. Even so, you'd think he'd notice something like that. No, because she leaned out of the open window and looked up at him, and his mind was elsewhere so he misremembered it. When the accident happened and the car mounted the kerb you slid down in the seat and Lauren got out to see what had happened, and it was messy and rainy and smoky and noisy, and nobody noticed that she hadn't been driving because why would they? She was in what should have been the driver's seat. But she couldn't go to the hospital with the others because she couldn't leave you, so she ran back to the car and *you* pulled away.

'When Lauren found out that Charlie Forester had died, you got rid of the car and told her that if anyone came to talk to her she would have to lie. Which she felt dreadful about. But why? You could have owned up. It wasn't your fault. That was the part I simply couldn't understand. But my partner told me something that stuck. He said that people sometimes keep bad relationships going just for the pleasure of hurting a partner, that cruelty becomes the only thing that pleases them. Is cruelty the only thing that pleases you?'

'I think you'd better go now, Mr Bryant,' said Aston, moving closer.

Bryant checked the big hand of his watch. 'Yes, I should be off soon. Bear with me for a moment more, though. Where was I? You enjoyed making Lauren feel bad. Every time she angered you, you brought it up again and increased her sense of guilt. But you pushed her too far. Eventually she decided to visit Sharyn Buckland and tell her the truth – that it was you who caused the accident, not her. I imagine that's when you decided she had to go. You got her drunk and took her to the park, which was virtually empty on such a cold afternoon. Lauren was a natural victim, empathetic and fragile. You enjoyed the power you had over her. You even told her what to wear. You dressed her as Titania, as your mother, and you said that everything was going to be all right, that you'd talk to Buckland and clear the whole thing up, and you gave her another drink – one to which you'd added a few crushed-up pills – am I right? What you hadn't expected was the thrill it gave you, seeing her looking so angelic. You alone had the power to send her to a beautiful, peaceful place. And you posed her just a little, although you probably didn't understand why you were doing it; it just made you feel more comfortable. But here's a funny thing: suicide can't be presumed – it has to be proven. And Lauren was found still wearing her glasses. People who kill themselves nearly always take their glasses off, and often their watches and rings. A little note of doubt was sounded at the inquest but nothing came of it. Then you went to see Sharyn Buckland, and watched her, trying to get up the nerve—'

'I only wanted to talk to her,' cut in Aston tonelessly. He was invading Bryant's space now, his arms at his sides. Flicking a quick glance at the door, Bryant carried on. It was important to appear oblivious to any threat.

'You followed Buckland, right to Helen Forester's flat. What did the two of them talk about in there? You had no idea, but you thought the worst. Were they going to the police, to say it was you and not Lauren who was driving drunk that night? Or perhaps they weren't even discussing that at all. You had no way of knowing. And you needed to find out. You hung around, trying to get a feel for what was going on. It must have been very frustrating. But this is where it gets interesting. You saw Helen Forester walking her dog. A very attractive woman, alone, keeping to a routine, whom you took to following.'

'I heard Helen Forester on the phone outside her flat,' Aston said, barely interested in his own story. 'She said, "What should we do about him, Sharyn? Is there any point in going to the police? It won't bring my son back."'

'So you killed her. You saw the light die in her eyes. And suddenly it all made sense. What you were doing wasn't wrong. The women didn't mind, in fact they were thankful for their release, and how you enjoyed the sensation! You stayed only long enough to make sure that Helen Forester was dead. The dog kept out of your reach but it wouldn't leave, because what you didn't know was that its master was also in the crescent with you, watching, but he was pathetically conflicted and powerless to act. So you ran off, leaving the dog behind, and as Jeremy Forester followed you out, the dog followed him. But you still had to take care of Buckland. And then – far more inconvenient – came a report in the news that you had been seen by a gardener.'

'If you've finished now,' said Aston, 'I think perhaps it's best if you go.'

Bryant walked around the desk, casually moving away from Aston. 'The last part of the puzzle was how you killed her, what you could possibly have used. We thought it might have been the dog leash except that we eventually found it in Green Park. You didn't leave anything behind except a few tiny pieces of what looked like lead shot. You hadn't planned to kill Helen Forester, so you had to make do with something that was already on your person. An item you might have had in your pocket. Then I remembered something I'd seen. That's why I came here – to find it.'

Aston slowly opened his fists. 'I believe this is what you're looking for.'

49

'THAT'S HOW ALL OF THIS BEGAN'

As Aston approached, he wrapped one end of the thin grey cloth tube around his left fist. 'I'm surprised you didn't spot it last time. Not much of a detective, are you?'

'I'm a bit of a bat when it comes to eyesight,' said Bryant. 'What is that?'

'We use them all the time in the library,' Aston said. 'Many of the larger books are too wide to hold open.' He held up the bobbled cord to demonstrate. 'It's a linen tube filled with small balls of lead. You lay it across the open page. It's heavy enough to keep the book flat while you work. They come in different weights and lengths. We have hundreds here. I've always got one on me. I find the seventy-centimetre one works best.'

'Trouble is, that one has a frayed end. You've lost some pieces of shot from it.' Bryant needed to keep talking. The library was mostly deserted at this time. He had no idea how long it would be before the security guard he and Maggie had dodged would appear. 'I couldn't see how you'd gained access to Clement Crescent. Then I remembered what a busybody old Mrs Farrier was. She saw you skulking about, didn't she? She wanted to know what you were up to. What did you tell her?'

'Do you know, I don't even remember. She invited me in for afternoon tea.'

'And that was when you discovered she had a budgerigar.'

Aston gave a mirthless chuckle at the thought. 'I guess I'm just full of good ideas. The old lady left her keys on the table while she went into the kitchen. I remembered those things from when I was a kid . . .'

'They're cuttlefish bones, Mr Aston. You wedge them between the bars of a cage and the birds like them because they're full of calcium. Best of all, they're very soft. The funny thing is that by pressing the key into the bone and taking an impression, you were replicating the exact method used by nineteenth-century burglars. That's how they illegally copied keys back then.'

'I knew that, of course. Kirkpatrick talks too much. A child could make one. The hardest part was finding any lead to melt into the impression. I had to buy some old toy soldiers and melt them down.'

'You could have used the book weights,' said Bryant. 'You missed a trick there. Not very improvisational, are you?'

Aston wrapped the book strap around his fists and flexed it. 'I improvised all the way. The name, the key, the cord, the women. Luck was on my side.'

'Perhaps your luck has finally run out.'

'No, I don't think so.' Aston took a step closer, towering over him. 'Old man falls down library steps. I'm sure it's happened many times before.'

'The stupid thing is, none of it should have happened at all,' said Bryant. He looked urgently towards the door, realizing how very far away it now seemed. It was essential to keep the conversation going. 'The boy wasn't hurt by your car. My analysis will show that when he bent down to pick up the toy truck he accidentally transferred the shard to his eye. You killed Lauren Posner for nothing. Not quite true – you killed her because you wanted to.'

Before Bryant had a chance to move, Aston released one

end of the heavy cord and whipped it around the detective's neck with astonishing speed. It was like being struck with a gaucho's *boleadoras*. Bryant suddenly found himself unable to draw breath.

Aston pulled the cord tighter. Bryant tried to get his fingers under it, but was too weak to gain a grip. He felt himself being lifted off the floor. Lights danced before his eyes. The door seemed a mile away now. *God,* he thought, *what a bloody silly way to die.*

The handle of the main door rattled as the shadow of a small woman appeared in its window. 'Arthur, is this the one?' called a thin, querulous voice. 'Are you in there or did I get it wrong again?'

Aston held on to the cord in silence and pulled tighter. Bryant could not move or call out.

'I should have written the number down, shouldn't I? I thought it was B230. Or was it A300? Or is that a motorway?' The handle rattled once more, then stopped. *No,* Bryant cried out silently, *don't go!* He watched in horror as Maggie's shadow slipped away.

Aston renewed his grip, pulling Bryant further off the ground. The detective felt his consciousness blur and fade.

With his last breath he kicked out his left foot, knocking over a tin wastepaper bin. Then came darkness.

'Some of us are still trying to do some bloody work in here, you know,' said Ray Kirkpatrick, removing his headphones and peering around one of the library stacks. The great bear-like English professor had been working around the corner of the large L-shaped room and now rose from his seat, thudding over. 'Do you want to put Mr Bryant down or do I have to tear your earholes off?'

Aston was so surprised to see someone else in the department that he froze, so Kirkpatrick punched him in the face. He struck with astounding force, breaking Aston's nose. Bryant fell to the floor, yanking the cord from his neck. For good measure, Kirkpatrick stood on Aston's windpipe until he blacked out.

'Could you be a bit more careful, Arthur? He might have killed you.'

'Very possibly,' wheezed Bryant, 'if he'd had a knife. That lariat wasn't doing the job very efficiently, I'm wearing two scarves.'

'It's a miracle I heard you.' Kirkpatrick gave Aston a boot in the head just to be sure he was unconscious. 'That bin went over during the three-second break between Cannibal Corpse and Decapitated Funeral. The next time you decide to get into a scrape, you might want to check that you've got some back-up first.'

'If you can't feel safe in the British Library,' Bryant said, rubbing his sore neck, 'where can you?'

'Ah, so this *is* the right room,' said Maggie, wandering in. 'Arthur, whatever are you doing sitting on the floor?'

Darren Link checked his Russian aviator's chronometer. 'Three thirty, on the nose,' he said. 'That's it, Islington's team is standing around in the rain like a bunch of King's Cross sploshers and the PCU's time is now officially up.'

He phoned John May. 'I'm sorry, mate, we're coming in. I'd quite prefer it if you unlocked the door. Save us doing a London knock. My sergeant did his back in ice skating and can't lift the battering ram.'

'Can't we just have five more minutes?' May pleaded. 'I tried calling Arthur but he's not answering his phone.'

'That's because he's old, deaf and mad as a bag of ferrets,' Link pointed out. 'Come in, number 231, your time is up.' He prodded his sergeant. 'Bassett, don't just stand there like a wet weekend, go and see if he's opening the door. Put your ear to it.'

Bassett lowered a tentative lughole on to the cold steel. 'I can't hear anything, sir,' he called back, and then fell in as the door swung open.

'Come on up,' said May wearily. 'We'll co-operate, I promise.'

Darren Link stepped over his sergeant and warily led his men into the building. 'Don't touch anything,' he told them. 'There's all kinds of weird stuff lying around this place.'

Bassett clambered to his feet and gave him an odd look. 'What's the matter?' Link asked. The sergeant held up his hand to show the palm covered with some kind of green fungus. He pointed to an upturned plate that had been left behind the door. 'For God's sake, wipe that off quickly,' Link warned. 'Bryant conducts experiments. It could be anything.'

'It's OK, it's cake icing,' said Janice Longbright, taking the plate away. 'We were hungry. Please, come in.'

She led the way to the operations room. When Link pushed open the door, he was amazed to see Arthur Bryant sitting surrounded by the other members of the PCU staff. A peculiar-looking woman in a rainbow jumper covered with costume jewellery was serving tea as if she was at home on an ordinary Sunday afternoon, and not in a barricaded police unit.

'How the hell did you get in here?' Link demanded to know.

'I came through next door,' replied Bryant. 'Your killer is in the basement. It's all right; he can't get out. We don't have a detention room any more so I've handcuffed him to a radiator. I was rather loath to do it, seeing as that's how all of this began, with another killer chained to a drainpipe. If that one hadn't got away we would never have had to close the roads under London Bridge Station.'

'What's he babbling about?' demanded Link. 'Is he ill again?'

'No,' said John May proudly. 'He's solved the case.'

50

'MADE RICHER BY YOUR FRIENDSHIP'

At 7 p.m. on Sunday the Caledonian Road was almost deserted, even though the rain had ceased and the clouds had cleared, leaving an ocean sky. In number 231 the lights had been lowered to a gentler hue, and only the unit staff remained. They had stayed to clear up after Link's arrival with the health and safety officer, but also because they enjoyed each other's company and had nowhere more important to go.

'Cheer up, Raymondo, have some Chateau Gumshrinker,' coaxed Bryant, opening a bottle of absolutely terrible Siberian burgundy and passing a glass to the unit chief. 'I guess your watercolour holiday will have to wait a while longer. Never mind, you have the remains of your life spread out before you in a rich panoply of disappointment.'

'I still don't know how you did it,' Land admitted. 'I mean I know, you've explained, but I just can't see it in my head.'

'It wasn't me,' said Bryant, pointing at his partner. 'We did it together. Aston's psychology didn't interest me; I thought he acted purely on instinct. If it hadn't been for John, it would never have occurred to me that when Aston took his girl-friend's life he had opened the Pandora's box of his own hidden feelings. A series of small nudges led him to kill again.'

He ticked off the points on his fingers. 'If he hadn't hung the family photograph above his desk. If he hadn't followed the nanny to Clement Crescent. If Mrs Farrier hadn't invited him in for tea. If he hadn't thought of copying the key to the gardens. If he hadn't seen Helen Forester walking the dog in her white tracksuit. If he hadn't had the book strap in his pocket.' He raised the wine bottle to the light. 'Can we bin this before it makes our teeth fall out and go over to the Scottish Stores instead?'

'Tell me something,' said May. 'Do you think those hallucinations of yours served a practical purpose?'

'Indubitably,' replied Bryant. 'I've spent all of my life trying to re-create London's history and imagine what its residents would tell me if they could reach out across the years.'

'So what have you learned?' Colin wanted to know.

'That the past is just a variation of the present, and that the future will twist the skein a little further. It's not about the city; it's about the people who inhabit it. If we stop talking to them – even the dead ones – we cease to learn about human nature.'

'You think we can actually improve?'

'With all my heart,' promised Bryant, placing his hand over his ratty cardigan.

'In that case I'm going to chuck out that bloody business manual.' Land rose with renewed determination and strode from the room.

'Blimey,' said Longbright, 'there's hope for him yet. Who's coming to the pub?'

Everyone rose. 'This is a tradition for you, I think,' said Steffi, pulling out her scarf.

'Pretty much,' said Longbright. 'It's been a pleasure having you with us. Will you be sharing what you've seen this week with your colleagues in Cologne?'

'I think not, no,' said Steffi, wrapping the scarf around her long pale neck. 'They would not appreciate your methods, which I still believe are ridiculous and highly illegal. But for myself, I am' – she sought the correct phrase – 'made richer by your friendship, so I thank you.'

'Then perhaps we'll see you in Germany one day, Steffi,' said John May.

'Please,' said Vesta, 'call me by the name my friends use. Swan.'

Raymond Land appeared in the doorway, looking shocked. 'Well, I did it,' he announced. 'I threw the manual out of the window.'

'That's a result, Raymondissimo,' said Bryant.

'It caught the pigeon right between the eyes,' Land admitted. 'That's put his beak out of joint.'

'This calls for a proper drink.' Renfield held out a hand to Longbright. Colin thought about doing the same but Meera shot him a look that could have punched a hole in a windscreen.

Arthur Bryant had gone on ahead in order to secure a table in the pub. As he stood at the edge of the kerb carefully refolding his striped scarf over his bruised throat, he watched in amazement as a slender woman with bobbed blonde hair materialized on the other side of the road, stepping with one silver high heel in front of the other, as if she was on a cat-walk. She wore a clinging, strapless silver gown, and a spotlight followed above her.

Bryant was transfixed. The woman glided along the pave-ment, past the kebab shop and the Achilles' Heels Shoe Repair Bar, past the Ladykillers Café and the Rooster Barn, singing as she went. None of the pedestrians seemed to react.

'"All I want is a room in Bloomsbury . . ."' she warbled in a high thin voice, but not even the people at the bus stop thought it odd. Passers-by behaved as if she wasn't there.

Bryant made his way across the road and watched in awe. As she approached he stood before her in the middle of the pavement, mesmerized.

'Twiggy,' he said. 'I'm dreaming again. It's 1966, isn't it? England has just won the World Cup and I'm in love with you!'

'Oi, mate, get out the bloody way, will you?' called one of the shoot wranglers, pointing back at the camera. 'It ain't 1966, we're shooting a Marks and Spencer commercial here.'

'Stone me, she looks good for her age,' said Bryant, watching a moment longer before heading for the pub.

'Maybe that'll finally cure your lucid dreaming,' said May, catching him up. 'Let me get you a pint.' He turned to the extravagantly bearded barman. 'What's good tonight?'

'I can heartily recommend the Spitalfields Colliery Brain-Smasher, squire,' said the barman, pushing his topknot into place.

'Tell him it's not the Middle Ages, you're not his squire and we'll have two regular pints of bitter,' said Bryant, tugging at his partner's arm. 'And a couple of Scotch eggs.'

Behind them the door opened and in came everybody else: Dan, Colin, Meera, Jack, Janice and Raymond Land, holding Crippen. Giles, Maggie and Kirkpatrick followed them in.

'Bugger, they'll want something celebratory and complicated,' said May. 'I'll never be able to remember the round. Have you got something to write the order down with?'

Bryant felt the top pocket of his overcoat and patted W. S. Gilbert's silver fountain pen. 'Don't worry, I think I can remember it,' he said.

8 p.m., back bar, the Scottish Stores, Caledonian Rd, London N1

KIRKPATRICK: Don't talk to me about property prices. London's now more expensive than living on Saturn. I read that a pair of knocked-through biscuit tins in Dalston sold to a pair of Russian mice for £750,000. I'm considering renting out the space under my sink to Italian students. Whose round is it?

MAGGIE: I bought my house in Highbury thirty-five years ago for £2,000. I wonder what it's worth now?

BRYANT: About £2,150, I should think. Your gaff is subsiding, Maggie. It's only the wallpaper that's holding it up. I'll just have a half. Make it a pint.

MAY: Arthur, did you take that pickaxe out of the electrics?

9 p.m., back bar, the Scottish Stores, Caledonian Rd, London N1

MAGGIE: Is anyone coming to the bus stop with me?

KIRKPATRICK: Only if you stop trying to score free bus trips by guessing the driver's birth sign. 'Best out of three' doesn't count.

MAGGIE: I'm heading to Waterloo Bridge to cast an urn of magical herbs on to the Thames. I won't throw the actual urn this time, now that I know tourist boats pass underneath. I'm going to ensure that it's a wonderful year.

BRYANT: Hm. I predict another year of Heraclitian ghastliness. Maggie predicts a year of Eudaimonian joy. Take your pick.

LAND: Knowing long words doesn't make you smart. My glass is empty.

MAY: So, whom do we believe about the year ahead? My partner, who kept a flea circus in his desk drawer until we made him get rid of it, or the witch who leaves her front-door key in a flowerpot? How many times were you burgled last year?

MAGGIE: Three. The thieves were looking for spiritual appeasement.

KIRKPATRICK: The thieves were looking for your credit cards, you daft cow.

10 p.m., back bar, the Scottish Stores, Caledonian Rd, London N1

KIRKPATRICK: Don't get me started on *The Mousetrap*. The detective did it, OK? Now you can go and see something decent instead. If you couldn't get your arse down to the theatre during its first sixty years you're never going to bother seeing it. And if you're willing to pay ninety squids to see *Phantom*, you deserve to be hit by a train. Twice. Right, whose round is it?

Colin held the pub door open for Meera, and for once she didn't tell him to stop being soft. The air was dry and clean, or at least clean for King's Cross, and the sky had cleared.

'Can I walk you to the station?' Colin asked, ready to back off if she tried to punch him.

'No, tonight I feel like celebrating,' Meera replied, turning up the collar of her black PCU jacket. 'I'm going to push the boat out and get a taxi.'

'Could you drop me off on the way?'

'I've a better idea,' said Meera. 'Let's go to yours.'

Colin looked as if he'd been hit with a house brick. 'Really?'

'Really. Come here.' There on the wet neon pavement in front of the Rooster Barn, she stood on tiptoe and kissed him tenderly on the lips.

Above them a rocket exploded in a shower of blue and silver stars.

Colin turned to see Renfield standing in the road with a milk bottle and a lit match, grinning.

'Jack,' he said, pointing.

'I know,' said Renfield, laughing. 'Got you. Good one, eh?'

'No.' Colin pointed more urgently. 'Behind you.'

Renfield's smile faded. 'What?' He turned.

'The unit's on fire,' said Colin.

On Monday morning, one week after the body of Helen Forester was found in Clement Crescent, Leslie Faraday's initiative was reversed by his superiors and the locks were taken off the gates of all London parks. Faraday was hauled before an investigative commission and questioned about his links with commercial developers.

Arthur Bryant stood at the entrance to Russell Square Gardens and looked across the sparkling lawns to the central fountain. The first commuters were heading to their offices, an Old English sheepdog was being walked and a businessman stood motionless with his briefcase in one hand, staring into the middle distance as if he had forgotten something important but trusted the park to remind him what it was.

'It's the closest I ever get to the countryside,' Bryant told his partner, who was just arriving with cups of coffee. 'How's the fire damage?'

'Trust me, you don't want to know,' said May, taking a sip. 'If you want to see some real countryside, my sister lives by the South Downs. The invitation still stands. Her turnip chutney's inedible but her heart's in the right place.'

'Thank you, but no.' Bryant looked about unsurely. 'The problem with all this space and greenery is that it slows you down and gives you too much time to think. You either find it peaceful or disturbing. I don't have time to reflect. There's still too much to do.'

'You know you could take it a little bit easier now,' said May.

Bryant looked horrified. 'And do what? Boredom is the enemy of age. Besides, we have myths to disprove.'

'What do you mean?'

'So long as people continue to judge us by the way we look, we need to show them just what we're made of.'

'So you want to go on? You don't want to turn back the clock after all?'

Bryant scrunched his face into something approximating a resigned smile. 'No. I have enough memories. Let's live in the present. How did that fire start, by the way?'

'Harry Prayer tried to cook some sausages in the microwave and it blew up.'

'And you believe that?'

'Well, he's a friend of yours. It's the sort of thing that usually happens to your friends. He's unharmed, by the way. Just in case you were concerned. Of course, you didn't help matters by leaving a pickaxe sticking out of the mains.'

'Hm.' Bryant sipped his coffee ruminatively. 'You don't think it odd that just after the body in our basement is identified as the US ambassador's son, the unit catches fire?'

'Are you saying there's a conspiracy?'

'Are you saying there's not?'

'I think we'd better head for the unit, don't you?'

'With all possible dispatch.'

Together they left behind the tranquillity of the park and walked back into the rushing pandemonium of the London streets.

Bryant & May will return.

ACKNOWLEDGEMENTS

London is like an old man's nostrils: alarmingly fecund, and you never know what you're going to find in there. Consequently, each Bryant & May novel contains more peculiarities than I'd ever intended to put in.

Last year councils decided to start charging personal trainers who use parks, a move opposed by 99 per cent of the general public. They then hired spies to look out for trainers and fine them. It's one of the reasons why I was drawn to writing about parks in *Wild Chamber*. The greenery is all around and barely noticed until it falls under threat. Naturally our moral guardians are forever seeking to monetize these special places. In my neighbourhood, three such areas remain in dispute as the council craftily outmanoeuvres beleaguered residents. Sometimes all that's being lost is sunlight or a view. But I remember the argument that was put forward when the first office block rose behind Tower Green and bisected one of the last unspoilt views in London – the one Anne Boleyn had from the execution block. The pro-development lobby said, 'You can't make money from a view.'

The Bryant & May novels are about Golden Age detectives in a modern world, and I've never enjoyed writing them more than I do right now. This is partly because surviving in London is more challenging than ever, but also thanks to a wonderful team who have now been with me for quite a while, headed by James Wills and Mandy Little, my agents, forever amenable, wise and honest.

Simon Taylor, my editor, has a uniquely laid-back style that perfectly gels with my own, and as time goes on we seem to read each other's thoughts about the manuscript. Kate Samano and Richenda Todd manage to locate the logic gaps in my narrative and come up with perfect ways of solving editorial problems. Cheers to PR guru Sophie Christopher for organizing me. A tip of the hat to Jan Briggs, Porl Cooper, e-book designer Martin Butterworth, the real Maggie Armitage and of course Pete for listening. Further thanks must go to the many libraries and bookshops that are foolish enough to keep inviting me back, and to the judges who recently described me as 'a new discovery'. It takes a long time to become an ingénu.

You can argue with me at www.christopherfowler.co.uk, where my website is updated every day of the year, or on Twitter @Peculiar.

Christopher Fowler is the author of more than forty novels (fifteen of which feature the detectives Bryant and May and the Peculiar Crimes Unit) and short story collections. The recipient of many awards, including the coveted CWA 'Dagger in the Library', Chris has also written screenplays, video games, graphic novels, audio plays, and two critically acclaimed memoirs, *Paperboy* and *Film Freak*. His most recent publication is *The Book of Forgotten Authors*, drawn from his 'Invisible Ink' column in the *Independent on Sunday*. Christopher Fowler lives in London, and Barcelona. To find out more, visit www.christopherfowler.co.uk or find him on Twitter @Peculiar

Discover Christopher Fowler's gloriously entertaining memoirs

PAPERBOY

'One of the funniest books I've read in a long time . . . this is the kind of memoir that puts most others to shame'
Time Out

'Anyone who remembers Mivvis, jamboree bags, streets with no cars, Sid James and vast old Odeons will love this Sixties retro-fest'
Independent on Sunday

'The book is fabulous, and I hope it sells forever'
Joanne Harris

'Paper-dry wit, natural charm, brutally funny anecdotes – Fowler's likeable memoir unearths the trail that led the schoolboy to become a writer'
Evening Standard

'Entrancing, funny, deeply moving and wonderfully written. Please read it'
Elizabeth Buchan

'An almost Morrissey-like lament . . . for a sixties childhood'
New Statesman

FILM FREAK

'Gold-plated writing: uproarious, then dark, and surprisingly moving' *****
Mail on Sunday

'An homage to pre-digital cinema, an elegy for a vanishing London . . . a tribute to friendship, gonzo-style. Two thumbs up for this triple billing'
Financial Times

'Charming, funny, perceptive . . . I found myself laughing loudly and lengthily. Above all, though, I was moved'
Daily Mail

'Brisk, chatty . . . trenchantly funny . . . he's so entertaining'
Daily Telegraph

'A master storyteller . . . a beautifully written and often hilarious book'
Sunday Express

Available in paperback and ebook.

Bryant & May
Hall of Mirrors

Christopher Fowler

It is 1969. You are invited to spend the weekend at a magnificent stately home. But beware – someone is harbouring murderous thoughts . . .

Among the party guests are young detectives Arthur Bryant and John May. In disguise and out of their depth, they're protecting a whistle-blower set to turn Queen's evidence in a massive bribery trial. And having recently experienced some 'local difficulty' in London, they need the weekend to go without a hitch.

It's Arthur who comments that it could be the setting for the perfect country house murder mystery – but the Golden Age was never like this. The house's owner – a penniless, dope-smoking aristocrat – is intent on selling the estate, complete with its miniature railway and hippy encampment, to a secretive millionaire, and the weekend has barely got going before events take a horrible turn. One of the group is felled from the sky, another goes missing and there's something grisly at the end of the garden. Bryant and May need help but the army has closed all the roads and it simply won't stop raining.

With their futures on the line, Arthur and John must go it alone. Amidst the murder, the madness and the macabre discoveries, they realize that, at the fag-end of the Swinging Sixties, the good times are drawing to a close and nothing is quite what it seems . . .

'A Machiavellian jokester'
Guardian

THE ROYAL HORTICULTURAL SOCIETY

——— ESSENTIAL ———

PRUNING &
TRAINING

THE ROYAL
HORTICULTURAL SOCIETY

─── ESSENTIAL ───
PRUNING &
TRAINING

DORLING KINDERSLEY
LONDON•NEW YORK•SYDNEY•MOSCOW
www.dk.com

A DORLING KINDERSLEY BOOK
www.dk.com

Special thanks to the staff of the
Royal Horticultural Society Publications

First published in Great Britain in 1999 by
Dorling Kindersley Limited, 9 Henrietta Street, London WC2 8PS

2 4 6 8 10 9 7 5 3 1

ISBN 0 7513 07335

Reproduction by Colourscan, Singapore
Printed and bound in Singapore by Star Standards Industries (Pte) Ltd.

CONTENTS

INTRODUCTION

AT THE SIMPLEST LEVEL, pruning and training aims to ensure that plants are as healthy and vigorous as possible, free of structural weakness, and at least risk of being infected with disease. With additional knowledge of how pruning and training affects the way that plants grow, the gardener can not only improve their natural appearance, but also enhance their ornamental value, create striking plant features, or increase crop yield and quality. Understanding the principles of a plant's response to pruning is absolutely key to realizing its full potential, but you should always bear in mind that, at any stage in its life, pruning causes some stress. It should never be done without good reason or without a clear idea in your mind of the intended effects of each and every pruning cut you make.

Trained clematis A twining climber, clematis eagerly clambers up and over a rustic tripod.

HOW PLANTS GROW

THROUGH PRUNING and training, a gardener can influence the ways in which a plant develops and performs. To do this effectively, it is essential to have a basic understanding of how plants grow in the wild.

PLANT GROWTH

For plants to grow, they must have air, water, nutrients, and light. Growth in height, or extension growth, is made by rapidly dividing cells behind the topmost (apical) bud. The apical bud imposes "apical dominance", producing hormones that move down the stem and inhibit growth of the side buds. These develop only when the leading shoot has grown away strongly, has been damaged, or removed by pruning. If this occurs, a lower sideshoot may reimpose apical dominance.

Parts of a plant
Cellular activity is most active at soft, green shoot tips, where hormones stimulate and control the plant's growth.

Apical or terminal bud ("growing point")

Leading shoot ("leader")

Sublateral, or sideshoot, develops from a bud on a lateral

Axillary buds form in the leaf axils

Apical or terminal bud of lateral shoot

A lateral shoot arises from a side bud (lateral, or axillary, bud)

Stems thicken and become woody as they age

Leaves and shoots develop from a point known as a node; the stem between nodes is an internode

Fibrous feeder roots absorb water and nutrients from the soil through fine root hairs

Roots thicken with age to form strong anchorage and may act as a food store

BUD ARRANGEMENT

Alternate buds arise singly at intervals on alternate sides of a plant's stem. Opposite buds occur in pairs at the same node.

ALTERNATE BUDS   OPPOSITE BUDS

INCREASING GIRTH

Another area of intense cellular activity is in the cambium layer, a band of cells that surrounds the stem just beneath the bark. As cambium cells divide and diversify, stem girth increases. They also form vascular bundles, which run the length of the stems, carrying water and soil nutrients to the leaves, and carbohydrates and plant hormones down the stem to the rest of the plant.

GAINING STRENGTH

Robust stems are formed by a process known as lignification ("becoming woody"), in which specialized strengthening tissue develops. It is stimulated by stem movement, such as that caused by flexing in the wind. This is why low stakes, or no stakes at all, are preferable during a tree's early years – this allows stem flexing and helps to produce strong trunks.

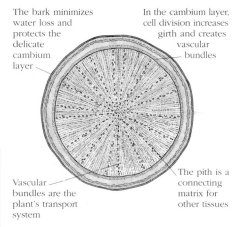

The bark minimizes water loss and protects the delicate cambium layer

In the cambium layer, cell division increases girth and creates vascular bundles

The pith is a connecting matrix for other tissues

Vascular bundles are the plant's transport system

Cross-section through a plant stem
Targeted cell activity in the stem ensures that it gains bulk and becomes strong, while carrying nourishment throughout the plant.

PHOTOSYNTHESIS

Plants manufacture energy by photosynthesis, a process that occurs mainly in the leaves. A green pigment, chlorophyll, traps the sun's energy, using it to convert carbon dioxide and water into sugars and starch, the food source of the plant. During pruning, the plant is deprived of leafy top growth, and the more of this material you remove, and the more frequently you prune, the greater the plant's demand for water and nutrients to fuel new growth. To ensure healthy regrowth, apply a balanced fertilizer after pruning.

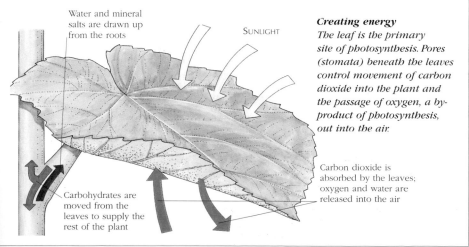

Water and mineral salts are drawn up from the roots

SUNLIGHT

Carbohydrates are moved from the leaves to supply the rest of the plant

Creating energy
The leaf is the primary site of photosynthesis. Pores (stomata) beneath the leaves control movement of carbon dioxide into the plant and the passage of oxygen, a by-product of photosynthesis, out into the air.

Carbon dioxide is absorbed by the leaves; oxygen and water are released into the air

HOW PLANT GROWTH ADAPTS

The aim of plants is to grow to maturity so that they can reproduce, usually by seed. Plants grow towards sunlight, branching to expose maximum leaf area to the sun to optimize photosynthesis; they extend their roots for anchorage and to exploit the soil for moisture and nutrients. Woody plants develop bark that is cold- and weather-resistant in order to survive from year to year and so maximize their potential for reproduction. Soft top growth, the site of photosynthesis, may be killed in harsh weather, and deciduous woody plants avoid this by dropping their leaves, to become dormant in winter. Plants can survive periods of cold, drought, and other adversities by regenerating from dormant buds on their tough, woody tissue. This ability, inherent in all woody plants to a greater or lesser degree, is the key to how a plant responds to pruning.

Dead wood is isolated by a natural barrier

Cut straight across the line between live and dead wood

Stem dieback (left)
A stub left by incorrect pruning dies back, but a natural barrier halts the die-back, permitting new growth from healthy dormant buds.

Renewal growth (right)
New growth from dormant buds at the base of this rose ensures survival if the main stems succumb to damage or disease, or die of old age.

LIFE-THREATENING DAMAGE

As a tree matures, so its girth increases and branches develop to expose the maximum leaf area to the sun. If all goes well, a tree naturally forms structurally strong branches. Sometimes, however, a young branch arises at a narrow angle to the trunk, creating a crotch that is inherently weak. As it gains weight and mass, the forces on the narrow crotch are such that it can be split in strong wind. If the damage has occurred at a large branch crotch on a single-trunked tree, neither the tree nor gardener may be able to remedy it, and professional advice should be sought; it may be necessary to remove the tree. By removing shoots likely to develop into such branches, through correct pruning and training in the early years, such damage could have been prevented in later life.

Split branch crotch
Wind has split this narrow-angled branch from the trunk, causing life-threatening damage. Corrective early pruning would prevent such branches from developing.

SURVIVING DAMAGE AND DISEASE

Many plants are able to limit the spread of disease, which can gain access through soft or damaged tissue. In response to infection, a plant produces chemicals that form a natural barrier across the stem, thus isolating the diseased portion from the main body of the plant. Woody plants respond to wounding in a similar way, by transporting protective chemicals to the wound site to isolate the damaged tissue and prevent the entry of disease. Scar tissue, or "callus", grows over the wound to form an air- and water-tight seal. When making pruning cuts, the aim should always be to reinforce the plant's own natural defences. Make cuts as small and clean as possible, at a point where the plant's defences are most active, at a node on the stem, or just beyond the branch collar (a slight swelling at the base of a branch where it meets the main trunk).

CROSS-SECTION THROUGH A BRANCH CROTCH

The bark ridge, where branch and trunk meet

Best place to cut

Branch collar

Cutting branches
Always cut just beyond the branch collar, at an equal and opposite angle to the bark ridge. Never cut into the bark ridge.

Target pruning
A small, clean cut was made just beyond the branch collar. Scar tissue, or callus, closes over the wound rapidly and keeps the plant's natural defence barriers intact.

BREAKING APICAL DOMINANCE

Hormones produced by the leading bud flow down the stem to inhibit the growth of laterals, or sideshoots. With the terminal bud intact (*right*), apical dominance is maintained, and vigour is directed primarily into further upward growth. When the terminal bud is removed (*far right*), the flow of these hormones is reduced. The topmost remaining bud then grows more strongly, but does not have absolute dominance and the buds lower down begin branching out. This universal principle is at the basis of many pruning cuts that promote branching, whether pinching out growing tips from soft stems, or removing the leading shoots on trees or shrubs.

UPWARD GROWTH

LATERAL GROWTH

HOW PRUNING WORKS

THE KEY FACT UNDERLYING all pruning and training techniques is that when material is removed from a plant or a stem is tied down to the horizontal, the plant will usually respond by making new growth elsewhere. Gardeners can prune to induce growth where and when it is wanted, and vary the direction, quantity, and vigour of this growth as desired.

RESPONSES TO PRUNING

Many plants will respond well to a variety of pruning techniques, but it is very important when choosing plants for special treatment to be sure that they will react in the desired way. It is not safe to assume that all plants in the same genus respond in the same way to pruning. They often do, but they may equally well vary widely in their growth habit and flowering season, two major factors to be taken into account when choosing suitable pruning techniques. Plants within a genus may also vary in their tolerance of pruning, so while one is stimulated by hard pruning, another may die of shock.

One species, two effects
Syringa meyeri *is naturally neat and bushy* (above), *with branches down to the ground, but it responds well to training as a clear-stemmed standard* (left).

THE GROWING TIP

Removing the terminal (apical) bud on a leading shoot breaks its apical dominance *(see p.11)*. Side buds lower down on the stem, often latent in leaf axils, are stimulated into activity and develop into shoots. If these in turn have their tips pinched out, and so on, the effect is a proliferation of growth. This is key both to creating dense, bushy growth and inducing new shoots that will grow, or can be trained, in the desired direction. Pinch pruning *(see pp.66–7)* uses this technique to great effect.

Pruning for bushy growth
This coleus shows clearly the effect of removing a terminal bud. A single-stemmed plant will branch freely if all its shoot tips are pinched out.

BEFORE   AFTER

SAME GENUS, DIFFERENT HABIT

Botanical classification groups plants into a genus according to shared characteristics, such as flower form and petal number. A genus includes a number of species, and within species there may be "cultivars", with their own distinct characteristics. The very different plants shown are both honeysuckles. *Lonicera japonica* is climbing, while *L. nitida* 'Baggesen's Gold' is shrubby. Since pruning needs depend on habit and flowering time, the requirements of species within a genus may vary considerably.

LONICERA NITIDA
'BAGGESEN'S GOLD'

LONICERA JAPONICA

HORIZONTAL TRAINING

Pulling a vertical stem down and tying it in horizontally has similar effects to removing the leading, or terminal, shoot (*see p.11 and opposite, below*). It reduces the sap flow so that the terminal bud loses much of its dominance. Instead of relentlessly pursuing upward growth, the stem diverts its energy into producing a number of sideshoots simultaneously from buds along its length; all will grow upwards with similar vigour and are much more likely to produce a good show of flowers and fruits. This technique is ideal for climbing and other long, flexible-stemmed plants grown directly up or along flat surfaces such as walls and fences, giving maximum coverage and an even distribution of flowers. It is also the principle behind cordon or espaliered fruit trees, where decorative forms are combined with increased yields.

MAXIMIZING FLOWERING AND FRUITING

Upward growth

Vertical stem
The natural tendency of this rose's unpruned main shoot and its sideshoot is to grow upwards toward sunlight. This means that a tall, leggy plant develops, with flowers produced only at the top of the stems and possibly out of sight.

Horizontal stem
Tying a shoot down allows sideshoots to grow out from buds in the leaf axils; these nearly always flower and fruit more freely.

WHY PRUNE?

BEFORE YOU MAKE A SINGLE CUT, there are two vital points to consider: the first is always to assess the whole plant, and the second is never to prune without a specific benefit in mind. Good reasons to prune include removing dead or damaged wood to ensure continued good health, improving flowering, or shaping young plants to a desired form.

MAINTAINING FORM AND EFFECT

One reason for pruning is to ensure a well-shaped specimen that is strong and healthy and that displays its desirable features to best effect. Most trees, for example, grow naturally with a single leader and an evenly distributed framework of branches above a clear trunk. Many need little, if any, pruning to produce this desirable form, but sometimes trees will produce two leaders – a situation that must be remedied if the tree is to be structurally sound at maturity. Many ornamentals are grown for desirable features such as attractively variegated foliage. If they revert, that is produce all-green leaves, pruning is needed to preserve the decorative qualities for which they were chosen.

Dual leaders (right)
If a leading shoot is damaged, a tree may produce dual leaders that form a narrow-angled crotch. At maturity, the branches may break away from the trunk (see p.10). The situation should be remedied as soon as possible by removing the weaker leader.

A well-formed specimen tree
Nyssa sylvatica *is grown as a central-leader standard; the lower branches have been cleared from the trunk to display the typical "starburst" habit to beautiful effect.*

Cutting out reversion
If not removed as soon as they occur, all-green shoots out-compete their variegated counterparts; they contain more chlorophyll and so are nearly always more vigorous.

SHAPING GROWTH

Pruning to shape growth can be as simple as cutting back to a bud that faces in the desired direction, but sometimes growth becomes unbalanced and more positive action is needed. In this case, it is essential to understand how pruning affects the vigour of regrowth. In general, the harder the pruning, the more vigorous the regrowth. Conversely, pruning lightly, or not at all, results in limited regrowth.

CORRECTING UNEVEN GROWTH

Tip-prune strong branches lightly

Remove any shoots on the clear trunk

Shorten weak growth by two-thirds

Year 1
This top-grafted cherry has become unbalanced. Prune the weakest shoots hard to stimulate vigorous regrowth; prune the stronger side lightly at the shoot tips only.

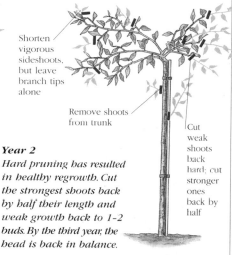

Shorten vigorous sideshoots, but leave branch tips alone

Remove shoots from trunk

Cut weak shoots back hard; cut stronger ones back by half

Year 2
Hard pruning has resulted in healthy regrowth. Cut the strongest shoots back by half their length and weak growth back to 1–2 buds. By the third year, the head is back in balance.

REMOVING SUCKERS

Suckers from roots or epicormic shoots on stems occur spontaneously or in response to damage. Suckers can cause nuisance by spreading beyond their allotted space. Cut them off at their point of origin and pare the surrounding tissue with a knife to take off any dormant buds nearby. New buds often grow around wounds made by removing epicormic shoots. They are best rubbed out before they grow, but otherwise, remove as soon as seen.

Suckers (left)
Willows are especially prone to producing root suckers; they seldom harm the tree, but may intrude where they are not wanted.

Epicormic shoots (right)
These arise from dormant buds on the trunk, often as an unwanted response to pruning. If not removed, they are likely to proliferate, taking energy from the tree.

Cut off at the point of origin

PRUNING FOR HEALTH

For many plants, pruning needs are very simple, since they require little other than the removal of dead, diseased, or damaged shoots to keep them in good health. Plants are often able to limit the spread of disease by forming natural barriers that isolate damaged tissue (*see pp. 10–11*). The aim of pruning out damaged tissue is to help the plant recover full health without breaching the natural barriers. Dead wood is removed because it can harbour infection. If a plant has already formed a natural barrier between live and dead wood, the general rule is not to cut below it, or the plant will have to expend energy needlessly by forming either scar tissue or another barrier further down the stem. In some cases, however, it is necessary to cut back into live, healthy wood. Some exceptions to the general rule are outlined here.

Frost damage
Cut back frost damage to live wood, but not when more frost is likely. Such cuts will expose new buds to further frost damage.

Snow-damaged santolina
Prune santolina back hard in early spring into old wood to stimulate new, bushy evergreen growth from the base.

Torn bark and jagged wounds may allow wood-rotting diseases to enter

Damaged branch
If a new branch at this point is desired, cut straight across below all damage, to a node, if visible. Do not breach the branch collar.

REMOVING DAMAGE

Branches that are partially broken, for example by lightning damage, the weight of snow, or the action of vandals or grazing animals, are best dealt with quickly because tearing injuries often leave large wounds that provide entry points for diseases. Damaged branches rarely mend if tied back in position. It is usually better to remove the branch (*see p. 23*), or shorten it to a suitable replacement shoot below the damage. Torn bark is unlikely to reunite with the cambium layer (*see p. 9*). If shoots fail to develop in the following growing season, remove the stub.

FEEDING AND MULCHING

While removal of dead, diseased, or damaged wood is always positively beneficial to the plant, other types of pruning inevitably remove healthy material in active growth. Removing leafy growth for purely ornamental reasons deprives the plant of energy-producing material (*see p.9*), while stimulating abundant flowering or fruiting makes considerable demands on the plant. If a plant is to remain healthy and be stimulated, rather than stressed, by pruning, it must have sufficient nutrients and water to fuel new growth.

- Use a complete fertilizer containing a balanced formulation of nitrogen, potassium, and phosphates, with essential trace elements.

- In spring, apply a balanced fertilizer to the base of the plant, using the recommended

rate. Make sure the soil is damp first. If repeated applications are needed, do not apply after midsummer; late soft growth is vulnerable to cold damage.

- Apply a mulch of organic matter (*see below*), 8–10cm (3–4in) deep, to conserve moisture and reduce weed competition. Do not allow the mulch to touch the stem.

MUSHROOM COMPOST   WELL-ROTTED MANURE

DEAD WOOD

When woody tissue becomes diseased, the tree or shrub responds by forming a natural chemical barrier to isolate the problem. In most cases, provided the disease is not too widespread, the infected part – deprived of nourishment by the barrier – eventually dies and is shed. If left in place, unshed dead wood provides a host for fungal rots as it decays, posing a health hazard to the tree.

The junction between dead and living tissue is often distinctly marked (*see p.10*) and this is the point at which dead wood is best removed. If the disease is still active, however, there may be no clear demarcation line. After making the cut, inspect the cut surface carefully. If disease or discoloration is still visible, more wood must be cut away.

Coral spot

Diseased wood
The branch shown here is infected with coral spot, a fungal disease that rapidly invades living tissue. The main stem is discoloured and dying back, but there is no clear demarcation line between healthy and diseased tissue.
The affected growth is cut back to clean living tissue that shows no sign of infection. A small, neat cut made with clean sharp secateurs will heal rapidly.

Healthy tissue

Dead patches in conifers
Remove dead material and disguise the resulting hole by tying adjacent branches to a cane inserted at the centre of the gap.

ORNAMENTAL EFFECTS

Several techniques can be used to enhance a plant's ornamental virtues. In some cases, trees with beautiful bark - in particular the birches - can be pruned to create multi-stemmed specimens, thus maximizing their most attractive feature. But the most obvious example is pruning to increase flower and berry production, which is often combined with training to a specific form to enhance a plant's decorative potential.

Pruning for flowering
Unpruned stems of Chaenomeles (left) *produce few flowers. Cutting sideshoots back to 2-3 buds creates free-flowering spurs* (right).

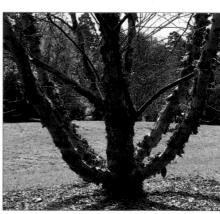

Multi-stemmed trees
Betula nigra *often takes a multi-stemmed form. Most birches can be made to do this by cutting back close to the ground in their early years.*

ANNUAL RENEWAL

Most shrubs flower more freely on young wood, either directly from new shoots, as with most buddlejas, or on lateral growth that arises from old wood. Ensuring the continuous production of fresh new shoots is key to consistent flowering. Annual removal in late winter or early spring of some of the oldest growth induces new shoots and allows light to reach the centre of the plant so that the wood can ripen.

Remove old, badly placed growth

Cut back last year's stems to 2-3 pairs of buds

Deciduous shrub flowering on new wood
Buddleja davidii *flowers on the current year's growth in summer. Cutting back hard induces strong straight flowering stems. Left unpruned, buddlejas may become leggy and tangled.*

PRODUCTIVE TRAINING

Growing plants against a wall or other support not only displays them to advantage, but may also improve the productivity of the plant. In most species, training stems to the horizontal breaks the apical dominance of leading shoots, causing them to produce laterals (*see p. 13*). In many plants, especially those in the rose family, the laterals produce significantly more flowers and fruit. This is the main reason why apples and pears are sometimes grown as cordons or espaliers. With a wall-trained pyracantha, the berries are revealed in all their glory by additional pruning in late summer to remove young shoots that would otherwise mask the ripening fruits.

Wall-trained tree
Training Magnolia grandiflora against a wall helps protect it from frost and aids good ripening of wood by summer sun. Well-ripened wood always flowers more.

Tie in shoots where possible to fill in the framework

Remove outward- and backward-growing shoots

Shorten protruding or crossing sublaterals to 1–2 buds; delay pruning shoots with buds until after flowering

When branches fill the allotted space, pinch out their shoot tips to induce growth of flowering laterals

Wall-trained shrub
The arching stems of pyracantha lend themselves well to horizontal training, producing a higher percentage of flowers and fruits as a result.

WALL SHRUBS

BUDDLEJA CRISPA
B. FALLOWIANA
CEANOTHUS (evergreen)
CHAENOMELES
CHIMONANTHUS PRAECOX
COTONEASTER HORIZONTALIS ♀
CYTISUS BATTANDIERI ♀
FREMONTODENDRON
FUCHSIA ARBORESCENS
MAGNOLIA GRANDIFLORA
PIPTANTHUS NEPALENSIS
PRUNUS MUME
P. TRILOBA 'MULTIPLEX' ♀
PYRACANTHA
RIBES SANGUINEUM
VITEX AGNUS-CASTUS

SPECIAL EFFECTS

Several pruning techniques can be
used – in conjunction with training –
for purely ornamental purposes. Topiary
has long been used in formal gardens to
create strongly architectural and geometric
shapes. The same skills and principles used
to create the complex and whimsical forms,
such as peacocks and chess pieces for large
gardens, can be used to train eye-catching
features for small spaces. Cones, obelisks,
and columns are relatively easy to produce,
since they require no intricate training, and
can usually be created from single young
specimens (*see pp. 52–3*).

Topiary forms
A clear-stemmed standard (left) *or elegant
spiral* (right) *in a container makes a perfect
centrepiece for a courtyard; a pair will flank
a path or doorway admirably.*

PINCH-PRUNED SHAPES

Similar – though more short-term – "topiary"
effects can be created relatively quickly by
pinch pruning (*see pp. 66–7*) rapidly growing,
evergreen subshrubs such as *Santolina* or, as
shown here, *Helichrysum petiolare*. Such
subshrubs, which produce soft, annual
top growth on a permanent woody base,
give attractive results in one or two growing
seasons. Once the desired shape has been
reached, with careful cultivation it can last
for several years. Here, three single-stemmed
young plants share a 23cm (9in) pot. They
are first trained upwards on a cane "wigwam"
and then, using the canes as a guide, all of
the shoot tips are pinched out each week to
form the shape and induce dense bushy
growth. The finished cone may reach a
height of 1.2–1.5m (4–5ft).

Helichrysum cone
*This pinch-pruned helichrysum makes an
unusual focal-point for a patio or courtyard
during summer. In cold climates, bring it in
for the winter for indoor decoration.*

FOR FOLIAGE EFFECTS

ACER NEGUNDO
  A. NEGUNDO 'FLAMINGO'
AILANTHUS
BERBERIS × OTTAWENSIS
  B. THUNBERGII ♀
CATALPA BIGNONIOIDES ♀
  C. BIGNONIOIDES 'AUREA' ♀
  C. SPECIOSA
CORYLUS MAXIMA 'PURPUREA' ♀
COTINUS COGGYGRIA ♀
  C. OBOVATUS ♀
ERYTHRINA CRISTA-GALLI ♀
EUCALYPTUS GUNNII ♀
INDIGOFERA HETERANTHA ♀
MELIANTHUS MAJOR ♀
PAULOWNIA TOMENTOSA ♀
PHILADELPHUS CORONARIUS
  'AUREUS' ♀
PHLOMIS FRUTICOSA ♀
POPULUS × CANDICANS 'AURORA'
RHUS TYPHINA 'DISSECTA' ♀
SAMBUCUS CANADENSIS
  'ACUTILOBA'
  S. NIGRA 'GUINCHO PURPLE'
  S. RACEMOSA 'PLUMOSA AUREA'
TOONA SINENSIS 'FLAMINGO'

ENHANCING FOLIAGE

Trees and shrubs that are known to respond well to hard-pruning (*see left*) can be cut back hard every year to produce specimens with much larger or more colourful leaves. Good results rely on feeding with a balanced fertilizer in spring to provide nutrients to rebuild the growth removed.

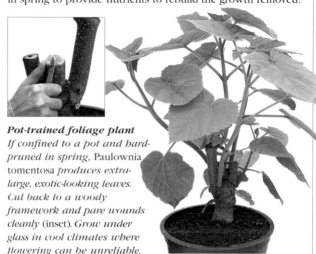

Pot-trained foliage plant
If confined to a pot and hard-pruned in spring, Paulownia tomentosa *produces extra-large, exotic-looking leaves. Cut back to a woody framework and pare wounds cleanly* (inset). *Grow under glass in cool climates where flowering can be unreliable.*

SPECIAL FUNCTIONS

Trees that naturally produce very flexible wood, such as apples, offer great potential for training and pruning to very "restricted" forms. The apple stepover, a variation of a cordon, is an extreme example. When bent over to the horizontal, the dominance of the leading shoot is overcome, inducing many flowering and fruiting sideshoots or spurs. Use it to form a decorative and productive edging to beds in the kitchen garden.

Flowering spurs are produced freely if apical dominance is overcome

Apple trained as a stepover
To support a stepover, insert 60cm (2ft) posts 1.5m (5ft) apart. Stretch stout wire horizontally between them, nailing it 5cm (2in) below the post tops. Prune summer and winter as for cordon apples (see p.128).

How to Cut Correctly

PRUNING CUTS SHOULD ALWAYS BE as small, clean, and neat as possible; the aim is to help the plant to heal its wounds rapidly. Young wood heals fastest, so prune shoots before they become woody and twigs before they become branches. Large wounds, especially those with torn or bruised tissue, allow easy access to disease-causing organisms.

Making cuts

A woody plant's natural defence system is at its strongest at the branch collar (a swelling where a branch joins the main trunk), at a fork on the branch, or at a node (bud or leaf joint). Bearing this in mind, do your utmost to make small, clean cuts at these points to speed natural healing. A slanting cut, if possible, is preferable, since rain cannot collect on a sloping surface. Water is a principal carrier of disease; many fungi and wood-rotting organisms spread by spores washed from the air and from nearby plant tissues by splashing raindrops.

CORRECT CUT   TOO SLOPING   TOO HIGH   ROUGH CUT

Good and bad cuts
A correct cut is made at a gentle angle, 5mm (¼in) above a bud, sloping down away from it. Do not leave stubs or torn tissue which will die back, or make steeply sloping cuts that breach the node's natural barrier.

Bud arrangements

All woody plants produce buds in one of two main patterns; these dictate how to make pruning cuts. Alternate buds arise at intervals on opposite sides of the stem. With these, it is possible to make the preferred sloping cut to the bud (*see above*), from which one new shoot will grow. Opposite buds arise in pairs from the same point at a node. A sloping cut would damage one or both of the buds from which two new shoots will grow, so here, a neat, straight cut above the bud is the only option.

Alternate bud (left)
Make a slanting cut at a point 5mm (¼in) above the bud. A gentle slope allows moisture to roll off the cut surface, and reduces the risk of disease.

Opposite bud (right)
Cut squarely across the shoot 5mm (¼in) above a node with a healthy pair of buds. Two strong, healthy shoots should then develop.

LARGER CUTS

Sometimes it is necessary to make larger pruning cuts, such as when removing the branch of a tree. These often take several growing seasons to heal, leaving potential entry points for disease. To reduce this risk, it is imperative to make cuts that heal with maximum speed. Make a smooth cut at the right point and scar tissue will grow from the edge to the centre, sealing the wound and preventing entry of harmful organisms.

REMOVING A BRANCH

For thick wood, always use a powerful tool such as these sharp loppers

Clean cut
Protective new wood – callus, or scar tissue – has formed rapidly with a clean cut.

Cutting to the branch collar
Make a clean cut just beyond the raised ring, or collar, at the base of the branch (see p.11 and inset). This ensures that the wound does not interfere with sap flow up the main branch or trunk.

Rough cut
Fungal spores that cause rots and cavities have invaded torn and jagged tissue.

WHEN TO PRUNE

TREES

Most trees are pruned when dormant, from late autumn to late winter. The wounds heal quickly once strong growth begins in spring. Some trees, for example birches, "bleed" if cut as the sap is rising, or is about to do so, and so are not pruned between mid- to late winter and midsummer. Cherries, which are prone to silver-leaf disease, are pruned in summer when the risk of infection is lower (*see pp.136–7*).

SHRUBS

Deciduous shrubs that flower before midsummer bloom on wood made the previous year. Prune just after flowering to promote new growth. Those that bloom after midsummer flower on the current year's wood; prune in late winter or early spring. Evergreens are usually pruned in spring after any danger of frosts has passed, but may be trimmed lightly after flowering to shape them or to remove old, flowered wood.

TOOLS FOR THE JOB

IT IS WELL WORTH buying the best tools that you can afford. Before you buy, make sure that the tools feel comfortable to use: check that they fit into your hand well, are easy to grip, and can be used without strain.

CUTTING TOOLS

The basic tools you will need for pruning are secateurs and, for heavier work, a pair of loppers or a long-handled tree pruner. Thicker branches are best cut with a saw. Use a pruning knife with a large down-swept blade to neaten any snags. Shears can be used on plants that need regular clipping over, and for hedges and topiary. Always keep cutting blades sharp, and look after your tools by cleaning and drying them after use. A final wipe with an oily rag will keep blades rust-free and in good condition.

TREE PRUNER

HAND SHEARS

The right tools
Ideally, have the appropriate tool to hand for every job. For best results, use a tool only for the tasks for which it was designed.

USING YOUR TOOLS CORRECTLY

Secateurs can be used for all soft growth and on woody stems up to 1cm (½in) in diameter. Always use them the "right way up", with the narrow, upper cutting blade nearer the bud or stem junction to which you are cutting so that the crushing effect of the thicker blade is confined to the tissue being removed. For thicker stems, to 2.5cm (1in), use a pair of loppers. A special pruning or Grecian saw designed for garden use is ideal for larger jobs; household saws clog up quickly when cutting green wood.

USING SECATEURS CORRECTLY

USING SECATEURS INCORRECTLY

Pruning with secateurs
Using the thin blade nearer the bud or stem junction (left) gives a clean, precise cut; reversing the position of the blades gives you less control and a tearing action (below left). Cutting an over-thick stem (below) blunts the blades and crushes stems.

USING SECATEURS INCORRECTLY

SECATEURS

LOPPERS

PRUNING KNIFE

GRECIAN SAW

POWERED TOOLS

Used with strict attention to safety, powered tools are ideal for some tasks. A nylon line trimmer makes short work of expanses of ground cover, and hedge trimmers are ideal for large hedges.

- Machines that use mains electricity must be fitted with a residual current device (RCD, or circuit breaker) to protect you should you accidentally cut through the flex. Never trim wet plants, or work in wet weather.
- Protective goggles are essential with power tools, and ear plugs are recommended.

PROTECTIVE GOGGLES

USING LOPPERS CORRECTLY

USING LOPPERS INCORRECTLY

Using loppers
A stem whose girth fits entirely within the bite of the loppers is easy to cut; the long handles exert extra leverage, so little effort is needed (far left). *A stem that is too wide for the blades to admit strains the loppers and is unlikely to make a clean cut* (left).

Pruning saw and knife
A saw with a curved blade (Grecian saw) is ideal for cutting thick wood or stubs in confined spaces (right). *Use a sharp knife to trim any rough edges on cuts large or small; the curved blade of a pruning knife gives greater control* (far right).

USING A PRUNING SAW

USING A KNIFE

ORNAMENTAL TREES

THE TREES that you plant in your garden form both
its most structurally important elements and an
enduring legacy. A wide range of trees is available
to suit most growing conditions, including a good
selection of smaller trees that are ideal for
relatively small modern gardens. Most need little
pruning or training once established, but the future
of a mature tree is often determined by the way
it is trained when young. It needs to have a
sturdy, well-balanced branch structure that will
remain safe and healthy into maturity and beyond,
as well as being pleasing to the eye. The
techniques of pruning, training, and grafting all
contribute to forming a sound structure that also
makes the most of a tree's ornamental virtues.

A beautifully formed tree *A tupelo tree will make an enduring contribution to the landscape.*

TREE FORMS

A WELL-GROWN TREE is trained when young to one of a number of forms. In most cases, training simply reinforces a natural habit, although sometimes, as with weeping standards, the shape is developed and maintained by pruning and training. To ensure a tree does not outgrow its site, always check its final dimensions before planting.

CHOOSING A FORM

In the nursery trade, standardized descriptions of tree form and size are used to help buyers make their initial choice. As a tree matures, some of the rigid form distinction made in the nursery may be lost. This is seldom a problem unless the tree's structural safety is threatened; the tree will look no less pleasing as it assumes a more natural, less formal habit of growth. But in very restricted forms, especially those such as weeping standards that are top-grafted, careful control is needed if the ornamental effect is to be conserved.

Young trees

Training usually begins in a tree's second or third winter. A very young tree most frequently consists of a single unbranched stem in its first year, known as a "maiden whip". Once side branches or laterals grow, usually in its second year, it is called a "feathered tree". Both forms can be purchased from specialist suppliers, so that you can train them yourself. But when selecting a tree, you must check that the tree you have in mind is suitable for training in the form you would like. Always check that the tree's height and spread at maturity fits the site. If the tree grows too large, your long-term investment is wasted, since it may have to be felled or endure costly tree surgery when it outgrows its allotted space.

Branched-head standard
Has a single, clear trunk that branches to form an open-centred crown. A common natural form, it can also be produced by top-grafting, or by cutting back a main stem to induce branching at a given height.

SUITABLE FOR
Albizia,
+ Crataegomespilus,
+ Laburnocytisus,
Malus, Prunus
cerasifera,
P. × subhirtella,
and some Japanese
flowering cherries.

Half-standard
Should have a clear trunk of 75-125cm (30-48in) and a compact crown of evenly spaced branches. The form is often lost with age, but a few trees, such as bay (Laurus nobilis), can be pruned to retain these proportions.

SUITABLE FOR
Acer platanoides
'Brilliantissimum',
Cornus kousa,
Eucalyptus gunnii,
Hoheria lyallii, Malus
floribunda, Prunus
serrula.

Feathered tree

The natural form of most young trees, with trunks clothed in branches almost to the ground. As they mature, many shed lower branches to develop into a central-leader standard.

SUITABLE FOR
Betula pendula, B. pubescens, Carpinus betulus, Carya, Cornus alternifolia, C. capitata, Ilex, Malus baccata.

Central-leader standard

Has a clear trunk of 1.5-2m (5-6ft) and a straight stem with a distinct leading shoot. A common form in nature, it can also be produced by removing the lower branches from a young feathered tree.

SUITABLE FOR
Aesculus hippocastanum, Alnus, Betula, Carpinus, Castanea, Crataegus, Davidia, Fagus, Fraxinus, Juglans, Laburnum, Liriodendron, Paulownia, Platanus and many more.

Fastigiate tree

An entirely natural growth habit, producing a narrow crown of, usually, upswept branches from top to bottom. Cannot be formed by pruning and needs no pruning to maintain. Many conifers grow this way.

FOUND IN
Carpinus betulus 'Fastigiata', Eucryphia × nymansensis, Fagus sylvatica 'Dawyck', Populus nigra 'Italica', Prunus 'Amanogawa'.

Bush

Most commonly created for fruit trees, to produce low-growing, productive trees that are easy to harvest. To achieve this form, fruit trees are grafted onto a dwarfing rootstock. Seldom seen as a natural form, except in relatively small trees, such as medlars and Hoheria glabrata.

SUITABLE FOR
apples, pears, plums, acid cherries, quince, medlar, and mulberry.

Multi-stemmed tree

Branching low down at or near ground-level, this form has several distinct stems or trunks and resembles a large shrub. A natural form, especially in trees reluctant to develop a single leader.

SUITABLE FOR
Celtis occidentalis, Cercis siliquastrum, Embothrium coccineum, Halesia, Nyssa sylvatica, Oxydendrum.

Weeping standard

Almost always produced by top-working, that is, grafting several buds at the top of a clear stem. A highly unnatural form needing maintenance pruning throughout its life. A few, naturally weeping trees can be trained to this form.

SUITABLE FOR
Betula pendula 'Youngii', Fraxinus excelsior 'Pendula', Morus alba 'Pendula', Pyrus salicifolia, Salix caprea 'Kilmarnock'.

BUYING YOUNG TREES

TO GIVE A TREE the best possible start, choose a small, sturdy specimen, no more than two years old. A ready-trained tree that is three or four years old may look better value, but it is more likely to suffer from post-planting shock after being moved, and fail to "grow away" well.

EARLY GROWTH

The ash tree (*near right*) is a good example of a well-trained tree at the end of its second growing season. Supported by a lightweight cane, it has a growing point at the apex of its single, straight shoot and is clothed with healthy leaves. The container is large enough to accommodate, without constriction, a root system capable of supporting the top growth. (The spread of the tree should never be more than 3–4 times the width of its container). In contrast, the gleditsia (*far right*) has been allowed to develop two leading shoots that will probably create a structurally unsafe fork at maturity. There is too much top growth for the constricted roots to sustain, and the tree is unsupported and growing at an angle.

Well-trained and neglected specimens
The ash tree (left) *is upright, vigorous, and healthy, but the gleditsia* (right) *is badly shaped and lop-sided.*

GRAFTED TREES

Many tree cultivars are produced by grafting a scion – a selected cultivar (in the form of a bud or length of stem) – on a rootstock from a compatible plant. The "graft union" can usually be seen as a swelling near the base of the trunk. A tree produced by bud-grafting grows away from the graft point as a single shoot. Where a section of stem is used as the scion, its topmost side bud grows out to form the leading shoot. Any growth that appears below the graft union is from the rootstock, not the desirable cultivar, and must be removed completely.

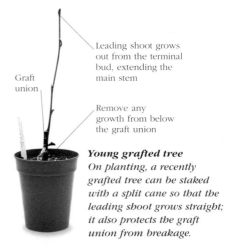

Graft union

Leading shoot grows out from the terminal bud, extending the main stem

Remove any growth from below the graft union

Young grafted tree
On planting, a recently grafted tree can be staked with a split cane so that the leading shoot grows straight; it also protects the graft union from breakage.

POT-GROWN AND BARE-ROOTED TREES

If you can, select and collect young trees in person, so that you can assess nursery conditions and look trees over for potential problems (*see opposite and below*). Transport them carefully, under cover or wraps. A tree transported on an open truck or roof rack, for example, with its foliage buffeted in the slipstream, suffers considerable stress. Bare-rooted trees are particularly vulnerable to damage during lifting and transporting.

Exposed to the air, the fine feeder roots begin to dry out and die. Generally, the roots of container-grown or rootballed trees do not need pruning when transplanting, but remedial action may be necessary with root-balled trees if damage has occurred. Before planting, cleanly cut away roots with ragged, broken ends or abrasions. Even up overlong, misshapen, or lop-sided roots so that there is a good spread emanating from the stem.

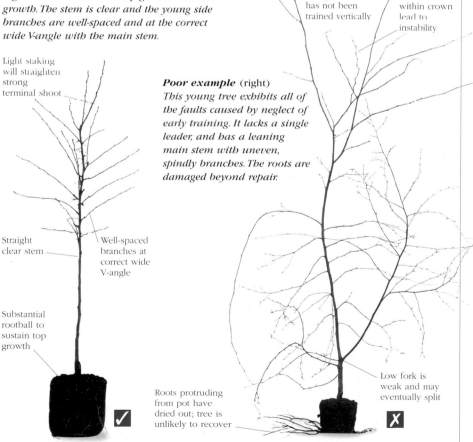

Selecting trees for purchase (below)
This short, sturdy, well-trained young tree has a good balance between top growth and root growth. The stem is clear and the young side branches are well-spaced and at the correct wide V-angle with the main stem.

Light staking will straighten strong terminal shoot

Straight clear stem

Well-spaced branches at correct wide V-angle

Substantial rootball to sustain top growth

Original leader has failed and its replacement has not been trained vertically

Weak shoots within crown lead to instability

Poor example (right)
This young tree exhibits all of the faults caused by neglect of early training. It lacks a single leader, and has a leaning main stem with uneven, spindly branches. The roots are damaged beyond repair.

Roots protruding from pot have dried out; tree is unlikely to recover

Low fork is weak and may eventually split

THE EARLY YEARS

IF NOT ALREADY in its final site, a two-year-old tree can be planted out and formative training can continue *in situ*, without further disturbance to the root system. For most trees, the best form to choose is one that is simply a well-shaped version of the habit the tree would naturally adopt, because this is the most likely to remain structurally sound until maturity.

FEATHERED TREES

Most evergreens are grown as feathered trees; the majority develop a neat conical shape naturally. The pruning of evergreens is done from late summer to before midwinter. A feathered tree is by far the easiest form to produce, since it requires little pruning other than to remove dead, diseased, or damaged wood. Check regularly for crossing shoots and cut them out. Look for shoots that form a narrow angle of attachment to the trunk and remove them too. The junction will be weak and in time may result in heavy branches splitting from the trunk at this point (*see p.10*).

Years 1, 2, and 3, winter
Cut off laterals at a narrow angle to the trunk and any that are not well-spaced or positioned. If laterals grow more strongly on one side, tip-prune weaker shoots to stimulate growth.

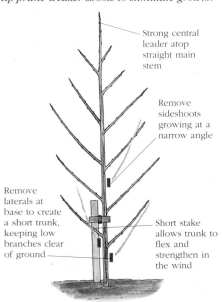

Strong central leader atop straight main stem

Remove sideshoots growing at a narrow angle

Remove laterals at base to create a short trunk, keeping low branches clear of ground

Short stake allows trunk to flex and strengthen in the wind

YEAR 1

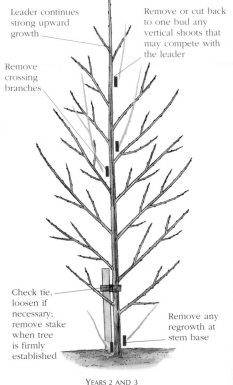

Leader continues strong upward growth

Remove or cut back to one bud any vertical shoots that may compete with the leader

Remove crossing branches

Check tie, loosen if necessary; remove stake when tree is firmly established

Remove any regrowth at stem base

YEARS 2 AND 3

CENTRAL-LEADER STANDARD

A central-leader standard has a length of clear trunk, topped by a crown through which the leader persists. Many trees take this form naturally; the lower branches die back and are shed as they are "shaded out" by the increasing density of branches above. The main danger in this form of training is that the leader may be damaged, or lost because another shoot overtakes it. Both of these problems can be rectified if remedial action is performed promptly (*see p.37*).

CLEARING THE TRUNK

The trunks of all standards are cleared in the same way, gradually over several years. If laterals are stripped away all at once, dormant buds break low down on the stem, producing unwanted shoots and inhibiting top growth. If removed when small, they leave little scarring. Another reason for removing laterals in stages is that their foliage helps to provide the tree with energy; laterals temporarily retained are known as "stem builders".

Years 1, 2, 3, and 4, winter
As a guide to clearing the trunk in stages, visualize the trunk, from the ground to the topmost lateral, divided approximately into thirds. To remove laterals, make small cuts that do not breach the branch collar (see p.11); as the swelling will be very slight, if visible at all, leave a stub of no more than 5mm (¼in). If shortening laterals, make correctly angled cuts to a healthy, outward-facing bud.

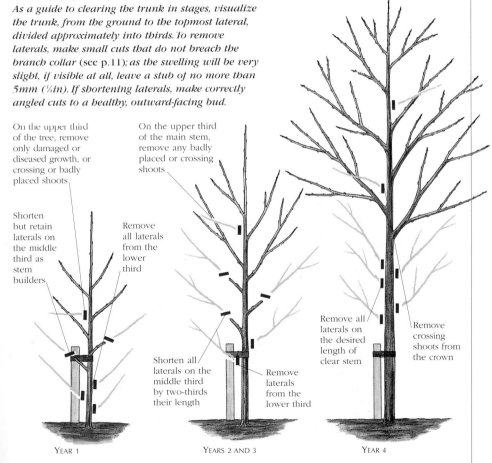

On the upper third of the tree, remove only damaged or diseased growth, or crossing or badly placed shoots

Shorten but retain laterals on the middle third as stem builders

On the upper third of the main stem, remove any badly placed or crossing shoots

Remove all laterals from the lower third

Shorten all laterals on the middle third by two-thirds their length

Remove laterals from the lower third

Remove all laterals on the desired length of clear stem

Remove crossing shoots from the crown

YEAR 1

YEARS 2 AND 3

YEAR 4

33

BRANCHED-HEAD STANDARD

Branched-head standards do occur naturally, many oaks adopting this habit with age as the leader loses dominance, for example. Pruning to form a branched head is used on trees that otherwise grow to considerable height, although this becomes less necessary, or possible, on older trees, which may tend to revert to upward growth. Training in the first and second years is the same as for a central-leader standard (*see p.33*).

BRANCHED-HEAD STANDARD

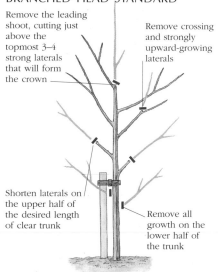

Remove the leading shoot, cutting just above the topmost 3–4 strong laterals that will form the crown

Remove crossing and strongly upward-growing laterals

Shorten laterals on the upper half of the desired length of clear trunk

Remove all growth on the lower half of the trunk

Year 3 or 4, winter
When 3–4 strong laterals have developed above the required length of clear trunk, remove the leader to create a branched head.

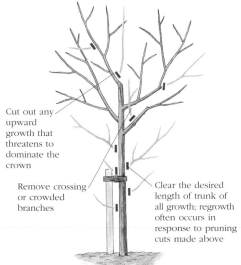

Cut out any upward growth that threatens to dominate the crown

Remove crossing or crowded branches

Clear the desired length of trunk of all growth; regrowth often occurs in response to pruning cuts made above

Year 4 or 5, winter
Check the overall shape before cutting, then make pruning cuts to restore or maintain a balanced, open-centred crown.

FORMING A LABURNUM TUNNEL

Plant one- or two-year-old feathered laburnum trees at 2–3m (6–10ft) intervals. Train over the arch, tying in early in the season while the wood is still supple. If insufficient laterals are produced to fill the spaces, tip back the leading shoot to encourage laterals to break. At the end of each subsequent growing season, reduce all laterals to within 2–3 buds of the main framework branches to encourage formation of flowering wood.

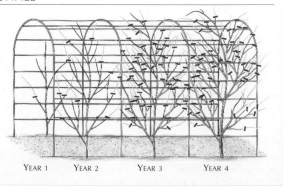

YEAR 1   YEAR 2   YEAR 3   YEAR 4

WEEPING STANDARDS

There are two types of weeping standard: natural and grafted. Trees that weep naturally first grow upwards, if well-staked, then arch at a height that depends on the species. With top-grafted standards, such as *Salix caprea* 'Kilmarnock', the branches all tend to grow away in the same horizontal plane and the crown can become congested. To avoid this, remove early on any shoots that cross the centre at awkward angles and, since upward growth spoils the weeping form, remove that too. Always remove any shoots growing on the clear stem; they are from the rootstock. Staking, with a tall, strong stake, is usually required for some years after the head has developed. The crown of a weeping tree often grows rapidly and may prove too heavy to be supported by the trunk until it has increased greatly in girth. Without support, there is a risk of the entire crown being damaged in strong winds.

Grafted weeping standard
Remove shoots growing on the clear stem, preferably by rubbing or pinching them out when still soft. Take off upward-growing shoots and weak ones, especially if growth is crowded.

NATURAL WEEPING STANDARDS

Some naturally weeping standards, like this *Betula pendula* 'Tristis', may form a squat, low-spreading mound unless trained firmly to the vertical in the early years. It is essential to support the leading shoot's upward growth until the wood has hardened enough for the stem to remain rigid. As the tree grows and while the leading shoot is still flexible, attach the leader to a vertical cane lashed to the main stake. Keep tying in until the leader reaches the required height; in this way the height of the trunk may be extended to about 4m (12ft). The weeping habit can then be allowed to develop naturally.

Raising the height of the main stem
Careful vertical training of the main stem to the required height allows branches to weep freely rather than trail on the ground.

Continue to draw up the leader gently but firmly until desired height is reached

Bamboo cane lashed to stake

Remove low laterals on the main stem

BETULA PENDULA 'TRISTIS'
YEARS 1 AND 2

BETULA PENDULA 'TRISTIS'
YEAR 3 UNTIL ESTABLISHED

MULTI-STEMMED TREE ON A LOW TRUNK

Some trees, such as this maple *Acer davidii*, are grown for their attractive bark. They are often pruned to produce a multi-stemmed specimen on a short trunk to display more of the bark's striations. Maples "bleed" sap, so are pruned when fully dormant, in winter. When young, they are prone to dieback and cold damage. Small cuts can be made to remove damage in late summer, but leave more substantial cuts until winter pruning.

Remove low laterals

Cut weak laterals to a bud at 2.5–5cm (1–2in)

Remove lower shoots to clear main stems

Year 1, winter
Prune to 50cm (20in), above 2 pairs of strong shoots. Tip-prune these by 10cm (4in).

Year 2, winter
Cut back dead or damaged wood to a healthy bud. Prune any weak shoots hard.

Year 3, winter
Keep main stems clear of low laterals; remove inward-facing laterals to open the centre.

MULTI-STEMMED FORM FROM A SINGLE STEM

This method is also used to display beautiful bark, but unlike the form shown above, is never used on grafted trees. It can be used to enhance the form of naturally multi-stemmed or low-branching trees; by restricting the number of stems and inward-growing laterals, a thicket is avoided. Some trees, for example *Celtis*, may not form a single stem in regions where summers are cool, but are equally attractive grown as multi-stemmed forms.

Year 1, winter
Cut back the stem of a 2-year-old tree straight across at 8cm (3in) above ground level.

Year 2, winter
Select 3–4 strong, well-spaced shoots to create a framework and remove the remainder.

Year 3, winter
Let laterals develop; remove any suckers and low laterals if clear stems are wanted.

TROUBLE-SHOOTING

If neglected, trees may produce two or more leading shoots in competition with each other, which must be dealt with if a central-leader specimen is desired. On this young tree (*right*), several shoots are clustered at the tree's apex. If all are allowed to develop, they will compromise the tree's structural stability at maturity. The topmost shoot will not always be the best choice as a leader; select the strongest and most upright shoot.

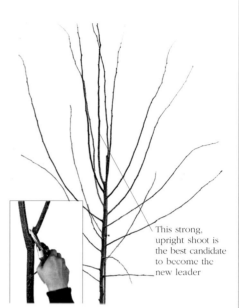

This strong, upright shoot is the best candidate to become the new leader

Competing leaders
Where competing leaders have formed (right), select the strongest, upright shoot. The topmost shoot may now not make the best new leader (inset); here, the lower shoot is stronger and straighter. Shorten vigorous low shoots by one-third to half of their length.

BROKEN LEADERS

If the leading shoot of a tree is "lost" – it dies back, is damaged by frosts, or is broken – prune it back to the nearest sound, strong lateral that can be trained vertically to take its place. If there are yet no laterals, prune to a healthy bud, and then train the resulting shoot.

DUAL LEADERS

On trees with opposite buds, the loss of a leader results in a pair of new ones. Select the shoot most easily trained to the line of the original main stem (here the right-hand shoot) and remove its competitor.

Attach new leader to cane

Cut back damaged leader

1 *Select a new leader and attach it to a vertical cane with soft twine at intervals of 25cm (10in).*

2 *Carefully cut the broken shoot with an angled cut, taking care not to damage the new leader.*

TWO LEADERS FROM OPPOSITE BUDS

STAKING

ALL BUT THE SMALLEST whips or young feathered trees need the support of a stake for the first two years until a strong trunk and good root system are established. The purpose of a stake is *not* to hold the tree up, but to allow it to develop a straight, vertical stem. Flexing in the wind is necessary to strengthen the trunk and, in most cases, a short stake and looser ties that permit this are the preferred option. There are a number of staking methods to choose from to suit the size and type of tree, the density of its crown, and the degree of exposure in the planting site.

SINGLE STAKES AND TIES

When planting a bare-rooted tree, insert the stake into the hole first and spread the roots around it – never drive a stake through the root system. For a straight stake (*below, left and right*), insert on the side of the prevailing wind so that the stem is pushed away from the stake. With a short angled stake (*below centre*), lean it into the prevailing wind. Stakes must be driven at least 60cm (24in) into the ground. Ties must hold the tree securely but not inflexibly and should be used with a spacer so that neither tie nor stake rubs against young bark; abrasions may affect the future health of the tree. Check ties regularly and loosen as the tree's girth expands; if they constrict the stem, the nutrient supply to the crown is reduced and may eventually be cut off if the bark is girdled.

Low, straight stake
A stake that is less than one-third of the tree's height permits strengthening by flexing. Use a tie and spacer to avoid chafing young bark.

Low, angled stake
Useful in exposed sites. Lean at a 45° angle into prevailing winds and attach by a belt tie in a figure-of-eight to avoid chafing the bark.

Tall, straight stake
Tall stakes with a tie and spacer are useful in the case of top-grafted trees or standards with dense, heavy, or weeping crowns.

Two-stake system

A pair of short stakes, driven into the bottom of the planting hole on either side of the rootball, can be used for most trees. This system is ideal for rootballed or container-grown trees, since the stakes can be sited so that there is little risk that they will penetrate and damage roots. The tree is secured with looped rubber ties, nailed to the stake, which allow the tree to flex freely in the wind, thus strengthening the trunk.

Pair of short stakes
A young tree is well-supported by low stakes on either side of the rootball and secured by soft rubber strips that enable to the tree to flex freely in the wind.

Guy ropes

A single stake is inadequate if planting a large tree. A sizeable crown effectively forms a sail and may blow out in strong wind, often snapping just at the top of a single stake. Guy ropes provide evenly distributed support until root growth is sufficient to support the weight of the crown, usually after two growing seasons. Guide the strong wire through low, sturdy forks in the crown of the tree and secure onto angled stakes.

Stabilizing a large tree
Thread the wire through lengths of hosepipe (inset) to protect the bark. Use angled stakes fitted with wire tension adjusters (below) so that the trunk is trained vertically.

ESTABLISHED TREES

ALTHOUGH ESTABLISHED TREES do not need regular pruning, all benefit from regular health checks throughout their life to identify and then to remove dead, diseased, or damaged wood. For most, the time to check and correct defects is in late summer and midwinter. A few, such as top-grafted weeping standards or those with variegated foliage, require more attention and may need pruning often to relieve congestion or remove reverted shoots.

UNEVEN GROWTH

The commonest cause of uneven growth is suppression by neighbouring trees or other shade-casting structures. If the prime cause remains in place, there is little point in remedial pruning. If, however, the offending structure is removed, the tree may be restored over several years. In the first year, prune weak branches hard and take off all suckers and dead, diseased, and crossing wood. In the second and subsequent years, reduce any overcrowding (which may result from the previous year's cuts) and remove or shorten other branches to enhance the shape. Remove only one or two branches in any one year; take them out in sections to reduce risk of tearing the bark (*see opposite*).

Year 1, winter
Tip-prune branch leaders on the stronger side to produce limited regrowth. Cut back the weaker side hard to stimulate vigorous regrowth that will balance the tree's form.

Year 2 onwards, winter
Strong new shoots have grown on the weaker side. In this and subsequent seasons, remove crossing shoots and any that will spoil the crown's symmetry if allowed to develop.

CUTTING OFF A BRANCH

You should only remove branches that are no higher than shoulder height and that are light enough for you to support safely. For your own - and the tree's - safety, any major pruning that has to be done from a ladder or involves removal of large branches should be undertaken by a professional tree surgeon.

CUTTING TO THE BRANCH COLLAR

1 *Reduce the weight of the branch first. About 30cm (12in) from the trunk, saw a quarter of the way into the branch from the underside to avoid the bark tearing if the branch breaks.*

2 *Cut squarely down from the top, 5cm (2in) beyond the undercut, until the section falls away. The final cut should now be much more controllable.*

3 *Make the final cut just beyond the branch collar, at an equal and opposite angle to that made by the branch's bark ridge (see p.11), to avoid damaging the tree.*

4 *Smooth any rough edges with a pruning knife. Wound paints are no longer recommended; they interfere with the tree's natural healing.*

41

THINNING REGROWTH

Hard pruning often results in the production of fast-growing shoots, known as epicormic or water shoots, from dormant buds under the bark around the site of the pruning wound. If left, they proliferate and divert energy from the rest of the tree, and seldom make safe and robust new branches. If they are carefully reduced in number, however, they can do much to improve the appearance of an awkward-looking, truncated stub.

Selected shoots are shortened back to a healthy bud

All surplus buds and wayward shoots have been cut or rubbed out

Before
This damaged branch has been lopped, giving it a clumsy appearance. Many new shoots have appeared. By careful selection, balanced regrowth can be developed.

After
Four strong shoots have been selected to form an open structure; each now has plenty of room to develop. Shorten them by at least half, varying lengths to avoid a "mop-head" cluster.

WITCHES' BROOMS

Many trees develop dense clusters of stunted twigs and foliage on their branches, usually as a response to infection by mites, insects, or fungi. These witches' brooms, as they are known, are harmless to the tree, but often look unsightly clustered in the crown, especially on trees of open, airy habit such as silver birches (*Betula pendula*). The affected branches can be removed at their point of origin, or to a suitable point below the affected area, at the junction of a main branch for example. This is best done when the tree is fully dormant and the witches' brooms can clearly be seen.

Witch's broom
Clusters of twiggy stunted growth can enhance a gnarled, picturesque appearance in a tree, but can be removed if found unsightly.

MAJOR SURGERY

On large trees, especially in urban areas, major tree surgery is an extremely dangerous task that should be carried out only by a qualified tree surgeon (arboriculturist). The work may involve crown reduction to reduce the overall size of a mature tree's canopy that has outgrown its space, and is often done in conjunction with crown thinning to remove congested growth. Crown lifting is used to remove the lower branches of a large tree that overhang and obstruct a path, driveway, or public highway, but may also be used to open up a view, or admit more light to allow plantings beneath. These operations are seldom necessary where proper species selection has been carried out in the first place; *always* check a tree's mature dimensions before planting.

LEGAL PRECAUTIONS

- It is essential, before any work is done, to check whether a tree is legally protected. If it is, you must obtain permission from the relevant local authority before felling or even pruning branches.
- If tree work is likely to affect overhead wires or underground cables and pipes, the relevant utility provider must be informed and the work carried out by a professional tree surgeon.
- The most bitter disputes between neighbours often arise from misunderstandings over boundaries. It is both wise and courteous to advise neighbours of your intentions if your tree borders their property; cooperation is essential if you must prune a neighbour's tree that encroaches on your garden. You are legally entitled to remove only as much of a branch that grows over a line drawn vertically upwards from your boundary. The cuttings are the property of the neighbours.

Crown lifting
Lower branches that obstruct free passage beneath them, block out light, or obscure road signs or street lamps are removed to create a longer length of clear trunk.

Crown thinning and reduction
Thinning the canopy admits light and air to the centre of the crown; crown reduction reduces the height and spread of a tree, for example to permit the passage of power lines.

CONIFERS

MOST CONIFERS ARE cone-bearing evergreens with needle- or scale-like leaves, and have strongly upright and dominant leaders that give rise to a typical conical habit. With few exceptions, they are best grown with minimal pruning. When mature, pruning is best avoided altogether unless to repair damage or remove reverted or wayward growth.

TRAINING A LEADER

The majority of conifers will naturally re-form a leading shoot if damaged when young or in early maturity. If damage occurs, select and train in a new leader as soon as possible. If injury occurs in later life, dual leaders often result. It is essential to remove one of them to produce a single-stemmed tree and to avoid dangerous narrow forks at maturity. Timing is critical, since most conifers are resinous and bleed profusely when cut. Pruning in autumn or midwinter keeps bleeding to a minimum.

Competing leader
To maintain a single-stemmed, central-leader tree, cut out the weaker or more crooked shoot cleanly at its base.

REPLACING A BROKEN LEADER

1 *On young plants, a broken leader can be replaced with a strong lateral that can be tied in to assume the dominant role.*

2 *Remove all damaged growth, cutting it back cleanly to a strong, preferably upright, shoot. The resulting small wound will heal quickly.*

3 *Tie the new leader to a cane pushed through the tree's centre. Remove the cane once the new leader is growing strongly upwards.*

SPLAYED SHOOTS

Wind, snow, ice, or occasionally the weight of an upright branch, can cause growth to splay out, spoiling the form of the tree *(see inset, right)*. First check that the branch has not split; if it is undamaged, it can be tied back in to the main shoot.

Dealing with splayed-out growth
Tie in undamaged shoots to the main stem, using soft material in case the tie is forgotten. Tarred twine or nylon tights are ideal.

DEAD PATCHES

Scorched or dead foliage should be removed completely *(see inset, right)*. Unless damage is very minimal, this leaves an unsightly hole, especially in formally shaped trees or hedges. New growth will not shoot from old wood, so disguise damage by tying in adjacent shoots across the hole, securing them with a cane tied to a main stem or branch.

Covering dead patches
Secure a cane to a main stem or branch. Draw neighbouring branches over the gap and tie them in. New growth will soon hide the cane.

DWARF CONIFERS

Dwarf conifers are propagated from sports (natural mutations) of the normal tree. Sports are often selected for a dense, prostrate, or upright habit. Pruning is usually unnecessary but sometimes a shoot reverts to the normal habit, which spoils the form and may eventually become dominant. All reverted growth must be cut out to maintain the distinctive shape for which the plant has been selected.

Removing reverted growth
The strongly upright shoot in this prostrate plant is removed at the point of origin, thus masking the cut within remaining foliage.

COPPICING AND POLLARDING

THE TRADITIONAL WOODLAND TECHNIQUES of coppicing and pollarding are similar and consist of hard pruning on a routine basis. Some trees respond to such treatment by producing vigorous new growth that is highly ornamental, such as larger than normal leaves or young stems in beautiful colours. These techniques are also used to restrict the size of large trees.

COPPICING

This entails the regular, sometimes annual, cutting back of a tree to ground level, when dormant, to obtain vigorous young stems. The tree has a full-sized root system, so regrowth of young, often richly coloured, stems is vigorous and leaves may be much larger or more colourful. Cutting to a low stump also makes it feasible to provide winter protection such as a mulch of straw to slightly tender trees like most eucalyptus. Not all trees respond well to such hard pruning.

Pollarded* Acer negundo *'Flamingo'
Cut back hard to a low framework in winter for larger leaves (see below) and a shrubby habit to suit confined spaces.

Pruning for foliage effect
By being pollarded to a very low stem, this Acer negundo *'Flamingo' has responded by producing fresh, cream-splashed variegated foliage. Many trees develop the most attractive foliage on the newest growth.*

TREES AND SHRUBS

The following respond well to coppicing and pollarding:

ACER PENSYLVANICUM
  'ERYTHROCLADUM' ♀ (red stems)
AILANTHUS (large leaves)
CATALPA BIGNONIOIDES ♀
  (large leaves)
CERCIS (flowers at eye-level,
  but do not cut every year)
CORNUS ALBA (coloured stems)
CORYLUS AVELLANA, C. MAXIMA
  'PURPUREA' ♀ (multi-stems
  and large leaves)
EUCALYPTUS (juvenile leaves)
FAGUS SYLVATICA ♀ (multi-
  stemmed)
PAULOWNIA (large leaves)
RHUS TYPHINA ♀ (large leaves)
RUBUS COCKBURNIANUS ♀,
  R. THIBETANUS ♀ (white stems)
SALIX ALBA and subspecies
  VITELLINA (coloured stems)

POLLARDING

Pollarding is much like coppicing, except that stems are cut back above a clear length of trunk. Willows and dogwoods are often pollarded to produce crops of young, vividly coloured stems in shades of yellow, green, or scarlet. When leafless, they provide welcome winter colour, growing to a height that displays the stems above other plantings. Stems are cut back before growth resumes in spring, securing the longest possible display. The technique is also effective in producing larger, more colourful leaves at eye level, or in maintaining eucalyptus, for example, in a state of perpetual juvenility – juvenile leaves are often more attractive than adult ones. Pollarding is also used to restrict the size of large trees, such as limes (*Tilia*), producing a compact crown that is ideal for a street tree. Both coppicing and pollarding are simple methods, but only a limited number of trees will tolerate such hard treatment: disease resistance is crucial to enable continual recovery from wounds.

***Established pollard* (Salix)**
Every 2–3 years, in late winter, cut back young stems to within 2cm (¾in) of the main stem.

***Pollarded* Catalpa bignonioides '*Aurea*'**
This tree, suffering from dieback, was pollarded in winter to a framework of 4–5 branches on a 1.2m (4ft) trunk (left). New growth bears a crop of larger, more colourful leaves (right).

WINTER

SUMMER

HEDGES

WHETHER FORMAL OR INFORMAL, hedges perform several important roles in a garden. Hedges give structure, and often form a backdrop to other plantings; they offer privacy and provide shelter from strong winds and sun, as well as filtering out noise and dust from nearby roads. They can also, if suitable species are chosen, create a haven for wildlife.

STARTING A HEDGE

Prepare a band of ground 1m (3ft) wide and plant 30–60cm (1–2ft) apart, in a straight line, alternating weak and strong plants. Shorten strong leaders and laterals by one-third and weak shoots by two-thirds. Cut back vigorous species such as hawthorn to 15–30cm (6–12in) to encourage a bushy base.

Providing support
New hedges need little support, except in exposed areas, when low wires and posts on the windward side may be necessary.

FORMAL HEDGES

Plants used for formal hedges must have a dense habit and tolerate clipping. From the early stages, the hedge sides should be cut at a slight angle (known as the "batter"), with the base as the widest point, to produce a tapered outline, with a flat or gently rounded top. This makes the hedge less vulnerable to damage by snow or strong winds, and allows more even distribution of light from the top to the bottom.

Tapered top
The shape of this hornbeam hedge permits light to reach the lower flanks, thus reducing foliage loss at the base.

Classic A-shape
This yew has been cut into a classic formal A-shape, which tapers gently to a neat, flat top.

Rounded top
Sloping sides and a rounded top give this conifer hedge a softer outline, and also reduce damage from wind and snow.

SHAPING FORMAL HEDGES

The aim of pruning and training are to ensure dense growth from the base to the top, and to produce a neat outline with a batter. When shaping, use a line or template as your guide; its almost impossible to do this accurately by eye, except on dwarf hedges, which look best with vertical sides. For most conifers and evergreens, only the laterals are pruned in the formative years. Do not shape the top until the desired height is reached.

Using a line
To achieve a level top, stretch taut string horizontally between two upright posts to act as a guideline for the highest part of the hedge, and cut the top along this line.

Using a template
To taper the top, cut a template (inset) of the required shape. Place on the hedge and cut following the line of the template, moving it along as you proceed; then cut the sides.

TRIMMING FORMAL HEDGES

Once the size and batter have been achieved, a hedge simply needs trimming to maintain its form, using a straight-edge or garden line as a guide. Frequency, degree, and timing of trimming depends on species. Most hedges are cut twice annually: when dormant and in midsummer for deciduous hedges, in late spring and late summer for evergreens. For conifer hedges, regular trimming is essential; few conifers break freely from old wood.

Using hand shears or trimmers
Keep blades of shears parallel to the line of the hedge so that top and sides are cut level and flat. Use a trimmer with a sweeping action to avoid cutting into the hedge and spoiling the shape.

49

INFORMAL HEDGES

An informal hedge is basically a screen of close-planted small trees or, more often, shrubs. Timing and techniques of pruning are much the same as for individual specimens, and should be accompanied by gentle shaping of the outline. Remove over-long or badly placed growths and trim back annually to keep within bounds. Trim large-leaved evergreens with secateurs; shearing will damage individual leaves, which then become brown and unsightly. For flowering or fruiting hedges, timing is critical if the display is not to be spoiled. The easiest to manage are shrubs such as pyracantha (*see p.65*) or chaenomeles (*see p.18*), which bear their flowers on laterals or spurs from older wood, rather than terminally on growth that will be removed by trimming.

Flowering hedges
Garrya (left) can be clipped as the catkins fade. Most other flowering hedges that bloom before midsummer are cut after flowering; those that flower from midsummer onwards may be pruned when dormant or in spring.

Semi-formal and informal hedges
Shape gently with secateurs. Cut back individual shoots to within the foliage canopy to disguise pruning wounds.

CONIFER HEDGES

Regular trimming of conifer hedges is essential to maintain a dense surface. If neglected, the usual result is a bare, woody, open centre with a fringe of foliage at the extremities. Such hedges are both unsightly and prone to splitting or collapse in heavy snow or strong winds. While minor localized damage can be remedied by tying branches over to conceal small gaps (*see p.45*), replacement is the best option for a badly neglected conifer hedge.

Section through a conifer hedge
Regularly trimmed conifers have a dense, even surface, but are leafless within; most will not produce new shoots from old bare wood.

RENOVATING HEDGES

Even well-maintained hedges may gradually edge their way beyond bounds. Beech, hornbeam, hawthorn, holly, and yew all respond well to hard pruning. Renovate deciduous hedges in midwinter and evergreen ones in spring. Cut the top and each side in different years to avoid undue stress, reducing to at least 15cm (6in) less than the desired height and width. Feed and mulch well in spring after each pruning.

Renovated surface
has produced
dense regrowth

Second side is now
cut back hard

Reducing hedge width, first year
Cut one side of the hedge back hard (right side), *almost to the main stems if necessary. Prune the other side* (left) *as usual.*

Reducing hedge width, second year
The renovated surface has produced dense regrowth. Cut the remaining surface back hard, by the same amount as the other side.

REDUCING HEIGHT

To re-create a dense, even top, reduce the height to at least 15cm (6in) below the desired height. If upper portions are very patchy, cut back harder than this. Use a straight-edge or garden line as a guide, to ensure that all plants are cut to the same height. Feed and mulch well after pruning; regrowth should disguise wounds within one or two seasons.

Leggy hedges
Thin, gappy top growth is unsightly and reduces the hedge's effectiveness.

PLANTS FOR HEDGES

FORMAL HEDGES
ACER CAMPESTRE ♥, BUXUS, CARPINUS BETULUS ♥, CHAMAECYPARIS, CRATAEGUS MONOGYNA, ELAEAGNUS, ESCALLONIA, FAGUS SYLVATICA ♥, GRISELINIA, ILEX, LAURUS, LONICERA NITIDA, PRUNUS LAUROCERASUS ♥, P. LUSITANICA ♥, TAXUS BACCATA ♥, THUJA PLICATA
FLOWERING OR FRUITING HEDGES
CHAENOMELES, FORSYTHIA, FUCHSIA, POTENTILLA FRUTICOSA, PYRACANTHA, RIBES, ROSA
INFORMAL HEDGES
AUCUBA, BERBERIS, CORYLUS, COTONEASTER, GARRYA, OLEARIA, PRUNUS CERASIFERA 'PISSARDII', P. CERASIFERA 'NIGRA' ♥, TAMARIX.

TOPIARY

A FORM OF TRAINING to create living "sculpture", topiary is a garden art traditionally used to produce a variety of geometric forms. Shapes such as cones, obelisks, and columns provide a strong, structural element in a design and are ideal for framing a vista, or as a contrasting foil for looser plantings.

__Shapes and effects__
Eye-catching forms are created by combining simple pruning and training; these need precise clipping and regular maintenance.

SPIRAL STEM   POODLE   BASIC CONE

CLIPPING TO CREATE SHAPES

The simplest topiary design is one close to the natural form of the plant. Plants used for topiary must have a dense habit, produce pliable growth, and respond well to close clipping. If a compact surface and crisp outline is required, they should also have small leaves. The species must be suitable for your soil type and climate; precise forms are quickly spoiled by dieback caused by frost and wind or unsuitable soil conditions.

Clip shoots back to a strong pair of buds. Avoid cutting individual leaves

1 *In the first year, a young box tree is clipped roughly to shape using secateurs. This will encourage the necessary dense, bushy growth.*

2 *Using a tripod of canes and wire hoops as a guide, in the second year the bush is clipped into a neat crisp cone with a dense surface.*

3 *In subsequent years, the finished plant is clipped two or three times a year, depending on growth rate, to retain a well-defined outline.*

MOP-HEAD STANDARD

A ready-trained mop-head standard like this sweet bay (*Laurus nobilis*) is expensive to buy, but it is relatively easy to create. Prune a young, straight-stemmed plant back to a cluster of sideshoots at the top of the stem, shortening these to outward-facing buds. Clear shoots from the stem. Keep the stem clear by rubbing off any new buds that emerge. As new shoots develop, tip-prune each to a bud facing in the desired direction, to build up a dense, compact head.

Tip-prune shoots

Stem cleared of shoots

Remove basal suckers

Standard sweet bay
In cool climates, standard bay trees will need winter protection, but if pot-grown, they can easily be moved into a cool greenhouse.

YEAR 1   YEAR 2

STEM EFFECTS

A mop-head standard of sweet bay or weeping fig (*Ficus benjamina*) can be enhanced by special stem effects. Stems are easily plaited when young; they eventually fuse together but will need support until growth hardens.

Barley sugar twist
Train one or two stems around a stout wooden pole, looping the stems beneath dowel pegs inserted in a spiral along its length. The pole is removed as growth hardens.

Plaited stem
Form a plaited stem simply by braiding together three flexible shoots. Select the strongest three on a multi-stemmed young plant, and remove the remainder.

PLANTS FOR TOPIARY

A number of trees and shrubs are suitable for topiary work. When clipping larger-leaved species, such as *Prunus lusitanica* or *Laurus nobilis*, take care not to cut individual leaves.

ARTEMISIA ABROTANUM ♥
BERBERIS
BUXUS MICROPHYLLA
  B. SEMPERVIRENS ♥
CRATAEGUS
CUPRESSUS SEMPERVIRENS
ELAEAGNUS ANGUSTIFOLIA
  E. FORTUNEI
FICUS BENJAMINA ♥
ILEX AQUIFOLIUM ♥
  I. CRENATA
JUNIPERUS COMMUNIS
LAURUS NOBILIS ♥
LIGUSTRUM OVALIFOLIUM
LONICERA NITIDA
MYRTUS COMMUNIS ♥
OSMANTHUS
PHILLYREA
PRUNUS LUSITANICA
SANTOLINA CHAMAECYPARISSUS ♥
TEUCRIUM CHAMAEDRYS

ORNAMENTAL SHRUBS

SOME OF THE most striking planting schemes rely on carefully chosen shrubs whose shapely form and healthy growth give pleasure all year round. Light pruning to shape, and the routine removal of dead, diseased, or damaged wood, may be all that some shrubs need to remain handsome and vigorous. However, for many popular shrubs, regular pruning is needed to enhance and maintain the quality of their ornamental features such as flowering and fruiting. Observe carefully when and where on their branches these shrubs flower, and on what age of wood. Your aim, then, is to remove old, unproductive wood in favour of the young, vigorous, and fruitful, thus encouraging the natural process of renewal.

Fragrant philadelphus *Most philadelphus need regular pruning to maximize flowering.*

BUYING A YOUNG SHRUB

YOU CAN BUY YOUNG SHRUBS as partially trained, container-grown plants from a garden centre, or as rootballed or bare-root plants from a nursery. Alternatively, you can propagate your own, using simple techniques such as cuttings or layering, which gives you control over growing conditions and an opportunity to begin immediately to train a well-shaped specimen.

WHAT TO LOOK FOR

Young plants should be vigorous and healthy, with no obvious signs of pests, diseases, or disorders caused by poor nutrition, such as leaf-yellowing. If grafted, check that the graft union is streamlined, so that scion and rootstock join smoothly and strongly, without a kink in the stem.

The root system must be large enough to support the top growth (*see far right*) and should never be potbound, since this will affect absorption of nutrients, which can lead to stunted growth. Avoid plants that have been encouraged to flower heavily for sale, or deadhead them as soon as possible.

Shoot tips are healthy, with no sign of scorch or dieback

New foliage is abundant and vigorous

Stunted top growth

Bare, leggy stems

Older leaves are glossy and healthy

Dead growth

Congested rootball

Good specimen
This camellia has healthy growth, glossy, disease-free foliage, and an attractive, well-balanced top growth that is supported by a substantial root system.

Poor specimen
This prostanthera has been in its pot too long; its rootball is compacted, and the compost is exhausted, resulting in leggy growth, and dead shoots at the base and centre.

PRUNING ON PLANTING

A well-chosen, healthy plant should need no pruning on planting except perhaps to tip-prune soft shoots to promote a bushy habit, or to shorten overlong shoots by no more than one-third of their length for a more balanced outline. Remove weak growth or damaged shoots and shoot tips, along with unnecessary canes and ties. Deadhead plants that have flowered, so that the plant uses energy for growth rather than seed formation. On rootballed or bare-rooted plants, which are planted when dormant, check for and cut away cleanly any damaged roots. Container-grown plants, which may be planted at any time of year, seldom need root pruning except to shorten any damaged roots to clean, healthy tissue.

ROOT-TO-SHOOT RATIO

An unbalanced root-to-shoot ratio – top growth that is far too large for the rootball to sustain – is the primary cause of poor growth after planting. A container-grown plant that has outgrown its pot will establish more quickly if, on planting, its top growth is reduced, either by shortening all stems by half, resulting in a bushy habit, or by cutting them back to the base, to encourage taller, more upright growth.

SMALL ROOTBALL

Deciduous cutting (below, left and centre)
A young forsythia naturally forms a single stem (left). *Cut the growing tip back, and it will develop a more bushy habit* (right).

Evergreen cutting (right)
Ceanothus and many other evergreens branch low down to form a balanced shape and seldom need pruning on planting.

UNPRUNED SINGLE STEM   PRUNED TO INDUCE BRANCHING   NATURALLY BRANCHING CUTTING

PRUNING SHRUBS

AS YOUNG SHRUBS GROW, routine tasks, such as the removal of dead, diseased, or damaged wood, should be dealt with as needed. Once shrubs have had a growing season in which to establish, and they have become dormant, formative pruning can start. The main aim here is to create a balanced shape and to develop their ornamental features.

FORMATIVE PRUNING

Evergreens tend to develop a neat habit and well-spaced branches naturally, so little formative pruning is needed. If necessary, take off cold-damaged growth and badly positioned or weak stems, then tip-prune overlong stems to balance the outline. Deciduous shrubs are much more likely to benefit from formative pruning. If a shrub is to be a permanent feature of some stature, especially if it flowers on second-year or older wood (*see below, right*), it needs to develop with an open centre to allow

penetration of light and air. Remove any crowded or crossing stems or shorten them to strong buds or young shoots facing in the desired direction. Shrubs that flower on the current season's growth are cut back to a permanent woody framework every year. They are pruned hard from the outset to develop a base of strong stems (*see below, left*) to support vigorous annual growth. The framework is usually near ground level, but if extra height is needed, more moderate pruning will produce a taller framework.

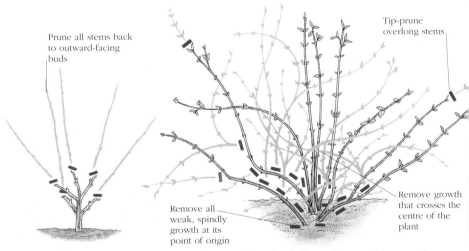

Prune all stems back to outward-facing buds

Tip-prune overlong stems

Remove all weak, spindly growth at its point of origin

Remove growth that crosses the centre of the plant

Developing a low framework
Remove weak or badly placed shoots, then shorten strong remaining stems to healthy buds at the desired height.

Formative pruning, shrub flowering on older wood
Early pruning ensures a well-shaped deciduous shrub with an uncluttered centre at maturity. Remove unwanted stems while they are still small and while the plant is young and its healing potential is at its greatest.

ESTABLISHED DECIDUOUS SHRUBS

Shrubs that flower on new wood will bloom after midsummer and are pruned back to a permanent woody framework in early spring. During annual pruning, aim to restore a balanced framework and an open centre. Remove dead or damaged wood as seen. Established deciduous shrubs that flower on second-year or older wood come into bloom before midsummer and are pruned immediately after flowering. Pruning aims to cut out some of the oldest wood each year, to encourage the production of young wood that flowers more freely.

Cut back flowered stems to non-flowered shoots

Cut out oldest flowered wood at its base

Cut weak or unhealthy stems to healthy tissue

__Deciduous shrub flowering on older wood__
Prune directly after flowering to create an open centre and a well-balanced framework of young, free-flowering wood.

ESTABLISHED EVERGREEN SHRUBS

Most evergreens need little pruning, but many will tolerate harder pruning to remove wayward branches or to renovate them. Pruning aims to remove diseased, damaged, or weak wood, to thin out congestion, and remove badly placed stems. Deadheading helps the plant divert energy into growth rather than seed. Evergreens are usually pruned in spring, when danger of frost has passed. Flowering evergreens may also be pruned lightly after flowering, to remove the oldest flowered wood, to trim to shape, or, in areas with heavy snowfall, to thin dense growth on which snow could accumulate and cause breakage.

Cut flowered shoots to outward-facing buds

__Pruning an established evergreen__
Immediately after flowering, deadhead all flowering stems, cut away any damaged wood, and thin out congested areas.

ROUTINE TASKS

CHECK OVER YOUR SHRUBS regularly and remove any diseased or damaged growth promptly before it becomes a problem. Other routine tasks include cutting out unwanted growth such as suckers, and deadheading. Where a shrub has become overgrown, hard pruning will give it a new lease of life.

REMOVING SUCKERS

The natural habit of many shrubs is suckering; sucker growth increases the plant's spread and replaces stems that grow old and die. If the plant is congested, it is the oldest stems that should be removed.

On grafted shrubs, sucker growth emerges from below the graft union. This growth is usually stronger than the desirable grafted cultivar and must be removed if the suckers are not to predominate.

NORMAL GROWTH

SUCKER

Identifying suckers (left)
The shoot from a desirable
Hamamelis mollis *cultivar* (far left) *is distinguishable from one arising from below the graft on the rootstock* (left).

Removing suckers (right)
Pull off sharply at the point of origin, on the stem or root. If pieces remain, nip them off with a sharp knife (inset) *without enlarging the wound.*

DEADHEADING

Though not essential, deadheading improves the look of some shrubs, and more importantly, diverts energy from setting seed into further growth. Spent flowers are cut off with secateurs, but for some shrubs, such as rhododendrons, it is safer to pinch them out with finger and thumb.

Spent flower cluster

Non-flowered sideshoot

Pinching out (left)
Spent rhododendron flowerheads are pinched out to avoid damage to new buds under the flowers (inset).

Cutting back (right)
On buddlejas, use secateurs to cut back a flowered cluster to a bud or young sideshoot.

REJUVENATION

If shrubs are neglected, they accumulate dead wood at their centre and produce fewer flowers from congested old wood. Provided that the plants respond well to hard pruning and are basically healthy, pruning gives them a new lease of life. They are best rejuvenated in the dormant season, although sometimes this results in the loss of a season's flowers. Since all plants have a finite lifespan, even shrubs that respond well to hard pruning when young may not do so as they age. Propagate favourite plants as insurance against losses, and always feed and mulch well after pruning.

Reinvigorating a shrub (Philadelphus)
Cut out dead, diseased, and crossing wood. Thin healthy shoots by half their number, to give the remainder room to develop.

DRASTIC RENOVATION

Several, mainly deciduous, shrubs respond well to drastic renovation when dormant. On vigorous plants, such as the lilac (*Syringa*) shown here, this can be done in a single operation. If you fear that the shrub may not respond well, and many evergreens do not, renovate over two or three growing seasons. Take special care if renovating grafted plants not to cut below the graft union and to remove any regrowth that appears below it.

Reduce the weight of top growth before cutting back main stems

Cut back main stems to form a low framework

Renovated lilac, year 1
Remove top growth first, then cut main stems straight across, to 30–60cm (1–2ft) above ground level. Work in sections to avoid tearing bark. Feed and mulch well.

Renovated lilac, year 2
Many new shoots are produced in response to hard pruning. Thin these to 2–3 strong shoots per stump to form a strong framework.

SPECIAL EFFECTS

MOST SHRUBS ARE PRUNED using one or other of the techniques described on pages 58–61. A few, such as hydrangeas, have individual pruning requirements, while others respond well – and their ornamental features are maximized – if they are pruned specifically to achieve a particular shape, such as a weeping standard or a wall-trained shrub.

STAGGERED PRUNING

Coppicing and pollarding (*see pp.46–7*) are frequently practised to produce vigorous young stems. In *Cornus alba, C. stolonifera,* and *Salix alba* cultivars young stems are brilliantly coloured in winter in shades of scarlet, egg-yolk yellow and lime green, an attraction that is dramatically enhanced when the shrubs are planted where the stems can be reflected in still water. A variation on the technique of coppicing, known as staggered pruning, takes this effect still further. Cutting the stems of neighbouring plants back to different heights results in successive bands of colour, giving the impression of a sloping bank rather than a dense thicket of regrowth at a uniform height.

SHRUBS WITH CANE-LIKE STEMS

Some shrubs, for example *Kerria japonica* and *Leycesteria formosa,* flower on cane-like stems that are produced annually from the base. The young canes add much to the overall effect, since they are beautifully coloured in intense shades of green. Cut back one in three of the main stems immediately after flowering for kerria, and in spring for leycesteria.

KERRIA JAPONICA

Pruning at different heights **(Cornus alba)**
Let the shrubs grow unchecked for their first season. In late winter or early spring, cut back the stems of some plants to 5cm (2in), those of the next band to 25cm (10in) and the third to 50cm (20in).

WEEPING STANDARDS

Many shrubs have arching or weeping branches which are shown off well if the shrub is trained as a standard. The shrub you buy may have been pruned to make bushy growth (*see below, left*). Remove up to three-quarters of the top growth, retaining a strong single stem furnished with laterals (*see below, right*). Train the single stem upright by tying to a vertical cane. When it has reached the desired height, pinch out the leading shoot to encourage branching. Tip-prune new laterals as they develop to create a well-branched head. Keep the main stem clear of growth by rubbing out new laterals as they emerge or, if you miss them at this stage, pruning them flush with the trunk.

Strong stem trained in as new leader

Cane assists vertical growth

BEFORE PRUNING

AFTER PRUNING

Initial training (**Buddleja**)
Before pruning, this Buddleja alternifolia *has bushy growth from the base of the plant* (far left). *After pruning away much of the top growth, a single stem remains* (left), *furnished with laterals to strengthen the leader as it grows. To assist vertical growth, the stem and leader are tied to a cane inserted into the ground.*

Remove old, weak and unproductive growth, especially if it is crowding the centre

Cut back flowered stems to non-flowering, upward- and outward-facing young shoots, or to a strong bud

The length of clear stem is sufficient to raise trailing branches clear of the ground

Established standard
Buddleja alternifolia *bears flowers on the previous year's wood and is pruned after flowering.*

WALL TRAINING

Numerous shrubs can be wall-trained in fans or espaliers or, less formally, by tying in to wires. Provide tough wire or trellis support. Plant shrubs at least 45cm (18in) from the base of the wall to avoid dry soil caused by the "rainshadow" effect of the wall. Cut single-stemmed plants back hard to encourage branching, then select 4–5 strong stems to form a well-spaced framework. Cut inward- and outward-growing shoots back to 1–2 buds to induce sideways branching.

***Initial training and pruning* (Ceanothus)**
If the shrub is well-furnished with laterals, space them out and tie in to the support. Shorten long laterals by a few buds to produce branches for balanced coverage.

Shorten stems that have reached the limits of the allotted space

Deadhead flowered growth and shorten outward-facing shoots

Check, reposition, or replace any broken or constricting ties

Tie in new growth and shorten weak shoots to stimulate stronger growth

Established shrub
As the shrub matures, older, less productive framework branches may be removed to make way for younger growth. Continue to tie in new growth and reduce inward- or outward-growing shoots to 1–2 buds.

PRUNING PYRACANTHAS

Pyracanthas are grown for the clusters of small white flowers in early summer and for the showy, red, orange, or yellow fruits that follow them. They are borne on spurs – fruiting sideshoots – on the old wood.

Pruning to shape and the shortening of outward-growing shoots on wall-trained shrubs is done in mid-spring; to display the winter-persistent berries at their best, pruning can be repeated in late summer.

Remove completely any weak, damaged, or unhealthy growth

Shorten vigorous new shoots to 2–3 leaves to encourage spur formation

Cut back fruit-bearing shoots to 2–3 leaves to expose berries

Wall-trained pyracantha
In late summer prune young shoots not needed for tying in to 2–3 leaves to expose ripening berries.

PRUNING HYDRANGEAS

Hydrangea macrophylla and *H. serrata* bloom in mid- to late summer on the previous year's wood. In warm climates, prune after flowering; in cool climates, leave old flowers in place over winter to protect growth buds beneath them and prune in spring. Cut out weak shoots and 1–2 of the oldest stems at the base. Shorten the previous year's flowered branches by up to 30cm (12in) to fat buds.

Shorten flowered stems to a pair of healthy buds

***Pruning* Hydrangea macrophylla**
Prune in spring; if frost-damaged shoots are cut to the base they will regenerate freely but will not flower until their second summer.

PINCH PRUNING

THE TECHNIQUE OF PINCH PRUNING is used to induce bushy growth by repeatedly nipping out soft shoot tips using finger and thumb. It is suitable mainly for subshrubs, such as fuchsias and coleus, which have woody bases and soft top growth. Combine it with training on wire frames or canes, and you can produce spectacular flower or foliage displays in many decorative shapes.

STYLISH SHAPES

With flowering plants, repeated pinching out delays flowering, because the shoot never has time to form a flower bud at its tip; its energy is diverted into forming sideshoots. If you cease pinching about two months before flowering, the last set of shoots, which all start into growth at the same time, will flower simultaneously. The striking result is well worth the time and patience taken to produce it.

Charm chrysanthemum
Grows naturally as a dense mound, so pinch pruning to form a sphere is a relatively easy procedure.

Chrysanthemum sphere
Train three or four plants of cascade chrysanthemums (above) around a large wire balloon frame. Tie in growth to fill spaces and pinch out surplus shoots.

Coleus standard
For fine foliage effects (right), *pinch prune to form a dense head on a clear-stemmed standard. This technique works well for pelargoniums, heliotropes, felicias, coleus, fuchsias,* Abutilon x hybridum *and* A. megapotamicum.

Fuchsia fan
Spread out and tie in fuchsia shoots to a framework of canes arranged and tied as a fan; for extra support, attach a semi-circle of wire netting to the frame before training.

Argyranthemum cone
Most plants amenable to pinch pruning can be formed into cones. Use three plants in a pot, as the more abundant growth makes it easier to pinch selectively to form a symmetrical shape.

PINCH-PRUNED STANDARD

Many subshrubs can be trained as standards, but coleus (*Solenostemon*) is one of the simplest. The height of the clear stem and head can vary according to the plant used and personal preference, but as a general rule, the most pleasing results are produced if the depth of the head is one-third to one-half of the total height. The head's density is dictated by the frequency of pinching, the size of the leaves, and the distance between leaf joints. Coleus, with closely spaced leaves, is perfect for creating a dense "lollipop" head.

1 *Plant a single-stemmed cutting in a 25cm (10in) pot. Insert a cane and tie the stem to it. Feed well. Allow a week or so for the plant to settle in.*

2 *Until the desired height is reached, pinch out all sideshoots, but retain the leaves from whose axils they grew. This foliage nourishes the plant and helps thicken the stem. Tie in the stem at intervals with soft twine as it grows upwards.*

3 *When the leading shoot reaches at least 20cm (8in) more than the desired height of the clear stem, pinch out the shoot tip.*

4 *At the head of the plant, pinch prune all new shoots when they have two to four leaves, until a bushy head is formed. Pinch or rub out all shoots that appear on the stem.*

5 *Continue to pinch as necessary to keep a neat shape. On flowering plants, stop pinching 8–12 weeks before flowers are desired.*

Most leaves are shed naturally from the stem; if not, pick them off carefully

SHRUBS IN CONTAINERS

ALL CONTAINER-GROWN SHRUBS need more care than those in open ground, since they have less access to nutrients and water. This is especially true of shrubs that are pruned annually to shape, as they rely on healthy, well-fed foliage to keep them looking good.

Standards in pots
Healthy, glossy foliage is essential for a fine-looking standard; good nutrition is vital to replace growth removed by pruning.

HELIOTROPIUM   VIBURNUM TINUS   NERIUM OLEANDER

ROOT PRUNING

When the roots of a mature shrub have filled a large container it may not always be practicable to pot it on into a larger one – or you may simply wish to keep it in a favourite pot. The old compost will have lost its structure and be depleted of nutrients. In these circumstances, root pruning is necessary. In spring, gently slide the shrub from its container while supporting the top growth with one hand. If the pot is full of

roots, it may be necessary to slide a long-bladed knife between compost and pot to free the rootball. Remove surface compost and loosen the roots with a hand fork to relieve compaction. Prune back about a quarter of non-fibrous roots by up to two-thirds of their length but retain fibrous roots. Repot using fresh compost, then prune the shrub to reduce top growth overall by approximately one-third.

Teasing out roots
Slide the plant gently from its pot (inset), then gently tease out the roots with a hand fork, shaking off as much old compost as possible.

Pruning roots
Shorten non-fibrous roots by up to two-thirds of their length. Leave as many fibrous roots intact as possible; these are the feeder roots.

MAINTAINING NUTRITION

To sustain good healthy growth on a shrub that is pruned annually, the plant must have sufficient nutrients to replace the growth that is removed by pruning. Apply a balanced liquid fertilizer 2-3 times during the period between the start of growth in spring and midsummer. Until plants reach maturity, they should be repotted into a larger pot each or every other year in spring. When they reach their final pot size, root prune on repotting if necessary to relieve congestion (*see opposite, below*). Otherwise, the top 5-10cm (2-4in) of compost can be removed and replaced with fresh compost mixed with a dressing of slow-release fertilizer at the manufacturer's recommended rate.

Demands of pruning and training
During the early years of creating, for example, this standard pyracantha, the demands on the plant's energy are great. It is vital therefore that some foliage is retained while the stem is being formed to allow the plant to manufacture the food it needs to grow and thrive.

Leader and laterals are continually shortened to create a bushy head

Laterals are shortened, but retained to fuel the growth of a strong upright stem

Remove any strong sideshoots that would otherwise compete with the main stem

All new growth is removed to clear the stem

Bushy head is kept in shape by pruning after flowering; further material is removed in summer to reveal the fruits

INITIAL TRAINING

TRAINING THE HEAD

MATURE STANDARD

INFORMAL BORDER PLANTS

A NUMBER OF SUBSHRUBS are commonly grown as informal border plants, as are bamboos and grasses. Subshrubs are generally smaller and more short-lived than other shrubs, with tender top growth and a woody base, and produce their flowers on soft but vigorous annual growth. Some bamboos and grasses are evergreen, but others die down over winter.

PEROVSKIA

A subshrub with aromatic grey-green foliage, perovskia produces spikes of blue flowers on white stems in late summer. Top growth dies back to a woody base in winter, but is left in place to protect the new spring buds from frost and cold winds. In spring, prune flowered stems back to within 3–4 buds of the old wood, varying the height of each cut.

Pruning an established perovskia
In mid-spring, as new growth is breaking, prune flowered stems. Perovskia becomes leggy if left unpruned and loses stem colour.

LAVENDER

Evergreen subshrubs, lavenders have aromatic, grey-green foliage and spikes of highly scented flowers in summer. They do not break freely, if at all, from old wood, so annual pruning is needed to keep plants compact and well-clothed with foliage. In warm climates they are pruned after flowering, but in frost-prone areas autumn pruning is restricted to deadheading, leaving top growth to protect next year's buds.

Autumn deadheading
In cold climates, deadhead in late summer or early autumn to keep the plant tidy and to harvest the last of the flowers for drying.

Spring pruning
When danger of hard frosts has passed, cut back hard, removing most of the previous season's growth. Do not cut into old wood.

PAMPAS GRASS

Cortaderia selloana (Pampas grass) is a large, clump-forming grass grown for its spectacular flower plumes, borne in late summer. As the plant matures, the crown often becomes congested with dead foliage, which can crowd regrowth and reduce its vigour. Burning off top growth used to be the routine advice, but this is risky; if the burn is not rapid and controlled, it simply destroys next year's growth buds. It is far safer to cut down the dead foliage and flower plumes as far as possible without damaging the new growth. This may be done in autumn in mild climates, but in colder regions, delay until spring. After cutting back, pluck out dried stem bases and leaves from the centre of the clump. Always wear stout gloves when handling pampas grass; the leaf margins are razor sharp.

Cutting back in spring
As new growth begins, use shears to cut the previous year's growth back as far as you can (inset) without damaging new growth.

BAMBOOS

With the exception of some dwarf species, which can be clipped annually in early spring almost to ground level, bamboos require little pruning. Most need only the routine removal of broken, frost-damaged, or discoloured canes in spring to keep them in good health. If a clump has become too dense, or if a species is grown for its attractively coloured young stems, the canes can be thinned in spring or late summer.

Pruning canes
Wearing stout gloves, use loppers to remove dead and damaged canes. Thin out the remaining canes by taking the oldest out at the base.

Clearing away
Taking care not to damage new shoots, clear debris from the base to let in light and air and allow new canes to grow unchecked.

Restricting spread
Dig a trench deeper than the main root system around the desired margins of the clump, and insert a barrier of rigid plastic or slates.

ROSES

THE OBVIOUS APPEAL of roses lies in their exquisite flower forms and divine colours and scents. They are also enormously versatile, which has undoubtedly contributed to their popularity as a garden plant. Roses are extremely adaptable, tolerating a wide range of soil types, and there are types to suit almost every climate. When deciding how to prune a rose, the many cultivars, the range of recognized groups, and their varying requirements can seem daunting. Simply identify the manner in which a rose grows and flowers, and match it to a training programme or pruning regime that best exploits its vigour, habit, and flowering performance, whether this is as a specimen plant, an informal hedge, or a cover for a variety of structures.

Rose arch   *With its pliable stems, 'Climbing Iceberg' is suitable for training over an arch.*

TYPES AND FORMS

THERE ARE SOME 150 species of shrub and climbing roses, along with thousands of cultivars of hybrid origin. Roses are extremely varied in the way they grow, with plants to suit almost every garden situation. Some produce only one flush of blooms in summer. Many others are repeat-flowering, from early summer until autumn (even, in warm climates, from spring).

MAJOR GROUPS OF ROSES

Roses are divided into horticultural groups according to their growth habit, flower form, and flowering season, all of which have a bearing on their pruning needs. Cultivars are nearly always labelled by category, which gives guidance as to their pruning requirements.

Modern bush roses
These include two major groups, the large-flowered bushes (hybrid teas) and cluster-flowered bushes (floribundas), as well as the more recently developed miniatures, and patio and polyantha bushes. These groups nearly all repeat flower.

Shrub roses
The shrub roses fall into three main groups: modern shrubs, which include ground-cover roses, old garden roses, and the wild or species roses and simple hybrids of them.
Modern shrubs These are a diverse group of 20th-century origin, and may flower once or repeatedly.
Old garden roses Among the most ancient plants in cultivation, old garden roses are mainly European plants that pre-date the mid-19th century. Most flower once in summer.

Climbing and rambling roses
This group is made up of climbers, which usually flower repeatedly, and ramblers, which usually flower only once, in summer.

Shrub: old garden, upright habit
Medium-sized shrubs with upright growth and a dense habit. They need light pruning, with thinning and occasional removal of old stems to stimulate the growth of new, free-flowering shoots.

EXAMPLES
'Belle de Crécy', Rosa gallica var. officinalis and 'Versicolor', 'Tuscany Superb', 'Charles de Mills', 'Duc de Guiche'.

Shrub: old garden, spreading habit
Spreading shrubs with thorny, arching stems. They are attractively informal; hard pruning to restrict size spoils the habit. They need light annual pruning to remove some of the older, flowered wood.

EXAMPLES
Albas ('Alba Maxima'), centifolias ('Tour de Malakoff'), damasks ('Ispahan') mosses ('William Lobb').

Shrub: modern

A "catch-all" group of diverse habit, size, and manner of flowering; includes ground-cover roses. They do not need hard pruning.

EXAMPLES

'Agnes', 'Buff Beauty', 'Fru Dagmar Hastrup', Jacqueline du Pré, 'Penelope'.

Modern bush: small

Miniatures are dwarf large- or cluster-flowered bushes, usually no more than 25cm (10in) tall; patio and polyantha roses are small cluster-flowered bushes. Their twiggy growth needs only moderate pruning.

EXAMPLES

Anna Ford, Cider Cup, 'Pour Toi', Sexy Rexy, Top Marks, 'White Pet'.

Standard roses

Roses from other groups top-grafted onto clear stems of 50, 75, or 110cm (20, 30, or 43in) to form standards. Weeping standards are ramblers or climbers budded onto rootstocks usually 1.4m (54in) tall. They are pruned every year.

EXAMPLES

Many bush, patio, miniature, polyantha, and ground-cover roses are trained as standards.

Modern bush: large- and cluster-flowered

Thorny shrubs of more or less upright habit, flowering repeatedly through summer on the current season's growth. They are pruned moderate to hard, according to type, to stimulate new, free-flowering shoots.

EXAMPLES

Large-flowered bushes (hybrid teas), for example Peace, and cluster-flowered bushes (floribundas) such as Iceberg.

Climbers

Thorny, long-stemmed, and of stiffly upright habit, these roses need support. They flower mainly on sideshoots from old wood and are pruned annually to stimulate more flowers.

EXAMPLES

'Aloha', Bantry Bay, 'Blairii No.2', Dublin Bay, 'Guinée', Handel, Leaping Salmon, 'Madame Hardy', 'New Dawn', Sympathie.

Ramblers

Often rampant growers, producing long, flexible stems from the base each year. Most bloom once, in summer. Entire flowered stems may be cut out after flowering.

EXAMPLES

'Albertine', 'American Pillar', 'Bleu Magenta', 'Emily Gray', R. filipes 'Kiftsgate', 'Seagull', 'Treasure Trove'.

75

SELECTING ROSES

WITH SO MANY CULTIVARS to choose from, the selection of roses is largely a matter of taste; the difficulty arises if you have room for only one. The best way to discover your own preferences is to visit established rose gardens and note the habit, height and spread, fragrance and colour of roses that appeal to you.

WHAT TO LOOK FOR

Roses are sold with bare roots, for planting in the dormant season, or in containers, for planting at any time when weather and soil conditions are suitable. They should have healthy, well-balanced shoots, and if they are in leaf the foliage should be glossy, of good colour, and free from obvious signs of pests, diseases, or disorders. Bare-root roses should have sturdy shoots and a good network of fibrous roots with no sign of damage or of having dried out. Standard roses should have a well-balanced head of strong shoots.

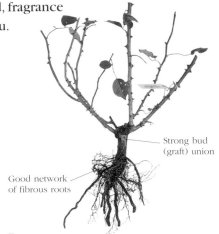

Strong bud (graft) union

Good network of fibrous roots

Bare-root rose
Avoid buying plants with weak, spindly top growth, spindly, damaged or dried-out roots, or a stunted system of scant roots.

Sturdy, well-balanced top growth

Moist compost free of weeds and moss

Vigorous foliage of good colour

Container-grown rose
Do not buy plants with spindly shoots, sparse or yellow foliage, weeds in the pot, or signs of disease such as rust or blackspot.

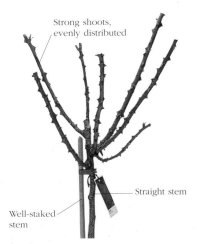

Strong shoots, evenly distributed

Straight stem

Well-staked stem

Standard rose
Avoid specimens with uneven top growth or weak, crooked stems; the head should have strong, evenly spaced shoots.

Basic techniques

All roses have alternate buds. Make angled cuts just above buds facing in the direction in which you wish new shoots to grow. To maintain an open centre, cut to outward-facing buds; on roses with arching shoots where inward- or upward-growing shoots are needed to fill the centre, cut to an inward- or upward-facing bud. If no bud is visible, cut to the required height and trim back the stub when a dormant bud breaks.

TOO RAGGED | BADLY ANGLED | TOO HIGH | JUST RIGHT | HEALTHY WOOD

Good and bad cuts
A ragged cut allows ingress of diseases. Angling the cut wrongly allows water to collect near the bud, encouraging rotting. Leaving a long stub may result in dieback (see below); to remove, cut back into healthy wood. A correct cut gives the best chance of a strong shoot developing.

Dead and damaged wood

The removal of dead, diseased, or damaged shoots is routine in the pruning of all roses. Crossing stems that rub are prone to damage and disease and should be shortened to a suitable bud or sideshoot. Make a clean, angled cut just above a bud facing in the required direction for a new shoot. With dead wood, cut to the demarcation line between live and dead wood to keep the "natural barrier" intact (*see p.17*). If shoots appear dried-up and light brown, and no clear demarcation between dead and live wood can be seen, dieback is probably the cause; cut back to clean, healthy wood.

Dead wood
Crossing stems
New shoot
Dead stub

Routine pruning
Take out damaged and diseased stems and any that cross each other or the centre of the bush. Cut out old unproductive wood completely. Remove any old stubs that have died back.

CUTTING TO A BUD

With a pair of clean, sharp secateurs, angle the cut cleanly across the stem not more than 5mm (¼in) above a bud on the same stem or in a leaf axil. The cut should slope gently so that the lower end of it is directly opposite the bud.

CLEAN, ANGLED CUT

ROUTINE TASKS

TECHNIQUES TO ENCOURAGE more, or finer, blooms vary according to the particular rose group, but there are several routine operations apart from pruning out dead, damaged, or diseased wood that are applied to all roses. Regular deadheading, the removal of suckers, and the renovation of neglected plants are the basic requirements for healthy, vigorous roses.

DEADHEADING

A rose's energy is diverted into seed production if hips are allowed to develop. Roses that bloom once in summer are pruned after flowering, removing faded flowers in the process. Repeat-flowering roses are stimulated to produce a second or third crop of flowers by deadheading. Always cut to the second or third bud down the stem, with a full-sized leaf, rather than just nipping off the flowerheads.

Large-flowered bush (left)
Cut to a strong, outward-facing bud or shoot below the faded flower to stimulate the production of a new shoot.

Cluster-flowered bush (right)
Cut away the whole flowered truss when flowers have all faded, making a correctly angled cut just above a bud.

REMOVING ROSE SUCKERS

Many roses are grafted onto a wild rootstock which may produce suckers that will weaken and eventually replace the cultivar if they are left in place. They usually occur at a short distance from the base of the rose, and are identifiable because their leaves are of a different shape and colour. Cutting them off at ground level simply stimulates them into growth; they must be traced to their point of origin and carefully pulled off at the root.

Finding the source (left)
Scrape away the soil gently and trace the sucker back to its point of origin.

Removing the sucker (right)
Pull the sucker sharply away from the root. This method is less likely to cause the sucker to regrow than cutting it off.

RENOVATING ROSES

Newly acquired gardens often contain badly neglected roses. Unless you replace or sterilize the soil you cannot plant another rose in the same place because of the risk of replant disease, so renovation is worth trying. The dormant season is the best time, even for roses that are normally pruned after flowering, although you may lose a season's flowers. All renovation work should be followed by a feed and mulch in spring. Autumn is also the time to trim back tall roses, especially in exposed sites, to reduce wind rock. The latter creates a gap in the soil, which, if it fills with water and freezes, damages the graft union and ruins the plant.

BEFORE

AFTER

Autumn trimming to reduce wind rock
Cut rose stems over 1m (3ft) tall back to a third or a half of their height in autumn so that winter winds do not damage the roots.

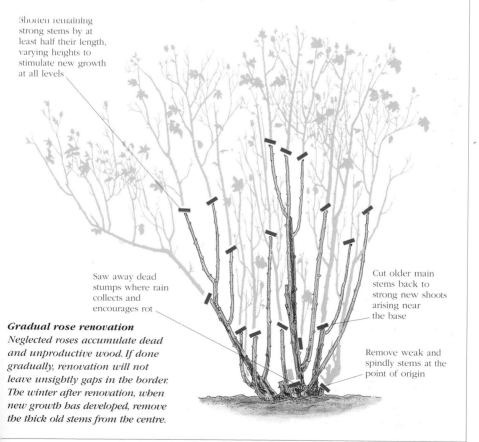

Shorten remaining strong stems by at least half their length, varying heights to stimulate new growth at all levels

Saw away dead stumps where rain collects and encourages rot

Cut older main stems back to strong new shoots arising near the base

Remove weak and spindly stems at the point of origin

Gradual rose renovation
Neglected roses accumulate dead and unproductive wood. If done gradually, renovation will not leave unsightly gaps in the border. The winter after renovation, when new growth has developed, remove the thick old stems from the centre.

MODERN ROSES

THE AIM OF PRUNING all modern roses is to encourage plenty of new shoots that will bear a succession of flowers throughout the summer. The two most important groups, the large- and cluster-flowered bushes, are pruned back annually to a low framework of main stems. Other modern roses generally need less severe pruning to give of their best.

BUSH ROSES

Hard prune modern bush roses immediately after planting to encourage growth from low down. If you are planting a container-grown plant in the growing season, just remove open flowers and damaged growth and prune hard next spring.

BEFORE PRUNING

Shoot tip is slightly damaged

Growth is already crossing and rubbing

AFTER PRUNING

Pruning a newly planted bush rose
Prune shoots to 8–15cm (3–6in) above ground level, cutting to outward-facing buds to form an open-centred bush.

LARGE-FLOWERED BUSHES

On established bushes, remove any dead or damaged growth as seen during the growing season and deadhead regularly. During the dormant season (in cold climates delay work until early spring), the main pruning consists of removing unproductive and unhealthy shoots and shortening what remains. Make angled cuts to outward-facing buds to avoid crossing stems. The harder the pruning, the fewer, but finer, are the next season's flowers.

Remove dead, diseased, damaged, and crossing shoots and cut any dieback to healthy wood

Established pruning
Retain only strong, healthy growth to supply vigorous shoots in the next season.

Shorten remaining stems to 20–23cm (8–9in) in height

POPULAR EXAMPLES

ALEC'S RED
ALEXANDER
BLESSINGS ♥
'DEEP SECRET'
ELINA
FREEDOM
JUST JOEY ♥
INGRID BERGMAN
PEACE
POLAR STAR
REMEMBER ME
THE LADY
TROIKA
WHISKY MAC

CLUSTER-FLOWERED BUSHES

Once large- and cluster-flowered bush roses are established, the major pruning difference between them is that the latter are not pruned so hard. The charm of these roses lies in the mass of flowers clustered in one head, so more buds are retained on a longer length of stem in order that they may develop into flowering shoots. On shoots that have carried large trusses of flowers there may appear to be no buds to cut to, in which case just cut to the approximate desired height. This should stimulate a dormant bud into growth and if a stub is left above it can be cut away.

POPULAR EXAMPLES

ANISLEY DICKSON
CITY OF LONDON
EVELYN FISON
ICEBERG
LILLI MARLENE
'MASQUERADE'
MATANGI
MOUNTBATTEN
ORANGES AND LEMONS
REGENSBERG
'THE QUEEN ELIZABETH' ✿
THE TIMES ROSE

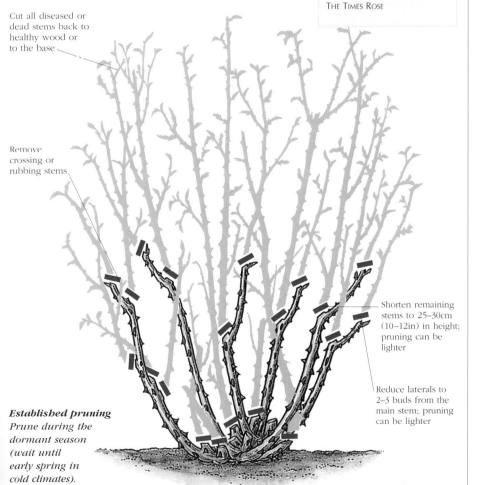

Cut all diseased or dead stems back to healthy wood or to the base

Remove crossing or rubbing stems

Shorten remaining stems to 25–30cm (10–12in) in height; pruning can be lighter

Reduce laterals to 2–3 buds from the main stem; pruning can be lighter

Established pruning
Prune during the dormant season (wait until early spring in cold climates).

81

MINIATURE BUSH ROSES

These tiny bush roses are scaled-down versions of large-
or cluster-flowered bushes and the principles of pruning
are the same as for their larger counterparts – deadheading
when flowering, and pruning when dormant. Prune hard
on planting, cutting back to 5–8cm (2–3in) above ground
level. Once established, and if growing well, prune lightly
as shown. If growth is poor, or in need of renovation,
prune harder, retaining and drastically shortening only
the strongest stems, as for larger bushes.

POPULAR EXAMPLES

ANGELA RIPPON
BABY MASQUERADE
DARLING FLAME
'EASTER MORNING'
'JUDY FISCHER'
PARTY GIRL
POUR TOI
'RISE 'N' SHINE'
SNOWBALL
STARINA
'SWEET FAIRY'
TEENY WEENY
YELLOW DOLL

Tip-prune main
stems to remove
the last of the
spent flowers

Remove dead,
diseased, or
damaged growth;
relieve congestion
by cutting out the
oldest stems entirely

Established miniature bush
*Bushes vary in height, so
prescribing an exact height
to which main stems should
be shortened is difficult. A
good rule of thumb is,
whatever the flowering
type, shorten main stems
by a half to two-thirds.*

Prune sideshoots
back to within one
or two buds of the
main stems

MODERN SHRUB ROSES

Many modern shrubs combine the vigour of a species rose with the repeat-flowering virtues of modern roses. They are pruned when dormant, in early spring. A few have a single flush of flowers and are pruned after flowering. Most shrub roses are bushy and vigorous, reaching heights of 1.2–2m (4–6ft), and need only light pruning (*see below*). Some are tall cultivars of cluster-flowered bushes and are pruned in a similar way (*see p. 81*), shortening main stems by only one-third to maintain stature. For the repeat-flowering hybrid musks, shorten strong stems by up to one-third, and sideshoots by one-half. For rugosas, prune when dormant, tipping back long stems and occasionally taking out an old stem completely.

Supporting modern shrub roses
Two low stakes with strong twine form a useful support for the stems of lax shrub roses and can be disguised by underplanting.

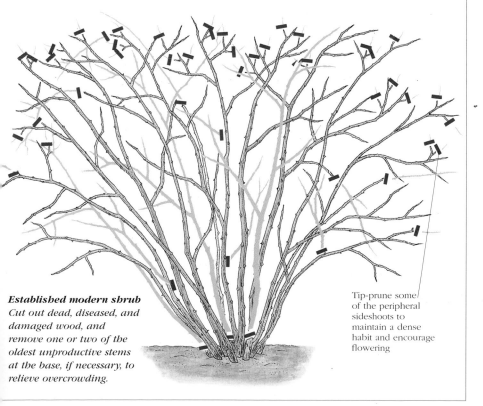

Established modern shrub
Cut out dead, diseased, and damaged wood, and remove one or two of the oldest unproductive stems at the base, if necessary, to relieve overcrowding.

Tip-prune some of the peripheral sideshoots to maintain a dense habit and encourage flowering

GROUND-COVER ROSES

There are two types of ground-cover roses: the modern shrubs, and the creeping ramblers. Both are pruned mainly to confine their spread. Modern shrub types have a spreading habit, and seldom exceed 60cm (2ft) in height. Prune repeat-flowering cultivars in late winter to spring, the rest after flowering, in summer. Cut out any dead or diseased stems, and tip-prune main stems, or shorten if overlong. Shorten laterals to keep an open centre. Rambler types are pruned after flowering. Cut overlong stems back to upright shoots to keep them within bounds.

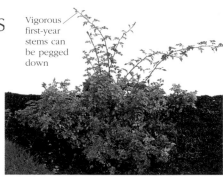

Vigorous first-year stems can be pegged down

Rambler-type ground-cover rose
The vigorous rambler type of ground-cover rose has long stems that will root into the ground, increasing the rose's spread.

STANDARD ROSES

A standard rose is created by top-grafting a selected rose onto a clear stem (heights may vary), which needs permanent staking. Standards are pruned according to the type of rose that forms the head, with the graft point being treated as if it were at ground level. The aim is to maintain a balanced head, free of crossing shoots and dead, diseased, or damaged wood. In areas with hard winters, autumn trimming is advisable to reduce the risk of strong winds damaging the head. Once-flowering roses are pruned after flowering; repeat-flowering types when dormant.

POPULAR EXAMPLES

LARGE-FLOWERED BUSHES
BLESSINGS, FRAGRANT CLOUD, JUST JOEY, PEACE, REMEMBER ME
CLUSTER-FLOWERED BUSHES
ANISLEY DICKSON, ICEBERG, MARGARET MERRIL, MATANGI
PATIO, MINIATURE, AND POLYANTHA
SWEET MAGIC, SWEET DREAM, 'THE FAIRY', 'TOP MARKS'

Remove dead, damaged, and diseased growth

Pruning in early spring
Prune stems that were reduced in autumn to remove oldest wood, create a balanced head, and promote vigorous new flowering shoots.

Sideshoots cut back to a healthy bud

Main stems shortened to suitably-placed buds and shoots

After pruning, early spring
On remaining healthy main stems cut back to 20–25cm (8–10in) from the graft union, and shorten their sideshoots to 2–3 buds.

WEEPING STANDARDS

A weeping standard rose is produced by top-grafting a rambler, climber, or trailing ground-cover rose onto a clear stem about 1.5–2m (5–6ft) tall. It is best left unpruned on planting and for the first two years to develop its form. Prune only to remove dead, diseased, and damaged wood, or to shorten weak shoots to a strong bud. The more rigid stems of climbers should be trained downwards by tying to a wire "umbrella" frame while still young. Once established, prune according to rose type: rambler (*see p.88*), climber (*see pp. 88–9*), or ground-cover rose (*see opposite*).

POPULAR EXAMPLES

'ALBÉRIC BARBIER' ♥
'ALBERTINE' ♥
AWAKENING
CHEVY CHASE
'CRIMSON SHOWER' ♥
'DOROTHY PERKINS'
'EMILY GREY'
'EXCELSA'
'FÉLICITÉ PERPÉTUE' ♥
'FRANÇOIS JURANVILLE' ♥
'GARDENIA'
'LEVERKUSEN'
'MINNEHAHA'
'NEW DAWN' ♥
PARTRIDGE
PHEASANT
'POMPON DE PARIS'
'SANDERS' WHITE RAMBLER' ♥
SUMA

Pruning a rambler weeping standard
After flowering, prune to remove oldest flowered shoots and reduce sideshoots. Shorten shoots that touch the ground.

Cut back oldest flowered shoots to just above graft union

Reduce sideshoots to 3–4 buds

Prune other flowered stems to an outward-growing replacement shoot

Tip-prune shoots that touch the ground

Cut or rub out suckers that appear on the clear stem throughout the season

OLD ROSES

THE OLD GARDEN SHRUB roses are mostly pruned in one of the two ways illustrated here, depending on whether their habit of growth is dense and upright, or more open and spreading. The majority flower in one glorious summer flush and are pruned as soon as this is over; those that are repeat-flowering are pruned the same way, but in the dormant season.

UPRIGHT HABIT

Forming dense shrubs, gallicas are typical of this group and bear fragrant flowers in summer. Prune lightly on planting, by tipping back overlong stems and taking out one or two stems if growth is crowded. Once established, remove dead and damaged growth in spring. After flowering, thin growth out by shortening laterals back to a main stem. Every one to three years, remove one or two main stems at the base. Gallicas make good informal hedges; clip hedges lightly when dormant.

Pruning a gallica rose
Routine pruning aims to maintain a dense habit while avoiding congestion. If neglected, gallicas can be hard pruned in late winter to early spring; cut out all but the most vigorous young stems.

Shorten laterals to a sideshoot or bud 5–15cm (2–6in) from a main stem

Completely remove one or two old, very woody stems at the base; remove all dead, damaged, and crossing stems

SPREADING HABIT

This rose group is distinguished by the long, gracefully arching stems typified by alba roses, which flower once in summer. On planting, lightly tip back long shoots. Once established, prune after flowering to remove dead, diseased, and damaged wood and thin crossing shoots. Cut back laterals and main shoots by one-third of their length. In autumn, shorten any very long, whippy shoots by up to a third, to avoid damage by winter winds.

Pruning an alba rose
Routine pruning aims to relieve congestion and renew flowering shoots. Neglected shrubs can be cut back hard; remove all but the strongest young shoots, then shorten them by one-third.

Reduce laterals by about one-third, cutting back to a healthy bud or sideshoot

Cut back old main shoots by about one-third

Remove low-growing shoots that will arch over to touch the ground

OLD GARDEN ROSES

UPRIGHT	SPREADING	CHINA	'HENRI MARTIN' ♥
GALLICA	**ALBA**	'CÉCILE BRÜNNER' ♥	'NUITS DE YOUNG'
'ALAIN BLANCHARD'	'ALBA MAXIMA' ♥	'HERMOSA'	'WILLIAM LOBB' ♥
'BELLE DE CRÉCY' ♥	'ALBA SEMIPLENA' ♥	'MUTABILIS'	**PORTLAND**
'CHARLES DE MILLS' ♥	'BELLE AMOUR'	'PERLE D'OR' ♥	'COMTE DE CHAMBORD'
'COMPLICATA' ♥	'CÉLESTE' ♥	**DAMASK**	'MARCHESA BOCCELLA' ♥
'DUC DE GUICHE' ♥	'GREAT MAIDEN'S BLUSH'	'ISPAHAN' ♥	'PORTLANDICA'
R. GALLICA 'OFFICINALIS' ♥	**BOURBON**	'MADAME HARDY' ♥	**PROVENCE**
'PRÉSIDENT DE SÈZE' ♥	'BOULE DE NEIGE'	'OMAR KHAYYÁM'	'DE MEAUX'
'TRICOLORE DE FLANDRE'	'LOUISE ODIER'	**MOSS**	'FANTIN-LATOUR' ♥
'TUSCANY SUPERB' ♥	'MADAME ISAAC PEREIRE' ♥	'CAPITAINE JOHN INGRAM' ♥	'THE BISHOP'
'VIOLACEA'	'VARIEGATA DI BOLOGNA'	'CRISTATA'	'TOUR DE MALAKOFF'

CLIMBERS AND RAMBLERS

AS THEY DIFFER in their mode of growth, climbers and ramblers have slightly different pruning needs. Ramblers tend to produce long, flexible stems annually from the base, with a single flush of flowers in summer. Climbers have stiffer, more upright growth and usually produce a succession of flowers from sideshoots that arise from a permanent woody framework.

WALL-TRAINED CLIMBERS

Tip-prune non-branching main stems by 5–8cm (2–3in)

Climbers are sold with longer shoots than those of shrub roses. These are not pruned, since this would remove the buds needed to produce plenty of new shoots. (It is most important not to prune climbing sports of shrub roses, since this makes them produce non-climbing growth.) Once growth begins, if the main stems are slow to branch, prune stem tips back to the first strong bud (make this an outward-facing bud on outer stems). This encourages sideshoots to develop. Fan out the main stems, space them evenly, and tie them in as nearly horizontal as possible. Cover the lowest supports well while young stems are still flexible; it is difficult to fill any gaps low down later on. No further pruning is needed until the framework is established, except to remove dead, diseased, or spindly growth.

Planting and training
Plant climbers 45cm (18in) away from the base of the wall. Remove only dead, damaged or spindly growth. Tie in stems as they grow.

WALL-TRAINED RAMBLERS

Ramblers produce their single flush of flowers most freely on one-year-old shoots and readily make new growth at the base each year. Plant 45cm (18in) away from the support. Remove weak, spindly shoots. Cut main stems back to healthy buds, 40cm (16in) above ground level, and train shoots to the horizontal.

Established wall-trained rambler
When plants fill their allotted space, thin and shorten excess growth after flowering. Then cut out one in three of the main stems at the base to ensure continued new growth. Remove stems in sections to avoid damaging remaining shoots.

ESTABLISHED CLIMBERS

Once a framework is established, pruning aims to confine spread and ensure production of new flowering wood. Overlong shoots can be shortened at any time; cut them back to a strong bud. In autumn, after flowering, to early spring, cut back flowered sideshoots by two-thirds of their length to stimulate growth of next year's flowering shoots. As main shoots become less productive, after about three years, cut them back to their base, or to a lower new shoot. Tie in all new growth and remove any dead, diseased, or weak shoots.

POPULAR EXAMPLES

'ALOHA'
ALTISSIMO ♀
COMPASSION ♀
DORTMUND
DUBLIN BAY ♀
'NEW DAWN' ♀
'PARADE'
'PINK PERPÉTUÉ'
SYMPATHIE
WHITE COCKADE ♀
'WILLIAM ALLEN RICHARDSON'

Prune flowered shoots by two-thirds of their length, after flowering

Shorten overlong stems at any time

Cut less productive stems back to a healthy shoot or bud after flowering

Routine pruning
Deadhead after flowering, and remove completely any unhealthy or spindly growth as soon as seen.

RESTRICTED RAMBLERS

Most ramblers are vigorous and too large for smaller gardens. The following are more restrained.
'ALBÉRIC BARBIER' ♀
'ALBERTINE' ♀
'CRIMSON SHOWER' ♀
'FÉLICITÉ PERPÉTUE' ♀
'GOLDFINCH'
LITTLE RAMBLER
'PAUL TRANSON' ♀
'SANDERS' WHITE RAMBLER' ♀
'VEILCHENBLAU' ♀

SPECIAL TRAINING

ONE OF THE MAJOR STRENGTHS of roses as a group is that they are amenable to training in so many attractive ways. They can be grown, for example, along ropes to create graceful swags, up vertical structures such as obelisks and tripods, and over pergolas, or they can simply be encouraged to scramble through trees or other suitable host plants.

SWAGS

Training a rambler or a climber with pliable stems on thick rope suspended between pillars makes attractive swags. Posts 2.1–2.5m (7–8ft) tall produce the best effect at eye level; make the rope 1.2–1.5m (4–5ft) longer than the distance between posts so that it dips about 60cm (2ft) midway. Plant roses 30cm (12in) from the base of each post. Allow them to reach the post top before training and tying into the rope with soft twine.

1 *In the first few years, prune according to the rose type. When the rose begins to crowd the rope, as here, more extensive pruning is needed to avoid spoiling the line of the swag.*

2 *Wearing stout gloves, carefully detach the rose stems from the rope and unwind them until each main stem with its sideshoots can be distinguished from its neighbours.*

3 *Prune each of the flowered stems back to a vigorous shoot, creating an L-shape in the direction of growth; sideshoots that follow the direction of the rope will be easier to tie in.*

4 *Taking care not to damage the junction between main stem and sideshoots, lift the L-shaped stems up to the rope and wind young stems around it, attaching with soft twine.*

PYRAMIDS AND TRIPODS

Roses suited to this form of training are the less vigorous climbers and any flexible-stemmed shrub roses. To cover the structure as quickly as possible, plant a rose at the base of each leg, about 25cm (10in) from the support, and splay out the stems around it. No initial pruning is needed other than removal of dead, damaged, or spindly wood. As growth proceeds, tie in the young pliable stems in evenly spaced spirals around the structure, as close to the horizontal as possible to encourage flowering laterals. Prune established roses as for climbers (*see pp.88–9*) or shrub roses (*see p.83*).

Cut back overlong shoots to a bud just below the top of the tripod

Cut back flowered shoots to a low, outward-facing bud

Tie in new stems that grow from the base to the horizontal, to fill any gaps low down

When growth becomes crowded, cut older stems back to young replacement shoots

SUITABLE ROSES

'ALCHYMIST'
'ALOHA'
'AMERICAN PILLAR'
BANTRY BAY
'BLEU MAGENTA' ♥
'BOULE DE NEIGE'
CHINATOWN ♥
CONSTANCE SPRY
DORTMUND
'GLOIRE DE DIJON' ♥
HANDEL
'LOUISE ODIER'
'MADAME ISAAC PEREIRE' ♥
'MUTABILIS'
'REINE VICTORIA'
SUMMER WINE
WARM WELCOME
WHITE COCKADE ♥
'VEILCHENBLAU' ♥

Pruning an established climber on a tripod
Cut back flowered shoots to an outward-facing bud or shoot. Cut back older stems to new replacement shoots lower down or remove completely, with new stems growing from ground level being trained in as replacements.

PILLARS AND PERGOLAS

Ramblers are obvious choices for large pergolas; for rustic pole structures, or pergolas less than 2m (6ft) in length, climbing roses are more suitable. Plant the rose 25cm (10in) away from the base of the pillar; prune as for ramblers or climbers (*see pp.88-9*). Train straight up the pillar, tying in shoots as they grow to wires or trellis fixed slightly out from the pillar. Remove sideshoots, to induce rapid upward growth. As the rose reaches the top of the pillar, guide and tie in stems to the horizontal along the cross pieces; use additional wires or battens for support if you want to produce a "roof" of greenery. Vertical stems cease to flower well after 2–3 years; if flowers are desired on both top and pillar, plant a second, less vigorous rose and train it spirally as for a tripod (*see p. 91*).

Main stems will reach canopy more quickly if sideshoots are removed

Stems at periphery can be taken round and tied in to pillar sides

Training a rose up a pergola pillar (right) *Avoid crossing and overcrowding as far as possible by spacing shoots evenly. Attach to wires using a "figure-of-eight" arrangement of soft twine to avoid constriction or chafing.*

Deadhead if practical; cut back to a low bud in a leaf axil

Tie in new shoots; staples make useful attachment points

On mature roses, cut out oldest stems at the base, teasing out in sections

FOR SMALL PERGOLAS

'ALBÉRIC BARBIER' ♥
'BLUSH RAMBLER'
'CLIMBING CÉCILE BRÜNNER' ♥
COMPASSION ♥
'COMPLICATA' ♥
'EASLEA'S GOLDEN RAMBLER'
'FRANCIS E. LESTER'
'GOLDFINCH'
HIGH HOPES
LITTLE RAMBLER
'NEW DAWN' ♥
'PHYLLIS BIDE' ♥
'SANDERS' WHITE RAMBLER' ♥
SYMPATHIE
'VEILCHENBLAU' ♥
WHITE COCKADE ♥

Pruning an established climber or rambler Take great care when pruning from a ladder. Use guidelines for pruning ramblers and climbers (see pp.88-9) but prune less hard.

TRAINING UP A HOST TREE

Ramblers and climbers are ideal for training up a host tree. Make sure that the tree is strong enough to bear the weight of the rose – a moderately vigorous climber such as 'New Dawn' would be suitable for a standard apple tree, while a rampant rambler such as 'Rambling Rector' needs a much larger woodland tree. Position the rose on the windward side of the host so that wayward shoots are blown into the tree. The shoots will make their way towards the sunnier side of the crown, so avoid a host on the sunny boundary of your garden if you want to fully appreciate the rose in flower. Plant the rose at least 1.2m (4ft) away from the tree base at the edge of the canopy, so that it is not robbed of moisture and nutrients by the tree. Twist or tie all the shoots to a stout rope anchored to a peg in the ground and tied at the other end either to the tree's trunk or to a low branch. For the first two or three years it may be necessary to secure shoots of climbers to the lower branches of the tree. Most ramblers should clamber unaided towards the upper branches.

Length of rubber hose threaded onto rope supporting rose protects branch fork

Formative training
Careful siting and initial training are needed to guide a rose to the lower branches; it will scramble up towards the light naturally.

PEGGING DOWN

Training rose stems horizontally by pegging them down to the ground was a popular technique in Victorian times. Any rose with flexible shoots is suitable for this method. Allow a growing season for the rose to become established, then, after flowering, carefully bend stems to ground level and peg them down or tie them to wires. In following summers, deadhead repeat-flowering roses regularly. In autumn, cut out all weak growths and 2–3 older main stems; peg or tie down strong young stems as replacements. Shorten flowered laterals to 10–15cm (4–6in).

Shorten all upward-growing laterals

Trim back leading shoots to limit spread

Pruning an established rose
Trim back leading shoot on each pegged-down stem to confine growth. Shorten flowered laterals to 10–15cm (4–6in).

CLIMBING PLANTS

AN INFINITELY adaptable group of plants in terms of garden design, climbers are indispensable when providing height and backdrops for other plants. They are also superb when grown in twining associations to provide year-round displays and combinations of foliage, flowers, and fruit. In the wild, climbing plants concentrate their energies on producing long, fast-growing shoots to scramble over other plants and obstacles in their quest for light. Pruning and training are vital when using climbing displays in the garden, to shape, direct, and sometimes restrict the plants' growth. Strong supports are also essential – all climbers need something to grow up, against, or through.

Wall-trained wisteria *The vigorous and highly ornamental wisteria is ideal for house walls.*

TYPES OF CLIMBING PLANTS

CLIMBING PLANTS have evolved a number of methods by which they support themselves on their upward quest for light. It is important to understand the way that they grow so you can provide appropriate support. Other aspects of growth, such as vigour and the ability to recover from pruning, also dictate the pruning and training methods needed.

CLIMBERS AND SUPPORTS

The way a plant climbs is not directly linked to its pruning needs, but does affect its training. It is important to choose climbers whose growth habit suits their intended support. A wrought iron obelisk, for example, would be so rapidly swamped by rampant climbers such as *Parthenocissus* or *Fallopia* (Russian vine) that the purchase cost of such a decorative feature would be wasted. If a tree stump is to be masked, a dense-growing evergreen is more useful than a deciduous climber that is bare in winter. It is equally important to choose methods of support that will enable a plant to climb or be trained successfully. An ivy will cling to and creep up a bare stone wall, whereas a honeysuckle needs guiding to wire or trellis before it can twine around them. Winter jasmine, like other scramblers, will never make its own way up a vertical support unaided; each stem must be individually tied in to gain height and coverage.

Stem roots (Hedera) *Plants such as ivy cling to any rough surface by means of small adhesive aerial rootlets that arise from the stems.*

***Hooked thorns* (Bougainvillea, above)** *Many plants, such as climbing roses, brambles, and bougainvillea, use sharp, sometimes hooked thorns to anchor stems to their host.*

***Self-clinging climbers* (Parthenocissus, left)** Parthenocissus *produces touch-activated adhesive pads, in the form of disc-like suckers at the ends of tendrils. They adhere to rough surfaces such as stone, brick, or tree bark.*

Twining stems **(Wisteria)**
Some stems will twine around any support they touch, but may need initial guidance.

True tendril climbers **(Passiflora racemosa)**
Tendrils are twining shoots that grow out from the stem; they will twine around any thin support, then coil up and shorten to tighten their grip, often thickening to secure their hold.

Twining leafstalks **(Clematis montana)**
Leafstalks wind themselves round each other and any support that they meet; tying in is only needed to guide and direct growth.

Leaf tendrils **(Cobaea scandens)**
Modified leaves or parts of leaves form tendrils that reach out in search of support; such plants usually climb rapidly unaided.

FIXTURES AND FITTINGS

Twining and tendril climbers need wire, netting, or trellis to attach themselves to. Clinging climbers adhere unaided to wood, tree bark, or masonry. Scrambling plants such as jasmine that throw out long stems, clambering over obstacles, need tying in to their support, whether trellis, laths, or wire. In nature, established stems that have died provide support for new basal shoots, but in gardens these are removed to reduce risk of disease.

VINE EYES (*INSET*) AND WIRES

SELECTING A CLIMBER

PERHAPS THE FIRST AND MOST IMPORTANT factor when choosing a climbing plant is to check that its height and spread are suitable for its allotted space. If you have continually to prune it hard to confine it to bounds, you make an unnecessary amount of work for yourself, and are also unlikely to achieve the best of the ornamental qualities, such as flowers or fruits, for which the plant is grown and valued.

BUYING YOUNG CLIMBERS

Climbers are usually sold as container-grown plants. The top growth should be healthy and undamaged, and free from any sign of pests or diseases. Look for a well-balanced framework of strong stems and fat, healthy buds; avoid buying plants with weak, spindly growth and dead or damaged buds. Check that the compost in the container is evenly moist, and that the surface is free of weeds and mosses – their presence indicates that the plant may have been in its container for some time, and may have suffered nutrient deficiencies. The compost should be full of healthy living roots, but the pots should not be so full that the roots are coiled around in the pot or protruding from the bottom.

Healthy green foliage, free of pests and diseases

Compost surface is free of weeds and mosses

Fat healthy buds at the base of strong stems

Well-formed specimen
The plant has strong, well-supported stems with a complement of healthy new leaves and fat buds at the base. The compost surface is free of weeds and moss.

Compost is evenly filled with healthy, pale-coloured, fibrous feeder roots

Strong healthy roots
The rootball is compact and the pale-coloured, healthy living roots fill the compost evenly. There is no evidence of coiling, constriction, or dead, brown roots.

ROUTINE TASKS

Early training and, often, pruning is essential to encourage climbing plants to produce plenty of strong shoots that will grow to cover the available space (*see pp.100–1*). Some climbers from then on need only minimal attention, so select them for sites where access to the mature plant may be difficult, as in the branches of a tree, or high on a wall. Other climbers need pruning to remove dead and diseased wood, or to take out old growth, thus inducing replacement shoots or increasing flowering potential.

Deadheading may also be required. The amount of time spent cutting back overlarge plants can be minimized if the vigour of the plant is well matched to the site. Pruning to enhance flowering is often an annual or twice-yearly task, and timing is crucial. While neglected specimens of short-lived plants are best replaced, others can be rejuvenated by pruning. Those that respond well to hard pruning can be cut down near to ground level and new growth retrained to restore the feature to its original beauty.

New growth

Dead flower stalk

Replacement shoots (left)
Unless changing the direction of growth, prune to a shoot that follows the line of the older stem.

Deadheading (above)
If dead flowerheads or flower stalks are unsightly, pick or snip them off, taking care not to damage any new growth.

Replacement stem

Flowered stem

Thinning growth
Pruning for flowering usually involves removing flowered shoots. This is often enough also to prevent congestion.

Tracing stems
It may be hard to trace stems to the point of origin. Cut a stem at its base, then tease out wilted growth in sections.

Shearing dense climbers
Large, dense, and vigorous climbers can conveniently be cropped back to their supports with hand shears.

INITIAL TRAINING

MOST CLIMBING PLANTS are trained along walls or fences. Many of the same principles apply to the various types of training, even though plants may differ in their individual pruning needs. For permanent climbers, time and effort spent developing a good basic framework in the early years will be amply repaid as the plant matures.

ON PLANTING

Before planting, cut out any dead, damaged, or weak growth. If only one stem is needed, remove all but the strongest. If strong stems are few and more are needed, pinch out their tips to encourage branching near the base. However, if there is only one stem (as with many clematis), do not check its growth until after the first growing season. Then, in late winter or early spring, cut it back almost to ground level to promote new basal growth. If the climber is to be trained against a wall or fence, plant it 25–40cm (10–16in) away from the structure. Secure

young stems to the support, using twine tied in figures-of-eight (*see opposite, below*). If necessary, use angled bamboo canes to guide shoots to their support. Tie the shoots to the canes and secure the canes to the wires or trellis. Little or no pruning should be needed in the first growing season. As the climber grows, train shoots to the support in the desired direction (*see opposite*). Provided that the climber is not one that is cut down every year, the next few years should be spent developing a well-spaced framework.

Tip-prune any vigorous leading shoots that have not branched to encourage them to do so

Shorten shoots not needed for tying in to 3–6 buds; the new sideshoots that result often flower profusely

Forming a framework
After the first growing season, pruning and training aims to develop a sound framework by tying in selected shoots before cutting out any surplus growth.

Shorten shoots where growth is sparse, especially at the base, to encourage branching

JASMINUM MESNYI

TRAINING IN STEMS

Guiding and tying in is crucial to obtain good coverage, particularly for wall-trained plants. Where the lower area of a support is to be covered, fan out some shoots from the start; gaps low down are difficult to fill later on. This will encourage twining and tendrilled plants to climb up the whole width of the allotted space, rather than straight up the middle. Always train some shoots horizontally to stimulate the production of flowers and fruit (*see p.13*). Cut back straggly shoots and any that grow in unwanted directions. Tie in as growth proceeds in order to cover the whole area.

INDOOR CLIMBERS

In cool climates, tropical climbers will thrive in a warm, humid conservatory. Those with aerial roots need tying in to a sturdy moss pole, kept damp by misting, to provide support.

Aerial roots

Moss pole

EPIPREMNUM

Achieving good coverage
Untended climbers will always naturally grow upwards rather than sideways and need careful initial training to ensure that the structure is covered as evenly as possible.

GUIDING AND TYING IN

Guiding in
Stems of twining and tendril plants must be guided into the support while still flexible.

Figure-of-eight ties
Twine tied like this allows for stem expansion and buffers stems against hard surfaces.

Neglected ties
Check and replace ties as necessary to avoid stem damage and constriction.

ESTABLISHED CLIMBERS

CLIMBERS TRAINED AS PERMANENT features against a wall or any other support need a certain amount of maintenance to keep them healthy and vigorous. Routine tasks can be done as soon as you see that they are necessary (*see p.99*), while the timing of pruning for shape and size depends upon the individual plant. Thinning and pruning old wood to induce the production of new shoots will also be needed as the plant matures.

MAINTENANCE PRUNING

Although the timing varies, maintenance pruning is generally best undertaken during the dormant season. When pruning to improve flowering, the age of flowering wood must be taken into account: plants that bloom on the previous season's wood usually do so before midsummer and are pruned after flowering, cutting back flowered shoots to buds or new sideshoots

that will bear the next year's flowers. Those that flower on the current season's shoots are pruned when they are dormant, cutting sideshoots to 3–6 buds to create flowering spurs. Evergreens are often pruned in summer, as are vigorous climbers, when it becomes necessary to restrict growth. Beware of pruning too hard; it induces excessive growth with few flowers or fruit.

Pruning in the dormant season
Basic maintenance pruning keeps plants in good condition and encourages vigorous growth while restricting their spread.

Tie in new shoots to fill gaps; remove dead, diseased, damaged, and unproductive old stems at their point of origin

Remove the weakest, crossing, or congested stems; cut shoots that are too long back to a bud

RENOVATION

Neglected climbers soon become overgrown and revert to upward growth which, when it becomes woody, is difficult to retrain. Dense, tangled growth may pull down supports and is likely to be full of dead wood, so that flowering and fruiting suffer. A plant that is moribund or suffering badly from pests and diseases is best replaced, but plants that are basically sound can be renovated in the dormant season. The easiest way is simply to cut the entire plant down, provided it will tolerate drastic pruning, and retrain the regrowth. If the plant will not tolerate drastic treatment or if you are unwilling to sacrifice the plant for the time needed for it to grow back, carry out stage pruning over 2–3 years.

TIMING OF PRUNING

AFTER FLOWERING

AKEBIA QUINATA
HYDRANGEA ANOMALA subsp. PETIOLARIS
JASMINUM NUDIFLORUM ♀
  J. OFFICINALE ♀
  J. POLYANTHUM ♀
LONICERA PERICLYMENUM
SOLANUM CRISPUM

IN DORMANT SEASON

ACTINIDIA KOLOMICKTA
AMPELOPSIS
LONICERA JAPONICA
PARTHENOCISSUS HENRYANA ♀
  P. QUINQUEFOLIA ♀
  P. TRICUSPIDATA ♀
VITIS COIGNETIAE ♀
  V. VINIFERA

Staged renovation

Over 2–3 years, cut back one in three of the main stems to ground level each year and tease out the severed top growth.

Clear dead, diseased, and damaged wood from the plant and remove any disease-harbouring debris from behind the support

Use loppers to cut back one in three of the main stems to the base

Tie in strong new growth to fill gaps in the framework

SPECIAL TRAINING

A NUMBER OF CLIMBERS have pruning needs that differ slightly from the norm, and some can be pruned in several ways according to the structure you wish to achieve. Their versatility allows them to be grown through trees and shrubs, up walls and fences, over arches, pergolas, and wire supports, and even as ground cover with no support at all.

BOUGAINVILLEA ON PLANTING

Bougainvilleas are best displayed and trained against a wall – plant in a warm conservatory in cooler regions. They flower on the current season's growth, from summer to autumn in cool climates and over a longer season in the tropics. Prune in late winter or early spring before growth begins. A well-spaced branch framework is essential, so on planting cut back hard to stimulate strong growth from the base.

Pruning on planting, spring
Select 4-5 strong shoots and shorten them to 15-20cm (6-8in), cutting back to a bud facing in the required direction. Remove all weak and spindly shoots. As growth proceeds, tie in strong new shoots in a fan shape.

Year 2, spring
Prune the previous year's growth by three-quarters, then tie in new shoots as they appear. Cut sideshoots back to 2-3 leaves or buds so that flowering spurs will develop. Repeat annually until the allotted space is covered.

ESTABLISHED BOUGAINVILLEA

Once the permanent framework has been established, the annual early spring pruning consists of tipping back any leading shoots that extend beyond the framework and shortening the previous season's sideshoots to 2–3 buds. This should leave spurs about 2–3cm (1–1½in) long, from which shoots will develop that will bear the current year's crop of flowers. During the growing season, remove weak, dead, and damaged growth as necessary. After flowering, deadhead by cutting back entire faded flower clusters to a young, non-flowering sideshoot. Old plants should respond to hard pruning, but are better replaced.

BOUGAINVILLEA STANDARDS

B. glabra and *B.* × *buttiana* cultivars are good for training as pot-grown standards. Take a single-stemmed plant and secure it upright with a stout cane. Shorten the leader on planting and clear the lowest laterals, leaving the rest as "stem-builders". In the first winter, shorten the leader and cut laterals back to 2–3 buds. In summer, pinch out the leader at the desired height and shorten laterals by a third. Repeat winter pruning in the third year and in summer remove laterals to create a clear trunk. Once a balanced head is formed, each year cut back all the previous season's laterals to within 2–3 buds of the branch framework.

Where shoots exceed the allotted space, cut back to a healthy bud or sideshoot

Deadhead faded flowers, cutting the entire truss back to a young, non-flowering sideshoot

If growth is crowded, cut out some older stems and tie in a young sideshoot to fill any gaps

Maintenance pruning
Once a bougainvillea has reached the desired size, shorten overlong shoots and cut out crowded stems in early spring. In summer, deadhead faded flower trusses and tie in new shoots.

Tie in new shoots where there is space to do so

CLEMATIS

Prune clematis according to flowering season and the age of the wood that bears the flowers. The many species, cultivars, and hybrids fall into one of three groups. The initial pruning and training is the same for all groups. Provide robust support of wires or trellis and on planting, pinch out the young shoot tips. Tie in young stems to the support, taking care not to snap them.

Group 1 This group includes species and cultivars that flower early in the year on the previous season's wood. They are pruned immediately after flowering, though most need only minimal pruning once they are established.

Group 2 Comprises the large-flowered hybrids which flower early in summer on the previous year's wood and again later on the current season's growth. With careful

pruning, the two periods virtually overlap, extending the flowering season. Prune in late winter or early spring before new growth begins.

Group 3 Clematis in this group flowers on the current season's growth in late summer. Prune in late winter or early spring, when buds show signs of growth.

CLEMATIS PRUNING GROUPS

GROUP 1 C. ALPINA ♀, 'BLUE BIRD', C. CIRRHOSA, C. MACROPETALA, C. MONTANA and cultivars

GROUP 2 'BARBARA JACKMAN', 'BELLE OF WOKING', 'DUCHESS OF EDINBURGH', 'ELSA SPÄTH' ♀, 'HENRYI' ♀, 'LASURSTERN' ♀, 'MARIE BOISSELOT' ♀, 'PROTEUS', 'THE PRESIDENT' ♀, VYVYAN PENNELL' ♀

GROUP 3 'ABUNDANCE', 'ETOILE VIOLETTE' ♀, 'GRAVETYE BEAUTY', C. ORIENTALIS, 'ROYAL VELOURS', C. TANGUTICA, C. VITICELLA

Thin dense growth, cutting back individual stems to healthy buds

Group 1
Give minimal pruning, immediately after flowering; cut back overlong shoots to a healthy bud. Congested plants may be thinned.

Cut weak or damaged shoots to strong buds or to the base

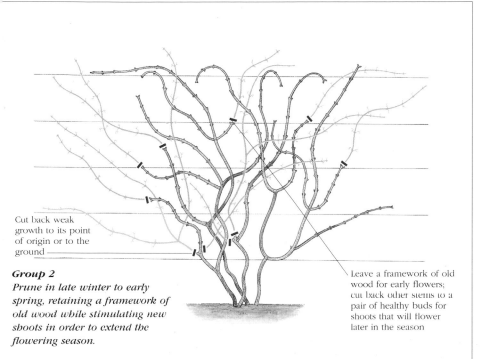

Cut back weak
growth to its point
of origin or to the
ground

Leave a framework of old
wood for early flowers;
cut back other stems to a
pair of healthy buds for
shoots that will flower
later in the season

Group 2

Prune in late winter to early
spring, retaining a framework of
old wood while stimulating new
shoots in order to extend the
flowering season.

Group 3

In late winter or early spring,
cut back stems to a pair of
healthy buds 15-30cm
(6-12in) above ground level

Remove all of the
previous season's growth
and all dead growth on
which buds are not
visibly breaking

Winter Jasmine

A deciduous scrambling shrub, winter jasmine (*Jasminum nudiflorum*) bears primrose-yellow flowers on bare branches in winter and early spring on the previous summer's shoots. It does not cling and always needs tying in to its support if wall-grown, but untied will cascade to great effect over a bank or terrace wall. In either case, annual pruning is advisable because otherwise new growth simply scrambles over old, dead wood, which builds up untidily, creating a haven for pests and diseases. Winter jasmine is pruned in early spring, immediately after flowering. On planting, cut back young shoots by up to two-thirds of their length to encourage strong growth from the base. To wall train, tie in the resulting shoots evenly across the support to create a framework of branches. In subsequent seasons, continue tying in shoots as necessary to extend or fill the framework and cut back flowered shoots to within 2–3 buds of the main branches, leaving the framework intact.

Building a framework
Cut back hard on planting to encourage the production of new shoots. Tie in new shoots evenly across the framework to achieve good even coverage. Remove dead, damaged, weak, and crossing stems altogether.

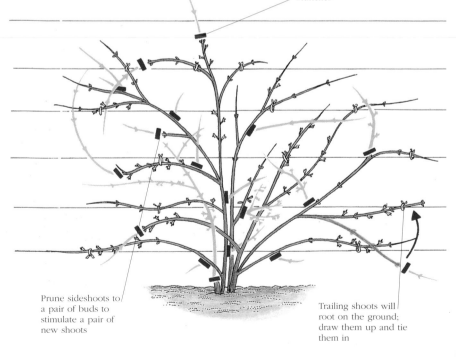

Prune vigorous unbranched stems to a pair of buds to encourage side branches

Prune sideshoots to a pair of buds to stimulate a pair of new shoots

Trailing shoots will root on the ground; draw them up and tie them in

CONTAINER-GROWN JASMINE

Jasminum polyanthum will tolerate the lightest of frosts if trained against a sunny wall, but in cool climates it is more often grown as a house or conservatory plant, much valued for its intensely fragrant white flowers. These are borne from late spring to early summer on the previous year's shoots and look well if the plant is trained to a wire hoop or on trellis. *J. polyanthum* is pruned immediately after flowering.

1 Jasminum polyanthum *remains quite small when confined to a pot but quickly becomes congested and is best pruned annually.*

2 *Detach the plant carefully from its support and gently untangle the stems, spreading them out around the pot. Check that the support is still sound and replace it if necessary. Repot or top-dress by carefully scraping away a shallow layer of compost and replacing it with fresh compost.*

3 *Prune all the long flowered shoots by cutting them back to non-flowering sideshoots or to a pair of strong, healthy buds.*

4 *Carefully retrain the plant over the frame, guiding the stems to the best effect and gently tying them in as evenly as possible around it.*

5 *Feed the plant to obtain vigorous new shoots. Guide these horizontally round the frame to stimulate flowering sideshoots.*

WISTERIA

In late spring and summer wisterias bear their drooping clusters of beautiful pea flowers on lateral spurs arising from old wood. Most are rampant climbers that can take seven years or more to begin flowering, and on very rich soils they tend to produce an excess of leaf growth at the expense of blooms. As ripe wood always flowers the most profusely, they benefit from the additional warmth that they receive when grown on a sunny wall. They are amenable to training in a number of ways, but the espalier form is perhaps the most perfect for displaying the hanging chains of flowers at their best. To maintain trained forms and enhance flowering, wisterias must be rigorously spur-pruned in two stages: in summer, about two months after flowering, and in winter.

Cut back leader to 75–90cm (30–36in)

Remove laterals to stimulate a strong new leader

Pruning on planting
Cut back the leader to a strong bud about 75-90cm (30-36in) above ground level, taking care not to cut below the graft union on grafted cultivars. Remove all laterals.

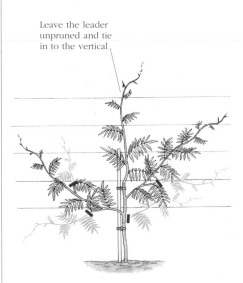

Leave the leader unpruned and tie in to the vertical

Year 1, summer
Tie in the leader vertically then select two strong laterals and tie them in at 45° angles. Prune any sideshoots to about 15cm (6in) long or to 3-4 buds to begin the formation of flowering spurs.

Cut back laterals by a third of their length to strong ripe wood

Year 2, winter
Cut back the leading shoot to about 75cm (30in) above the topmost laterals. Lower the pair of laterals that were trained to 45° to the horizontal and tie them to the lowest wires. Cut back by a third of their length.

Continue to tie in leading shoot

Train the next pair of strong laterals to a 45° angle

Tie in new leading shoot of each lateral

Cut back leader to 75cm (30in) above topmost lateral

Lower topmost pairs of laterals and tie in to horizontal

Cut back all laterals by one-third

Year 2, summer, until space is covered
Tie in the leading shoot and lowest laterals as they grow. Prune sideshoots arising from the laterals to 3-4 buds. Select the next pair of laterals and tie them in at 45° angles.

Year 3, winter, until space is covered
Shorten the leader to 75cm (30in) above the topmost pair of laterals; lower the latter to the horizontal and tie in; prune all laterals by a third of their length to strong ripe wood.

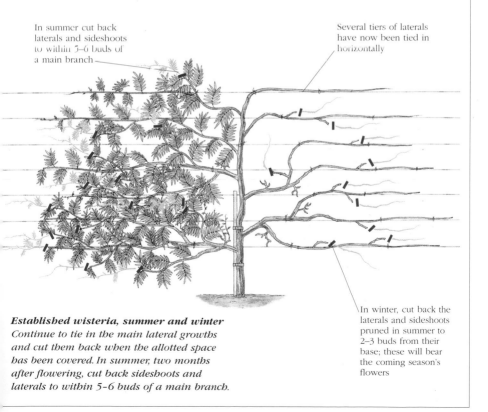

In summer cut back laterals and sideshoots to within 5–6 buds of a main branch

Several tiers of laterals have now been tied in horizontally

In winter, cut back the laterals and sideshoots pruned in summer to 2–3 buds from their base; these will bear the coming season's flowers

Established wisteria, summer and winter
Continue to tie in the main lateral growths and cut them back when the allotted space has been covered. In summer, two months after flowering, cut back sideshoots and laterals to within 5-6 buds of a main branch.

111

GRAPE VINES

As rampant climbers, grape vines (*Vitis vinifera*) can be trained in a number of ways. In cool-summer climates, cultivars are grown under glass to guarantee a good crop. Pruning is imperative to keep vines under control and fruiting well; where space is limited the "rod-and-spur", or cordon, system (as shown here) is the most suitable. Grapes are borne on new wood arising from wood made the previous year, so annual pruning back to a permanent "rod", which may be productive for decades, is required. For good-quality fruit, do not allow the plant to fruit at least until its third year; it must become fully established if it is to bear increasingly heavy crops. Thereafter, fruiting is controlled by pruning and thinning to produce fewer but finer bunches of grapes. The main pruning is done in midwinter to reduce sap "bleeding", with some summer pruning to control vigorous leaf growth.

Cut back the leading shoot to a strong bud

Rod-and-spur system: Year 1, winter
Plant vines in late autumn or early winter. Before midwinter, cut back the leading shoot by two-thirds, to a strong bud on ripe wood at or near the lowest wires; cut back harder if the wood is unripe. Remove any laterals.

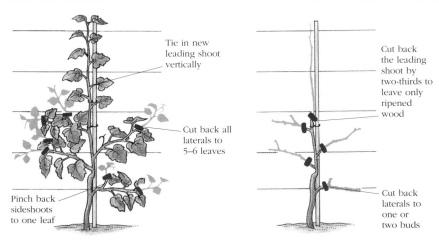

Tie in new leading shoot vertically

Cut back all laterals to 5–6 leaves

Pinch back sideshoots to one leaf

Cut back the leading shoot by two-thirds to leave only ripened wood

Cut back laterals to one or two buds

Year 1, summer
Allow the leading shoot to grow unchecked and tie in vertically. Cut back each lateral to 5–6 leaves. Pinch or cut back to one leaf any sideshoots on the laterals, including any that emerge after laterals have been shortened.

Year 2, winter
Cut back the leader by two-thirds of the summer's growth, or more if necessary, to leave only ripe brown wood. Prune back laterals to one bud if it looks strong, or two if it doesn't appear to be so.

Tie in the leader vertically as it grows

Cut back leader by half to two-thirds to leave only ripe brown wood

Year 2, summer
Tie in the new leading shoot vertically. Cut back each lateral to 5-6 leaves of the current season's growth. Pinch back to one leaf any sideshoots arising from the laterals. Remove any flower trusses that form.

Year 3, winter
Cut back the leader by a half to two-thirds, with the top bud facing the opposite way to the previous year's. Shorten laterals to one bud if it is strong, two if not. In spring, reduce new growth from each spur to two shoots.

Spring pruning allowed two shoots to grow at each spur; pinch out the weakest

Lower the leader in midwinter and retie vertically when buds break in spring

Established vine, summer
Prune laterals without flowers to 5-6 leaves, those with flowers to 2 leaves beyond the last truss. Pinch out trusses to one per lateral for dessert grapes, one every 30cm (12in) for wine. Pinch back sideshoots to one leaf.

Established vine, winter
Cut leader back to a bud below the top wire; tie it to the horizontal to encourage shoots to break low down. Prune laterals to one bud if strong, two if not. If spurs become congested, saw off the oldest section with a pruning saw.

VERTICAL FEATURES

Training climbers on arches, pyramids, and pergolas lends a strong vertical element to a design. Choose plants that will be capable of covering the structure without swamping it, and, if vigorous, will tolerate hard pruning to restrict their size. Some, such as *Cobaea scandens*, can be trained close to a support, while others, for example honeysuckle, develop into a cascading feature. Where winter appearance is immaterial, herbaceous climbers, such as *Canarina*, that die down to the ground or those that tolerate severe pruning and produce vigorous basal stems that will reach the height of the structure in one season (for example *Clematis viticella*) are the easiest to manage. For more permanent plantings, such as wisteria or *Clematis montana* and its cultivars, spiral flexible stems round for the first 2–3 years to produce a well-spaced and free-flowering framework. The support should be well furnished with wires, netting, or trellis.

Training climbers on an arch
Fit the arch with plastic netting to provide attachment for climbing stems. Trim back overlong shoots to maintain shape and keep the pathway through the arch clear.

Long shoots are spur-pruned annually to within 2–3 buds of main stems

***Pergola-trained* Passiflora**
Plants such as Passiflora *that flower on spurs are ideal for a pergola; the main shoot is trained horizontally and flowering sideshoots hang from wires. Clothe bare pillars with annuals, roses, or small shrubs.*

MIXED PLANTING EFFECTS

When mixing two or more climbing plants together, choose combinations that will prolong the season of interest or provide eye-catching contrasts of colour or form. Site the plants on different sides of an arch and train them so that their stems entwine; on a wigwam structure, grow one plant up each leg of the support (*see below*). In the latter case, a vigorous climber can be planted in the centre of the wigwam and trained vertically so that it cascades from the top to meet the plants that have been trained up the sides. It is easy to cut the wrong stems when pruning intertwined plants, so select plants with similar or complementary pruning needs; for example, train a permanent woody-stemmed, spring-pruned climber up one side of a support and clothe the other with rapidly growing herbaceous or annual climbers.

GOOD COMPANIONS

ASARINA with a white-flowered ROSA or CLEMATIS
JASMINUM POLYANTHUM with HOYA CARNOSA
LONICERA PERICLYMENUM 'BELGICA' with CLEMATIS 'JACKMANII' or C. 'POLISH SPIRIT'
RHODOCHITON with HUMULUS LUPULUS 'AUREUS'
VITIS VINIFERA 'PURPUREA' with annuals such as LATHYRUS ODORATA or TROPAEOLUM MAJUS
WISTERIA SINENSIS with a pink rose such as 'NEW DAWN'

TRIPOD PLANTED WITH MIXED CLIMBERS

One *Passiflora caerulea* planted beside each leg of the tripod

Clematis viticella planted centrally

Prune all trailing sideshoots of passion flower back to within two buds of horizontal stems

Clematis with Passiflora, training
Train and tie in the lateral shoots of Passiflora *to make permanent horizontal arms along the wires. The clematis climbs unaided.*

Pruning, early spring
Cut back trailing sideshoots of Passiflora *to two buds from main stems first, then prune clematis to 15cm (6in) above ground.*

FRUIT TREES

THE DESIRE FOR full-flavoured fruit that has not been
treated with chemicals has stimulated a revival of
interest in the traditional skills and pleasures of
fruit-growing. Many cultivars for the garden have
both ornamental and cropping potential, a bonus
that helps justify their pruning and training
demands on the gardener. Pruning and training
play a major role in fruit tree cultivation; all fruit
tree forms need careful shaping and regular
maintenance pruning to maximize yields of high-
quality fruit. The introduction of dwarfing
rootstocks that produce small, compact, and easily
managed trees has brought fruit tree cultivation
within reach of those tending even relatively small
plots – extensive orchards are no longer necessary
to enjoy fully the fruits of your labours.

Apple espalier Decorative and productive, an espalier needs systematic pruning and training.

FRUIT TREE FORMS

THOUGH MOST FRUIT TREES can be trained into almost any shape, several distinct forms have been developed that are sympathetic to the growth habits of the individual trees and suit various garden situations and sizes. All fruit trees – in whatever form you choose – need careful pruning and training if they are to be both ornamental and maintain high-quality yields.

SELECTING SUITABLE SHAPES

When choosing a fruit tree form, there are three main factors to consider. Growth habit is the first. If you want to grow an apple on a wall, the espalier form is ideal, because it suits the way most apples fruit – on short sideshoots, known as spurs. Secondly, consider the space available. Many fruit trees cannot pollinate themselves and must be grown with compatible pollinating partners to secure a crop. If space is limited, several cordons can be sited in the same space needed by just one fan or bush. Thirdly, take into account how much time and attention you are prepared to devote to your trees. Free-growing forms, like a bush or half-standard, are relatively easy to shape and maintain, needing one annual pruning in winter. More elaborate forms, like an espalier or cordon, need precise training in their early years, and a pruning programme that may stretch over several weeks in summer. Even when established, these are high-maintenance specimens.

Fan

A decorative heavy cropping form, ideal for wall-training or growing on posts and wires.

Needs moderate maintenance.

SUITABLE FOR apples, pears, plums, apricots, peaches, nectarines, sweet and acid cherries, figs.

Espalier

Must have the firm support of a wall, fence, or strong posts and wires. Needs intensive training and high levels of maintenance, but very productive.

SUITABLE FOR apples and pears. Most other fruits, especially stone fruits such as peaches or plums, are unsuitable for training to this form.

HOW ROOTSTOCKS AFFECT TREE SIZE

Fruit trees are grafted onto rootstocks that vary in vigour, thus controlling, and often dwarfing, the tree's eventual size. The same cultivar is often available in different sizes; ensure the rootstock suits both site and desired form.

| M27 | M9 | M26 | MM106 | MM11 |

Cordon

Ideal for growing several cultivars in a small space, and thus ensuring good pollination. Excellent for good yields of high-quality fruit.

Moderately high maintenance.

SUITABLE FOR apples that bear fruit on spurs (not those few that fruit at branch tips such as 'Lord Lambourne') and pears.

Dwarf pyramid

Similar to the pyramid, but 1.5–2m (5–6ft) tall. Needs a dwarfing rootstock. A productive form that can be planted 1.2–1.5m (4–5ft)

apart. Pruning must be disciplined, but form is simple to train and maintain.

SUITABLE FOR apples on M27 or M9 rootstocks. Pears on 'Quince A' or 'Quince C' rootstocks.

Pyramid

The tapering form allows fruits on the lower branches to receive plenty of sun. A compact, easily maintained form, about 2.5m (8ft) tall, suitable for confined spaces.

SUITABLE FOR ideally, plums grafted onto the rootstocks 'Pixy' or 'St Julien A', but will suit most plums except for strongly upright growers.

Stepover

Essentially a modified cordon that is bent over at right angles and trained to the horizontal on strong posts and wires (see p.21). An attractive form to use as low edging in the kitchen garden.

SUITABLE FOR spur-bearing, not tip-bearing, apples. Few other fruit woods are flexible enough to bend at right angles without breaking.

Half-standard

A bush tree on a taller clear trunk, 1.3m (4½ft) high, and suitable for a large garden. Ideal form if growing for ornament and cropping. Needs a vigorous

rootstock. Its height can make pruning and harvesting difficult.

SUITABLE FOR apples, pears, plums. Especially useful for older cultivars to be grown in traditional orchards.

Bush

The most widely used form for a large variety of tree fruits. Structurally strong, productive, and fairly easy to train and maintain. Although quite short (grown on a clear trunk up to 90cm/3ft tall), it spreads widely, so needs considerable space. Available on a wide

range of rootstocks.

SUITABLE FOR apples, pears, quince, plums, acid cherries.

SELECTING A FRUIT TREE

ALWAYS BUY FRUIT TREES from specialist fruit nurseries. They supply strong, healthy, well-trained stock and will give you reliable advice on the suitability of your intended site and whether the particular tree you want is self-pollinating or needs another cultivar nearby in order to set fruit.

BUYING YOUNG TREES

Specialist nurseries often sell young trees on which early form-training has already been done. The alternative is to buy one- or two-year-old trees to train yourself. In either case, use the same criteria when choosing a fruit tree as for selecting ornamental trees (*see p.30-1*), but check also on the vigour, position, and direction of growth of any laterals, since these are crucial to building up a strong branch framework.

Young untrained trees
In the first year, a tree will develop as a single stem or "maiden whip" on which laterals may form (when it is known as a "feathered maiden"). A two-year old feathered tree will have plenty of laterals from which to make a selection when forming a branch framework.

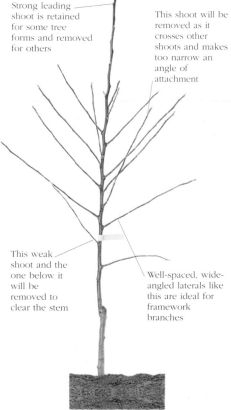

Strong leading shoot is retained for some tree forms and removed for others

This shoot will be removed as it crosses other shoots and makes too narrow an angle of attachment

Single, strong shoot well-clothed in healthy leaves

Straight, vertical stem

This weak shoot and the one below it will be removed to clear the stem

Well-spaced, wide-angled laterals like this are ideal for framework branches

Graft point

ONE-YEAR-OLD MAIDEN WHIP

TWO-YEAR-OLD FEATHERED TREE

PARTS OF A FRUIT TREE

The pruning of fruit trees is one of the most skilled and well-understood of pruning techniques; it has, after all, been practised for centuries. It is an art that has its own precise vocabulary for describing different parts of the fruit tree, and a little time spent familiarizing yourself with the most important terms will be rewarded by a better understanding of the techniques and, consequently, healthy and productive trees.

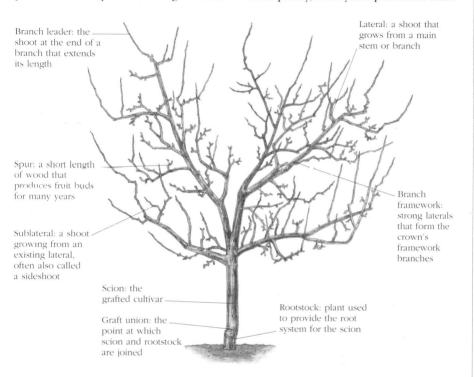

Branch leader: the shoot at the end of a branch that extends its length

Lateral: a shoot that grows from a main stem or branch

Spur: a short length of wood that produces fruit buds for many years

Branch framework: strong laterals that form the crown's framework branches

Sublateral: a shoot growing from an existing lateral, often also called a sideshoot

Scion: the grafted cultivar

Graft union: the point at which scion and rootstock are joined

Rootstock: plant used to provide the root system for the scion

BUDS AND FRUIT-BEARING GROWTH

A growth bud varies in appearance slightly, but is generally a narrow pointed bud that will develop into a new shoot or spur. A fruit bud contains next season's flowers, and is more fat and rounded than a growth bud. The graft union is the point at which the scion (cultivar) is grafted onto the rootstock. It should be 10–30cm (4–12in) above soil level. A spur is a short-jointed shoot that bears fruit buds rather than growth buds, often for many years.

GROWTH BUD

FRUIT BUD (APPLE)

GRAFT UNION

SPUR

BASIC TECHNIQUES

THERE ARE THREE MAIN aims when pruning and training fruit trees: to influence the direction of shoot growth, ensuring structural strength and the desired shape; to protect the tree's health by prompt removal of dead, diseased, and damaged wood, as well as crossing and crowded branches; and to maintain a good balance between cropping and growth. Every pruning cut you make should have at least one of these aims in mind.

RESPONSE TO PRUNING

The skill of fruit tree management lies in using pruning and training to influence the balance between growth and the formation of fruit buds. The pruning season is during winter dormancy, or in summer for stone fruits such as plums and peaches. To maintain the size and balanced shape of a mature tree, the most important rule is to prune weak shoots hard and stronger growth lightly. After hard pruning, the roots have fewer buds to feed, so these have good growth potential, resulting in strong new shoots but few fruit buds. Little or no pruning leaves a smaller ration of nutrients per bud, yielding an abundance of small fruits at the expense of the young growth that would in time bear future crops. The nature of pruning depends on the state of the tree – whether it lacks strong new growth, or is growing well but cropping lightly – and on where new growth is needed to replace old wood nearing the end of its useful life.

Strong shoots
Tip-pruned shoots produce extension growth and fruit buds; moderate pruning increases branching and reduces fruit-buds; hard pruning gives strong growth at the expense of fruit buds.

LIGHT PRUNING   MODERATE PRUNING   HARD PRUNING

Weak shoots
With light pruning, weak shoots form fruit buds but do not grow much longer.
With moderate pruning, growth and fruit bud development are both encouraged.
With hard pruning, strong growth is formed at the expense of fruit buds, but this may be necessary if replacement shoots are needed.

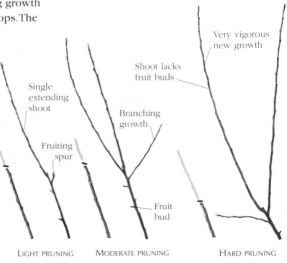

LIGHT PRUNING   MODERATE PRUNING   HARD PRUNING

MAKING CUTS

Narrow blade nearest the bud

Cutting to a bud (left)
Approach with the secateurs from the opposite side to the bud to avoid damage from closing blades

Replacing shoots (right)
Choose a strong shoot growing in a direction that enhances the tree's shape; cut in line with its growth.

Replacement shoot

Old, worn-out wood

SPUR FORMATION

Long laterals

Pruning laterals
To stimulate formation of fruit buds near their bases, shorten long laterals to 5-6 buds, weaker ones to 2-3 (left); leave short ones unpruned. Prune branch leaders by up to a third of their length, cutting to a bud (right). The fruits develop close to main branches, reducing risk of breakage.

Branch leader

SPUR THINNING

Crowded fruit buds

Unproductive old growth

Space between fruit buds will allow fruits to develop

Older spurs have been removed in favour of younger wood

Before thinning
After several years, spur systems become congested and overcrowded, leaving too little room for fruits to develop properly.

After thinning
Older, more complicated growth has been cut out, leaving younger wood where possible. Weak spurs have been removed completely.

SUMMER PRUNING

All formally trained tree forms are pruned in summer using the basic technique shown below to restrict growth and encourage fruit buds to form. It also discourages later, secondary growth, which may be vulnerable to frost damage. Pruning starts when the lower third of new shoots becomes woody and growth begins to slow, but precise timing depends on the weather. Shoots will become ready for pruning over a 2-3 week period.

TRAINED FRUIT TREE: SUMMER PRUNING

1 *Before pruning, new laterals have grown rapidly on this apple espalier, and are now ripening from the base. If not pruned, they can shade fruit from ripening sun and rapidly outgrow their site. All new shoots 15–23cm (6–9in) long are shortened when the lowest third of the shoot has turned woody. New shoots emerge from the trunk and main branches, as well as from existing laterals and spurs.*

2 *Shorten new shoots (left) growing from the trunk and main branches to three leaves above the basal cluster.*

3 *Shorten sideshoots (right) from existing laterals or spurs to one bud above the basal cluster of leaves.*

4 *After pruning, good form is restored to the espalier branch, and more sun can reach the ripening fruits. Pruning cuts made in summer also stimulate the development of future fruit buds. If any secondary growth does occur, prune shoots back to a bud at the base in mid-autumn to avoid frost damage.*

SECURING THE HARVEST

Blossom thinning
If fruit trees bear only every other year, remove 9 out of 10 flower trusses a week after flowering.

Before fruit thinning
If crowded fruits are all allowed to mature they will be small and sour, and their weight may break branches.

After fruit thinning
Excess fruits have been removed to leave room for the remainder to develop to full size and sweetness.

PREVENTING BRANCH BREAKAGE

Young trees need a supporting stake, at least until established. To avoid branches breaking, loop them up with soft twine tied to a stout cane that is lashed to the vertical stake.

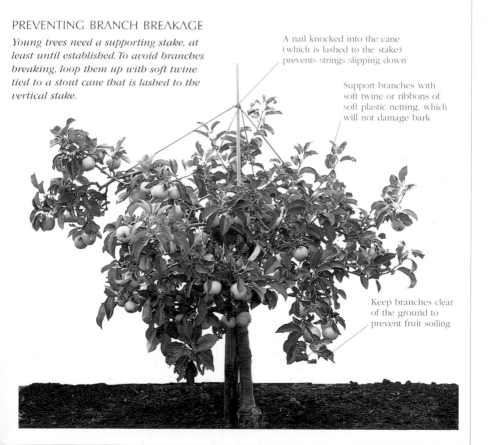

A nail knocked into the cane (which is lashed to the stake) prevents strings slipping down

Support branches with soft twine or ribbons of soft plastic netting, which will not damage bark

Keep branches clear of the ground to prevent fruit soiling

125

APPLE BUSH

ONE OF THE MOST useful apple tree forms, the apple bush is also one of the easiest to train. A wide range of rootstocks is available (*see p.118*), giving a range of heights in the mature trees, but to accommodate their spread they must be planted at least 2m (6ft) apart, even on the most dwarfing of stocks.

FORMATIVE TRAINING

The aim is to create a branched, open-centred crown with 8–10 branches radiating from a short trunk, about 60–75cm (24–30in) above ground level. Start in winter with a feathered two-year-old tree that has three or four strong, wide-angled, and well-spaced laterals 60–90cm (24–36in) from the ground. This form is also suitable for pears, plums, cherries, peaches, and nectarines, though stone fruits are pruned in summer.

Training an apple bush form
Most apples are spur-bearers (see p.118); a few are tip-bearers, fruiting on longer shoots. Pruning differs according to fruiting habit.

Prune the leader to just above the topmost of 3–4 strong laterals, which should radiate outwards

Shorten laterals by two-thirds of their length

PRUNING ON PLANTING, WINTER

Shorten by half laterals selected to become main branches

Prune other shoots to 4–5 buds and remove badly placed or crossing shoots

YEAR 2, WINTER

Shorten branch leaders by a quarter of the previous season's growth

Prune strong laterals to 4–6 buds, weak ones to 2–3 buds

YEAR 3, WINTER, FOR SPUR-BEARERS

Shorten branch leaders by a quarter of the previous season's growth

Leave all sideshoots unpruned unless badly placed or crossing

YEAR 3, WINTER, FOR TIP-BEARERS

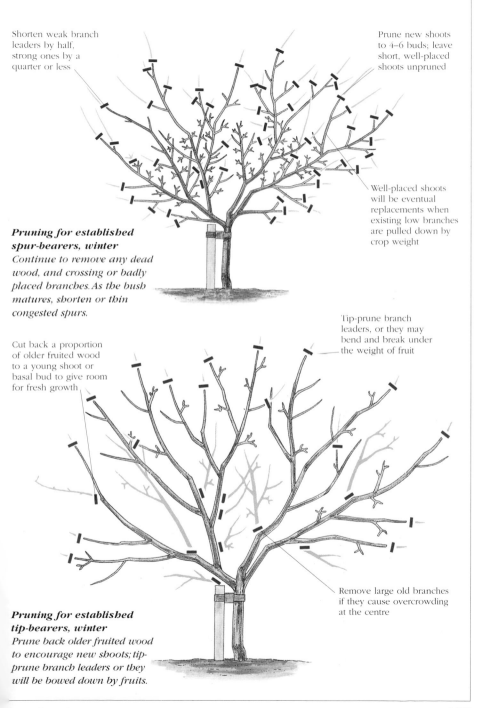

Shorten weak branch
leaders by half,
strong ones by a
quarter or less

Prune new shoots
to 4–6 buds; leave
short, well-placed
shoots unpruned

Well-placed shoots
will be eventual
replacements when
existing low branches
are pulled down by
crop weight

**Pruning for established
spur-bearers, winter**
*Continue to remove any dead
wood, and crossing or badly
placed branches. As the bush
matures, shorten or thin
congested spurs.*

Tip-prune branch
leaders, or they may
bend and break under
the weight of fruit

Cut back a proportion
of older fruited wood
to a young shoot or
basal bud to give room
for fresh growth

Remove large old branches
if they cause overcrowding
at the centre

**Pruning for established
tip-bearers, winter**
*Prune back older fruited wood
to encourage new shoots; tip-
prune branch leaders or they
will be bowed down by fruits.*

127

APPLE CORDON

A CORDON CONSISTS of a single main trunk along which the laterals are pruned in summer and winter to produce fruit-bearing spur systems. This style of pruning is suitable for spur-bearing cultivars only. Cordons are ideal for small gardens, since several pollination-compatible cultivars can be grown to yield substantial crops in a relatively restricted space.

TRAINING AND PRUNING

You can either buy ready-trained cordons from specialist suppliers or begin with a feathered maiden or two-year-old tree with well-spaced laterals *(see p.120)*. Cordons need strong horizontal support in the form of a set of wires, 60cm (24in) apart, stretched tautly between strong uprights 2.2m (7½ft) tall. These can be freestanding or fixed 10–15cm (4–6in) away from a wall or fence. Space individual plants 75cm (30in) apart; if a double row is required, space at 2m (6ft) apart. Plant at an angle of 40–45° to the ground, tying the stems to a bamboo cane lashed to the wires. Shorten long laterals to create fruiting spurs, but do not cut the central leader until it reaches the top wire, when it should be pruned back to a weaker shoot in late spring.

CORDON FRUITS

All apples, except tip-bearers, can be grown as cordons. The technique is also suitable for pears. Cordons are often used to produce fruits for exhibition, as the technique combines maximum exposure to sunlight with all the vigour from a large root system directed into top growth restricted by pruning.

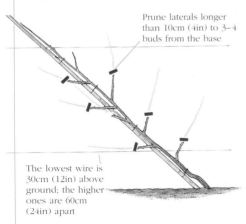

Prune laterals longer than 10cm (4in) to 3–4 buds from the base

The lowest wire is 30cm (12in) above ground; the higher ones are 60cm (24in) apart

Pruning on planting, winter (above)
Plant the tree at a 40–45° angle to the ground. Tie it to a 3m (10ft) long bamboo cane lashed to the wires. Leave the leader unpruned; shorten long laterals to 3–4 buds.

Year 1, summer (below)
As they ripen, prune new laterals from the main stem back to 3 leaves above the basal cluster; prune sideshoots from existing laterals to one leaf to initiate spur formation.

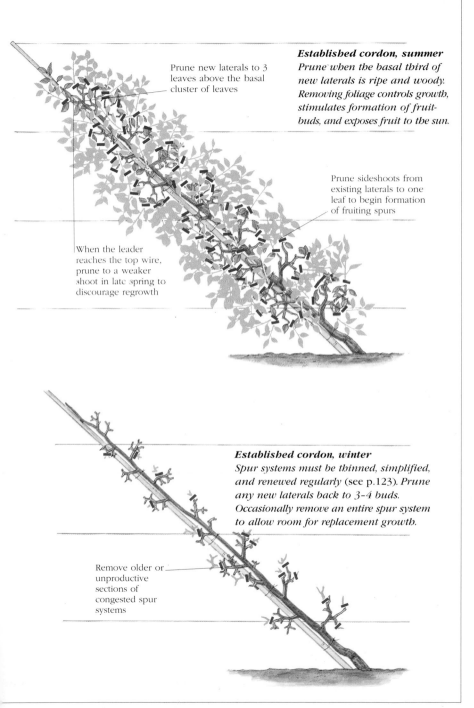

Established cordon, summer
Prune when the basal third of new laterals is ripe and woody. Removing foliage controls growth, stimulates formation of fruit-buds, and exposes fruit to the sun.

Prune new laterals to 3 leaves above the basal cluster of leaves

Prune sideshoots from existing laterals to one leaf to begin formation of fruiting spurs

When the leader reaches the top wire, prune to a weaker shoot in late spring to discourage regrowth

Established cordon, winter
Spur systems must be thinned, simplified, and renewed regularly (see p.123). Prune any new laterals back to 3-4 buds. Occasionally remove an entire spur system to allow room for replacement growth.

Remove older or unproductive sections of congested spur systems

129

APPLE ESPALIER

THE BEAUTY of the espalier form lies in its formal symmetry, so you should aim to produce pairs of branches of equal length as nearly opposite to each other as possible. An espalier's productivity results from the reducing effects of horizontal training on apical dominance. Espalier training is ideal for spur-bearing apples and pears, but unsuitable for stone fruits.

PRUNING AND TRAINING

Espaliers must have firm support in the form of a wall or strong fence with taut, horizontal wires set 45–60cm (18–24in) apart and 10–15cm (4–6in) clear of the wall. For three or more tiers, a vigorous rootstock is necessary. Two-tiered, freestanding espaliers can be used as fruit-bearing "fences" or dividing barriers. Precise early training is essential; this is easiest with a maiden whip, but if you can find a feathered tree with one or two pairs of nearly opposing laterals you have a head start. Training is done in two stages, with the laterals first trained diagonally to keep them growing strongly, then lowered to the horizontal at the end of the growing season.

Prune the leader with an angled cut to a strong bud. Shoots from below the wire form the first tier of branches

Year 1, winter
On planting, cut back the leader to a strong bud 5–8cm (2–3in) above the lowest wire. This bud will produce a new leading shoot.

Lower laterals to the horizontal at the end of the growing season

Pinch out all other laterals to 2–3 leaves

Prune the new leader to a good bud above the next wire

Cut back to the main stem all laterals pinched out in the summer

Year 1, summer
Using canes tied to the wires, train the leader vertically and two opposing strong laterals of equal vigour at a 40° angle to the ground.

Year 2, until all tiers are formed, winter
If growth is weak, prune laterals back by a quarter of their length. Remove all the other laterals that were reduced in the first summer.

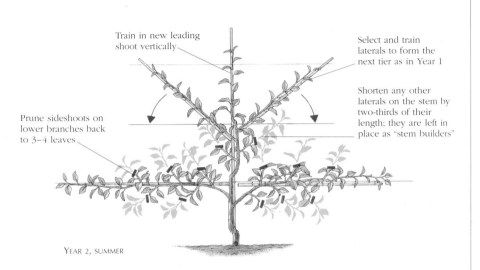

Train in new leading shoot vertically

Select and train laterals to form the next tier as in Year 1

Shorten any other laterals on the stem by two-thirds of their length; they are left in place as "stem builders"

Prune sideshoots on lower branches back to 3–4 leaves

YEAR 2, SUMMER

Year 2, until all tiers are formed, summer
An espalier establishes gradually and the lowest tiers fruit before the topmost tiers are formed. As each tier is created, those below are summer-pruned (above) to produce fruiting spurs when the basal third of the sideshoots is ripe.

Established espalier, summer
Regular summer pruning is vital (below), otherwise the main stem directs energy into strong upper growth at the expense of lower tiers. As spur systems become more complex, thin them as shown on p.123 in winter.

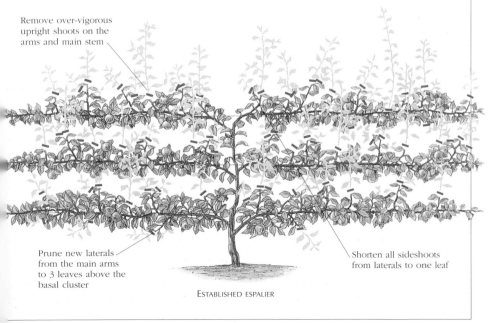

Remove over-vigorous upright shoots on the arms and main stem

Prune new laterals from the main arms to 3 leaves above the basal cluster

Shorten all sideshoots from laterals to one leaf

ESTABLISHED ESPALIER

131

PEAR DWARF PYRAMID

THE DWARF PYRAMID is ideally suited to the pear's spur-bearing habit and can also be used for spur-bearing apples. As only 2m (6ft) is needed between trees it is a perfect form for small gardens, though if the trees are closely planted precise training and regular summer pruning are essential to maintain the compact size and shape.

PRUNING AND TRAINING

Formative pruning and training concentrates on overcoming the naturally upright habit to reduce vigour, and on forming an open branch structure that radiates evenly around a strong central trunk. Begin with a young feathered tree with wide-angled laterals and encourage this growth habit by cutting to outward-facing buds on the undersides of the shoots. Make your first priority the establishment of strong lower branches; vigorous shoots on the upper part of the stem must be removed. The pyramidal shape should admit sun and air to all parts of the plant without any overshadowing.

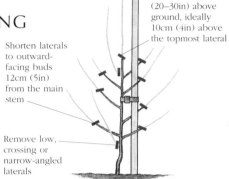

Cut the main stem to a bud 50–75cm (20–30in) above ground, ideally 10cm (4in) above the topmost lateral

Shorten laterals to outward-facing buds 12cm (5in) from the main stem

Remove low, crossing or narrow-angled laterals

Year 1, winter
Dwarf pyramids need permanent staking, so on planting insert a sturdy 2m (6ft) post that will support the tree at maturity.

If the new leader does not grow straight and vertical, tie it to the stake

Cut back all vigorous upright shoots to one bud

Year 1, summer
Aim to maintain a strongly upright and vertical leading shoot and to reduce any upward-growing shoots from the laterals.

Prune sideshoots to 2–3 buds to begin spur system formation

Prune maiden laterals and branch leaders to 15–20cm (6–8in), cutting to outward-facing buds on the underside of the shoots

Year 2, winter
Cut the central leader to a bud, leaving 25cm (10in) of new growth. Choose one that faces the opposite way to the previous year's cut.

Leave leader unpruned

Year 2 and after, summer
Begin pruning when the basal third of sideshoots has ripened. Prune sideshoots from winter-pruned laterals back to one leaf and any shoots arising directly from the main stem back to three leaves beyond the basal cluster.

Prune new growth on branch leaders back to 5–6 leaves of the previous summer's growth

To maintain the desired height, shorten the leader to one bud of the previous summer's growth

Year 3 and after, winter
Ongoing pruning aims to maintain the size and compact shape. As the tree matures, spur systems will become overcrowded and should be thinned (see p.123) to allow room for replacement growth and the ripening of the fruit.

Reduce overgrown spurs and thin out overcrowded spur systems

PLUM PYRAMID

THIS FORM, when grafted onto the dwarfing rootstock 'Pixy', reaches no more than 2m (6ft) tall and, at spacings of 2.5–3m (8–10ft), is ideal for smaller gardens. A compact form which needs permanent staking, it suits all types of plums, including gages, damsons, and bullace.

PRUNING AND TRAINING

Plums fruit at the base of one-year-old wood and along the length of two-year-old and older wood, so young growth is not routinely pruned as with apples and pears. As plums are susceptible to silver-leaf disease, winter pruning is avoided to reduce the risk of infection and any pruning that must be done during dormancy is delayed until early spring. It is easiest to begin with a feathered tree, as all but the lowest laterals can be used for branch formation. Always make angled cuts to outward- or upward-facing buds whose direction of growth will reinforce the pyramidal outline.

Cut back the leader to a strong bud 1.5m (5ft) above soil level

Prune laterals that will form main branches by half their length

Remove all laterals less than 45cm (18in) above soil level

Year 1, early spring
On trees with upright habits, cut laterals back to outward-facing buds; on spreading habits, cut to upward-facing buds. Check ties regularly.

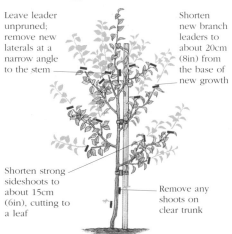

Leave leader unpruned; remove new laterals at a narrow angle to the stem

Shorten new branch leaders to about 20cm (8in) from the base of new growth

Shorten strong sideshoots to about 15cm (6in), cutting to a leaf

Remove any shoots on clear trunk

Year 1 until maturity, summer
Prune when the basal third of sideshoots is ripe. Continue to cut to upward- or outward-facing buds, as in early spring pruning.

Until the pyramid reaches desired height, shorten the leader to leave about one-third of the previous season's growth

Year 2 until maturity, early spring
Keep spring pruning to a minimum. As the tree matures, delay shortening the leader until late spring to discourage regrowth.

Established pyramid, summer
Summer pruning must be done
every year or the pyramidal form
will rapidly be lost. It is most
important to control upper growth
or it will shade fruit on the lower
branches. Thin out less productive
growth to relieve congestion.

Weak regrowth from leader
is shortened to 2.5cm (1in)
of the previous year's
growth in late spring

When the bases of
new shoots are ripe,
shorten branch leaders
to 20cm (8in) and
strong sideshoots to
15cm (6in)

Where growth
is congested,
remove
some older
unproductive
sections, cutting
back to strong
shoots

Remove any dead,
diseased, or
damaged growth,
cutting to a sound
shoot or the point
of origin

Remove over-vigorous
upright growth
completely

CHERRIES

SWEET AND DUKE CHERRIES fruit at the base of one-year-old and older wood. Usually two compatible cultivars are needed so that cross-pollination occurs. Since dwarfing rootstocks are not readily available, sweet and duke cherries are best for large gardens. Choose acid cherries for limited space: they are smaller, self-fertile, and fruit almost exclusively on the previous year's shoots.

SWEET OR DUKE CHERRY FAN

A fan trained against a sunny wall, on a system of horizontal wires, is ideal for sweet or duke cherries; the wall's warmth helps the fruit to ripen in cool-summer climates. Allow an area about 2.5m (8ft) in height by 5m (15ft) wide. As cherries are susceptible to silver-leaf disease, formative pruning takes place at bud-burst in spring. Start with a feathered maiden, and plant in autumn to midwinter. In early spring, cut the leader back just above the topmost lateral. Select 2–4 strong laterals, and shorten to 40cm (16in) from the main stem. Tie them to canes attached at 45° angles to the wires. In midsummer, select and tie in shoots from sublaterals to form the ribs of the fan, aiming for even development on each side. Use well-placed sideshoots to fill the framework. Shorten surplus sideshoots to one leaf and remove all growth below the lowest wires. To encourage branching, shorten the ribs in the early spring of the second and third years to leave 60–75cm (24–30in) of the previous year's growth.

Established fan, early summer
Prune to control growth in early summer and again after harvest. Remove young sideshoots that grow out from, or towards, the wall; thin the rest in spring to about 10cm (4in) apart.

In early summer, when they have 8–12 leaves, cut back laterals not needed to fill the framework to 6–7 leaves; pinch out regrowth and after harvest prune these laterals back to 3 leaves

Leave branch leaders alone until they fill allotted space

ACID CHERRY BUSH

Although acid cherries are self-fertile, you still need 5m (15ft) of space for a bush form 4m (12ft) high. Start with a feathered maiden. In early spring, cut the leader back to the topmost lateral, about 90cm (3ft) above ground. Shorten 3–4 well-spaced laterals by two-thirds to an outward-facing bud; these will form the main branch framework. Always cut to a pointed growth bud, rather than to a fat fruit bud. Shorten low or narrow-angled laterals to two buds. Pinch out regrowth to two leaves during the summer. In the second spring, on each lateral, shorten 2–3 strong sideshoots by half, to a bud that will produce a balanced crown. Remove badly placed shoots and low and previously shortened laterals. In the third spring, prune branch leaders by a quarter to a bud that will grow to fill the framework.

Established bush
Prune partly in spring, partly after harvest. On older trees, in spring, when growth buds are clearly visible, cut back 1-2 branches or branch sections each year to encourage new growth. Alternatively, delay until after harvest when up to a quarter of the fruited shoots are cut back.

Shorten to a sideshoot or leaf over-vigorous upright growth that will crowd the centre

Cut back one in four fruited shoots to a replacement shoot near their base, but leave any that have made plenty of fresh growth beyond the fruited portion. this growth will fruit well next year

Clear stem of 75–90cm (2½–3ft), with a low stake that will not chafe lower branches

Always remove growth that is downward-pointing on lower branches

137

FIGS

FIGS NEED LONG, HOT SUMMERS to fruit heavily. In warm countries, figs are grown as informal bush or half-standard trees. To crop well in cool climates, they need a very favoured site and are pruned to be very open to let in light; the fan form is ideal for this, on a warm, sunny sheltered wall, but even there winter protection of netting filled with bracken or straw is advisable.

FRUITING HABIT

The fig has an unusual fruiting habit – figs at three stages of development are present all at once. First to ripen are overwintered embryo figs, produced in the leaf axils the previous year. Those formed in spring on new growth ripen next. In hot climates, they make up the main, late summer crop; they seldom ripen well in cool-summer regions. Meanwhile, new embryos form in the upper leaf axils, to overwinter and ripen the following summer. In cool climates, pruning concentrates on encouraging embryo figs to form and giving them the best ripening conditions.

FRUITING DEVELOPMENT

On this unpruned shoot, a fig at the base that overwintered from last year is now ripening. Above it figs that form this spring will be next to ripen, if summer is long and hot. Embryo figs, forming in leaf axils at the tip, will ripen next year.

FIG FAN

A fig fan needs an area 2.1m (7ft) high by 4m (12ft) wide, and strong horizontal wires. Start with a 2–3 year-old plant with sturdy laterals. Build up a framework in the same way as for cherries (*see p.136*); aim to produce six main ribs either side of a main stem over 2–3 winters; use laterals to fill out the framework. Prune figs in early spring, and in cool climates again in summer. In early spring, remove some older wood and cut a few young shoots back to one bud to boost new growth. Remove vigorous and overcrowded laterals.

Established fan, summer, cool climates
In summer, once the framework is complete, pinch back all new shoot tips to 5–6 leaves to stimulate new sideshoots.

FIG BUSH

Start with a two-year-old fig with 3-4 well-spaced laterals of equal vigour arising from the main stem at about 45-90cm (1½-3ft) above ground. A bush is ideal for containers, but in this case the trunk should be 40cm (16in) high to give stability. Plant and prune in late winter-early spring, or in cool climates when severe weather is over. Form a bush with 8-10 main branches arising at or near the trunk, as for an apple bush (*see p.126*). Prune established bushes in spring, and in cool climates again in summer, by pinching out new shoot tips when they have made 5-6 leaves. In cool climates, spring pruning aims to keep the bush as open and spreading as possible. In warm climates, the reverse is true. Cut spreading branches back to upright shoots and leave growth in the centre to give protection from sun scorch.

Thin badly placed shoots and any that crowd the centre of the bush

Cut bare or leggy shoots back to one bud, or 5–8cm (2–3in) to encourage new growth

Established bush, spring, cool climates
First cut back any frost-damaged growth to healthy wood and aim to make all other cuts to maintain an open, spreading habit.

Pinch back new shoots to 5–6 leaves to encourage embryo fruits to form in the leaf axils

CITRUS FRUITS

MANY CITRUS TREES are grown for their ornamental value as well as for their fruit. In warm regions, they may crop for up to six months of the year in growth cycles of 4–6 weeks, and pruning may be done at any time. In cool climates, citrus trees must be protected from cold and frost. Prune young trees from spring to late summer, established trees at or after harvesting.

BRANCHED-HEAD STANDARD

In cooler climates, grow citrus trees under glass or in pots which can be transferred to a sheltered, sunny outdoor site during the summer. Citrus in containers look best as branched-head standards on a trunk of 1–1.5m (3–5ft). Feed young plants regularly each month during the growing season. Remove any shoots or suckers on the stem as soon as they develop. In spring, shorten any shoots that have been cold-damaged. For well-established plants, reduce watering to a minimum for 3–4 weeks during early summer; this will promote flowering when watering resumes (citrus trees become dormant at temperatures below 13°C (55°F), or in drought conditions; the onset of rain or resumption of watering usually results in flowering within four weeks).

TRAINING A CITRUS STANDARD

Cut back leader to a strong bud

Leave new young laterals unpruned to thicken the stem

Remove all other laterals and subsequent regrowth from the main stem

Remove stake and tie as soon as the tree is well established

Shorten all laterals by one-third of their growth

Remove all previously shortened laterals

Stage 1
A young, unbranched plant is lightly staked and the leader tied in to ensure vertical growth. Shorten all laterals by one-third of their length.

Stage 2
Once the desired height of the stem has been exceeded, prune the leader back to a strong bud. Remove the previously shortened laterals completely.

Stage 3
Select four well-spaced shoots from which to develop the head; tip-prune each by 3–4 leaves. Prune subsequently as for a bush tree (see opposite).

CITRUS BUSH

Cropping citrus trees are grown as bush trees on a trunk of at least 50cm (20in). The trunk is cleared gradually (*see p.34*), and once the desired height of clear trunk has been achieved, the crown is formed in much the same way as for a branched-head standard. Begin with a young unbranched plant; when it reaches 90–120cm (3–4ft) high, cut back the leader to 60cm (2ft). Select 3–4 strong laterals, at angles of at least 40° to the main stem, to form the branch framework. Shorten them in early spring to about 30cm (12in) from the main stem. In subsequent springs until established, shorten new branch leaders by one-third of their growth, and tip-prune sideshoots by 3–4 leaves.

Established bush, at or after harvesting
In general, prune mature trees as little as possible; remove dead or diseased wood regularly, and any crossing branches that could cause chafing damage.

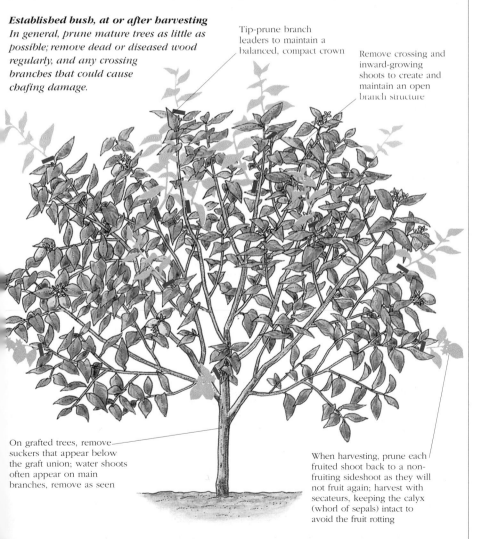

Tip-prune branch leaders to maintain a balanced, compact crown

Remove crossing and inward-growing shoots to create and maintain an open branch structure

On grafted trees, remove suckers that appear below the graft union; water shoots often appear on main branches, remove as seen

When harvesting, prune each fruited shoot back to a non-fruiting sideshoot as they will not fruit again; harvest with secateurs, keeping the calyx (whorl of sepals) intact to avoid the fruit rotting

SOFT FRUITS

THE TEXTURES and flavours of sun-warmed soft fruits is a pleasure that even a small garden can afford. You don't even need to grow them in a traditional "model" fruit garden, for many are equally at home in the ornamental garden, especially when trained to restricted forms. Soft fruits are generally cool-climate plants that enjoy sun, but dislike humidity and stagnant air. Most are prone to viruses, but in the case of those that are, new stock is usually available with virus-free certification. Left unpruned, all soft fruits will crop after a fashion, but with correct pruning and training you can establish a regular cycle of renewal pruning, removing the old to make way for the new, that guarantees healthy, fruitful plants which bear luscious, flavourful crops of the best possible quality and quantity.

Gooseberries *A bush fruit, the gooseberry is naturally shrubby and compact.*

BASIC TECHNIQUES

WITH THE EXCEPTION of autumn-fruiting raspberries, all woody soft fruits crop on stems that are at least a year old. This makes pruning fairly simple: on cane fruits and, to a lesser degree, blackcurrants, fruited wood is cut out after harvest; on other bush fruits it is shortened, or "spurred back", annually to a semi-permanent branch framework.

SOFT FRUIT FORMS

Cane fruits, raspberries, blackberries, and hybrid berries produce new stems annually from the base, to replace fruited canes as they die. Pruning speeds up replacement, and training the new shoots makes harvest easier. The shrubby bush fruits, such as currants and gooseberries, fruit on sideshoots arising from one-year-old or older wood. Pruning aims to encourage the production of sideshoots and ensures regular replacement of fruiting wood.

Bush
Pruning and training aims to create a crown of well-spaced branches, to admit light and air to the centre; a short stem or "leg" keeps fruits clear of the ground.
SUITABLE FOR *red and white currants, gooseberries.*

Single cordon
An ideal form for spur-bearing fruits, giving high yields in restricted spaces. It is easy to net (all soft fruits attract birds), and is either grown singly, or in rows trained on posts and wires.
SUITABLE FOR *red and white currants, gooseberries.*

Multi-stemmed bush
The natural form of blackcurrants. They produce new shoots from the base each year to form an upright multi-stemmed bush. Pruning aims to ensure continued replacement of year-old wood, which is the most productive.

Canes: raspberry
Raspberries produce suckers freely, often at a distance from the original planting site. Pruning speeds production of new canes, and by selecting only well-placed replacements, aims to confine plants to bounds.

Canes: blackberry and hybrid berry
Canes develop from a more or less central point. They are separated and trained apart to receive light and air and to make harvest from the often thorny stems easy.

ROUTINE TASKS

There are two main pruning periods for soft fruits: winter and summer. Prune in winter to develop and improve a plant's shape, remove badly placed or old, unproductive growth in favour of young wood, reduce overcrowding, and open up the centre of the bush. Do it as late as possible in the season, so that any bird damage to buds can be taken into account when deciding what to cut out. Summer pruning is only necessary for trained forms, to restrict growth and maintain the shape and structure. Soft fruits are particularly prone to serious virus diseases. Grub out and burn affected plants before starting to prune other plants. Remember that secateurs and other tools can spread viruses, so disinfect thoroughly by dipping them in household disinfectant before and after pruning each plant. Aphids and other sap-sucking insects also spread virus diseases, so look for them and then control them immediately.

CANE FRUITS

Pruning cane fruits
Fruited canes are cut out with a straight cut across the stem at ground level, carefully avoiding young growth that is being retained.

Removing unwanted suckers
All canes begin as suckers from the roots or base of the plant. Hoe out any too far from the row, or remove (as above) for propagation.

BUSH FRUITS

Renewal pruning
With bush fruits (particularly blackcurrants) a proportion of older wood is taken out each winter to keep the centre open and increase the proportion of the plant formed by one- and two-year-old shoots. The latter fruit in the summer, while new shoots that will fruit the following year are developing. Cut fruited shoots back to the base or to a strong sideshoot low down.

BLACKBERRIES

ALTHOUGH DESCENDED from woodland plants, the blackberry (*Rubus fruticosus*) and its cultivars, and hybrid berries – loganberries, tayberries, and boysenberries (crosses between blackberries and other *Rubus* species) – need a sunny site to produce good crops of well-ripened fruit. All are temperate fruits, and are cultivated, trained, and pruned in the same way.

TRAINING METHODS

Blackberries and hybrid berries fruit on sideshoots arising from long, vigorous canes produced in the previous year. Pruning and training has several aims. Canes are trained to allow maximum exposure of the fruits to the ripening sun and to make harvesting easy; training also keeps fruits clean and clear of the ground and prevents stem tips from self-layering. They are pruned to encourage continuous production of vigorous healthy shoots, removing the old to make way for the new. These fruit are not certified to be virus-free, as raspberries are, so avoid buying any with mottled leaves or dwarfed growth.

Fan (for less vigorous cultivars)
Fruiting canes are spread out and new canes tied in to the central space, to be lowered and tied into position once fruited canes have been cut away.

Alternate bay
Ideal where several plants grow along a wall. Train young and fruiting canes towards each other in the spaces between plants, or bays; the canes in each bay fruit in alternate years.

Rope (for cultivars with pliable stems)
Fruiting canes twisted into "ropes" are tied to the lower wires; new canes trained up the middle and along the top are allocated to the lower wires after fruited canes are cut out.

Weaving (for cultivars with pliable stems)
Fruiting canes are trained in a serpentine manner on lower wires; new ones are taken up the middle and along the top, to be lowered after fruited canes are cut out.

ESTABLISHED PRUNING

The aim is maintain an annual succession of year-old, heavy-cropping canes. Once all berries have been harvested, cut out fruited canes and tie in new ones. If there are too few new canes to fill the space, retain a few old ones, cutting back their sideshoots to 2.5cm (1in). Pull out any growth springing up too far from the row as soon as seen, or it will quickly become a nuisance. Canes may be bundled together for added winter protection and retrained in spring. At the end of winter, tip back canes by 15cm (6in).

FORMATIVE PRUNING

Plant one-year-old plants in early winter or, in severe climates, in early spring. Shorten the original cane to 20–30cm (8–12in) above ground on planting, to stimulate basal growth, then remove it completely in summer. New shoots, which are tied in as they develop, fruit in their second summer. Routine pruning takes place in autumn, after harvest, to remove all fruited canes, and again in late winter or early spring, tipping back to encourage sideshoots and remove any frost-damaged growth.

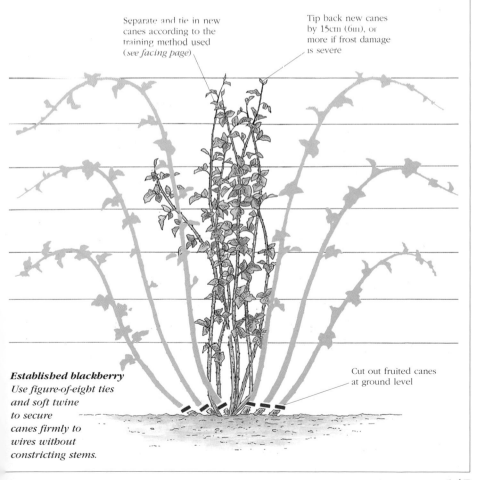

Separate and tie in new canes according to the training method used (*see facing page*)

Tip back new canes by 15cm (6in), or more if frost damage is severe

Established blackberry
Use figure-of-eight ties and soft twine to secure canes firmly to wires without constricting stems.

Cut out fruited canes at ground level

RASPBERRIES

NUMEROUS RASPBERRY CANES are produced directly from the mass of fibrous roots just below soil level. The canes of summer-fruiting raspberries grow one year and crop the next, after which they are removed at ground level. Autumn-fruiting raspberries produce canes that fruit at the end of a single season, from late summer to the first frosts, and are then cut to the ground.

TRAINING SYSTEMS

Open posts and wires systems are widely used for training. Good support is essential, especially for summer-fruiting cultivars, which must survive winter weather.

Scandinavian system

Suitable for less vigorous summer-fruiting cultivars, the Scandinavian system is ideal for a large, sheltered area where you want to grow a quantity of plants. With this training method, the canes are not tip-pruned. The canes are planted centrally and 3–4 of the strongest from each plant are woven along wires and around each other. Tie in if necessary. New canes fill the central space, protected from wind and possible damage during harvesting. When the fruited canes are cut away, the replacement canes are woven into place.

Post-and-wire system

A compact, secure method, posts and wires are good for windy areas. The fruits receive maximum sun. Fruiting canes are tied in on one side of the wires; do not weave them in and out or they may chafe. New canes are loosely looped in round the wires.

VIRAL DISEASES

Raspberries are very prone to viral diseases, for which there is no cure. Plants showing symptoms – short, weak canes, yellow-blotched foliage, and sparse, small or distorted fruits – must be dug up and burned. Remove any suckers that grow from overlooked fragments. Do not replant raspberries for several years where virus-infected ones grew.

TRAINING METHODS

Scandinavian system
Drive 1.5m (5ft) posts 60cm (2ft) into the ground, in two rows 90cm (3ft) apart, with posts set at 3m (10ft) intervals. Add diagonal support struts; run a single wire along each row.

Post-and-wire system
Stretch taut three wires at heights of 75cm (30in), 1m (3ft) and 1.5m (5ft), between two end posts or stapled along a line of 4–5 posts. Tie canes in on one side of the wire.

PLANTING AND PRUNING

Cultivation for summer- and autumn-fruiting raspberries is the same, except for pruning. Established summer-fruiting cultivars are pruned in late winter and after fruiting; autumn-fruiting raspberries in late winter.

Summer-fruiting raspberries

Plant as single canes, usually 60cm (24in) long, between late autumn and early spring. Shorten to 25cm (10in) on planting. Prune out the stumps in midsummer (*see right*). Tie in new canes as growth proceeds. Pinch out any flowers that appear, to conserve energy for next year's crop. Make sure the canes are well-supported over winter, tip-pruning them as winter ends (but not if using the Scandinavian system, *see opposite*). As soon as cropping has finished, cut fruited canes out at the base. Retain about eight strong new canes per plant, and tie in. Unless required as new plants, young canes emerging more than 20cm (8in) from the row should be removed by hoeing lightly.

Autumn-fruiting raspberries

These are bought as single canes and planted and pruned as for summer-fruiting cultivars. In summer the new canes will both grow and bear their first crop. As the canes grow, shorter cultivars such as 'September' will require no support, but more vigorous ones such as 'Autumn Bliss' need training to guard against wind damage. At winter's end, before any sign of growth, cut all canes to the ground. As the next year's young canes grow, remove weak and damaged growth. Do not tip-prune, since much of the fruit is borne at the top of the canes. Replace old plants when cropping declines.

Year 1, summer for summer fruiting
The original cane of this summer-fruiting raspberry was shortened to 25cm (10in) on planting, during the dormant season. Its stump is pruned in midsummer.

ROUTINE TASKS, SUMMER-FRUITING RASPBERRIES

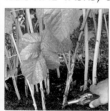

Fruited canes
Cut out at ground level, taking care not to damage current season's new shoots

Tying in new canes
Tie new canes 10cm (4in) apart, looping in with a continuous length of string.

Looping over
Bend very long canes over, tying to the top wire to avoid wind damage in winter.

Tip-pruning
At the end of winter, tip-prune canes by about 15cm (6in) to the same height.

CURRANTS

THE PRUNING of blackcurrants is very simple; all that is needed is the annual removal of older, less productive wood in favour of younger, more free-fruiting growth. Red and white currants fruit at the base of one-year-old laterals and are spur-pruned to a permanent framework of branches, with old wood only taken out in the event of disease, old age, or overcrowding.

BLACKCURRANT BUSH

Blackcurrants fruit most freely on shoots formed the previous summer, which are smooth and tea-coloured. Some fruit is borne on the grey, shaggy two-year-old wood, but this is often worth sacrificing in favour of young growth. Begin with a certified virus-free, two-year-old bush with 3–4 healthy shoots; it will crop in its second summer after planting. Plant when dormant, with the nursery soil mark about a thumb's width below ground. On vigorous, well-established bushes you can cut out entire fruited stems at harvest, tidying up what is left in winter. Aim for a balance of one- and two-year-old wood, retaining more of the latter on weak bushes to fill them out.

Years 1 and 2, winter
Immediately after planting, prune all shoots back hard to within one bud above soil level. In the second year, remove only weak or damaged shoots or those that are growing horizontally or downwards.

Established bush
Prune at any time between cropping and late winter. Cut out all dark, three-year-old or older wood at the base.

Retain strong two-year-old wood with plenty of new sideshoots

Remove less productive two-year-old wood with few sideshoots

Prune low, horizontal branches to a strong upward-growing shoot to restrict spread

Cut out older wood at the base

RED AND WHITE CURRANT CORDON

In winter, red and white currants are hard-pruned to form spurs which fruit annually. These can be grown as an open-centred bush, as for gooseberries (*see pp. 152–3*), and are also ideal trained as cordons. For this you will need a wall, fence, or pair of 2m (6ft) posts, fitted with horizontal wires at 30cm (12in) intervals. Begin with a one-year-old, single-stemmed currant. Plant it in winter, staking it with a cane tied to the wires. All cordons are pruned in summer and winter each year. In time, older spur systems will need thinning as for apples (*see p. 123*). The leading shoot must be pruned back to a bud to restrict height once it reaches the top wire. Pinch out or shorten shoots that are growing towards the wall.

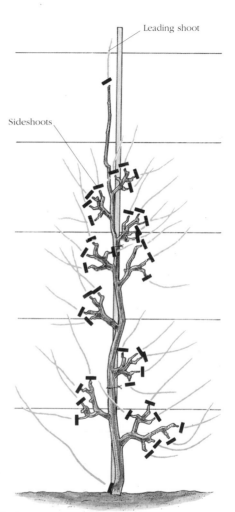

Leading shoot

Sideshoots

Pruning on planting
In winter, cut back the leading shoot by half its previous year's growth (left). If a lower shoot is stronger, train this in instead. Cut back all other shoots to one bud.

Year 1 onwards, summer
When new shoots have at least seven or eight leaves, prune back to five leaves (right). If they have developed any sideshoots, pinch them out altogether or shorten them to one bud.

Year 2 onwards, winter
Prune new growth on the leading shoot by a quarter each winter, cutting to a bud on the opposite side to last year's cut. When it reaches the top wire, prune new growth to one bud. Cut back all summer-pruned sideshoots, and any new ones, to one bud. Cut back to their point of origin any new shoots less than 10cm (4in) from the ground. Thin mature spurs when necessary.

GOOSEBERRIES

THE GROWTH HABIT of gooseberries varies between pendent and upright, according to cultivar. Usually grown as a bush, gooseberries can be pruned in two ways: either on a loose renewal basis, or spur-pruned to a permanent framework. The latter makes standard, fan, and cordon (*see p.151*) forms possible. Gooseberries fruit on year-old shoots and older spur systems.

GOOSEBERRY BUSH

The aim is to produce a bush 1.2–2m (4–6ft) tall with a strong framework of branches on a short leg. Start with a one-year-old plant with at least three strong shoots. Prune in late winter or just as buds burst in early spring; the later pruning reduces the impact of bird damage. In late winter after planting, shorten all shoots by about three-quarters; if this has already been done in the nursery, trim by 2–3cm (¾–1¼in). If the cultivar has a pendent habit, always cut to an upward-pointing bud. Sideshoots should develop during the next season, from which 8–10 are selected to form the main branches.

Prune all shoots back by three-quarters

Year 1, winter
In late winter, after planting, prune back each shoot by three-quarters to an outward-facing bud. On pendent cultivars, prune to an upward-facing bud.

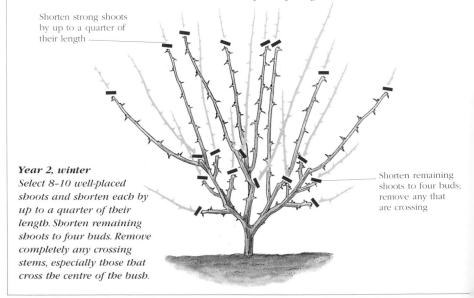

Shorten strong shoots by up to a quarter of their length

Year 2, winter
Select 8–10 well-placed shoots and shorten each by up to a quarter of their length. Shorten remaining shoots to four buds. Remove completely any crossing stems, especially those that cross the centre of the bush.

Shorten remaining shoots to four buds; remove any that are crossing

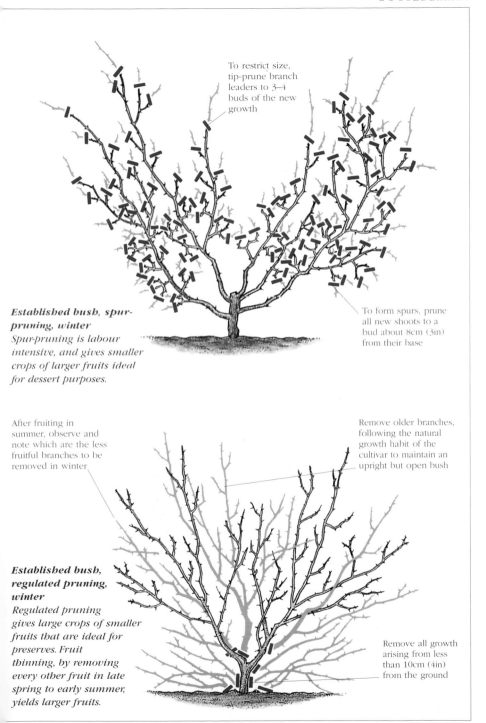

To restrict size, tip-prune branch leaders to 3–4 buds of the new growth

Established bush, spur-pruning, winter
Spur-pruning is labour intensive, and gives smaller crops of larger fruits ideal for dessert purposes.

To form spurs, prune all new shoots to a bud about 8cm (3in) from their base

After fruiting in summer, observe and note which are the less fruitful branches to be removed in winter

Remove older branches, following the natural growth habit of the cultivar to maintain an upright but open bush

Established bush, regulated pruning, winter
Regulated pruning gives large crops of smaller fruits that are ideal for preserves. Fruit thinning, by removing every other fruit in late spring to early summer, yields larger fruits.

Remove all growth arising from less than 10cm (4in) from the ground

GLOSSARY

Adventitious bud Latent bud on a stem or root, often invisible until stimulated into growth.
Angle of attachment Angle at which a shoot develops from a main stem.
Apical bud A bud at the tip of a stem.
Apical dominance Controlling influence of the apical bud over the growth of a stem, which restricts development of lateral buds. **Axil** The upper angle formed where a leaf stalk or sideshoot joins the stem.
Axillary bud One that occurs in an axil.

Basal Growing at the base of a plant.
Basal cluster Lowest cluster of leaves on a shoot, at or around its point of origin.
Basal shoot A shoot arising from near or at ground level.
Bleeding The oozing of sap through a cut or wound.
Blind shoot A shoot that does not form a terminal flower bud, or one where the growing point has been destroyed.
Branch bark ridge A fold in bark where a branch joins the trunk, sometimes visible.
Branch collar A thickened ring of tissue at the base of a branch; a primary site of natural barriers.
Branch leader The leading shoot of a branch, where length is extended.
Break Used to describe new growth from a bud, such as the emergence of a shoot.
Bud A condensed shoot containing an embryonic leaf, leaf cluster, or flower.

Callus tissue Protective tissue formed by mainly woody plants to seal off a wound.
Cambium layer A layer of tissue beneath bark which produces new cells to increase the girth of stem and roots.
Coppicing Regular pruning back of trees or shrubs close to ground level to stimulate growth of vigorous shoots.
Crotch Angle between two branches, or between a branch and the trunk.
Crown Branched part of a tree above the trunk.
Crown lifting Removal of low branches to produce a taller clear trunk.

Crown reduction Making a crown smaller by cutting back the longest branches.
Crown thinning Removing crowded growth from the crown of a tree to admit more light, reducing wind resistance from heavy branches.

Deadheading The removal of spent flowers or flowerheads.
Dieback Death of shoot tips that spreads down the stem, due to damage or disease.
Disbudding Removal of surplus buds to promote better quality fruits or flowers.
Dormancy State of temporary cessation of growth and slowing down of other life processes, usually during winter.
Dual leaders Competing leaders of equal strength.
Dwarfing rootstock In grafting, using roots of a smaller-growing plant than one grafted onto it to limit size of top growth.

Epicormic shoots Shoots that develop from adventitious buds, often at the site of pruning wounds.
Extension growth New growth made during the growing season.

Feathered maiden One-year-old tree that has developed lateral shoots (feathers).
Framework Permanent branch structure of a tree or shrub.
Fruit bud Bud from which a flower, followed by fruit, develops.

Graft union The point at which rootstock and scion are united.
Grafting Making an artificial union between the top growth of one plant (scion) and the roots of another (rootstock) so that they function as one plant.

Internodal cut A cut made between two nodes or growth buds.

Latent bud A bud that fails to develop in the season it was formed and remains dormant until stimulated into growth.

Lateral Side growth that arises from any root or shoot.

Lateral bud Bud that will form a sideshoot.

Leader A plant's main, usually central, stem.

Leading shoot The main central shoot of a plant, or of a main branch.

Maiden A tree in its first year.

Maiden whip A tree in its first year, without lateral branches.

Natural barrier Internal chemical barrier produced by a plant to halt the spread of infection through the rest of the plant.

Occlusion Process by which a pruning cut or wound is sealed over with callus tissue.

Pinch pruning Method of pruning whereby shoot tips are removed with finger and thumb.

Pollarding Regular pruning back of main branches of a tree to the head of a main stem or trunk, or to a short branch framework (*cf.* coppicing).

Regulated pruning Occasional removal of sections of branches, or whole branches, from large woody plants to prevent congestion and stimulate younger growth. **Remedial pruning** Removal of dead, diseased, and damaged wood to protect plant health.

Renewal pruning A system in which older growth is regularly removed in favour of younger growth.

Replacement shoot Strong young shoot left to grow where it will develop to replace old growth removed by pruning.

Rib Main branch of a fan-trained tree.

Ripe wood Mature, hardened wood.

Root-to-shoot ratio Proportional size of the root system to the top growth.

Secondary growth Growth that appears after pruning in summer.

Self-fertile A plant that produces viable seed when fertilized with its own pollen.

Sideshoot A shoot growing out from a stem.

Silver leaf A disease that attacks a wide range of shrubs and trees, especially *Prunus* and *Malus* (cherries, plums, apples), causing leaves to have a silvered or leaden appearance.

Soil mark The usually visible point on a plant's stem showing the original soil level before the plant was lifted in the nursery.

Sport Natural mutation of plant or part of a plant that differs from normal characteristics of habit, shape, size, form, or colour.

Spur A short shoot or branchlet bearing flower buds, as on fruit trees.

Spur-bearing Bearing flowers and fruit on short shoots along the length of stems.

Stem builder Shoot on a main stem retained temporarily so that its leaves can nourish stem growth.

Stub Portion of stem remaining between the point where a cut is made and the next area of active growth below it.

Sublateral Sideshoot from a lateral shoot.

Target pruning Removing growth with as small a pruning cut as possible, so as not to breach a plant's natural barriers.

Terminal At the tip of a stem or branch.

Tip-bearing Carrying much of the fruit crop at or near the shoot tips.

Tip-pruning Pinching or cutting out shoot tips to encourage sideshoots to develop, or to remove damaged growth.

Tipping back See *tip-pruning*.

Truss Compact cluster of flowers or fruits.

V-angle The crotch or angle between a branch and the main stem.

Vegetative growth Non-flowering, usually leafy, growth.

Water shoots Sappy, fast-growing epicormic shoots, usually arising at the site of damage or pruning cuts.

Whip A single-stemmed young tree that has not yet developed lateral branches.

Wind rock The destabilization of a plant's roots by strong winds.

✿ The Royal Horticultural Society's Award of Garden Merit.

INDEX

ACKNOWLEDGMENTS

Dorling Kindersley would like to thank Diana Vowles and Lesley Malkin for editorial assistance; Sonia Charbonnier for additional DTP design; Angela Anderson for picture research; Alice Fairman for overseas liaison; and Ella Skene for compiling the index.

Photography credits
All photography by Peter Anderson, except for the images on the pages specified below (b=below, l=left)

Eric Crichton Photos 14 bl, 19 bl
John Glover 116
John Finler 94
Andrew Lawson 54
National Trust Photographic Library:
  Neil Campbell-Sharp 2-3, 6
Derek St Romaine 72

Illustration
All artworks by Karen Cochrane, except for those on pages 7, 27, 55, 73, 95, 117, and 143, which are by Sarah Young